EDITED BY BROOKE. M. MIKELBANK

The Last Day

Toby Mikelbank

Published by Toby Mikelbank, 2024.

THE LAST DAY

First edition. October 27, 2024.

ISBN: 979-8227390783

Written by Toby Mikelbank.

Dedication

To my wife Amy, who supported this wild idea and the long hours that were required at the computer. To my daughter Katlin, for tons of technical support for her non-techie Dad. To my daughter Brooke for editing this book. To my son Logan, for challenging me to make this book better with creative ideas. To Ken Cooper, for helping me with my difficult questions about Revelation. To my Lord and Saviour Jesus Christ, for being so incredibly patient.

Chapter 1 - The Vacation

The crowd swelled like the sea. A stormy and violent sea. It was getting larger too, a panicked mass, all moving as one toward the park exit. Weston looked behind him to make sure the Miller clan wasn't getting separated. They weren't. Allyson and the kids were being jostled and shoved, but they were close behind and determined to stay together despite the aggressiveness of the crowd.

For now, they were trapped inside this press of bodies, and there was nothing to do but pray they didn't lose their balance and get trampled. This was a ride that hadn't been described on disneyland.com. The Magic Kingdom: Mass Exodus.

This trip had been planned for almost a year, and Allyson stated that was because it took that long to save up for the admission price of five tickets. At $220 each, plus hotel, meals, and travel expenses, the Millers had had to amass quite a sum for the privilege of entering Mickey's gates. Now, after spending three days and nights here, the allure had begun to fade.

Maybe it was just part of getting older, but nothing seemed the same to Weston as it had when he was a kid. Instead of gawking in wonder as movie characters made their rounds, like a child would, Weston noticed with irritation that they were late according to the scheduled time on the placards. This was likely because he could see several cast members putting out their cigarettes and arguing as they came out of the 'Employees Only' area. Instead of marveling at the wonders in Tomorrowland, Weston kept noting with annoyance that the estimated wait times hovered over one hour.

Well, that was just the way life was, right? As you grew up, your perspective of the world around you changed. Became more realistic. Anyway, he had found that it had been more enjoyable experiencing the park through his children than experiencing it himself as a child. They loved it.

His twelve year old son Dylan was still at that age when trying to act cool was not more important than just experiencing life. He was enjoying himself but kept wanting to go back on the same rides repeatedly, which wasn't practical at Disneyland. Charlotte, his youngest, well, she was simply ecstatic. She lit up like a Christmas tree at each new bend and corner of the park, especially in Fantasyland. To her, it seemed to offer endless thrill and adventure. Being just eight, she was the ultimate demographic for the Disney machine. Her squeals and giggles were like medicine to Weston, helping soothe his irritation from the admission and food prices, massive crowds, and endless lines. The exception was Braden, his seventeen year old son. He seemed more interested in girls that walked by than anything the park had to offer.

At any rate, it was a beautiful, typical Southern California day. The sky arched deep blue; there was not a cloud in sight. It was warm but nowhere near the triple-digit heat coming later in the summer. Everyone was dressed casually in T-shirts and shorts.

The park was beautiful and seemed full of adventure and life. He could hear the happy cries of children on rides in the distance. He noticed little sparrows would flutter from one tree to the next. The foliage was quite dense and added to the mystique of the park. The kids were eating ice cream cones, and everyone looked happy. Weston had to admit it was nice to get out of his routine, get his kids out of theirs, and get them all into a different environment. *At least I'm not in the office. At least they're getting a break from school.*

But now, everything had changed. The magic mood had turned from the pixie dust variety to the darker Fantasia kind. Cell phones everywhere began to chime in unison; an Amber alert, but not for another missing kid this time. Today was different. People all around him were opening their phones. Weston grabbed his from his pocket, fumbled with it, and read:

(!) National Alert.

This is not a test. The National Wireless Emergency Alert System is broadcasting this message at the federal, state, local, tribal and territorial levels to alert and warn the public with the following information. Please see the enclosed link:

As Weston clicked on the link with his thumb, the message opened:

"Incident at White House. President Fauser dead. Stay tuned to your local news."

Weston was startled. Douglas Fauser was a young President, only two years into his first term. He showed real promise as a leader, a quality the last few Presidents had not possessed. He was a mesmerizing speaker and had managed to unite liberals and conservatives more than had been done in decades. There had been some excitement again in politics in America, some hope for the future, but now he was gone.

Something had happened at the White House. This was hard to process and unexpected. Too much reality while strolling through Fantasyland on a sunny day with your kids.

What could it have been? Weston couldn't recall a President dying in office in his lifetime. It said there was an 'incident.' Fauser couldn't have been more than forty-five, and the word incident implied an unnatural death. An accident, or worse, an assassination. He had a foreboding, sick feeling in his stomach.

The television next to them at the ice cream kiosk had some information. The news said there were plumes of smoke rising from the White House. Weston saw a pile of shattered sandstone. He stared at the screen in shock. Clearly it had once been the White House, but now it looked like something a giant had tried to step on and crush.

Many people didn't know, but the White House had steel support beams inside, which were added much later on. This was probably why some of it was still holding up; whatever had happened to it had clearly been large in scale. Weston thought of 9/11 right away.

Something must have exploded inside it or flown into it, he thought.

His next thought was of his kids; they were all holding now melting ice cream cones, staring fascinated at the images. He wanted to shield them from these kinds of things, and now it was right in front of them, demanding attention. He suddenly didn't feel good about being in a place like this at all. Disneyland was a very public location, and this looked like a terrorist attack. Were they even safe?

Act normal, don't upset them, he thought. *Let's just leave.*

"Ally, I was thinking, why don't we just head back to the hotel? I'm just so tired; I didn't sleep well last night...I remember I saw they had a pool. It's so hot, don't you think, swimming maybe?" he said.

Allyson stared at him for a second, caught off guard. Who knew where her thoughts were at this moment? Then, understanding.

"Well, we have pretty much seen everything..."

Weston noticed more people had phones in hand and were moving towards the front entrance. A few here, a group of five or ten there. Power walking with a new purpose: holding their kids' hands too tightly. He read the same thing in each face: dull disbelief and growing concern.

"No, Mom, please!" Charlotte begged, bending towards her and dragging out each word.

Braden and Dylan looked sick and worried, still watching the TV screen, but Charlotte seemed unaffected.

"Mom, we still have to do Bibbidi Boutique! You promised!" she pleaded.

"I know, honey, but your Dad's right. We'll go swimming, maybe order a pizza..."

Charlotte pouted, unconvinced that any other experience could be had that would justify leaving the park.

"Alright, well, let's get going; it's already two o'clock," Weston said, feigning surprise as he looked at his watch.

He had to prod the boys away from the television, and Charlotte reluctantly followed as Weston and Allyson began walking towards Main Street USA. The kids were now a mess of melting ice cream, but as they followed behind, they started slurping up what remained on their hands.

Since they were already in Fantasyland, he had thought reaching the exit would not take long. It was a straight shot. Unfortunately, more and more people seemed to have the same idea. Additional groups began to pour in from each side street and park section. Soon a large, slow-moving crowd had formed.

It was difficult, but Weston kept trying to look at his phone while shuffling along. He could see footage on YouTube showing a Learjet flying into the White House, and there had been some kind of explosion in the air even before the plane crashed.

The news anchor was interviewing an expert who was saying it was a terrorist attack since the size of the explosion was too large to be from a plane crash. It had to be an air-delivered bomb.

A Learjet packed with explosives?

I thought they had air security around the White House, a no-fly zone or something? Weston remembered.

It didn't seem possible that something like that could get through.

They were now past the magic castle. It took forever as thousands tried to enter through a bottleneck maybe twenty feet wide. He could now see Walt holding Mickey's hand in the main plaza.

Disneyland employees were communicating into walkie-talkies and gesturing to the crowd to take their time and remain calm. The hierarchy had apparently resolved itself to the fact that everyone was going to leave early. The problem now was that so many people were trying to exit that they were making little progress, and people in the crowd were getting agitated.

"It isn't fair!" Charlotte complained. She was still trying to make her case. "We can go into Tomorrowland. There's so much time to do that. Everyone's leaving!"

"I'm sorry Char, it's time to go," replied Allyson.

"I don't understand why we have to leave," retorted Charlotte, greatly exaggerating the word why.

Suddenly, a shove came from the side.

"Hey!" Weston gasped as he took the force of it.

"Move!" the voice came from a young bodybuilder type who looked ready for anything, especially a fight.

Best to let this pass, thought Weston.

Muscles glared at him, then shoved ahead without another word.

They were now on Main Street. Almost there. Weston was getting tired of shuffling his feet. It was more work than regular walking.

Now phones everywhere began beeping again as a new National Alert came in:

(!) National Alert.

This is not a test. The National Wireless Emergency Alert System is broadcasting this message at the federal, state, local, tribal, and territorial levels to alert and warn the public with the following information. Please see the enclosed link:

It was harder this time, with the movement of the crowd, but Weston clicked on the link again:

"Terrorist attack confirmed at Busch Gardens Tampa Bay. Multiple dead. Recommend shelter in place until further notice."

The dam burst.

A collective gasp came from the crowd, and Weston could hear women crying and men shouting. Like a roller coaster climbing that first peak, then rounding the top and gaining speed, the crowd surged forward, anxious to get out. Everyone began shouting and pushing. It had hit much closer to home now; Disneyland could be next.

Screams penetrated the air. Weston immediately thought of his kids and tried to look behind him. He was getting jostled and shoved from every direction. He managed to grab Ally's hand.

"Ally!" he screamed, "Hold on!"

The crowd seemed to be a living, menacing thing. There was pushing and shoving from all sides. It threatened to take one down to the ground where you would be crushed.

"We're here!" Ally cried, "What is it?"

"It's bad!" he replied.

I can't say more; don't scare the kids even worse, he thought. *Just hold on.*

Some Disney employees were yelling now and gesturing wildly, but it was too late. A deep kick in the Achilles heel sent a wave of pain through Weston. He moaned. His eyes watered, but he had to focus. Over and over, he would lose his balance, as bodies collided and backed off and collided again. There was more kicking into his legs and shins as people attempted to move faster than they were able. Everywhere there was screaming and crying.

We might all die because of this stupid crowd, Weston thought.

"Kids?" he shouted. He couldn't turn around now to see.

"Yeah!" responded Ally. It was enough.

The crowd was really moving now. Too fast. A fifty something woman fell to the pavement to his right, moaning as she slammed into the ground. Bodies plummeted over her and around her like a herd of animals. It was hard to see what happened.

"West!" shouted Ally as their hands, locked together, were forced apart. He shouted her name, but she was gone. The mass of people was surging now. Stampeding.

He saw the main gate. It was getting difficult to breathe and more than once, he was pressed in so tightly that he couldn't. Claustrophobia was setting in. If he didn't get space soon, he would lose his mind. It was like a human anthill. Everyone piled on top of each other. He could smell the breath and body odor of those around him.

One thought would not stop coming: *are they still behind me? Are they ok?*

They passed the entrance sign. It was starting to thin out a bit now. As people moved in different directions in the parking lot, the heightened panic seemed to dissipate. Now that there was more space, people began running freely in various directions.

As soon as he was able, he turned around. He couldn't see his family anywhere. Wave after wave of park goers piled out of the gates. Weston started to panic, thinking the worst. Maybe they had all been trampled? He had to go back inside, crazy as it was, and find them. He couldn't stand the thought of his wife and kids in trouble and him not being there. He started to push his way against the flow of people.

A large group of Japanese tourists, old school cameras dangling from their necks, moved around him like flowing water. They were all yelling excitedly. He stared ahead intensely into the crowd. Another large group moved past him. Weston cried out Ally's name.

Like an incoming tide that loses its force in the sand, the next large group quickly spread out, running with their children. Ally and his kids were behind them.

They all ran to each other and hugged. Ally and Charlotte were sobbing.

Chapter Two - Home

They headed out of Southern California on Interstate 5. Dusk was settling in as they sped northward through flat desert. With the sun setting over the Southern Coast ranges, the light hit the mountains and flashed erie streaks across the sky. The clouds were turning shades of red as the sun made its final effort to give its light. It was a calming sensation speeding across the desert, being in control again.

Weston pressed the accelerator a bit more in their Grand Caravan. There was absolutely nothing out here. It was so deserted they might as well have been on the moon. They needed to get home; it would return a sense of normalcy and security to everyone.

What a way to end a vacation, he thought.

Ally had reviewed her cell phone now and was up to speed. Of course they couldn't talk about it, not in front of the kids. Fortunately, none of them were asking any questions. The boys sat silently, and even Charlotte had moved on from her stay at Disneyland campaign. Everyone looked exhausted.

They're probably trying to process what just happened, Weston thought.

But the kids were resilient, thank God. Weston would have to spend his own time processing what had almost happened to some or all of them.

I think that lady got trampled to death.

How many others had there been? Would they ever even find out? He hated losing control of a situation that badly. He decided he would not let it happen again.

It was dark now, and Weston could only see as far as the headlight beams extended onto the road. However, in the distance, an oasis of powerful lights shone on the horizon. As they drove closer, it looked like one of those mega gas stations with a few other buildings clustered around it. Maybe a restaurant? What a strange microcosm of humanity out in the middle of nowhere.

There hadn't been much out here in the last hour, and he was starting to feel hunger pangs. They'd run out of snacks in the car on the way down to SoCal.

"Dad, can we stop to eat?" Braden asked, reading his thoughts.

"Yeah, let's stop?" he suggested, turning towards Allyson.

"Sure," she answered.

He could see the layout more clearly as he pulled off the interstate. The brightly lit gas station had dozens of pumps, restrooms, and a large variety of artery-clogging foods inside. But he wanted to eat something real. One of the buildings looked like a restaurant. Pulling through a maze of curbs to get to it, he saw a sign that said 'Rosita's.' It didn't seem open, but he pulled the car to the front door.

Closed.

No one seemed to be inside. There was no hope of an authentic meal here.

"I guess we'll grab something when we get gas," he stated.

In the station, everyone dispersed to restrooms and snack aisles. Weston was determined to find something remotely healthy. As he perused the aisles, he realized a Quest bar and some cashews would be tonight's fare.

"I just wanted some Mexican," he grumbled to himself.

From behind the counter, a large flat screen TV was on. Weston couldn't hear what the newscaster was saying, but he read the closed caption underneath:

"We're recommending..at this time...shelter in space...to be in for prevention attacks further. I mean long and until further. Eminent..."

Weston was always annoyed at how bad closed captioning was, even with all the technological advances happening around them.

"...because the runway at Joint Base Andrews was compromised in the explosion...military could not, could not most likely not intercept, it was not in time...since three Learjets encroached...their place, as though and it took time..."

They were showing a pile of concrete and wreckage on a long runway somewhere, surrounded by emergency vehicles, presumably the runway at Joint Base Andrews they spoke of. There seemed to have been more to the attack than was first realized.

This thing must have been highly coordinated, Weston thought.

"Dad," called out Charlotte, "can I get these, plleeeaasse?"

She was holding a pack of Twinkies. He gave her a disapproving look. Char dropped the pack with much emphasis and moved on down the aisle. The rest of the family seemed to be rounding up their provisions and slowly moving towards the register.

Now the news had moved on to Busch Gardens:

"...at least true suicide...bombers had had hit it the park Busch Gardens and....projections one hundreds or hundred has died...yes, and died. Local hospitals are treating dozens and more...Atlanta is reporting dozens of explosions reporting now there are explosions..."

Oh, no, he thought. *So this was a coordinated attack on America, everywhere.*

Now he REALLY wanted to get home. At least at home, he had...

"Weston," Ally called out, annoyed, "can we go?"

She was gesturing at the screen and the kids. They were glued to it again like before, and he knew they shouldn't be watching this.

"Sorry," said Weston.

He'd been completely unaware of his surroundings for a second there. He moved forward to the register. Suddenly, something on the bottom right aisle caught his eye. It was a red Scepter USA five gallon gas can. It had a weird green valve at the top. He paused. It was ridiculously priced at $39. He shook his head and moved forward again. A voice in his head now spoke.

"Get it."

He slowed down.

What was that? Was that me?

Whatever he had heard, or thought he heard, it didn't seem like it had come from him, but inside his head, nonetheless. He paused for a moment before moving forward again.

"GET IT."

Louder this time.

OK, what was happening?

Weston had never experienced anything like this. It was like something was talking to him. People would say God, but Weston didn't believe in God. At least not an involved God. He wasn't an atheist; he was more agnostic. Something had set this whole crazy world in motion, but whatever it had been, it clearly wasn't involved with this planet anymore.

"West, LET'S GO, please!" Ally was clearly annoyed now. Eyes wide, motioning at the TV again.

He turned around and returned to the gas can without thinking.

"What are you doing?" she demanded.

"I'm just going to get this," he stated.

His voice was monotone now, and he surrendered to the idea that he was getting the stupid container. Ally just sighed and moved towards the register.

He walked towards his family with the container and plopped it down next to all the bars, crackers and drinks his family had procured.

"Can you add in five gallons of gas for this, too?" he inquired of the clerk.

"Certainly. Total is $108.50." said the clerk.

Ally let out a big sigh.

The kids were already running out the double doors, chimes ringing as they went through.

Back in the van, Ally was driving now. She was unusually silent. Braden spoke from the back seat:

"Dad, that gas SMELLS!"

Ally glared at Weston.

"I know, bud. I just thought it might be a good idea," he replied.

"But you're up there, and I'm back here, and it really smells," Braden fired back.

"I can't breathe," chimed in Charlotte.

"It was $39, West." Ally declared, emphasizing the nine.

"I know, I know," he said, trying to placate her.

He didn't know why he bought the can. They already had one at home. And now he had bought another one that they didn't need. He could see why his wife was upset, but that voice. It was so weird, like he was being told.

It was nothing, he told himself.

The memory of it was already fading, and he closed his eyes and laid back in his seat. Best to forget the whole thing and get some sleep. They had at least six more hours to go.

He was awakened by a hand gently placed on his. It was Ally. He started quickly and looked around. All was dark except the faint glow of the dashboard and weak beams of light pushing out in front of them as they raced down the interstate.

"What's up?" he asked. As he said it, he looked behind him. The kids were all asleep.

"Something's wrong," Ally stated, keeping her voice quiet.

"What?" he asked, thinking she meant they had managed to get lost. Ally was notorious for her lack of direction in the car.

"The power's off," she stated.

He chuckled. "You mean the streetlights, the local Walmart?"

He was just being smart, because he was irritated. There was nothing around them but miles and miles of orchards.

"I'm serious," she retorted. "We just passed a town. A real town. There was not one light on."

"I don't know," he said, "maybe they lost power. What are you so worried about?"

"West, it did have a Walmart. Everything was dark," she explained.

"It's the power," he replied. "Like you said."

He was growing more and more disinterested in this conversation. He was also annoyed that she woke him up for this.

"But I thought it was weird, so I turned on the radio," she said.

He pressed the radio ON/OFF button. Static. Next button, static, and the next. They were all presets to their local channels. He grabbed the band selector.

"Those were stations we only get at home," he mumbled, turning the dial to the right.

As he moved through all frequencies, there was only lifeless static.

A sick feeling began in the pit of his stomach. Did this have something to do with the attacks? Had power gone off in the area for some reason?

"Where are we?" he asked.

"I just saw a sign that said Coalinga," she responded.

"Well, I think we'll hit Stockton or Modesto in a couple of hours and be back in the bigger areas. We'll see up there everything's probably normal again."

Weston was wrong about hitting Modesto. He saw that you could only get there on the 99. But as they drew closer and closer to

Stockton, the absence of light was noticeable. Typically, you would see occasional county lights on the outskirts and steadily increasing brightness as you moved into the neighborhoods.

There was nothing.

The only reason they could tell they had reached the city was from the freeway signs whizzing by in the reflection of their headlights.

"West, the power's off here," Ally whispered.

"Let me check my phone," Weston reached for his Android with annoyance.

After pressing the power button, his screen reassuringly lit up. He went to his browser and typed.

Nothing.

Weston noticed he had no bars in the upper right corner of his screen. In tiny letters at the top, it said 'no service.' He checked if he was in airplane mode or had deselected cellular data/roaming or something like that, but nothing helped. The phone continued to say, 'no service.'

"Hmmm," he complained. "I've got no internet. I don't know what's going on."

"At least we know how to get home," Ally said positively.

As they buzzed past exit after exit, there continued to be no visible light coming from the sides of the freeway. He strained, but it was difficult to see anything beyond their headlights. It was a dark night with no moon, and Weston felt a moment of panic. They were in a tiny, fragile lifeboat on an enormous dark sea. He was convinced their vehicle would now somehow lose power, too. Then, this encroaching darkness would swallow him and his family. He felt they would cease to exist in it. He shook off these irrational fears.

He stared out the passenger window. He couldn't be sure, but occasionally, on the outskirts of the beams, he thought he could see movement on some of the streets.

As they rounded a gradual curve on the freeway, they could now see the flashing of the lightbars on several police cars.

Finally, some law and order, he thought.

As they drew closer, he saw they were parked at one of those large strip malls with seven or eight big box stores. As they sped by, Weston noticed in the blue glow of the flashers large groups of people going in and out of one of the stores through broken windows.

"They're looting!" he exclaimed, a little too loudly.

Suddenly, the kids started to stir.

"What?" Ally replied, "No. I don't think so...West, you woke the kids," she scolded next as she noticed them rousing from sleep.

"I saw it," he countered. "The police weren't even doing anything!"

"Where are we?" asked Dylan.

"Dump land," Braden retorted.

"Dad, I have to go to the bathroom," requested Charlotte.

The strip mall was on the edge of the city, and already they were moving back into the country again. Now they would hardly see anything until they reached Sacramento in an hour.

"We're almost to Sacramento, guys," Weston replied. He was relieved they hadn't seen the looters. "Can you wait, honey?"

"I'll try," responded Charlotte.

Weston was starting to feel stressed. Apparently, there was a widespread power outage, and he had just seen a mob breaking the law. His kids needed to use the bathroom, but now there was no place to go with the power out.

He glanced at the gas gauge - only one eighth of a tank left. The anxiety increased. There was no way they would make it home on that.

The gas can!

Relieved, he remembered the annoyingly overpriced gas can he had bought earlier. Five more gallons should get them home.

As they drew nearer to the city limits of Sacramento, things were similar to those in Stockton. There was a complete absence of any man-made light. The only difference was the odor of smoke permeating the van. In the distance, he could see a strange glow. Multiple fires lit up the night sky.

"West, look at those fires," exclaimed Ally.

"Dad, what's going on?" Braden asked in a concerned tone as he stared out the window. "Why are there no lights?"

"I think it's just a power outage, son," Weston replied quickly.

"And why are there fires?" Braden continued.

"Probably 'cause of the power," Weston said, doubting his own words.

Weston could see large fires billowing up in several areas of the city with thick black smoke. He knew that meant structure fires.

This was NOT good.

"Dad, I HAVE to go!!!" announced Charlotte.

"Char, can you go if we pull over here?" he asked, meaning on the side of the freeway.

"DAD!" Charlotte responded in horror.

"West, let's just get off at the next exit and find a place…" Ally suggested.

"Ahh, I don't know…" his voice trailed off. The freeway had been his security blanket this whole time. Nothing bad had happened on the freeway. Bad things seemed to be happening off the freeway. He felt uneasy about exiting. Anything could be going on out where they couldn't see.

"Ally, I don't think - " he spoke uneasily.

" - Honey, it'll be fine," she responded as she gently eased the wheel to the right and took the next exit.

They slowed down on the freeway ramp and stopped at a stop sign. Ally looked both ways. To the left, she could see the road winding off into a maze of houses; it was nothing but inky blackness. To the right was a tiny strip mall, and further down appeared to be a small gas station. Weston noticed several cars parked on the side of the road, but not in front of any house or business. Apparently, they had run out of gas and been abandoned. The lights were out everywhere.

"Honey, the station's not open anyway. She can't use their bathroom," Weston said.

"Let's just see," Ally replied as she turned right.

She drove onto the street and made a left into the small parking lot. Several cars were in the parking slots, but the owners appeared missing. As they peered into the gas station windows, nothing stirred inside.

"It's closed. Can we go?" Weston questioned.

"I just wanted to try - "

BANG! Something slammed into the back of their van. The noise startled everyone. Another BANG. Something was hitting their minivan hard. Weston whirled in his seat and saw several dark forms running behind them. Another group emerged from the right and began moving towards his passenger side.

"GET OUT OF THE VEHICLE!" screamed a masked man. "GET OUT OF THE VEHICLE!"

Weston saw a large man, clothed in black, with a ski mask. He had a bat in his right hand, which he pointed at them. The man was walking briskly towards the van. Behind him, more figures emerged from the darkness. It was difficult to see how many. Suddenly, Weston's window exploded, shattering glass chunks all over him. Part of the window continued to hang in place in the frame.

Charlotte was screaming, a high-pitched wail.

"GO! GO! GO!" Weston yelled.

Ally stomped the gas pedal to the floor, lurching the van forward but also hard to the left. They were experiencing torque steer. Ally had lost control of the wheel.

Everyone was thrown to the right in their seats, and now a telephone pole appeared dead ahead in the headlights, closing fast.

We're going to hit that pole, and this mob will get us, Weston thought.

Ally grunted as she fought to regain control. She shimmied her hands on the wheel to get it straight again. The van sped by the pole, missing it by inches. A shower of rocks now rained down, some landing on the car and others hitting the street.

As they raced out of the parking lot and onto the main street, there was a loud crash. Sparks erupted from the chassis as it slammed into the space between the gutter and the street. The remainder of the broken window collapsed into Weston's lap from the force of the impact. Ally continued to hold the pedal to the floor. They began to pick up speed as she moved them towards the freeway entrance ramp.

"Good, good, good," Weston was chanting to himself.

"What was that?" Ally cried.

Charlotte and Dylan were crying.

"We're ok, everything's ok, kids," Weston soothed, "Braden?"

He gave Braden a look, which he understood to mean he was the oldest and needed to comfort his younger siblings.

Braden turned in his seat. "Guys, we're good. Mom and Dad got this! Mom, way to Earnhart it!" Braden exclaimed.

They were back on the freeway again and moving fast. The wind was blowing hard in Weston's face from the broken window. The noise was incredible, but Weston was thankful they were in control and moving again. Suddenly, the gasoline light came on.

"Honey, we've got to refuel," stated Ally in a panic.

"It's ok. We've got the gas can in the back," he replied.

"Oh, my gosh," Ally cried, remembering. "Have I told you that I LOVE you?"

Weston refueled on the side of the freeway while Ally helped Charlotte find a spot where she could go to the bathroom. She crouched right next to the van, so no one passing could see them. Only a few cars raced by in the darkness, headlights growing bright and then fading again. A few minutes later, they were moving again. Several interchanges later, and after passing through a series of darkened intersections without incident, they finally pulled into their beehive of a neighborhood. Up ahead they saw their green-colored Craftsman-style home. It had never looked so good as they pulled into the driveway.

Chapter Three - The Power

When Weston woke up the next morning, he glanced at their alarm clock.

Nothing.

There was still no power. He sauntered downstairs to scrounge up some breakfast. There was still half a gallon of cold milk. Last night they had emptied a few things from the fridge, put them in a large Coleman cooler, and dumped the contents of the icemaker on top. The ice was already melting, leaving a pool of water at the bottom of the cooler.

That won't last long, he noted.

He ate some cold cereal, careful to take just a little milk. The majority would be used by the kids when they awoke later. He rechecked his cell phone. No service. The only change was that the battery was now at twenty-two percent. That wouldn't last long either.

Weston was supposed to return to work today, but with all the power off, it was obviously not going to happen. His desk job depended entirely on a working computer, and he was sure the office would not be open. It was too far to drive anyway without verifying over the phone that things were resuming, and the phones didn't work.

The kids were also supposed to return to school, which wouldn't happen either.

He could hear them stirring upstairs. Soon, everyone would be up, and with the power off, there would be little to do. Hopefully it would come back on in the next couple of hours. Weston had no idea what to do besides basic chores around the house and yard.

As the kids came downstairs, everyone scanned the Coleman cooler and the cupboards for breakfast. Weston stared at them wistfully as they made their way to the dining room table. They were all growing up too fast. Braden had his mother's good looks, dark hair, and was getting taller and more broad-shouldered. He was coming into his own and would soon be a man. But Weston was worried he had not adequately prepared him for the realities of life. And he was spoiled by his mother. It was a rumor among the other children that he was the favorite. Deny it though she tried, the belief held among them.

Dylan, being a pre-teen, was entering an awkward phase physically and socially. He looked like a smaller version of Weston. At 5'10 and 160 lbs, Weston had never been the biggest guy in the room but had always kept in decent shape. Even though he was in his early fifties, he still kept himself up with a routine of weights and running. Fortunately for Dylan, he looked to be headed down the same path as his father, of neither being too thin nor too fat.

Charlotte was more of an amalgamation between Allyson and Weston, although Weston thought she looked more like her mother. This being the case, his friends had once chided him that Charlotte had definitely 'dodged a bullet.' She was a sprite little thing of sixty pounds, with chestnut hair like her mother and similar mannerisms, the main one being that she usually moved her hands in the air when she talked.

No one seemed to be much in the mood to talk. Everyone had figured out the power was still off, which was just another reminder of the crazy events of last night. No one wanted to think about that. Weston was worried the power wouldn't come on today either, which would mean another night of uncertainty. He was starting to see that their safety and security were fragile without electricity. At the very least, it was a huge inconvenience.

Water was an issue, too. While they still had cold running water, by the time they had finished taking their morning showers, the hot water was gone.

After several hours straightening up and doing chores, Weston noted the power had still not come on. He was starting to get restless. He felt that everyday normal life could not resume again without him and his family being supplied with electricity. They were in a holding pattern, not really living, just waiting for the power to make life normal again. He did not even know where their electricity came from, but just assumed it would always be supplied. His whole life, there had never been a time when it wasn't there; every light switch had always turned on and every outlet had always powered his devices to life.

How did people ever live like this, he questioned.

About four o'clock, probably due to boredom, Ally began rustling up some canned stew, which they heated slowly on the burner portion of their propane barbeque grill. About an hour later, the clan gathered at the table and slowly ate the stew. It wasn't fancy, but at least it was hot.

"Mom calls you Brae-bear all the time," Charlotte observed while they were eating.

Braden got an annoyed look on his face.

"So?" he countered.

"I have nicknames for all of you," Ally piped in, "even your father."

"But you use Braden's the most," Charlotte noted.

Weston wondered if Charlotte was probing, sensing favoritism towards Braden from their mom. Weston had chastised her more than once on this issue.

"Hopefully, the power will come back tonight," Weston stated, trying to change the subject.

"Dad," Braden replied condescendingly, "you should have bought that Costco generator."

"So you could play Need for Speed 23 with the girl in it?" Dylan spoke up, provoking his brother.

"Quiet, dork-a-tron!" Braden hissed.

"All right, you two," Ally interjected, "since you've got so much energy, clear the dishes, both of you!"

After dinner, Dylan wanted to play Mexican Train, which he and Charlotte loved. Everyone sat around the table, matching up and moving the tiles into long trains. They passed the evening with more of a sense of normalcy. Ally brought out a couple of candles as the sun began to go down, and flashlights were dispensed. It was going to be another night without power.

Soon, the kids began yawning, and Ally suggested they all go to bed. As the kids moved off to their rooms, Weston realized he was exhausted. He decided to make the rounds, check all the doors, and head off to bed. He peeked his head into each kid's room and gave them a hug. As was about to leave Charlotte's room, she said:

"Dad...wait."

"What is it, Char?" he asked at the doorway, trying to leave.

"Why did the people try to hurt us?"

He paused. How to explain all that was bad in the world to someone so young and good?

"They just made bad choices. Some of those people were probably not bad people; they just started hanging around the wrong people," he tried to explain awkwardly.

"But doesn't your behavior show if you're good or bad?" she questioned.

He hesitated. "Yes, I suppose it does," he relented.

"Then they were bad people," she reasoned to herself.

"Try to get some sleep, sweetie. You're very safe here," he promised.

"Goodnight," she replied sleepily.

Later, Weston and Ally sat in bed and talked.

"There was some scary stuff last night," Ally said.

"Yeah," Weston answered.

"I guess when the lights go out, some people take advantage of it."

"Let's just hope it stays away from here," he said.

"Let's hope it doesn't happen again," she replied.

"I think we're safe here. This is a better area than those areas....just the same, I should probably keep the gun nearby."

He went into his closet and grabbed his Smith and Wesson SD9 9mm handgun. It had a metallic slide with a black grip and trigger. He had added a tactical LED light on the bottom rail. Holding it in his hand felt, well, sort of reassuring. Could he ever actually use it on someone though?

"Just please be careful with that," she motioned towards the gun, waving her arms for emphasis.

"I will," he promised.

"Anyway, 911's down, so we need a backup," he added, trying to justify the gun.

"Do you think the power will come back on tomorrow, West?" Ally questioned.

"I think so, honey," he lied.

Weston was starting to doubt it would come on anytime soon at all. He was beginning to wonder what had really happened to the world in the last twenty-four hours.

The next morning, he awoke to the same thing. Daylight was seeping through the windows, but every electronic device in the house continued its peaceful sleep. That is, except for his cell phone. It was still alive, but now its battery was hovering at five percent. Weston was already feeling restless, and the day hadn't even begun. He needed to do something about their situation, not just sit here all day again.

"Honey, I think we should start storing what water we can," he declared.

Ally gave him a concerned look. "Do you think this is long-term?"

"I don't know. I just know I want to be prepared. And the first thing we could run out of is water. In an outage, I don't think it just keeps running to the houses day after day. Let's store it in containers."

He moved toward the window, glancing outside. No one was out on the street except his older neighbor, Rick. He was rearranging some items that were laid out in his driveway.

"We're really not prepared for this at all," he complained, staring out the window.

"West?" she said.

He turned and stared at his wife of nineteen years.

Had it really been that long, he thought.

With her beautiful features, chestnut shoulder-length hair, and slender build, he was just as attracted to her as the day he had met her. She sauntered over to him at the window, giving him a tight hug. At first, he tensed, but her touch began to relax him.

"We're going to be fine," she whispered.

"Mm-hhh," he grunted, unconvinced.

"I bet Rick is happy," she added playfully, "he's been waiting for this sort of thing to happen for years."

Weston chuckled. "Yeah, probably."

Suddenly, he had an idea.

"Hey, maybe I'll go talk to him. See if he knows anything?"

The thought animated him. Rick was kind of a know-it-all who didn't come across as one. He was ex-military. He might have some good ideas in a crisis.

Ally gave him a mischievous look.

"You ready for another sermon?" she inquired.

"Agh," he waved his hand, walking out of their bedroom, "it'll be fine."

Weston walked out his front door into his yard. The sun was bright, causing him to squint. As he walked across his lawn towards Rick's house, he could see the shock of white hair and stocky build bent over assorted camping gear on the driveway. Rick was the only man Weston had ever met who could be both fierce and friendly simultaneously.

Many of the neighbors avoided him and called him Ranger Rick behind his back. But, for some reason, Weston had always felt drawn to him. Rick looked up and noticed Weston coming towards him.

"Weston!" he said, giving him an enthusiastic greeting and the usual firm handshake.

"Hey, Rick," Weston returned.

"You all holding up ok? You need anything, MREs, gravity filters -"

" - No, no, we're ok. Thank you," he answered.

"Well, what's the word?" he asked.

"I was hoping you could tell me?" Weston replied.

"Seems like the whole world's gone to heck in a handbasket," he answered.

Rick had never spoken an actual curse word in Weston's presence. Weston just stared expectantly at him. If anyone knew something, he knew it was his neighbor.

"Actually, I have heard something."

Weston wasn't surprised. He continued staring.

"My buddy John, his son works for SMUD, and since yesterday, his son has been gone."

"Mmhhh," Weston encouraged.

"Well, he called John this morning and said the Roseville Energy Park plant was attacked, and they've got a lot of people over there."

"Attacked?" Weston questioned, a sick feeling beginning in the pit of his stomach.

"It's got two big Siemens turbines...one of them got damaged by an explosion. Once it got damaged, they had to shut the system down. He's sure it was an attack," Rick explained.

"Wait, they don't know what happened?" Weston asked.

"People know, but not John's son. It's just rumors; everything's hush-hush, need to know only. But he saw the turbine room; it was an explosion, maybe a bomb," Rick said.

Attacks even here, thought Weston.

Suddenly, he felt very unsafe. He glanced around the neighborhood, scrutinizing it for anything unusual.

"Rick," said Weston, "how long do you think this outage will last?"

"Could be days, could be weeks," Rick declared.

"Weeks..." Weston responded dully.

That was a punch in the gut. They needed to do something.

"What are you going to do, Rick?" Weston asked.

"Shelter in place, fill every container with water. You should have already filled your bathtubs with water."

"Wait, how long will the water last?" Weston remembered he needed to know that.

"Until that water tower on Westpark Drive runs out. We're still being gravity-fed, but once that's gone, with no more pumps running...." His voice trailed off.

"That could be any time!" Weston exclaimed. "I've got to get back home."

He started to turn back towards his house.

"Weston, you need to get some go bags ready. Plus a firearm and any gas you can scrounge up," Rick warned.

"What do you think is going to happen? The attacks are over now. We just need to get power again," Weston stated.

"Something much worse is coming. You need to get ready for it, and you need to get right with the Lord, too," Rick lectured.

Weston began tuning out after that last part. He had heard this before. He and Rick had had several debates before about religion, and about the end of the world. He believed that God was not involved in the affairs of humanity, and Rick's belief was that Jesus was coming back soon to this planet.

"I know you don't believe me, Weston." Rick added, "But I'm telling you, next they'll digitize the currency, CBDC, and then they will have total control, despotism...and then, the final events will happen rapidly."

"Rick, I don't think - " he began.

" - Central Bank Digital Currency. Look it up. Then it won't be long. When you see our currency digitized, you'll know I was right about this," Rick interrupted.

"Thanks, Rick, for the information," Weston said, trying to change the subject. "I really need to store up more water, so I'll talk to you later."

He turned around and walked back to his house.

"Then you'll know I was right," Rick repeated, more to himself than to Weston.

Bud Collins ran his fingers through his thinning hair, letting out a sigh. He stared out the window at his substation field. He didn't like the look of it at all. The LPT, or Large Power Transformer, sat lifeless in the gravel field bed.

At least they didn't hit that, he thought.

The turbine room nearby was a different story. Most of the siding and framing had been blown away in the explosion, leaving huge black streaks on the remaining white walls. Currently, there was a swarm of technicians moving over and around one of the SGT-800s.

And there was another problem. There were two soldiers now stationed here, walking around his facility. He couldn't even tell what branch of the military they were from. More than likely, they were Blackwater; private security. He had heard of these guys before. They had no identifying patches or logos at all; and they were armed to the teeth.

He had not asked for them, and had not been involved in corporate's decision to send them here. A fact he resented deeply. Being left out of the loop entirely, as though he were not actually in charge, was hurtful. The soldiers, or whatever they were, had just showed up yesterday, and they would not engage with him at all.

The technician was staring at him, waiting for an answer. Bud was nervous. He had never spoken to someone so important before.

"Yes, let him in, Bob," Bud replied.

A few moments later, Governor Edward Thompson walked in with a small entourage of staff and security in tow. He looked haggard, exhausted, and highly annoyed.

"Hello, Governor, I'm Bud Collins," he greeted, extending his hand nervously.

"Are you in charge of this facility?" asked Governor Thompson, skipping formalities. He did not return the handshake.

"Yes, sir. I - "

" - What exactly is going on here? This region has been without power for days. Why?" he demanded.

"Governor, as you probably know, four days ago, an explosion took place here - "

" - How?" Thompson interrupted with annoyance.

"A drone penetrated the perimeter. It was loaded with an explosive charge," Bud explained.

The governor turned towards one of his staff members for further explanation, ignoring Bud.

"Sir, even though this is restricted airspace, it is possible for someone to hack in and then fly a suicide drone into the area," the staff member advised, "we know some of the other attacks happened this way."

"Was the step-up transformer damaged?" another of Thompson's staff interjected.

"The LPT? No, thank God," Bud responded.

"Why does that matter?" asked the Governor.

"Governor, if that Large Power Transformer out there had been hit, we could be looking at months before we could get our station back online," he answered.

"Months?" the Governor exclaimed in total disbelief.

"Fortunately," interjected Bud, "the shrapnel from the bomb missed that device entirely. What we are looking at, though, is that one of our SGTs was hit. Our turbines. Without them, nothing happens here."

"So, what do we need to do? What can I get you?" the Governor asked in a calmer tone now.

"The compressor casing was compromised, and several vanes were hit, as well as several lines on the fuel system. We need replacement parts from Siemens. We cannot get them from anywhere but Siemens," he answered.

"How long?" asked Governor Thompson resignedly.

"Two weeks - "

" - Two weeks!" he exploded. The original irritation was back.

"Sir, as you know, many other substations were hit locally and nationally, and we are simply waiting in line for these components," he responded.

The Governor was staring at the destroyed turbine building now.

"We'll see about that. My people are not waiting that long," he grumbled.

He turned to face Bud.

"Thank you for your work here. I'm sorry. The stress of these times..."

"I understand, sir," Bud empathized.

"My staff will work on this. I promise you that. Get Clint here the contact information for the people you're dealing with at Siemens," the Governor instructed.

"Yes, sir. Thank you, sir," he replied.

The Governor took one last look at the substation field. He looked pensive as he spoke.

"The times in which we are living. Thank God this wasn't worse. I can assure you, things are going to change though," he declared.

"Change?" Bud asked.

The Governor looked out towards the Blackwater guards.

"Things ARE going to change," he stated with authority. With that, he turned and walked out, staff in tow.

Several more days passed without incident at the Miller house. They began to settle into a routine of meals, chores, and board games. Food was not a problem as Ally had stored tons of flour, pasta, and canned vegetables. But they all longed for some pre-power outage food. Weston was dying for In-N-Out.

The propane tank on their gas grill seemed to be holding up fine, and there was a spare in the garage. Water, however, was becoming the biggest concern. Weston had filled every available container, including the bathtubs, but they were going through it fast. He continued refilling every container as they used it, but he kept looking at the various faucets in the house, anticipating that they would run dry any second.

Finally, on day six, the water stopped flowing.

Ally shot a concerned glance at Weston as she tried a different faucet, only to get the same result. The water was gone. Ally motioned for Weston to follow her into their bedroom, out of hearing of the kids.

"The water's gone now. What do we do?" she asked Weston worriedly, closing the door.

"We'll be fine, Ally," he answered.

"You always say that," she snapped, waving both arms.

His temper began to rise. He wanted to say something in retaliation, but held his peace and tried to calm himself.

"Sorry," she stated, "I'm just really scared and freaked out."

She started to cry.

"It's ok, Ally. I feel the same way," he replied, calming himself, "I'm sure everything will return to normal soon. Rick said there are lots of people working on the power. I think it will be anytime now."

He reached out for her and pulled her in.

"I think we're going to be ok...but I think we need to probably become a little more like Rick," he chuckled.

Ally was crying, but out came a weak laugh. She wiped her eyes.

"You're probably right," she agreed, "let's be more like Rick."

It was two o'clock in the morning. Weston was on his right side, snoring lightly. Weak beams from a full moon penetrated through their window blinds, spilling light into their bedroom. Outside, the only sound was the soothing rhythm of crickets.

Suddenly, a bright light burst on in the room. A radio began blaring 'Tutti Frutti, Oh Rudy' downstairs in the kitchen. Weston sat straight up, heart racing. Ally started up next to him.

"What the..." she cried, "Get the gun!"

They both half-fell out of bed, trying to meet this new emergency. Weston moved towards the hallway; his heart was racing and he felt dizzy. He willed himself to calm down. He needed to find the weapon; where was his 9mm? Why couldn't he remember where he had put it?

He could hear Braden stumbling down the hall, mumbling to himself.

Suddenly, Ally started laughing hysterically.

"What?" he whirled around towards her.

She would not stop laughing.

"What is it?" he demanded.

"The power...Weston...the power's on!"

He suddenly realized what was happening. They had left switches and radios in the on position by accident, probably because they had turned them on and off so many times to check them. And now, at two o'clock in the morning, SMUD employees had finally managed to get power back.

God bless them, Weston thought.

He was overjoyed. Life was going to go back to normal now!

"The power's back on!" he repeated back to her.

She squealed with delight, and they jumped into each other's arms, squeezing each other like they hadn't in a long time. Weston lifted her up and whirled her around. Ally laughed and threw her head back, hair twirling behind her.

The power was back on, and life was going to be good again.

Chapter Four - Inclusion

Weston sat at his desk at work, typing away a narrative on his computer. It was a four-part resolution strategy on how he planned to resolve a high-dollar claim. A sea of adjusters sat typing and talking on phones all around him.

Worker's Comp, he sighed.

He had been back to work for only a few days, and he was already burnt out. His whole job was about selling the illusion of control to clients. The illusion being that they had any control over what would happen on these claims. The file he was working on had started as a simple back strain. Now, four years later, and with the insertion of a notorious applicant attorney, it had morphed into a nightmare of multiple orthopedic injuries: diabetes, hypertension, heart damage, and even cancer. What frustrated Weston the most was if the incident had happened at home, he knew it probably would have resolved itself in a few months.

He rubbed his hands on his face and twirled around in his chair.

I need a microbreak already, he thought.

Standing up, he looked around the office. He was in a sea of cubicles, in a room about three hundred feet wide by two hundred feet long, on the fifth floor. Not that you would know there was any view outside. Weston was far from any window or natural light. His existence for the next eight hours would consist of staring at his computer screen, typing, and constantly adjusting his ergonomic chair due to nagging back pain.

As he glanced around, he noticed that Natalie from HR was making the rounds with an intern. They were only one aisle away and would reach his row shortly.

Great, he thought.

He was sure he knew what they were coming to say. He quickly sat back down and began reading his resolution strategy, but he couldn't focus. He knew there was going to be trouble with Natalie. Everything had been changing at work in the last year, and none of those changes were good.

"Weston?"

He whirled in his chair. In front of him stood Natalie with her intern.

"Oh, hi, Natalie. What's up?" he feigned surprise, a sick feeling rising in his stomach.

"Weston, we wanted to come by, to talk to you again about Tolerance and Wellness," she looked unnaturally giddy as she spoke. "We wanted to give you another opportunity to accept your pins."

The intern was silent but glared at Weston.

The last thing he wanted today was confrontation. He just wanted to get back to work. Why did this stuff have to be forced on him? It wasn't even related to what they were doing here.

She stared at him coldly. She displayed a wide smile, which seemed inappropriate for the tone of their conversation. Her eyes were dark and lifeless.

"Weston," she repeated as though she had not heard him. "We are here to make sure you receive your Binary Shame - "

" - I know," he interrupted, now irritated. He knew he shouldn't fight back, but he had difficulty controlling his temper once provoked.

"Weston - "

Why did she have to keep starting every sentence with his name?

" - are you saying that you will not wear these pins?" she asked.

"Yes," he stated curtly. "I will not take or wear the pins. Can I get back to my job now, or is there anything else?"

Natalie glared at him. Without a parting word, she turned and walked away, her intern in tow.

Exhausted, Weston exited his work building with all his other co-workers. It was the end of the day, and he was glad to be working again and making money. But after almost two weeks away, it dawned on him how much he really hated this job.

As he moved out of the main entrance and into the parking lot, he was shocked to see an armed security guard standing under the eaves of the building, watching all the workers leave. The guard had a rifle slung from his shoulder, and he was in all-black military-style fatigues. Weston could not tell what branch of the armed forces he was affiliated with. He noticed his weapon was an AR-15, complete with an extendable buttstock, red dot scope and tactical light on a rail underneath. He also had a large Glock on his hip. The guard nodded reassuringly as Weston walked by. Weston tried not to gawk at him.

He got into his car, turned the ignition key, and started the engine.

What is going on here, he thought to himself. *Are there going to be more attacks?*

He suddenly felt more unsafe than ever.

That night, Weston lay in bed with Ally. After talking for a while, he began watching the news. Of course, it was all about the attacks. Nothing else had played for weeks, and he imagined it would be like this for a while. The newscaster was discussing the attack on the White House, and an animated video was playing in the background showing what had occurred. It had the cheesy look of CGI that programmers had not fully completed yet. Little pixel-looking airplanes moved on the screen like chess pieces. There was a blue background meant to simulate the sky.

In the video, three white blocks were shown flying through the air. They were supposed to be the Learjets used in the attack. After a time, Jet One split from the others, while Jets Two and Three continued on. Jet Two could be seen moving directly under Jet Three in tight formation.

The animation began to focus solely on Jet One. It proceeded to lose altitude more and more. Eventually, trees and buildings could be seen, and it slammed into the ground. It had clearly hit a runway of some sort. This created an explosion that looked like something from one of those cheesy Nintendo games Weston played as a kid. The words *Joint Base Andrews* appeared on the video in the caption below.

The video returned to Jets Two and Three, continuing to move through the air. Suddenly, two darker blocks emerged behind them. They had that sinister, sharp look of fighter jets. At first, these fighter planes stayed behind Two and Three, but then they moved to the front. Eventually they both took flanking positions.

As they did this, Jet Two pulled hard left and slammed into one of the fighters, causing another Nintendo explosion. Now tracers of light could be seen shooting out of the nose of the remaining fighter towards Jet Three. It was firing bullets at the terrorist plane, trying to shoot it down, but it was too late. The video ended with Jet Three flying into a blocky looking building that was obviously meant to be the White House.

The reporter concluded the segment by saying that Hezbollah had claimed responsibility for the attack, and sources close to the former Vice President, now President Lutrell, were blaming Iran.

The segment moved on to President John Lutrell's speech at a podium with the Pentagon in the background. He stated he and the Congress were now considering the nation's options, which included a declaration of war against Iran.

Weston yawned. It was getting late. He still couldn't wrap his head around the reality that the White House was gone, that all this had happened. There had been dozens of simultaneous attacks on the power grid and public places. They had all been carried out by drones or suicide bombers. Hundreds of Americans were dead, and thousands injured.

They had all seemed so safe for so many years. Weston didn't feel that he or his family were very safe anymore at all.

As the week went by, Weston eased more and more into his old routine. He would get up before sunrise and work out. Sometimes Ally would join him. The workout consisted of either lifting weights, or going for a run. He stayed motivated by the fact that he sat at a desk all day long and had done so for most of his life.

He knew the reason Ally didn't share his obsession with exercise was because she spent most of her day running around doing household chores and dealing with home life. Home life was a term inadequate to describe the whirlwind of activity involved in being a stay-at-home Mom. Its duties involved cook, launderer, teacher, chauffeur, event planner/coordinator and occasional grief counselor. With kids aged seventeen, twelve, and eight, there was never a dull moment, nor time to slow down. Braden had Ju-Jitsu, Dylan piano lessons, and Charlotte western horseback riding.

He would then make the one hour and ten minute commute to his job in the downtown area. If an accident occurred, you could easily add on another twenty minutes. For some reason Weston could never understand, Fridays were always worse.

On weekends Weston would go in the opposite direction and attempt to stay in bed for as long as possible. He tried to do as little as Ally would allow. Usually the family would go see a movie, run to a local park, or do some other activity they could all agree upon.

On this Sunday they were out shopping. Rick had made Weston a list of things to get if you wanted to be a 'prepper,' and Weston was excited to acquire some new stuff. When he was a kid, he had gone backpacking a lot, but the gear had changed since then. As he perused the camping aisle at Walmart, Ally and Charlotte said they would meet him and the boys up front once they were all done.

Weston bought a Sawyer Filtration straw and a Platypus gravity camping filter. Additionally, he purchased backpacks and twenty degree mummy bags for each of them. Lastly, he procured several four man tents, each weighing about five pounds. There were other odds and ends thrown in as well. When they met everyone else up front, Ally had several large cases of water and an assortment of dehydrated foods.

As they left the store, something caught Weston's eye. He was surprised to see a guard at the front entrance in black fatigues armed with a rifle.

The next morning, Weston was working his way through a bowl of grape nuts, with little enthusiasm. Sitting at the kitchen table, he tried not to think about the day ahead of him. The kids were all at the table as well. Ally was packing lunches at the kitchen island. Braden and Dylan were having some fiery discussion about some historical figure, John Sutter, and about how bad he was.

The TV in the kitchen was on, but the volume was low, and a closed caption was running below the screen. It was news as usual. Weston was feeling irritated from all the commotion in the kitchen. He was trying to read their mail.

Someday, none of them will be here anymore. Enjoy it now, he told himself.

This thought made him feel a little better.

"Ally?" he called out.

"Yes, West," she answered.

"Can you please call that fund company? What they sent here states we lost $800 in the last six months," he complained.

He glanced at their 401K performance sheet that had recently come in the mail.

"I'll try," she stated, "you know how they keep refusing to talk to me."

As she was talking, Weston stared at the TV. A news anchor was talking with the Federal Reserve building in the background. They were cutting to a live feed of the Fed chairman, who was already beginning his speech nearby.

"I'll probably need you to call them again to give me permission," she continued.

He read the closed caption at the bottom of the screen, annoyed as usual by its inaccuracy.

"....and because of that fact...these terrorist activities are activities, they came from were funded in a way we can't control..."

"So, I'll text you the number. Can you call on your lunch?" Ally asked.

"...And that is the reason reason that today, we are making the announcement for the full implementation... implementation of CBDC..."

"Honey, are you listening?" Ally questioned.

"Wait!" he interrupted, "Turn it up. Turn up the TV!" he yelled.

Everyone turned and stopped talking, staring at Weston. Since no one went for the remote, he pushed towards the TV and turned up the volume manually.

" - we will put a stop to these attacks, when we have control. Central Bank Digital Currency will be that medium of control, a new weapon in America's war on terror. But it's more than that, it's a new way of life for every American," the chairman stated.

Weston stood, glued to the TV. Everyone else stared too, bewildered at Dad's behavior.

"And fortunately, other nations have already paved the way. We cannot afford to be left behind in the critical area of currency technology in this global economy. In the past, America has set the standard, and we will continue to do so for the future. May a higher power bless you all," he stated, ending his speech.

The anchor cut back in, finishing the segment by stating that implementation of FedNote would begin as early as next month.

Weston continued to stare as the program moved on to a raunchy talk show called Jack Springer: Fights and Fury. Scantily clad guests began throwing chairs at each other on a small stage.

"Honey?" Ally said.

Weston stood in front of the TV, deep in thought.

"ARE YOU OK?" she demanded. Apparently, she had been talking to him.

"Yes," he assured her.

"What is it?" she queried.

"Oh, it's just that Rick told me this digital thing...that it would happen someday," he answered.

"Digital what?" she asked.

"It's nothing," he stated calmly. "They're just putting everything on a card. I've gotta go."

He said goodbye to the kids, who had resumed eating. He gave his wife a squeeze and a kiss and walked out the door.

His neighbor Rick had been right.

When he got to his desk that morning, an urgent email awaited him among all the regular emails. Its subject line read: 'Required meeting - 10am.' It was from HR. As he opened it, he saw that he was required to attend a meeting at that time with his boss. It stated he had the option to request his union rep to attend. Weston had an immediate feeling of dread in the pit of his stomach. He forwarded the email to Bess Thompson, his union rep, and requested she be there.

Around 9:50 he got up from his desk and made his way to the third floor. After searching for a few minutes, he located Conference Room 3D and knocked lightly as he slowly opened the frosted glass door.

Inside was a small conference table with several people seated at the far end. Weston immediately noticed Natalie and the intern were both there, smiling and laughing about something he couldn't make out. The other two were Bess Thompson, his union rep, and his supervisor, Ellen Hoffert. Everyone quieted down as he entered the room.

"Please have a seat, Weston," Ellen invited, motioning with her hand.

Reluctantly, he sat down.

This is going to be bad, he thought.

"Weston, we are here to meet today...well, it has been brought to our attention...that you have had multiple issues recently with Tolerance and Wellness," she stated.

Weston sat in his chair and stared at Ellen, waiting.

Natalie broke in.

"Weston, you have refused to wear your required pins. Binary shame and MAP Ally, to be specific. And there is this issue with your email signature," she said, smiling.

"You have repeatedly refused to note your personal pronouns on your email signature," Ellen finished Natalie's thought.

"I don't need a pronoun, Ellen. I use my name, which is a noun. I like nouns better," he answered curtly.

"Very funny, Weston. But in all seriousness - " Natalie broke in. Her smile had finally faded.

" - I'm not kidding," he interrupted. "I already have a pronoun on my email signature, anyway. It says Senior Claims Adjuster. And above that is a noun: my name. If that's not enough, then maybe - "

" - Look, I don't think we need a grammar lesson here today. We all know grammar is triggering anyway. I think the point is, Weston, that you are in violation of company policies. We're here to remedy that." Bess Thompson interrupted.

"Is there an issue with my work? Because, if I recall, I led the unit in settlements last month."

"That may be the case, but that is not why we are here today," Ellen stated.

"One of the requirements of working here, Weston, is that you wear these pins," chimed in Natalie.

The rest of the group remained silent, waiting.

"You call this policy...tolerance," he emphasized that last word, "but you're telling me I should be ashamed because I am - " he raised his hands to make quotation marks, " - BINARY. So you are not being tolerant of me!" he raised his voice.

"This is a stubborn - "

" - And do you people even know what a MAP is?" he stated incredulously. He was angry now. "You want me to wear something stating I agree with the most sick, twisted - "

" - How dare you!" Natalie interrupted, emphasizing each word slowly. She had risen to her feet. All eyes turned to her.

"Love is love," she explained, talking to him as though he were a slow, ignorant child, "and love comes in many, many different and exciting forms, Weston."

There was a crazed look in her eyes now. Several droplets of spit flew from her mouth as she spoke.

"You WILL wear these pins," she demanded in a commanding tone, "symbolizing that you FULLY agree that an adult can be attracted - "

" - Screw this!" Weston shouted, pounding the table with his fists. Everyone turned towards him; wide-eyed. Natalie stopped.

"You people are creating problems that aren't real...you are... weaponizing language! Bess, back me up here! I was hired to do a job...This is very simple. I was hired to do a job, and I AM DOING THAT JOB!"

He was furious now.

"This prissy little pin show is...stupid, a waste of my time. It was not in my hiring contract, and it has nothing to do with any real work being done here. What do these people even DO?" he asked, motioning towards Natalie, "We're here to handle claims. They're getting paid to harass us. It's insane."

"Weston," Bess replied in a soothing tone. He suddenly noticed she had been cradling a large packet of papers in her hands. She continued:

"Weston, our policies of Tolerance and Wellness were put into place for a reason, and they are very important to the life and health of this company. We stand strongly behind these ideals and we believe in them firmly. They are more important than even the work we do here. They are for the protection of everyone."

"Almost everyone," Weston retorted.

"Weston," she went on, "unfortunately, due to your insubordination in this matter, I'm afraid we have no other choice... but to terminate you, effective immediately."

Natalie sat back down. Her smile had now returned. She stared at Weston with satisfaction.

"What?" he exclaimed.

"Ellen will help you return to your desk... and pack up any essentials," she stated curtly.

"Really?" he mused. "Really..." he repeated in wonder.

"We thank you for your service," Bess added.

With that, they all stood as one, waiting for Weston to stand as well. He took their queue and awkwardly rose.

"I'll email you the separation paperwork," Bess stated with finality.

They all turned and exited the conference room. Weston remained standing at the table in total shock. As Natalie passed by, she cast a hateful glance at him. Under her breath, she muttered one word:

"Cis-freak."

At home, Weston and Ally were sitting at the kitchen table. The kids had long since gone to bed. Ally was crying.

"I just don't understand. Why would they fire you...fire you over this?" she asked between snivels.

"I don't know," he responded flatly.

What was he going to do now? Besides the fantastic retirement (which he was in danger of losing due to his termination status - he would call calPERS regarding that) and great benefits, he had been pulling in almost $100k a year. His only backup plan was to work for his brother-in-law Bill, who ran his own construction company doing punch-out work. He doubted he could pull in even half of his old salary doing that though, and there were no benefits.

Ally read his thoughts.

"Maybe you should just go work for Bill for now. It seems like this movement has taken over white-collar work," she stated while gesturing with her hands in exasperation.

"Yes," he agreed, "if we can make it work."

"We can make some cuts. Stop eating out. Less entertainment. Stuff like that," she stated.

"I'll call Bill," he said with resignation.

It was decided.

Chapter Five - Dreams

It had taken Weston longer than usual to fall asleep. There was too much on his mind. He relived the meeting, picturing Natalie's inappropriate smile, lifeless eyes, and final parting insult. He still could not wrap his head around the fact that his company had actually fired him over nothing.

Ally had long since drifted off, snoring lightly. Weston continued to stare at the ceiling, finding shapes in the popcorn texture. The house was dark and silent, but a slight breeze was blowing outside, which made a soothing sound. The maple tree next to the house occasionally rocked against the window, being blown by the wind.

I need to prune that, he thought to himself.

His eyelids were getting droopy now. Slowly, slowly, he began drifting off to sleep.

In his dream, he suddenly awoke. He could tell something was very wrong. Everything looked strange. He was standing at the edge of an ocean, but all the colors were wrong. The sky was a turbid green, menacing and dark. The land was crimson-tinted and was smoldering in some areas. There were no trees or greenery. Everything looked like he was viewing it through stained glass. The ocean looked dark blue.

Suddenly, several enormous explosions occurred. The noise was deafening, and Weston started in surprise and crouched down, covering his ears. It barely helped. Immense cataracts of water were erupting into the sky. He gazed upward at them in awe. Large, jagged rocks were spinning and flying through the air, some slowing down and descending back to earth, others continuing their trajectory upward to unbelievable heights. The scale of it was beyond comprehension.

Movement near him caught his eye, and he turned toward it. In the distance, large groups of animals and people could be seen running away from him. They were moving up a distant hillside to higher ground. Both man and beast were much larger than he was. Nevertheless, all looked terrified as little children running from an angry parent.

"Why are you running?" he yelled.

His words sounded distorted, empty. He could tell they did not reach more than five feet beyond him. The group continued running into the nearby foothills, out of sight.

Within seconds, water was upon him. Not a creek or river but an ocean of water. He was submerged instantly, but strangely, the force of it did not move him at all. He seemed now to be hundreds of feet beneath its surface, yet he continued to breathe as he normally would on land. Every other living creature was not so lucky, however.

As his vision adjusted to his new environment, Weston was horrified. Every few feet, as far as the eye could see, floated the bodies of man and beast. Some hung upright, others sideways, and many hovered upside down. All had one thing in common though; as the gentle current of the ocean swelled to the right, each body gently pulled in that direction. Then slowly back to the center, and then to the left. Gradually, ever so gradually, all of them were sinking downward into a nightmarish abyss. Weston had the thought that they were performing for him, performing some kind of macabre dance. A flash mob from a hell that he wanted to get out of, but he could not wake up.

Nearest to him floated an enormous man. Weston turned to look at him. He guessed he must have been nine feet tall, maybe five to six hundred pounds. He was all sinew and muscle. The dead man was clothed in a purple tunic, a one-piece outfit with a sturdy belt at the waist. His long hair flowed in the opposite direction of his body, exposing a slash of a mouth and a vicious face. His arms floated straight out at his sides while his hands bent downward at the wrists, making weird little waving patterns due to currents. It was almost like he was waving at Weston, but his eyes were closed. His lips were open, and his face was bloodied and lifeless. Sea water made its way in and out of his torn lips.

Weston continued to stare at him. Suddenly, the man's eyes opened, and he looked at Weston. Out of his distorted lips came a single phrase:

"Two horns," he moaned.

Weston leaped up in bed, gasping for air. He was back in his bedroom again. His heart was racing. Next to him, Ally turned, starting as well.

"Honey, what's wrong?" she exclaimed, turning on a bedside lamp.

He continued to struggle to breathe, not responding to her.

"What is wrong?" she demanded, "Did you have a nightmare?"

"Yes...yes," he choked out.

Tears were streaming down his face. He couldn't believe how vivid the dream had been. He was covered in goosebumps, and his mind was whirling. He needed to calm down and stop being so emotional.

Breathe, just try to breathe, he told himself.

He took several deep breaths. Slowly, he began to relax. The sound of his pounding heart started to recede a bit.

"What WAS it?" she urged.

"A dream," he uttered, "a dream...but SO vivid. There were bodies floating everywhere....and a flood."

"What?" she asked in surprise.

Suddenly, he had an idea.

"Ally, do we have a Bible?" he asked.

"What?" she repeated, dumbfounded.

"A Bible," he restated.

"I think so," she answered slowly, "on the bookshelf...from our wedding day."

He slipped on a robe, grabbed his flashlight, and moved towards the living room. He was starting to calm down now.

"West, what's this about?" she questioned.

He continued into the living room downstairs and found the bookshelf. He started moving the beam of the flashlight over books. The bookshelf was full and Weston noticed with annoyance that they had begun stacking additional rows of books in front of the old ones, making it difficult to see what they had.

Then he caught a glimpse of it. It was a large white Bible buried behind several hardback novels and magazines. He dumped a clump of books off the shelf onto the floor, and shimmied the Bible out of its spot.

Ally followed behind him.

"Weston!" she exclaimed as the books made a loud thud.

He ignored her, flipping through several pages. He had to find it. It had been years.

Thirty years, he thought.

He flipped through Genesis four, five, and six. Then he found it. Genesis seven. It was entitled, 'The Great Flood.' Weston began reading, "Then the Lord said to Noah..."

Finally, in verse eleven, he found it.

"In the six hundredth year of Noah's life, in the second month, the seventeenth day of the month, on that day *all the fountains of the great deep were broken up*, and the windows of heaven were opened."

"What are you reading?" Ally inquired, coming over to him.

"I saw this!" Weston declared incredulously.

A surprised laugh escaped her lips.

"You what?" she asked.

"In my dream. All the fountains of the great deep were broken up. I just saw huge fountains of water shooting up into the sky...in my dream," he repeated.

"West, it was just a dream. I'm sure it was vivid, but..."

"Like I was there. This was something more," he reflected. He was sure of it.

He looked at her now and hesitated before speaking.

"What does two horns mean to you? Anything?" he asked.

Ally's face changed from concern to a knowing smile.

"Honey, come back to bed. You're under so much stress right now. It's all going to work out with this new job. Just come back with me to bed and get some rest."

"Ok. ok," he relented.

Perhaps he was overreacting. It was just a dream after all. Dreams were not real. But something was nagging at the back of his mind. Why would he have dreamed about Noah's flood when he hadn't heard that story since he was a teenager? It had been that long since he had been to church. He must have been fifteen when his father, angry at the pastor, had declared, 'We're never going back.'

Weston couldn't remember what the disagreement had even been about, but true to his word, his father had led the family steadily away from any form of religion. None of them had ever thought about church again.

Ally was right, though; he was under an enormous amount of pressure and stress. Stress did strange things to the body and the mind. He just needed to get some rest. He knew he would be thinking more clearly in the morning.

He put the Bible down on the coffee table and followed Ally back upstairs to the bedroom. After a while, he drifted off to sleep again.

The second dream was worse. He and his family were running through a dark tunnel. Every hundred yards or so, there was a green lamp on the wall. It provided just enough light to show the way to the next fixture. The walls were glistening with condensation and oozing dark fluid. They were covered with cabling and machinery, and seemed to provide no adjoining corridors or other way out. So they continued running forward, because something was coming up behind them.

Weston glanced over his shoulder as they ran. He was terrified at what he saw. An army was chasing them. Thousands of soldiers, armed to the teeth, scrambling over each other trying to reach them. Each soldier had a crazed look in his eyes, and some screamed at the top of their lungs. It made Weston think of what the Japanese must have looked like during their kamikaze charges of World War II.

And there was something worse. Some soldiers were different from the rest. Instead of a human head and face, they had the face of either a wolf or a hog. These unholy fusions between man and beast shouted just as their human counterparts did. In fact, they seemed to be in charge, barking orders and spurring the army forward.

"Hurry!" urged Weston to his family.

Ally and the kids all looked terrified as they glanced back at him. Each one tried to pick up the pace. Weston stayed slightly behind. Not that he could do anything to protect them, but his protective instincts kicked in, nevertheless. If one of these hybrid soldiers caught up to them, he would somehow fight them, even though he possessed no weapons.

Up ahead, something was different. They could see that the next lamp was now a dull red instead of the usual green. As they ran towards this light, they could see two tunnels ahead. The one on the right was wide, and the one on the left was narrow. The wide tunnel exuded very faint light. The narrow tunnel was absolutely pitch black. The main tunnel shifted into these two; there was no third option to choose from.

"GO RIGHT?" yelled Ally.

It seemed wrong. Weston didn't feel good about the wide tunnel at all. It felt like a trap.

"No!" he shouted back, out of breath, "The narrow one!"

"Left?" she questioned him.

"Go left, Ally!" he demanded.

The army was closing in behind them. He could hear squeals of delight from the pig soldiers and the stomping of thousands of feet. He was sure those feet would trample them.

Allyson was hesitating.

"Go left! Left!" he shouted in frustration.

As Ally neared the tunnels, she veered to the left without losing her stride. Dylan, Charlotte and Braden followed her and disappeared into the black. Weston came up right behind them and flew into the tunnel. The opening was so narrow he barely fit.

There was now no light at all. His whole family was shouting. They had to slow down to a trot because they kept hitting the walls, which had closed in on them dramatically.

Behind them, the crazed army had severely bottlenecked and was struggling to get through, as each soldier was loaded with weapons and gear. The soldiers roared in frustration and anger, beating at the concrete walls and pounding on the man or beast in front of them.

"Follow me, follow me!" shouted Ally.

Her voice sounded far away. Weston was panicking because he was falling further behind. He couldn't close the gap between him and his family because he kept slamming into walls. The tunnel had changed from a straight shot to a confusing maze. The floor was also starting to slant up and down at various points. Weston felt utterly turned around. If only there were just a little light.

Up ahead, a dim light materialized. In the distance he could see his family. He began pushing his legs and lungs to catch them. As he drew nearer to Braden, who was in front of him, things changed again. There was a door jam ahead, with no apparent door. One by one, he watched his family run through it. He saw Braden run through and readied himself to pass through as well. Suddenly, a large steel door came down from the door header and slammed shut. He was so close to passing through it that he could not stop in time and slammed into the steel. He collapsed onto the concrete with a painful thud. With the wind knocked out of him, he could do nothing but try to force some air into his lungs and pick himself up off the ground.

He could hear soldiers closing in behind him. He pulled and pounded on the door but there was nothing to grab; it had no doorknob. He pushed on it with all his might, but it would not give. Weston screamed in frustration.

Suddenly, he heard a growl, and he whirled around. A soldier with bulging muscles and a wolf head had just entered the room. It was no more than ten feet away. Its eyes were large and filled with need. Its jaws were twitching with excitement. In its right hand, it held a machete. In its other hand was a pistol. It wore camo fatigues and a torn A shirt.

As it edged closer, he noticed a glittering object was dangling around its bulging neck and bouncing on its chest. It was a small ornament, about the size of a tangerine, dangling from a faded chain. A white lamb with two prominent horns protruding from the lamb's head.

Additional soldiers now piled in the small room behind the wolfman. He held up his hand and growled at them, letting them know he would be the one to make the kill. He grinned and moved slowly towards Weston, raising the machete.

Weston cowered in fear, but managed to utter a single word.

"Why?"

Wolfman grinned.

"Wide is the gate Weesstonnn…" it growled mockingly, gesturing towards the two tunnel entrances.

With that, it lunged.

Weston leaped up in bed for the second time, tears streaming down his face, heart racing.

The next day at work, Weston moved a trowel of mud over a drywall patch. Bill came over and took a look.

"Don't worry about the lift-offs," he instructed, speaking of the lines the edge of the trowel made as he smoothed it over the patch, "they'll sand off easily."

"Gotcha," Weston returned.

They had been doing drywall all week. Weston had done it as a teenager, but this week had been a steep learning curve, as it had been years since he had worked with his hands. But he was enjoying the freedom of not having to be at a desk all day.

As Weston smoothed over additional patches, he brooded over the meaning of the dreams. The first one seemed fairly straightforward; it was a vivid presentation of Noah's flood. The waters bursting forth out of the ground, the people and animals fleeing, and the bodies in the water had made Weston feel like he was there. It had been many years since he had attended church, but he was sure what he had seen was Noah's flood. It was one of the more well-known stories in the Bible. But the real question was, why had he seen it?

What Weston could not understand was the message 'two horns' from the drowned giant. He could not recall ever hearing that phrase in a church setting or Bible reading.

The second dream was less clear and more frightening. Being chased down a tunnel by a horde of hybrid man-beast soldiers had no context for Weston. But choosing between a wide tunnel and a narrow tunnel seemed familiar. He remembered a phrase he had heard when he was a kid about wide is the gate and narrow is the way. He was pretty sure that was from the Bible.

But again, at the end of the dream, there was a strange similarity with the mystery of the two horns. Wolfman had a lamb with two horns on his necklace. So, here was additional information that was not in the first dream: the two horns were on a lamb. He had no clue what any of it meant.

After work, as he drove home, he continued pondering the dreams. They had been so vivid that he was beginning to wonder if they had come from God. This was a quandary for Weston, because he did not believe that any higher power was involved in human affairs. He just could not believe, with all the evil in the world; all the wars, the poverty, the suffering, that there could be a God who was engaged with Earth's affairs. If He did care, then why did He allow such things?

But the dreams seemed like a message. Choosing between a wide tunnel and a narrow tunnel had to be a reference to this statement in the Bible that he remembered. He had never had dreams like this in his life, and they had shaken him badly. He made a decision then and there, that if there was a message for him in all this, he would listen to it, whatever the source.

That night, in his study, Weston opened his wedding Bible again. Ally and the kids were all asleep. He began by re-reading the story of Noah's flood. As he reviewed it, he was struck by the vividness of his dream again. While not necessarily sequential, each scene seemed true to the Bible. But he felt like there must be more to it. Why did he even have a dream about Noah's flood? And what was the message of 'two horns' all about?

After half an hour of further study, Weston grew frustrated. The Bible was too large a book and covered too great a diversity of topics and time-periods for him to understand. He could not find the answers to his questions. He recalled a similar feeling of exasperation as a child. It was simply too difficult to find what he was looking for.

Suddenly, he had an idea. He could ask Google questions, and maybe it would direct him to the passage in the Bible he was looking for. He typed in Google, 'Noah's Flood.'

Multiple webpage results appeared, and he began reading them. One caught his eye in particular.

"As in the days of Noah, so also will the coming of the Son of Man be." He clicked on it.

He read: "But as the days of Noah were, so shall also the coming of the Son of Man be. For as in the days that were before the flood they were eating and drinking, marrying and giving in marriage, until the day that Noah entered into the ark, and knew not until the Flood came, and took them all away, so shall also the coming of the Son of Man be." Matthew 24:38,39.

It was becoming clearer. A correlation was made in the Bible between the Flood and the second coming of Jesus, which Rick kept saying was coming. As Weston read on, the commentator stated that Jesus was saying conditions at the end of time would be the same as they had been right before the flood.

He Googled, 'What were conditions like before Noah's flood?' He had no idea.

He was led to Genesis 6:5: "And the Lord saw that the wickedness of man was great in the earth, and that every intent of the thoughts of his heart was only evil continually."

He understood the message. It was hard to deny the negative change in society that had taken place since his childhood. Since his parent's childhood, the shift was incredible. As kids, his parents had watched The Adventures of Rocky and Bullwinkle on TV. Weston's children were watching The Walking Dead.

Next, he focused on the second dream. He Googled, 'Wide is the gate.'

Immediately, the message became clear. "Enter ye in at the straight gate; for wide is the gate, and broad is the way, that leadeth to destruction, and many there be which go in thereat. Because strait is the gate, and narrow is the way, which leadeth unto life, and few there be that find it." Matthew 7:13,14.

Was this the allegory of the tunnel dream? It seemed so. Weston and his family had chosen the narrow way, which seemed less inviting and more difficult. But why had Weston not made it through? At any rate, he seemed to have received a message to choose between two paths. And it seemed clear at this point he was not taking the right one. Otherwise, the dream would not have been necessary.

Finally, he typed in what intrigued him most. He Googled, 'two horns.' Three rows down, he could see the search engine prefill 'two horns like a lamb...'

That was it! He clicked the link.

"And I beheld another beast coming up out of the earth: and he had two horns like a lamb, and he spake as a dragon." Revelation 13:11.

Weston was getting tired. This last verse meant nothing to him at all. He really should be getting some rest. He had another hard day ahead of him tomorrow, and he was sore from today.

I'm going to see what Rick has to say about all this, he decided.

With that, he went to bed.

The next day after dinner, he saw Rick out in his front yard, and figured this was his chance. As he approached, Rick gave his usual friendly greeting and a firm handshake.

"You get that go bag ready, Weston?" Rick started in immediately.

"Yes, yes, Rick," Weston answered. He had actually prepared one for each family member, and they were sitting in the garage.

"Good, good. Something's coming I tell ya," he prophesied.

"That's actually what I wanted to talk to you about, Rick," said Weston.

"Really?" Rick answered in surprise.

"You know I'm not really into this stuff - "

" - Yeah."

"Well, I had this dream. Two dreams. They were so intense, and they kinda shook me up."

Weston told him about both dreams. Rick listened attentively.

"I think these dreams are from the Lord," he declared, "I think He is trying to warn you of what's coming. To get ready."

Weston hesitated. It was hard for him to accept where this was going.

"Rick, the dreams were incredible. I just don't know if I believe that God would personally interact with me, or anyone, like this. I believe this world was created by intelligent design, but I am an agnostic. We just can't know how it happened, who did it," Weston stated.

"Weston, have you ever read the Bible?"

"Parts, yeah. I mean, mainly when I was a kid. Not anymore."

"The reason I ask is, it describes what we see around us very accurately. More accurately than the other religious books that are out there. Better than the Qur'an, the Vedas, the Tripitaka, the Sishu Wujing - "

" - The what?" Weston asked.

"Those are the holy books of Islam, Hinduism, Buddhism, Confucianism. The other main religions that offer an alternative to Christianity."

"But all these religions lead down the same path. I mean, there can't just be one way," Weston reasoned.

"There is one major difference between all of them and Christianity. Do you know what it is?" Rick inquired.

"No," Weston admitted.

"There's a quote that sums it up well. It says: "The principle that man can save himself by his own works lay at the foundation of every heathen religion."

"But those are legitimate beliefs. They can't all be wrong," Weston challenged.

"What I'm trying to say is, every, and I mean EVERY, religion other than Christianity tells you you've got to summon up something within yourself, to save yourself. Christianity teaches that you were born sinful, and that someone else has to deliver you from this condition. You can't do it yourself," Rick explained.

"Rick, I'm not a sinner. I've never hurt anybody. Ally and I are good people. We're raising our kids better than we were raised, I know that much. Jesus probably died for really sinful people, the drug addicts, murderers, etc. Not us." he said.

"I'll stop you right there," Rick said. "Do you think you're good enough to go to Heaven?"

Weston paused for a moment.

"I do. Yes," he stated firmly.

"How are you going to get there?" Rick questioned.

"What?"

"After you die, how are you going to get to Heaven? You won't be alive anymore, and it's more than likely really far away."

Weston chuckled. "That's a silly question."

"Not really. I'm a practical man, Weston. I would like to know exactly how you plan on arriving at Heaven, and once you get there, how you plan on being allowed inside?"

"I don't know, Rick," Weston was starting to feel exhausted by this conversation. He felt like he was being outwitted and he was growing tired.

"Grace," Rick stated plainly.

"Grace?" Weston repeated.

"That is how you will get there. You actually don't deserve to be there."

"Thanks," Weston replied sarcastically.

"Neither do I, Weston. Nobody does. It is God's grace alone that would allow you into Heaven. And, He has outlined how you can obtain this. It is arrogant and presumptuous to think you can just enter the presence of your Maker without even bothering to learn what the conditions for entering into His presence are. The Bible says if we came near Him in our present state, we would be destroyed."

"So, how do you think we get to Heaven then?" Weston questioned.

"Accept that Jesus died on the cross for YOUR sins. Repent of your sins and ask Him to save you. Spend time in His Word and prayer. He will change you more and more as time goes on. It's called being 'born again.' And by His grace alone, He will resurrect you when He comes and bring you to Heaven, even though you will never deserve it."

"Is that what the Bible says?" Weston queried.

"Yes, it is," Rick replied.

"The thing is, with me, I'm just not sure the Bible can be trusted."

"Now we're back to what I was trying to say in the beginning," Rick declared. "Because the Bible is the only source that describes the human heart correctly, that it is desperately wicked, and that there is nothing within man that he can summon from within to save himself from that wickedness, we can know that the Bible is the only religious material that is giving us the truth."

"Hmmh. Makes sense, I guess. I don't really know - "

" - And before 1947, many more people mocked the Bible than they do now."

"1947?" Weston questioned.

"The Dead Sea Scrolls were found in 1947. It took them years to go through them all, but once they did, do you know what they found?" Rick asked.

"I don't know," Weston admitted.

"They found portions of all books of the Bible, except one. They found that the age of those books was over a century before Christ, and they found that they were the same as the translations that you can buy in a bookstore today.

That would be amazing in and of itself, but one of those books, Daniel, literally contained a time prophecy specifying exactly when Jesus would come...before He came. They dated the age of that book of Daniel to over a century before Jesus came. It's a slam dunk, Weston. And I haven't even talked about the time prophecies," Rick stated emphatically.

"A slam dunk..." Weston repeated.

"The book of Daniel itself was written six centuries before Christ. But the one they found must have been a copy. So, over a century before Jesus came, this copy of the book of Daniel was saved with the other Dead Sea Scrolls. It specified what year Jesus would come. And we know historically, He did come in the year that it outlined; A.D. 27. That was the year of His anointing. There is no way to explain it."

"You've given me a lot to think about..."

Weston remembered the two horns. He was feeling like he had taken in all the information he could for the time being.

"Does the term two horns mean anything to you, like, on a lamb?"

Rick looked at him and grinned. "I remember your dreams had that in them...and I know exactly what it means."

Weston grew excited.

"Really! Really? You've got to explain this to me - "

" - Weston, I hate to stop this, but right now, I'm late for something. Why don't you, Ally, and the kids come over for dinner this Thursday? Kathleen makes incredible enchiladas."

"Ok," Weston replied disappointedly. "Ok. I'll check with Ally. I think we can make it."

He had really wanted to know what the two horns meant.

Chapter Six - The Talk

President John Lutrell shifted in his chair, looking down at his hands. He was getting frustrated. He and his cabinet were at the Pentagon, listening to the morning briefing. It had been gridlock for weeks, and he was getting tired of it. The constant disagreement and lack of any forward movement.

General McCarthy was getting worked up, as he did each day, about retaliation against Iran, whom he felt was fighting a proxy war through Hezbollah.

Other members of his staff disagreed, and the arguments began to escalate.

Finally, his chief-of-staff Tim Blain interrupted.

"Folks, we can all agree a response is needed...the time for arguing about that is over. We're sitting here having these meetings in the Pentagon! We just need to decide the level of that response and to whom it is ultimately directed. Correct, John?" He turned his gaze to the President.

President Lutrell realized all eyes were on him. He was not used to this, being in charge of making the call. And he knew Tim's bent on this; he was trying to push him to act.

When he was Fauser's vice-president, he hadn't made decisions of any kind. At first, when Doug died, he believed he would enjoy being in the captain's chair, finally in charge. Of course it seemed morbid, given the circumstances. But after only a few weeks, the constant stress was already taking a toll. He wasn't sleeping much, his appetite had waned, and he was having trouble staying focused.

He ran his hands through his thinning gray hair. He knew what he wanted to do. He just didn't know if it was what he should do.

"We have that satellite intel on the Hezbollah base in Chabahar? It's still current?" he inquired.

"Rock solid, Mr. President," answered General McCarthy. "Two days ago."

"Ok...ok. Let's send a team. Let's clean it up."

"Yes, sir!" McCarthy answered enthusiastically.

"Mr. President, you realize that might elicit a response from - " his Secretary of State Judy Nguyen stated.

" - They have already destroyed the White House, Judy," Lutrell interrupted. He had raised his voice and now the whole room had gone silent.

The Secretary of State looked surprised at the reprimand. She stared down at the conference table in front of her.

He felt bad, but he knew he was right. Terrorists had wiped out the White House, attacked the whole country, and they were squawking like a bunch of chickens, afraid to retaliate! He hated to admit it, but he was enjoying the power at his fingertips. The power to make life-altering decisions. To hand out some payback to evil-doers.

"General..." he said.

McCarthy had looked away, but turned back to face the President.

"Who do we have in the region?"

McCarthy understood him correctly to mean what Carrier Strike Group. His face lit up.

"Group Five, USS Ronald Reagan, is closest. They could be there within the week," answered the General.

"Let's get them over there...let's do it."

Judy looked unhappy, but continued to be silent and stare at the table.

"Give me a report tomorrow, please. I think that's it then," he stated as he looked around the room. Everyone was silent. They seemed to be contemplating the ramifications of his order. Lutrell stood up from his chair.

Immediately everyone in the room stood up, and slowly began exiting. General McCarthy was beaming.

As Lutrell moved towards the exit Secret Service came up alongside him. Tim moved towards the President, motioning with his hand towards a tall, well-dressed individual.

"Mr. President? John?" he called out, "I have someone that wants a quick meeting. Ambassador Bianchi. Is that ok?"

"Ok, ok," John stated, reaching out and shaking Ambassador Bianchi's hand.

The Secret Service agent remained at his side. People continued exiting the conference room all around them.

"How can I help you today, Mr. Bianchi?" President Lutrell inquired.

He was anxious to get on to his next appointment; racquetball with his lawyer.

"Mr. President," Ambassador Bianchi began, "I have come on behalf of the Holy Father. He wishes to extend a message to you."

Bianchi glanced at the agent at his side, as well as Tim Blain.

"Privately, if I may? If at all possible," he asked.

"Mr. Bianchi, any message you have to convey, I assure you these gentlemen can hear," the President instructed.

"Fine," Bianchi stated in a defeated tone.

He hesitated.

"His Holy See wishes to see you personally as soon as possible. There are multiple issues he desires to address, and wishes he hopes to convey. He hopes to come here, to meet with you, perhaps as early as next week?"

"Next week," Lutrell repeated with surprise. "Is there an urgency?"

"I'm afraid there is, Mr. President," Bianchi replied.

Lutrell paused for a moment. The Pope, coming to see him, and only a few weeks into his Presidency! Something important must be in the pipeline. Quickly he realized, though, it was probably to stop him from moving forward with any Middle East aggression. The Pope was probably anticipating American retaliation in the Middle East. Suddenly, Lutrell's enthusiasm cooled.

"I'll have Tim check the schedule - "

" - Mr. President," Bianchi interrupted forcibly, "it is difficult for me to properly emphasize the importance of this meeting."

He had placed his hand on President Lutrell's wrist. John looked down at this and then looked back into Ambassador Bianchi's eyes. They held a strange urgency.

"Please, President Lutrell," he pleaded.

Lutrell hesitated.

"Ah, Mr. Ambassador, we will definitely make this a high priority. I'm sure we will be able to make it work...okay? Get with Tim on the details, yes?"

Bianchi seemed to relax again, and a twinge of embarrassment came over his face.

"Thank you, Mr. President. I am sorry," he stated, gesturing towards the hand that had grasped Lutrell's wrist. "I truly thank you."

"Of course," Lutrell replied. He walked away, annoyed, with his staff in tow.

Tommy 'Nighttrain' McCaine sat back in his host chair at WKPI headquarters. Computers, monitors and microphones surrounded him. He took a pull off his vape pen and rolled his eyes. There was no one in the studio to see this act of annoyance. His current caller had stayed on topic for about twenty seconds, but was now droning on about aliens.

The topic in question was Starshield, SpaceX's latest satellite program. Tommy had been discussing Starlink, and it had morphed into a discussion on its successor, Starshield. For almost a week now he had been fielding calls on the topic.

His radio show had always dealt with issues on the fringe, and Starshield was no different. Over the last few days, calls had ranged from mild defenders to zealous critics. This kind of stuff was a magnet for conspiracy theorists and tin-foil hat wearers. Tonight, everyone was universally attacking the program. This was all as Tommy would have it, since he believed there was more to the space program than met the eye.

"Well, thank you, caller," Tommy interrupted, hitting the call end button as they started reliving their latest alien abduction.

"Next caller, what's your name?" Tommy asked.

"Sean."

"Hello, Sean. Well, what's your take on the purpose of Starshield?" Tommy asked.

"You have to ask yourself why Starlink has launched over five thousand satellites in about five years - "

" - mmmhhh," Tommy encouraged.

" - and they have plans to launch seven thousand more. But the real issue is, if you go to Starshield's own website, it says right on there that they have a surveillance package capability."

"Ah-huh. Cameras in the sky. How do you feel about that, Sean?" Tommy prodded.

"Not good. What if they turn 'em on me? This seems like the road to despotism. It has not been very long since millions were killed by Comm - "

" - it's even more than Communism, Sean. What if I told you it was to do something we haven't ever seen before."

The caller seemed thrown off.

"Ah, like what?"

"Global control, Seany boy. Why do you think the internet was even created in the first place?" he questioned, raising his voice. He was getting worked up.

"The plan is even crazier than you think, but you were headed in the right direction when you brought up Communism...Stalin, Pol Pot, Hitler, they were all thinking small. What's going on now behind the scenes, it's bigger. It's gonna make Mao look like a thug with a born to lose tattoo on his chest holding up the corner liquor store. It's bigger..."

He noticed that time was up now, commercials were set to go in ten seconds.

"Well, folks, we've got to take a quick commercial break. We'll be right back with our discussion on Starshield. Call in to Nighttrain at 855-423-7494, that's 855-423-7494."

Tommy hit the button to move to commercials. He sat back, ready to enjoy the next five minutes, when from his left he noticed his station manager was motioning for him to come out. He sighed, exited the booth, and went out into the hallway.

In the hallway, his station manager Tony was waiting with two men. They were fit-looking guys in dark suits. Tommy took one look and smelled government agents.

"Tommy, these gentlemen insisted on having a word with you...in private," Tony stated. He had a defeated look on his face, like he had already had badges pulled on him to make this happen.

Tommy hated the government and he hated government agents. He had spent a good part of the last twenty years railing against them, dealing with government conspiracies on his radio show, and he didn't mind standing up to them at all. He knew how to handle these types.

"No problem, Tony," he replied smoothly, "gentlemen, what can Nighttrain do for you this evening?"

"Mr. McCaine," stated the older agent, glaring at Tony, who took the hint and started to walk back to his office. "We wanted to come by tonight and just make a very simple, reasonable request."

This outta be good, Tommy thought.

"Oh, yeah, what's that?" he questioned.

"Your topic. Starshield. It's a sensitive subject. You've been talking about it for some time now. We would prefer that you cease these discussions on the air." he stated flatly as he motioned toward the sound booth.

"We would prefer that I cease these discussions?" Tommy repeated back mockingly.

"Yes."

"Who's 'we?'" he asked defiantly.

The older agent paused. "I need to know if you will move on to a more palatable topic."

"Palatable?" he grinned.

Tommy was highly annoyed. No one told him what to do, and he was unafraid of these goons. They were clearly trying to intimidate him.

"Look, I don't know where you guys are from, and you haven't shown me identification. You know I have freedom of speech, right? The 1st amendment. You ever heard of the 1st amendment," - he pointed a finger towards the agent's chest - "you don't tell me what I can and can't talk about. I'll talk about clown posse armies invading Polish suburbs in the dead of night if I want to talk - "

" - You've been asked.... I'm noting your refusal," interrupted the agent. He nodded to his companion, indicating it was time to leave, "I think this meeting has been successful."

"Successful?" Tommy chuckled, "I just told you I won't comply, you moron. I have rights. I won't stop talking about Starshield. In fact, I think now that you've pushed me and tried to mess with my rights, I'll do a whole 'nother week on Starshield, maybe an entire month on nothing but - "

" - Good day," the younger agent stated flatly as they turned to leave. They no longer seemed interested in anything he had to say.

"Whatever," Tommy shot off, staring at them in disbelief.

The agents walked out the front door.

Jerks, he mused.

He laughed, and went back into the studio.

His show, set in a late time slot, always got out at 12:30 am. Tommy was used to it. He knew it was placed there because of the unpopularity of his views, but he didn't care. He was fighting against the establishment, and that meant a life of struggle, not one of ease. He was never going to be popular, but he was doing what was right.

Tommy wondered about the two men again as he got in his car and started his long commute home. He was sure they were CIA or NSA. They hadn't even put up much of a fight with him, which he thought was strange. The whole thing had seemed more like a performance.

As he started down the winding roads of Butte Mountain towards his home in the valley, he noticed a set of headlights come up behind him in the distance. They were a little ways off, and as he pushed through turns and switchbacks, they would disappear momentarily behind mountain bends.

He slowed down to fifteen MPH on one unusually sharp turn. As he pulled out of it, he noticed the vehicle was much closer.

Whoever is back there is really moving, he thought.

The road was straightening out, and he was getting close to halfway down the mountain. Several more switchbacks were coming up, but soon it would straighten out for good. The headlights now glared in his rearview mirror. The moron had his brights on, and he was going a lot faster than Tommy. The vehicle looked like a large truck.

"I guess this idiot HAS to pass me," he grumbled as the truck moved in behind him.

Instead of passing, the vehicle slammed into his trunk with a resounding crash.

"Ugghhh!" Tommy gasped in surprise, losing control of the wheel.

As his hands came off the steering wheel, his car began slowly veering towards the ditch on the right. The drop-off was probably one hundred feet down. He quickly grabbed back onto it and readjusted.

"What!" he yelled.

He was so shocked he couldn't process what had just happened. He laid on his horn as hard as possible, announcing his disapproval to the other driver.

Immediately, the vehicle sped up and slammed into him again. This time his left hand pushed awkwardly into the steering wheel, making a crunching sound. Fire seared through his left hand and wrist. Tommy roared in pain. He struggled to focus on the road ahead. He took several deep breaths, but the pain would not subside.

As they passed a large rural light, the only one around, he could see the vehicle more clearly. It was a black F250 truck. It had a bull bar on the front. It started to move towards him again.

"They're trying to kill me!" he moaned in disbelief.

He floored the engine, and his 2024 Malibu began accelerating. The speedometer needle slowly pushed toward the right. Trees and guardrails sped by with frightening speed. His hands shook; he knew he was going way too fast to be safe, but what choice did he have?

He gazed in his rearview mirror. It was hard to see out of it. The mirror had been knocked slightly downward, but he could tell he was outdistancing the truck. His head cooled, and his breathing slowed, but the pain still throbbed in his wrist.

I can make it, he thought.

He was going to make it. He just had to think. If he could get to town, there would usually be a cop sitting at the BP station. He could actually try to make an emergency call right now, even though the roads were windy. He carefully looked down and reached into the center console to grab his cell phone. He just needed to....

BANG!

The Ford slammed into his Malibu with enormous force this time. The Malibu lifted slightly and shuttered. Sparks flew out the back, shooting a meteor shower over the hood and windshield of the truck. The truck didn't even look damaged from the little he could see. His car was not faring so well. It was making a high-pitched groaning sound and struggling to maintain sixty MPH. Something was clearly damaged. All he knew was he needed to get this stupid car moving.

The truck was now overtaking him on the left side. To his right, Tommy noticed a large gulley going several hundred feet down. Great. Mr. Death wasted no time and again slammed into his driver's side now, creating a loud noise. The subsequent impact sent his car flying into the guardrail on his right and his head flying into the side window. A sharp pain surged through his left temple. His vision blurred momentarily.

Thank God that guardrail was there, he thought.

Tommy had had enough. He screamed in anger, punched the accelerator, and turned his wheel sharply left, forcing it into the metal door of the F250. The vehicle reacted by pushing slightly over towards the cliff wall flanking the road. He whooped with satisfaction. If they were going to try to take him out, he wasn't going down without a fight.

He noticed smoke was now pouring out the back of his car, and he was only going fifty-five MPH instead of sixty. Tommy looked at the dashboard in dismay. Multiple warning lights had gone off, giving him information that couldn't help him. He was pretty sure he wouldn't be able to get away from this truck unless something drastically changed.

He couldn't slow down because he knew whoever was inside would easily finish him off if he left the vehicle, and they were still in the middle of nowhere. It was probably those agents he had met earlier. In horror, he noticed there was no guardrail for at least several thousand feet ahead. He had to outrun them.

Tommy stomped on the accelerator one more time. The Malibu moaned and shuttered, but it increased speed slightly. As he did so, the Ford, seeming to anticipate this move, plowed into his driver's side again with even more force than before. Tommy's head slammed into the side window again, and he saw his tires suddenly move out into nothingness. He lifted up impossibly in his seatbelt as the car suddenly turned into a rollercoaster, pulling downward towards the ground as gravity took over. A gasp escaped his lips as he felt the pull of freefall in his gut. Tommy could see trees rushing past him in the Malibu's headlights as the ground raced towards him. His final thought was that he wished he couldn't see what was coming, so he closed his eyes as the forest floor rushed up to meet him.

The Malibu slammed headfirst into the ground with a deafening crash.

Weston was embarrassed. He was going for his third round of enchiladas. Rick had been right; his wife Kathleen was a fantastic cook. Ally shot him a disapproving glance as he picked up two more enchiladas and another serving of sour cream and guacamole.

Oh, well, he thought, *I burn tons of calories at my new job anyway.*

As he sat back down, Rick finished answering Ally's question about how he and Kathleen had met.

" - and so there was a bar called The Oasis, outside the Marine Base - "

" - Wait!" Weston interrupted, "You guys met at a bar?"

"We weren't always Christians, Weston," Rick answered.

"But we've been married thirty-eight years now," Kathleen stated, giving Rick a loving glance.

"Why don't we move to the living room, everybody," Rick suggested, "Kathleen has some scones for us, right dear?"

Weston groaned. He had already eaten too much.

As they sat down, the kids went into the backyard to play. Rick resumed the conversation.

"So, Weston, you were very interested in those two horns on the lamb."

"Yes," Weston replied quickly, eager to know more.

"And I can see why, after hearing about those dreams," Rick said.

"So this comes from the Bible, Revelation 13:11, which says, 'Then I saw another beast coming up out of the earth, and he had two horns like a lamb, and spoke like a dragon.'"

"I read that, but I don't understand it," Weston stated.

"Why don't we pray first?" Rick asked, looking around the room.

Rick and Kathleen seemed quite comfortable with this idea and quickly bowed their heads. Weston and Ally suddenly felt awkward but followed suit. Rick offered a short, to the point prayer for guidance. It seemed like it was over before it began.

"Let me set the stage for you, Weston. Revelation twelve is, in a way, the crux of the book. It is a sequential outline of the history of the world from the time of Christ's first coming until the time of his second coming. Revelation twelve gives a general outline of all that history, and then with each continuing chapter, it just keeps giving you more and more detail on what chapter twelve said," Rick explained. "Once you get to Revelation twenty, it is all about after Jesus came, so we will just focus on chapters twelve through nineteen."

"OK," Weston noted.

"I'm going to explain a few things to you, but I really want you to read this book, and then let me know if you have any questions," Rick stated as he handed him a book entitled 'America in Bible Prophecy.'

"So, in order to understand who your lamb is, we have to start with chapter twelve. Chapter twelve starts with a woman clothed with the sun - "

" - Uh-huh," Weston noted.

"She gives birth to a child, and a dragon tries to kill it. This child is caught up to God's throne. So, this was John the apostle describing God's church. A woman in Bible prophecy represents a church or religious body. Good or bad. But in this case, it is good; she's clothed with the sun. She wasn't a church like you or I think of a church today, but she was God's people for that time. So, you have to unlock the symbolism in Revelation, which that book I gave you will help you do. The neat thing is, everything you need to understand the symbols is already in the Bible, it's all there, especially in Revelation's sister book, the book of Daniel - "

" - Why was Revelation even written with all these symbols?" Weston interrupted.

"Because when John wrote it in A.D. 95, he was imprisoned by pagan Rome. Since much of this book is about Rome, he could not just come out and plainly say what God needed to convey. Rome would have destroyed the book; they are not pictured in a flattering light here," Rick explained.

"That makes sense," Weston agreed.

He was starting to feel that Rick knew what he was talking about.

"So, the dragon is the devil. The child is Jesus. Jesus came from the woman, the church of that day, which was the Jews. So, the devil tried to kill Jesus once he finally had access to him. And how did he do this? The Bible tells us in Matthew 2:16; Herod, a ruler representing pagan Rome, sent soldiers to Jesus's last known location and killed all the children two years old and younger."

"I know this story," Ally chimed in.

"It goes on to tell us that with Jesus gone, ascending back to Heaven, the devil turned his attention towards the church."

"But Christians aren't really being killed anymore, right?" Weston questioned.

"For the first couple centuries, Rome killed them in great numbers. It was a massive persecution, and an untold number died. Crucified, torn by wild beasts, killed in the Colosseum at Rome. The Christians went underground, into the catacombs. But after a while, the devil did something even worse," Rick answered.

"What could be worse?" Weston said, chuckling.

"Have you ever heard the saying, if you can't beat 'em, join 'em?" Rick asked.

"Sure," Weston replied.

"The devil joined the church. He was unable to exterminate Christianity. So, he joined it. This is where Revelation thirteen comes in, and your lamb beast."

"Ok," Weston replied reluctantly.

"John sees a new beast in this chapter, unlike any other in the Bible. You see, there are several beasts seen in Daniel and Revelation, and the Bible tells us they represent kingdoms, ruling powers - "

" - Oh," Ally stated with surprise. "I thought they were things we were going to see at the end of time?"

"No," Rick replied, "as we'll see shortly, every beast, or kingdom in the Bible, has already come to power in Earth's history."

"Wow," Weston stated, surprised at that.

"This same beast is also described in Daniel seven, 2 Thessalonians two and also in Matthew twenty-four. Let's start with Revelation thirteen, and you tell me who you think it is."

"Alright," Weston stated doubtfully.

"These are just a few of the characteristics:

The whole world worships the beast

He speaks haughty and mighty things

He utters blasphemy against God

He makes war with God's people

He has authority over all

All worship him

His reign continues for forty-two months," listed Rick.

"Ahhh, I have no idea," Weston replied slowly.

"Daniel seven puts it this way:

He comes up from among the ten horns

He rises from the Great Sea, which means the Mediterranean Sea

A man is in charge of it

It would pluck out three of the ten horns when it came about

It would make war with the saints

It would emerge from the fourth beast

It would speak great words against the Most High

It would intend to change times and law

It would continue for a time, times and half a time," Rick continued.

Weston just shrugged.

"I still don't know," he stated defeatedly.

"First, let's tackle those weird time periods. They are actually mentioned seven times in Daniel and Revelation. They are called a time, times and half a time, they are called forty-two months and they are also called 1,260 days. The first one is the most confusing, but a time just means a year. The Jewish year had 360 days; not 365.

So when you add up all these calculations, they all come to the same number; 1,260 days, which is three and a half years," Rick stated.

"Gotcha," Weston indicated.

"But these prophecies would not make sense if they lasted three and a half years. The thing is, when you study the Bible, you find when God makes a prophecy, He designates a day for a year. I could give you multiple examples. So the period this beast maintains power is not one thousand, two hundred and sixty days, but one thousand, two hundred and sixty years.

Now Daniel seven said this beast would emerge from the fourth kingdom. A lot of people nowadays think this beast has not arrived on the scene yet, but the fourth kingdom Daniel saw was clearly an empire of the past. He saw four empires in succession; Babylon, Medo-Persia, Greece, and then he saw the mighty Roman empire," Rick declared.

Weston's mind was beginning to uncloud.

"What power emerged out of the Roman empire, made war with God's people, had a man as its head, demanded and successfully caused the world to worship it, and continued for 1,260 years?" Rick asked.

Ally knew.

"Not the - "

"The Papacy...the Roman Catholic Church," Rick finished. "And we have only looked at five of the nine characteristics. The others make it more lock-tight. You see, during the Dark Ages, the papacy ruled the Earth. They held sway over the civilized world; controlled kings and nations. They tortured and killed anyone who would not assent to her authority. Historians agree they wiped out around fifty million people. The greatest mass murderer of the modern age, Chairman Mao, was not even able to kill that many. Hitler, Stalin and Pol Pot combined, those notorious villains, only managed to kill fourteen million combined," Rick stated. "It's a staggering number.

If you average that out, that is one hundred and seven people being tortured to death every single day of the Dark Ages."

"I don't know anything about the Dark Ages, but I've heard references to it before," Weston admitted.

"You heard that saying, those who don't know their history - "

" - are bound to repeat it," Ally finished Rick's thought.

"Right," Rick continued, "and so the real story of Revelation is that history, as we know it always does, will continue to repeat itself. The devil, through these entities, will repeat his tactics until the very end."

"The lamb beast?" Weston pressed.

Rick laughed.

"I'm getting there," he replied, "Revelation thirteen shows the sequential history of the Papacy, and then it dies off. We know that it dies off because of an earlier reference to a mortal wound that ends up being healed, and we know it dies off because this lamb beast has to be the one now to cause the world to worship the Papacy once again. Clearly the Papacy doesn't have the power that it once had.

Now here's the cool part. The Bible indicates after the Papacy dies off, then he sees the lamb beast emerge. The Papacy died off in 1798, when Napoleon's general, General Berthier, took the pope captive and ended their reign."

"Okay," Weston said.

"The lamb beast also comes up out of the earth. Every other beast came up out of the sea. The Bible tells us the sea represents multitudes of people, centers of civilization. So, coming up out of the earth would, of course, stand for the opposite; arising from an unpopulated area. So, you have to ask yourself, what nation came up out of a less populated region of the world around 1798, and is so powerful, it can compel the world to worship the first beast?"

The answer was obvious. Weston and Ally glanced at each other.

"The United States," Weston answered reluctantly.

"Yes, Weston. America. We made our Declaration of Independence in 1776. We adopted our Constitution in 1787, and we were recognized as a world power some time later. These things were taking place as the Papacy was dying off. We arose from the New World, an area that was very much unpopulated, when you consider the enormous numbers of people in the Old World. In America, it is estimated there were maybe only one million Native Americans on the entire continent. So, it makes sense the Bible would see this beast arise up 'out of the Earth;' the only beast in prophecy to do so."

"But didn't you say the lamb beast would emerge after the Papacy died off?" Weston questioned, "1787 is before 1798."

"True," answered Rick, "but you're forgetting about the War of 1812. It wasn't until after that, when it ended in 1814, sixteen years after the Papacy's deadly wound, that we were seen as a legitimate nation to be reckoned with. The British finally let their 'colony' go for good."

"I guess it makes sense," Ally reasoned, "if there was going to be a nation powerful enough to compel the whole world to worship the first beast, as it said, it would be us. We are called the world's policeman."

"Think about how powerful we are. We came to Europe's rescue in WWI and WWII. We used the atomic bomb to end WWII. We enforce embargos on entire nations, forcing them to submit to our will. We have the most powerful military in the world. All this from thirteen tiny colonies in the middle of nowhere," Rick stated.

"But what is it with the two horns?" Weston asked.

"Yes, the two horns...what brought us here," Rick laughed, "in the Bible, horns represent powers. You will notice every beast that has horns also has crowns. What gave America her power, was the thing that was totally unique about her, unique from every other nation that had ever been founded."

"Which is?" Weston plied.

"Two things; two horns. Civil and religious liberty," Rick replied, "it was revolutionary. It was totally new. No one had ever done it. And that is still today what makes America stand out. We have a Constitution and a Bill of Rights, and every American has civil and religious liberty. Now, other nations have since followed suit, but we were definitely the first. Notice also, we are the only beast with no crowns, meaning, we have no ruling monarch or despotic leader over our people. We are ruled, in theory, by ourselves."

"Wow," Weston said.

"So, why...how could America do these bad things?" Ally asked, "I've read about the mark of the beast when I was a kid; doesn't it say it would kill those who don't comply?"

"Yes," Rick answered, "Ally, don't you think you're already beginning to see the change from lamb to dragon?"

"Well, just in my lifetime...yes," she admitted.

"During Covid-19, people's constitutional rights were suspended, because the government determined it was for the 'common good' to do that. That phrase comes from the Preamble to the Constitution. People lost their jobs because they wouldn't get a shot. But the government has shown repeatedly that they will suspend or take away your rights, if they think what they're doing best serves the general welfare and common good of America. It's happened in Puerto Rico, Hawaii, Alaska, California, Tennessee. The list goes on. It's happened many times, and it will happen again," Rick stated.

"I mean, I just lost my job because of this. This stuff is happening now... the intolerance. All because I wouldn't wear a PIN," Weston stated.

"I'm sorry, Weston," Rick replied, "and we can only expect more to come. We are seeing movements sweep the nation that are intolerant to any dissenting opinions. And those movements are taking over every institution of America."

Ally yawned. She was fascinated by all of this, but it had been a long day.

Rick took the hint.

"Well, we've covered a lot of ground here. I think this is all our brains can handle for now, especially after those enchiladas," he joked.

"Which were amazing," Weston declared, "yeah, we should probably get going."

Everyone slowly stood up to leave. As the kids joined Weston and Ally from the backyard, they exchanged goodbyes and promised to come again soon.

As Weston exited the front door, he turned to Rick.

"By the way," he stated, "you were right about the CBDC thing. The money."

"Yep," Rick answered matter-of-factly, "it's gonna go down real soon now, I think."

Chapter Seven - Church

When Weston came home after work, Ally showed him what they had received in the mail. It was a letter from the Federal Government. It said Central Bank Digital Currency, called FedNote, was officially digitizing the U.S. dollar in order to build 'an open, inclusive, interoperable and innovative currency service system for the digital economy.'

The letter also included two FedNote debit cards: one for Weston and one for Ally. It stated both cards were linked to the same account. Weston noticed the cards were like a driver's license, in that there was a small photo on the card. The photo had clearly been pulled from the DMV; it was their driver's license photo.

The letter also announced that the public had thirty days from the date of the letter to turn in all cash for deposit and funds from other accounts into their FedNote account. It also said any existing debit or credit cards would be voided by the date in the letter.

"What happens to cash that doesn't get turned in?" Weston asked.

"It says any form of cash not turned over by November 11th at one of the designated FedNote locations will cease to be valid currency!" Ally read with surprise.

"I don't think we have any loose cash anyway, do we?" Weston asked.

"We only have a couple of hundred dollars here. I'll make sure we get it into this new account."

Ally paused.

"West, didn't Rick say this digital currency was going to be a really bad thing?" she asked.

"He did," he answered.

"I guess we have no choice anyway," she said resignedly.

"No choice," he replied.

Weston was thinking. Rick had told him this was the road to despotism. And he had read that China had already been using it for some time in conjunction with their social credit system. Citizens were being punished for behavior that the state deemed inappropriate, and the way the state was punishing them was by freezing their personal bank accounts and/or deleting funds. Could it now happen here? Weston would have once thought this impossible, but now, things seemed to be moving in the same direction. Add to that the intolerance movements taking over every area of American life, and...

The lamb speaking like a dragon, he mused.

The Bible had said, 'and that no one may buy or sell, save he who had the mark...' He realized this prophetic statement was no longer much of a stretch. They were now going to be able to control, for the first time in history, what everyone on the planet bought and sold. He had read that almost every country was preparing to implement a similar digital currency.

Daniel and Revelation had outlined with remarkable accuracy the succession of kingdoms, as well as the history of the Dark Ages and the rise of a final powerful kingdom, which Weston now understood to be the United States. It had done so in the exact order that the events took place. The Bible had then foretold something that seemed impossible when it was written: that worldwide money transactions could somehow be controlled. There was now every reason to believe this prediction would also come to pass.

He knew what they had to do.

"Ally?"

"Yeah?" she asked.

"I think we should go to Rick's church," he declared.

"Ok," she replied matter-of-factly.

They all met up in the parking lot of Rick and Kathleen's church that Saturday morning at 10:30 am.

People were streaming into the main entrance as the couples exchanged greetings.

"Well, should we go inside?" Rick suggested, nodding towards the entrance.

"Ok. Lead the way," Weston answered.

He was nervous as they walked into the foyer. He hadn't been in a church since childhood. A middle-aged gentleman, probably a greeter, stood in the double doorway and shook their hands as they walked in. He gave them an enthusiastic greeting and handed them a bulletin, offering to help them find a seat.

"Oh, it's ok, Ted, they're with us," Rick stated.

The greeter nodded as Rick led them through the foyer and into the sanctuary. As they walked through another set of large doors, Weston was impressed by the expansive, modern-looking sanctuary. The pews were crowded, and he was wondering if they would even be able to sit down.

They were somehow able to squeeze all seven of them into the third row from the back. The service seemed about to begin. A musical group was taking up their positions on the stage. Weston was just beginning to acclimate a bit and relax when a face popped up in front of him.

"Good morning!" the stranger said. He reached out his hand.

"Good morning." Weston returned reluctantly.

"I'm Pete," the man continued, "so glad you were able to join us today."

Weston nodded. He introduced Pete to his wife and kids.

"Weston," Rick explained, "this is our head Pastor, Pete Clark. He runs things here."

"Well, now, I don't run things," Pete shot back, "you know that. God's running it, and I'm just trying to keep up!"

Weston chuckled. He could tell that Pete was one of those personalities that could control the room whenever he entered it.

"Well, I'd best be going. It's about to start," he stated, "great to meet you all."

As the band began to play, the congregation started singing. The Millers grew slightly uncomfortable; they seemed to be the only ones not participating. Weston was actually enjoying the songs, but he just was not familiar with any of them. Even though all the words were displayed on a large screen behind the stage, he and his family just stared ahead.

The sermon was given by Pete, and the subject surprised Weston. It was on the two beasts of Revelation thirteen! He looked over at Rick and whispered, "Did you have something to do with this?"

Rick shook his head '*no.*'

Some of it was hard to understand, but it was also becoming a bit more familiar. The timeline of Christ's first coming through His second coming was pointed out in more detail, and it was starting to make more sense. The second beast compelled the world to worship the first beast because the first beast no longer had the power to force worship of itself. But the issue never seemed to change throughout history; the first beast demanded worship from beginning to end. In the end, those not following God had the mark of the beast, and those loyal to God had the seal of God. It seemed everyone was actually given a mark. The mark could be in the forehead or the hand, but the seal could only be in the forehead.

He looked over occasionally at Ally and the kids. Ally seemed to be soaking in every word; the kids were also listening attentively.

After church, they were persuaded by several members to stay at a potluck held in the fellowship hall. They packed into a large room filled with members and guests, all sitting at fold-up tables stacked side by side.

The food was delicious, including the main entree, some kind of fried chicken.

"This chicken is so tender," Ally commented.

"Actually, it's not chicken," Kathleen answered, "it's a vegetarian dish."

"Oh, my," Ally laughed in surprise, "well, it still is really good. What's it made of?"

"I'm not sure. Probably chickpeas, bread, and some different spices," Kathleen stated.

"How long have you guys been going here?" Ally asked, changing the subject.

Kathleen looked over at Rick with a questioning look.

"Probably ten years?" she answered.

"And what made you guys pick this church, if I may ask?" she inquired.

"Ally," Weston said. He felt it was too personal of a question.

"Oh, no. It's fine, Allyson," Rick interjected, "ask anything you want to. Well, you see, Revelation twelve indicates the last day church would have two characteristics, and we believe we're living in the last days. It would keep the commandments and have the spirit of prophecy. Seventh-Day Adventists do both. They keep the ten commandments, and they have prophecy seminars around the world."

"Aren't all churches really focusing on prophecy nowadays, though?" Weston countered.

"There are a few that do," Rick answered, "but the interesting thing is, prophecy interpretation falls into just three camps: preterist, historicist, and futurist. I believe the historicists are the only ones getting it right, and Adventists are that. The crazy thing is, pretty much all Christians were historicists once and believed like Adventists do on Daniel and Revelation."

"So, what changed?" Weston asked.

"Let me give you a little history lesson," Rick said.

"Here we go. He's a history buff," Kathleen chided her husband, giving him a playful elbow in the ribs.

Rick made a face at her.

"I love history, so sue me," he shot back, "so, the Protestant Reformation was succeeding...exploding. People were protesting against the abuses of the Catholic church. The deceptions, the robbery, and the brutal murders of untold millions. People started actively fighting against it. Many were reading the Bible and identifying the Pope as the Antichrist because he fit every single marker outlined by God's Word. This reformation was spreading throughout Europe. It was so successful that the Pope called together the Council of Trent in 1540 to try and figure out how to deal with the problem," Rick explained.

"So, what did he do?" Weston questioned.

Other people from nearby tables were starting to quiet down and listen.

"Five things," he answered,

"1) Establishment of the Jesuits

2) Tradition declared above the Bible

3) Establishment of the index of forbidden books

4) Revival of persecution and

5) Counter systems of prophetic interpretation. Number five was the game changer; it literally transformed the world we live in today."

"How?" asked Ally.

"The Pope appointed two Jesuit priests; Francisco Ribera and Louis Alcazar, to come up with alternative theories on Daniel and Revelation, since those books were pointing to him as the

Antichrist," Rick replied, "Ribera invented futurism. Remember I said only three concepts exist today on prophecy? So, futurism came from Ribera. He said the saints will disappear in a secret rapture, and a future anti-Christ figure will appear at the end and rule for three and a half years after the saints are raptured away."

"Uh-huh," Weston nodded.

"Alcazar invented the other concept, preterism, or some call it predorism. He said Daniel's little horn was not the Pope, but Antiochus of Epiphanes, a Greek ruler from before Christ's time, and that 666 referred to the pagan Roman emperors of the early centuries," Rick continued, "well, the new ideas worked; it took some time, but now every Protestant denomination believes preterism or futurism."

The thought of that seemed absurd to Weston.

"You mean to tell me that every Christian church out there is called a Protestant church, because they were protesting against the Catholic church, and now they've been fooled into believing something invented by the very entity they were protesting against?" Weston exclaimed.

"Every church except this denomination," Rick stated matter-of-factly.

"That seems hard to believe," he mused.

"I'm not trying to be rude, but...do you guys not like Catholics? I've heard Seventh-Day Adventists don't like Catholics. I know Jesus said to love all people," Ally asked hesitantly.

Kathleen and Rick looked at each other and laughed.

"If we hated Catholics then I guess we'd have to hate ourselves," Rick declared.

"Rick and I were both Catholic most of our lives. Our families are Catholic," Kathleen explained, "and we have a lot of Catholic friends."

"Oh," Ally stated in surprise.

"Actually, Catholics are some of the most sincere Christians in the world right now. Much more even than a lot of the evangelical world, which has become extremely liberal. Interestingly as well, a large percentage of Adventists are former Catholics," Rick stated. "It's not the people we're talking about here...you see, it's the system they're in. The Catholic system is part of what the Bible calls Babylon, in Revelation eighteen. And God says, come out of her, MY people. You see, we believe God's people are in the Catholic church, in every church, in every worldwide religion. God is wanting people of every persuasion to come out of non-biblical systems of error, and become part of what He calls His 'remnant,'" Rick explained.

"Well, not to be rude, but is it really necessary to follow God a certain way, go to a certain church?" Weston wondered, "I mean, you said Adventists keep the ten commandments...is that necessary?"

"You want me to break the sixth commandment if I get angry with you, Weston?" Rick said playfully.

"What's that?" he asked.

"Thou shalt not murder..."

"Oh, well, I guess, of course not," he realized, "but...people are keeping that commandment anyway because it's a law in America. You would go to jail if you broke it."

"Right," Rick stated, "and that brings me to another point. The last six commandments deal with relationships between people. Most of them are laws of the land, with consequences if they are broken. But, the first four commandments deal with our relationship to God. There are no laws of the land governing those. Do you think it's ok to break those commandments?"

"Umm," Weston wasn't sure what to say.

"How about the first commandment; thou shalt have no other gods before Me?"

"Ah," Weston felt confused, "I guess you can't, no, probably not."

"How about commandment number two, no idol worship?"

"No, I don't think it's ok to worship an idol, definitely not," Weston laughed.

"Taking God's name in vain, number three?" Rick continued.

"No, you obviously can't do that either..."

"Number four, keep the seventh day holy?" Rick asked.

Weston hesitated. It was hard to explain why the fourth commandment differed from the other three, even though it was in the same group. But people didn't keep that one anymore, right?

Just then Pastor Pete walked up.

"You going easy on this family, Rick?" he joked.

"Ah, you know Pete, I'm breaking 'em in," Rick bantered.

"Well, if he gets to be too much, you just let me know," Pastor Pete said to the Miller family as he raised a playful fist at Rick. He stood by and listened for a moment.

"So," Rick continued, "the fourth commandment, can you break it?"

"I don't think it's the seventh day anymore. Isn't it the first?" Weston inquired.

"There's no change of day recorded in the Bible," Rick stated with certainty.

"Then it was changed later. A change was made. I don't know, at some point a change must have been made - "

" - In honor of the resurrection," Ally added.

"No record of that either," Rick replied with a slight smile.

"Then what happened?" Weston asked, exasperated.

"In 321 A.D., pagan emperor Constantine made the first official law, ordering folks to start observing Sunday instead of Saturday. There was a popular pagan religion in Roman society at that time, called Mithraism. They worshiped the sun. Constantine hoped to combine these pagan believers with the Christians in his realm. They were tired of fighting and killing the Christians, so he decided to try getting everybody to join hands and sing kumbaya around the campfire. And his law wasn't the first. There were subsequent laws reaffirming that Sunday must be kept instead of Saturday," Rick answered.

"Wait," Ally questioned, "if they had to make a law..."

Her voice trailed off.

"Then that means there were people keeping the Sabbath on Saturday, three centuries after Christ," Rick finished her thought, "and we have Christ's own words as proof. He told his disciples in Matthew twenty-four, speaking of the destruction of Jerusalem in 70 A.D., to pray that their flight would not be in winter, or on the Sabbath. If He had changed it, why would he admonish them to still keep it holy, almost forty years in the future?"

Rick paused for a moment, and then continued on.

"So, the Catholic church themselves have made some comments on this Sabbath/Sunday issue," he stated.

"What'd they say?" Weston asked, surprised.

"You wouldn't believe it if I told you...but I'll tell you. Their comments are what actually convinced me about the Sabbath," Rick answered, "Let me read you this - "

" - You have this stuff on you?" Weston interrupted.

"Never know when you might need it," he countered, pulling a small booklet out of his suit jacket pocket, "here we go."

He opened the pamphlet and read:

"It is well to remind the Presbyterians, Baptists, Methodists, and all other Christians, that the Bible does not support them anywhere in their observance of Sunday. Sunday is an institution of the Roman Catholic Church, and those who observe the day observe a commandment of the Catholic Church."

"They said that?" exclaimed Ally.

Rick continued reading.

"Of course, the Catholic church claims that the change (from Saturday to Sunday) was her act... and that act is a MARK of her ecclesiastical authority in religious things."

The whole table was silent, including Weston's kids. The last quote was the real shocker.

"Sunday is our MARK of authority...the church is above the Bible, and this transference of Sabbath observance is proof of that fact."

Weston stared down at his food. He was in absolute shock.

"Her mark?" he questioned, looking up at Rick.

"Her mark," Rick held his gaze. "In their own words. The mark of the beast."

Chapter Eight - The Decision

Adele Schleizenger started her morning commute from Novato into downtown San Francisco in the dark. It was necessary to leave this early. Otherwise, she would be late for her corporate job at Wells Fargo.

As she moved past San Rafael, traffic was already slowing, and she was still at least eighteen miles from the city.

I'm barely going to make it on time, she thought.

She stared ahead at the sea of brake lights, twisting and turning on the bends of Highway 101. The slow pace never ceased to annoy her.

Sequoias and coast live oaks edged the sides of the rolling hills that bordered the freeway. It was quite beautiful here if you could just get used to the congestion. Anyway, she didn't plan to live here forever. It was just hard to pass up a Bay Area salary.

As she continued to move southbound, she could see the towers of the Golden Gate Bridge in the distance. After about ten minutes, she made her way off the peninsula and onto the bridge itself. She could see the city, and the Bay Bridge off to the left, moving over into Oakland.

She always marveled at the Golden Gate whenever she drove over it. With two towers standing almost eight hundred feet tall, a span of nearly nine thousand feet, and main cables over three feet wide, it was a feat of engineering. She had also read that the bridge was retrofitted with seismic isolators, some kind of oversized bushing, and energy defusion devices, too. These were all there for earthquake protection. Still, whenever she was on it, she wanted to get off the bridge as quickly as possible.

Adele was zoning out at the wheel when she heard a strange sound on her phone. Three metallic beeps in quick succession. Then, a voice came through the speaker stating, "Earthquake, earthquake," followed by three more metallic beeps.

She looked down at her Android in the center console. The MyShake app had opened on her screen. It said *Shake Alert. An Earthquake has been detected. Shaking expected.* A stick figure man dropped to the ground with the words *drop, cover, hold on,* in large words on the screen. Below it said *Projection: 8.5.*

Adele looked around. There was no way to follow these instructions in the car, and no one around her was slowing down, or could stop, as they were in the middle of the bridge. She looked down at her speedometer; everyone was going sixty MPH.

In the next instant, she heard a strange noise, like distant freight trains. The bridge began to gently sway, first to the right, then to the left. Cars around her began slowing down, some losing traction and skidding and some crashing into each other. She also slowed and tried to stay in her lane. The car in front of her slammed into another vehicle, and she swerved to avoid them. Everyone screeched to a halt.

Adele glanced over to her left and saw the northbound portion of the bridge swaying as well. She had been through an earthquake before; the feeling of the very ground moving under your feet was the most unsettling thing she had ever experienced. Fortunately, she was on the bridge, and Adele could not feel any shaking at all. But the swaying was scaring her and she was starting to feel ill from the motion. This was the last place she wanted to be during an earthquake. The ocean had to be at least three hundred feet below her.

The shrill beeps from the phone continued to ring out as the swaying worsened. Adele closed her eyes and tried to push through the rising panic.

Earthquakes don't last more than thirty seconds, she told herself. *I can get through this.*

Her head was feeling dizzy, and nausea was overtaking her. The swaying, rather than starting to slow down, was only getting worse. The freight train noise was getting louder, and she was scared. Adele heard screams coming from the cars around her.

Adele opened her eyes again, and she was sorry she did. The bridge was moving like some giant snake that slithered on the ground, swaying impossibly from side to side. Vehicles around her were losing traction. She heard tires skidding on the pavement. A van next to her slammed into her passenger side, blowing out her side window. She screamed as glass flew across her arms and lap. She looked at the other driver. They seemed as scared as she was.

Something new caught her eye. In the distance she could see huge plumes of smoke billowing from the downtown area. It was on fire.

How much longer can this possibly last, she wondered.

It must have been at least a full minute now.

Suddenly, the noise stopped. It was over. The swaying went from a violent side to side motion, to a gentle wave, then to a complete stop. Adele began sobbing.

Up ahead, she could hear horns beeping, and slowly traffic started moving forward again. There were multiple wrecks on the roadway. Cars were threading their way through; the normal three-lane highway was down to one lane. Adele wiped her eyes and edged forward. She had to avoid multiple car crashes as she slowly proceeded towards the south end of the bridge and the Presidio.

She wasn't sure what her plan was going to be. Clearly, she could no longer go to work downtown; it appeared there were multiple fires. She hoped none of her co-workers had gone in early today. She decided the best course of action was to get to the Presidio and try to turn around. As she made her way back into the northbound entrance of the bridge, it became obvious that everyone had the same idea. Normally, at this time of day, northbound traffic would be minimal, but now she saw this was going to take some time.

No matter, she thought.

She would be taking the day off and could go home and relax, watch a movie or something.

After about five minutes, she decided it would take her at least another fifteen minutes just to get off the bridge. Adele turned on the radio to try and get some information. Most stations were off the air, but KQED was on and was saying the quake had gone beyond what seemed possible. It had reached an 8.7 and clocked in at just over two minutes. The radio host was saying this was unprecedented and considered impossible, based on the size of the San Andreas fault or something.

She made a quick move into the fast lane and was able to speed up a bit. It occurred to her that she should try to reach her brother who lived near Golden Gate Park, to see if he was ok. As she reached for her phone, the MyShake beeping tones began again, with the same message; *"Shake alert. An earthquake has been detected..."*

Dumb app, she thought, *we just had the big one.*

Suddenly, the whole bridge started violently rocking up and down. Adele was pushed up and caught mid-air by her seatbelt.

"No," she yelled as she tried to hold on to the wheel.

The sound of freight trains was back, but now much closer than before. The noise was deafening. She tried to stay in her lane, but the roadway lurched upward and then down again. Every car around her lost control and smashed into each other, coming to a stop on the road.

Weston was getting ready to go back inside the house. He and his family had run out onto the front lawn after the first earthquake. It had lasted well over a minute, which was unusual, but he had to get going to work. He wanted to check for damage around the house, and then get moving. They had a big remodel project going that he wanted to make some real progress on today.

As the second set of tremors came on, Charlotte screamed and everyone froze in place, crouching towards the ground.

"Hold on," he reassured, "it's ok."

It really was going to be ok. The earthquake must be a really big one, but it was not very dramatic in Roseville. The ground was swaying, setting them off balance, but it wasn't violent.

Still, Weston thought, *it must be a tremendous quake at the epicenter.*

The fact that they could feel it to this extent, was amazing. Weston had never felt an earthquake at all.

He looked at the kids. They all looked sick and scared. He thought he should say something funny, get their focus off what was happening.

"Weeble's wobble, but they don't fall down," he exclaimed, turning towards them.

The kids hardly seemed to notice he had spoken. Ally gave him a disapproving glance.

Oh, well, he thought, *I never claimed to be a stand-up comedian.*

Adele self-assessed, and determined she hadn't sustained any injuries in the pileup.

It was hard to see out the windshield because it had cracked. She decided the best thing to do was stay buckled, hold on to the wheel, and ride it out one more time. She knew aftershocks were common; she had just never heard of one being even worse.

The violent rocking still had not stopped. She couldn't understand why it was shaking the whole bridge now, when the first time the bridge seemed to absorb the shockwaves. Something must have changed, or maybe something got damaged in the first quake. Suddenly, an ear-splitting whining noise, like metal on metal, rang through the air. Adele looked up towards its source. One of the large cables on the side of the bridge was flapping violently.

That can't be good, she worried.

The cable continued to whip up and down, along with the whole bridge. Suddenly, there was an enormous explosion, and it seemed to come loose. She could only assume that because it was clearly now moving away from the roadway. Looking up, she could see it for just a moment, ascending out of sight into the air. Now dozens of the vertical cables extending upward began to snap all around her. The entire northbound section of the bridge suddenly dropped several feet and tilted towards the bay. Adele screamed as she momentarily hung in the air, held only by her seatbelt. She slammed back down and hit her head on the side door. She saw stars for several seconds and felt a sharp pain in her temple.

The roadway was now tilted about ten degrees down towards the water. It seemed miles below them. Adele could see ships that had passed under the bridge making their way into the bay. She clung tightly to the wheel. Her head was beginning to feel a little bit better but the rocking would not stop; it had to have been over a minute now.

I have to figure out how to get off this bridge, she thought.

She looked ahead; she had at least five hundred feet to go before she could reach the peninsula.

I'm not going any further in this car. I can make it on foot, she decided.

Suddenly, there was an enormous crash as the loose cabling finally made its way down onto the roadway. She instinctively closed her eyes and covered her head with her arms. Screams rang out through the air. She opened her eyes and saw the large orange cable sliding off the edge of the roadway, over the side into the ocean. It easily scraped off the thick pedestrian railing as it went over.

The shaking stopped.

"Thank you, God," she breathed through clenched teeth. Adele had never been so thankful for anything in her whole life. She looked around her; both sides of the bridge seemed beyond any hope of repair. The entire northbound section was sagging heavily towards the bay. She turned around. She could still see plumes of smoke coming from downtown.

Their hands are full in the city, she thought.

No help was coming. It was time to get out of here.

She reached for and pulled the release handle for the driver's door.

Nothing.

Apparently, it had been damaged in the crash. Adele vaulted herself over the center console and opened the passenger side door. It came open with tremendous effort, as it was also damaged. As she set foot on the pavement, she almost slid over the edge, which was only fifteen feet away. She quickly grabbed the door of her car and stopped herself.

This is going to be harder than I thought, she assessed.

Adele began making her way towards the peninsula ahead, clinging to car after car. As she passed vehicles, people had varying reactions to her. Some looked at her and seemed to consider following her example, while others just gazed ahead, seemingly unaware of her presence.

Adele had read about this, the different reactions to life-threatening situations. Some took charge of their situation, and others just froze in fear, accepting their fate. Adele had never been a lay-down-and-die kind of person. Twenty years of Tae Kwon Do had kept her physically and mentally fit, ready for any challenge. And this appeared to be the mother of challenges.

In the distance, she could hear an army of sirens and helicopters over the bay, but she knew none of them would be able to reach these trapped commuters. Not for a while, anyway. They would mainly focus on the city. It was likely absolute chaos there. Not that things were peachy here.

The roadway continued its tilt little by little towards the bay. Occasionally, more vertical cables would explode off their moorings and the entire roadway would drop several inches, inducing screams from the people inside their vehicles. Soon, all the cars would slide off into the ocean. Adele knew she didn't want to be around when that happened.

She looked back and saw that several other groups had followed her example and were also heading towards land. She tried not to look towards the edge as she picked up the pace.

Up ahead, she could see that several big rigs and moving vans had collided. There was no way she could pass without moving over to the right, towards the edge.

Great, she thought sarcastically. *Let's just get this over with.*

Adele made her way around a smashed white passenger van. She could see she had about two feet of clearance between the van and the edge of the bridge. Cautiously, slowly, she inched towards the edge. As she moved closer, she got down on her butt and scooted forward. She rounded the edge of the van and looked over the side. A wave of nausea overtook her.

Bad idea.

She could see she would have to stand up and ease herself around the van. There was only about a foot of clearance. Far below her, she could see an armada of boats and ships moving towards the bridge.

Are they coming to try and help? she wondered.

She wasn't sure what they could possibly do. She felt vertigo as she stared down and quickly closed her eyes to regain her bearings.

Don't look down again, she commanded.

She stepped forward and slowly eased around the vehicle. Suddenly, a metallic wail filled the air, and the roadway dropped again. It caught Adele off balance at exactly the wrong time. At the same instant, the van bounced. She lost her grip and her footing and began struggling, desperately flailing her arms and legs to try and grab something, but nothing was within her reach. She gasped as the sensation of falling pushed into her abdomen, and she watched the bridge pass in front of her.

She knew she would die when she hit the water. People came here from all over the world to die, to commit suicide on this bridge. It was very tall, and she had heard that at this height, hitting the water was the same as hitting concrete.

Help me, she moaned out to God.

There was nothing left to try but prayer.

She let out a gasp as she slammed into the large net below her. Her body bounced slightly up again, then settled back down onto the network of ropes. Her mind seemed unable to process what had taken place. She was not dead. She found herself caught in a huge net made of thick rope.

"I am not dead," she stated. She started laughing.

"Thank You, God," she yelled out, when suddenly the entire net pulled off its tiering and started swinging away from the bottom of the bridge towards the ocean.

Adele screamed as she started plummeting a second time towards one of the piers. Fortunately, both arms were intertwined within the pattern of rope, or she was sure she would have flown off. With teeth clenched and eyes closed, she continued to swing to her left in a wide, long arc. Her grip on the ropes was like iron.

The sick feeling of falling was over again, and she swung gently back and forth. She dared to open her eyes. She was not dead, yet again. But her view made her sick to her stomach. She was successfully clinging to the net, which had come undone on one side, and she was hanging down towards the ocean below. Fortunately, one part of the net was still attached to the bridge above.

This was that suicide net, she realized.

She had read about it but had forgotten it was there. It had saved her life.

She looked below her and tried to assess how far she was from the water. Probably at least a hundred feet. There was no way she was going to jump. A large boat gunned closer to her, and a man on the deck shouted out to her.

"Hey lady, jump! I gotcha," he yelled.

"No," she yelled back.

No way.

She was afraid of heights. There was no way she was going to do that. The thought of it gave her nausea. She would just have to climb her way back up and make her way under the bridge. She believed she was strong enough to do it. She had once done ten pull-ups when challenged by an ex-boyfriend.

"Lady!" the boatman screamed, "Come on!"

"No," she repeated weakly.

She began climbing the net, square by square. She had gone several feet up when another loud wail ran out above, and the entire bridge shifted again. The net thrashed in the air, and Adele screamed as her grip was threatened. She clenched with everything she had, as it tried to shake her off into the bay.

She opened her eyes. The net had come undone even further, and she was hanging lower. Adele was now closer to the water but still much too far to jump. She took a deep breath and reassessed. Even though she was exhausted, she would have to find the strength to climb back up to the bottom of the bridge. She strained, but she could see a walkway underneath. She was sure that could take her all the way to land.

"Hey!" the annoying boatman screamed, "Hey, look out!"

She turned from looking at him to above her where he was pointing. The white van she had passed earlier had moved out over the edge and was now falling directly towards her. In seconds, it would hit her and the net, killing her instantly.

She released her grip and experienced the awful sensation of gravity pulling her down again as she accelerated toward the water.

Squeeze everything together, she thought.

She pulled her arms and legs tight and closed her eyes.

It seemed like only two seconds before she hit the water with an enormous crash. She plummeted down like a missile into the cold depths.

She was alive!

Now she was pushing her arms and legs upward, upward towards the surface. She needed air. An enormous explosion pushed her body sideways and hurt her ears. She opened her eyes and saw the white passenger van sitting in the water about two feet away.

That was so close, she shuddered.

As she made her way up, the van began its descent downward. She could see the surface now, and the boat with her boatman. She pushed hard for the final few feet and broke the surface, gasping for air.

A buoy was already within reach. The boatman was motioning towards it.

"Lady, grab the buoy!" he shouted.

He was laughing in disbelief at the extraordinary feat of survival he had just witnessed.

She wrapped her arms around the red and white buoy, totally exhausted. It took her last bit of strength just to hold on as they hauled her into the boat with the help of another net and several men.

As she collapsed onto the deck, shaking and heaving, her boatman ran to her and threw a wool blanket around her.

"Lady," he continued to laugh in amazement, "are you alright?"

His eyes were wide with wonder. She stared back at him. It took all her strength just to speak. Her voice was shaking from the cold.

"I'll be moving to Kansas," she announced with finality.

Weston and his family sat with a small group of other new church attendees in Pastor Pete's office. It was Monday evening, and as Weston gazed out the window, he could see that it was growing dark outside. Fortunately, the pastor had scheduled these meetings, or 'new believer Bible studies,' as he called them, at 7 pm. This way everyone still had time to get home, shower, and eat dinner before coming out.

In the last month, they had covered many topics. Daniel chapter two outlined the kingdoms of the world from Daniel's day until Christ's second coming: Babylon, Medo-Persia, Greece, Rome, and the ten kingdoms that Rome split into. It was fascinating, especially when they learned that archaeology had proven that Daniel was written before Greece was even a power.

Matthew twenty-four was an exposition by Jesus on specific things that would happen before He came back. Weston was learning Jesus was not one to sugarcoat things. He was especially surprised to learn that before Jesus came back, someone or something would impersonate Christ Himself to deceive as many as possible. Fortunately, there were markers given so that a person could determine if it was the real Christ.

Tonight's topic was the origin of sin. Chapters were read in Isaiah and Ezekiel that were clearly describing Lucifer, or the devil, and his fall.

"But why would God make a devil?" an older gentleman asked.

"That's a great question," Pastor Pete replied, looking over towards his head elder. "Elder Andre, you want to tackle this one?"

Elder Andre was a tall, imposing African-American gentleman. He stood about 6'3" and looked to be about two hundred pounds, all muscle. He had made a comment once about playing 'football in college' to Weston. He had a confidence about him that Weston was drawn to.

"Well, you see," started Elder Andre, "there was no discord, no evil, in Heaven...at first. The Bible indicates though, at some point, it could have been thousands of years, it could have been millions of years...but, at some point, His top man, Lucifer, started fostering envy and pride. When you read this passage in Isaiah 14:14, where he says, "I will ascend to the heights of the clouds, I will be like the Most High." It's clear that he was jealous of God and wasn't satisfied with his current position. Eventually, this turned into a full-on rebellion."

"Why didn't God just destroy him?" Weston's son Braden asked.

Weston was happy to see that his son was taking an interest in all this.

"You see, son," Andre replied, "God operates on the principle of free will for all of His creatures. He loves His creation and He desires them to love Him in return. If He had snuffed out the devil, His creation would have become afraid of Him. They would have started serving Him out of fear rather than love."

"I guess that makes sense," Braden stated.

"Lucifer, now Satan, was basically saying, I'm proposing an alternative system to what God's doing. Whoever wants to try it my way, follow me. God must have said, if you want to go I won't stop you. It's like the saying we've all heard, 'if you love something, let it go.' Well, at some point, these two groups could no longer abide together, and there was war, according to Revelation twelve. And since that time, Satan has been causing misery down here on Earth for thousands of years," Andre explained.

Something was troubling Weston. It was a question in his mind, a question that had always been there. He realized it was what made him agnostic in the first place.

"Elder, I just don't understand, though. Why does God allow so much sin and suffering here on Earth? If He's all-powerful, why doesn't He stop the evil things that happen in our world? Stop the devil?" Weston asked.

"Well, let me ask you a question as well. Why did God allow sin and suffering in Heaven, in His very presence?" Andre countered.

Weston had never thought of it that way.

"I'm not sure," he hesitated.

"For the reason I stated before," Andre replied quickly, "turn to Revelation twelve."

They all turned there in their Bibles or on their phones and read about war in Heaven.

"So, you see," Andre continued, "the question is not why does God allow suffering here on Earth, but why did He allow sin and suffering in Heaven, in His own backyard? We see from the way He dealt with evil in Heaven, a principle that carries through in everything. He gives all creatures free will to follow Him, or to not. He allowed suffering in Heaven. He allowed war, possibly even death, in Heaven. Death, destruction, and suffering always come in conjunction with war. If you think about that, it means that the misery of sin has reached every part of this universe, even God's own presence. We cannot expect to be insulated from something God was not even insulated against...but when He comes, He will make all things right. Justice will be meted out. Until then...these are just the rules of the game."

Heads nodded in agreement. For the first time in his life, Weston felt satisfied on the issue.

"And that's why it's so important that God is not only a God of love, but a God of justice," Andre continued, "when bad things happen to good people, they want justice. And so does God. But He needs us and the whole universe to see what sin really is. Unfortunately, for us here on Earth, time had to be given to Satan for his principles of rebellion to be carried out to their full fruition. I think we can all agree those principles are no good."

Heads nodded again. A few amens rang out.

After the meeting, the car was silent as they drove home. They had been going to church for about a month and attending Bible studies with the pastor. Weston was wondering where everybody's head was at.

"So," he began.

Ally turned to look at him. "Yes?" she asked.

"What do you think about all this stuff?" he ventured.

She turned back to glance out her side window at the streetlights going by. The kids were all watching the two of them.

"I've lived my whole life working to be as self-sufficient as possible," she began, "I've always believed being a good person, following a set of rules, was enough."

"Mm-hhh," he understood.

"I believe these people know what they're talking about. Jesus is the only way. I know in my heart of hearts, that a Savior is needed, that we don't have the goodness or the power within ourselves to really change ourselves."

"I agree with that," Weston concurred.

"When I was young, we went to church. I told you about the bad things that happened - "

" - I know," he stated.

"So, I didn't want anything to do with Christianity again. I know you had a similar experience. But what these people believe, it makes sense to me. And they seem so genuine," she said.

"I think so, too," he agreed. He looked towards the backseat. "What about you guys?" he said to the kids, "You have a say in this too."

Braden, Dylan, and Charlotte exchanged glances.

"We like the church, Dad," Dylan stated.

"And we agree it's the truth," Braden added.

"Ditto," Charlotte chimed in.

"So, let's keep going to these studies," Ally said.

"Ok...we'll keep going to the studies," Weston decided.

Chapter Nine - All the way

The sun was setting over the Cascade Range in Northern California, giving the snow on Mt. Shasta a pleasant pink hue. Below the snow line, thick forest wrapped the mountain all the way down into the foothills below.

An enormous storm-front could be seen to the west. Cumulonimbus clouds filled the sky, from north to south, as far as the eye could see. At least fifteen towers were gracefully floating in slow motion toward the forest, each with their imposing anvil shape.

The overshooting tops were white and lovely, contrasting the vast dark towers where warm air was soaring upward, being sucked in by the shell clouds like some vacuum cleaner of the gods.

The difference between positive and negative charges in the upper clouds and the lower clouds demanded a release. Occasional bolts, blue and white, could now be seen shooting from cloud to cloud, then to the ground, and even upward into the sky. Explosions of distant thunder racked the air, echoing throughout the surrounding countryside.

As the massive storm front made its way over Mt. Shasta, all its power was suddenly unleashed. Sixteen jagged bolts came down in red, yellow, cyan, blue, violet, and even green onto the mountain. The entire sky appeared to be one massive flash of light. The deafening roar of a thousand bombs filled the air and continued without ceasing. Seemingly unsatisfied with the first display, hundreds of brilliant blue bolts now probed the timbers at random points, apparently looking for weaknesses in the forest.

The armada began to pick up speed over the mountains, increasing its intensity with each passing minute. Trees everywhere exploded as they were kissed with electricity, and small forest creatures, terrified for their lives, fled in all directions.

The titans continued to make their way east, towards the forests bordering Oregon and upper Nevada. In their wake could now be seen more anvils approaching, and something even worse. A huge wall of fire raced across the ground as far as the eye could see.

President Lutrell waited anxiously in his conference room near corridor five in the Pentagon. They had eventually set up a permanent office here since it was close to the heliport outside. Given that his job involved so much travel with Air Force One by helicopter, it was convenient for him and his staff. Everything had been set up in a series of conference rooms: his office, a presidential podium with chairs for reporters, and even a gym.

Lutrell and his staff watched the Pope's AgustaWestland AW109 helicopter descend in the rain onto the heliport for landing. Three small panels at the bottom of the aircraft opened slowly, exposing the landing gear. As the sleek craft touched down, a passenger door opened, and several Swiss guards emerged, dressed in business suits, followed by the Pope himself.

As the entourage made its way through the Pentagon's halls towards them, Lutrell and his chief-of-staff, Tim Blain, made quick small talk. Everyone stood up as the newcomers walked in.

Lutrell immediately recognized Ambassador Bianchi, who reached him first and extended his hand.

"Mr. President," he spoke with joy, "it is so good to see you again."

"Likewise, Mr. Bianchi," he returned the greeting.

"It is my great pleasure to introduce to you the Holy Father," he beamed, moving out of the way and motioning towards the Pope, who was slowly but nimbly making his way into the conference room. "Pope Antony Giordano."

President Lutrell smiled as he shook hands with the Pope.

"Mr. President," the Pope began in slow, broken English, "thank you... for meeting me."

"Of course," Lutrell returned.

The Pope began speaking rapidly to his interpreter in Italian. The interpreter addressed the President, as the Pope continued to rattle off words.

"His Holiness is grateful for this meeting," he paused, "he would like to address issues with you now, in private... Perhaps, there is a meeting place?"

"I would like my chief-of-staff, Mr. Blain, present..."

As this was conveyed back to the Pope, a look of consternation came over his face. He spoke swiftly in Italian again. Lutrell already knew what he was saying.

What was it with these people and only meeting one on one?

"His Holiness has come a long way, President Lutrell," the interpreter struggled with his name, "and he has such important matters to discuss with you. If you could reconsider..."

"Fine," he relented, "let's just get going with it."

He had argued this point before with Ambassador Bianchi and was too tired to continue with it.

Pope Giordano smiled and shook his head as the interpreter conveyed agreement to meet privately. He and the Pope moved into an empty conference room, interpreter in tow.

As the three of them sat down, Lutrell studied the Pope. His aged face was graced by a full head of grey hair, parted at the side. He appeared thin, but not frail, in his white cassock. His movements seemed slow but steady. He appeared advanced in years but looked confident and good-natured, with a near-constant smile.

Lutrell motioned for Giordano to begin. This was after all, a meeting initiated by him. Lutrell was curious about what was important enough to bring him halfway across the globe. After several seconds of speaking in Italian, his interpreter caught up in English.

"I am deeply concerned about the aggressions taking place in Chabahar and Kerman. There has been much loss of life from the air strikes of your military. I am worried about the Iranian people," he said.

President Lutrell tensed. So, this was the reason for the visit? He immediately went on the defensive.

"I think you mean surgical air strikes," he corrected, "we are worried about the Iranian people as well. They have been taken hostage by terrorists within their own government."

The Pope listened as the interpretation came back to him, and then waved his hand dismissively. He continued to speak through his interpreter.

"I do not understand such things. I am just a simple man who wants peace. Peace, as well as healing for this tired Earth."

Lutrell nodded in agreement at that last part. If they could move away from the subject of the Iranian war, perhaps this wouldn't descend into an argument. The Green movement was something they could all agree on.

"Yes, your Holiness. America is currently making great strides in Green energy. We are 100% committed."

"Yes, yes. But enough is not being done. Currently climate change is ravaging your Western United States, yes?" the Pope countered.

He was clearly referring to the unprecedented wildfires ravaging every Western state except Utah.

"Yes," Lutrell admitted, "we are moving many fire personnel towards the west. We are hoping for containment by next month."

This was an optimistic assessment at best. Lutrell knew it was totally unrealistic. Actually, so many lightning strikes had occurred in California, Oregon, Washington, Nevada, Arizona, Colorado and

Idaho that they had their best scientists studying this phenomenon for an explanation. Due to this event, they were experiencing the worst wildfires in American history, and there was no comprehensive plan to get them put out. Over a thousand had already died.

"I pray this will be so," the Pope stated, placing his hands together in prayer. "Even so, measures should be put in place to put our nation's, and the Earth's, health back on track. We only have one home. We must take care of her."

"Yes, I agree," Lutrell nodded, "we are doing what we can, I believe."

"And yet, I know we can do more. During the COVID-19 epidemic, when all the movement of man finally slowed down, mother Earth was able to for the first time heal. It was a beautiful time," he went on, "but this is about even more than global warming, President Lutrell. I believe these calamities... are judgements from God."

Lutrell was somewhat shocked to hear this. He had never considered the possibility.

"God is displeased with the state of things," the Pope continued, "and I believe He is making that displeasure known."

"I see," Lutrell said somewhat reluctantly. He was not sure where the Pope was headed with this.

"So, what are you proposing?" he asked.

"My predecessor's encyclical called for Sunday to be implemented as a weekly day of rest, in order to save the environment. In this way, our societies can finally adopt a lifestyle that is eco-sustainable. I have been working with many different cultures and religions of the world, they are ready to move forward with this idea. To unite together, despite religious differences."

Lutrell hesitated. "What you're asking for, it sounds like a violation of what we refer to here as separation of church and state. We don't enforce religious laws."

"Mr. President, as you know, separation of church and state is not spelled out in words in your Constitution. It is more of this... idea, when the 1st Amendment says your Congress shall make no law respecting an establishment of religion, or the free exercise thereof," the Pope stated.

"Technically, you are correct - "

" - This Sunday law would have nothing to do with religion at any rate. It would be for the healing of the Earth...for the healing of families. Your culture is suffering, yes? It is sick with vice and sin. And the healing of mother Earth falls in line with, as you say in your Preamble, the common good, the general welfare. If these disasters continue, it would be detrimental for both these things. Can we agree that we are at the point where something must give on this separation concept?" the Pope insisted.

"Yes, I suppose," the President suddenly felt a bit light-headed, "I would actually love to do it, and I agree with it in principle."

The strange feeling quickly passed.

What was he thinking, agreeing with this so easily?

He spoke up again.

"However, however...I do not see how such a law could pass in my country."

A change came over the Holy Father's face. The gentle man of peace seemed gone. As Lutrell stared at him, he now appeared to have hard edges, looked more young and vibrant, and had a darkness in his eyes that alarmed Lutrell.

"La Protesta e finita," muttered Pope Giordano, staring into Lutrell's eyes. His voice seemed to have changed into someone else's.

His translator stared at the Pope for several seconds before recovering. As he resumed translating, the Pope placed his hand on his arm to stop the interpretation. The warm smile and gentle demeanor returned as quickly as it had left.

"We do not know what the future holds for our two nations. I only know that once I was a simple boy in a small fishing village, and now I am an old man, praying for peace. I am sure we will discuss these matters again soon," he stated with finality.

With that, Pope Giordano stood up to leave. President Lutrell suddenly realized he had lost control of the meeting and that the Pope had set the tone the entire time. The Pope had also decided when it was over, not Lutrell. A tide of anger welled up in him, as he realized he had been outclassed by a more experienced statesman.

He quickly forced a smile and extended his hand to the Holy Father. As they shook hands and left, he wondered what had come over him. He prided himself on taking control and being the one in charge. It was almost as if Pope Giordano had cast some kind of spell over him.

Weston was nervous. The church was singing Hymn 100 and was finishing up the last chorus. He was standing up on the platform with several other church members. He had been asked to do the scripture reading for the morning church service. Weston had always been terrified of public speaking and hadn't had to do anything like this in years. As his turn drew nearer, the old feelings of fear were returning. As he looked out at the congregation, he saw no one was looking at him.

But in a few minutes, that is going to change, he worried.

He estimated there were two hundred people seated opposite him. As the singing ended, the elder in charge asked everyone to be seated. Then another church member stood up to the podium and made the offering appeal. Weston noticed the service went by much faster when you were up on the platform than it did when you were in the pews.

Before he knew it, he was next. His breathing started to increase as he thought about going up to the microphone. He was beginning to panic. He realized he should pray.

He began: *Lord, You know I'm not good at this sort of thing. I'm really nervous. Please help me to calm down and do a good job for You. Amen.*

As he finished his prayer, he noticed Pastor Pete, who was sitting next to him, was motioning for him to go up.

He stood up and stiffly walked to the microphone. The scripture that was to be read was conveniently on the rear projector screen, should the presenter ever forget. Today's verse was Psalm 91:9-11.

Weston looked down at his Bible, which he had bookmarked to the correct page, and began to read:

"Because you have made the Lord, who is my refuge, even the Most High, your dwelling place, no evil shall befall you, nor shall any plague come near your dwelling. For He shall give His angels charge over you, to keep you in all your ways. They shall bear you up, lest dash your foot against a stone."

Weston glanced at the crowd. All were watching him and listening attentively. As he kept reading, the ending seemed especially meaningful:

"Because he has set his love upon Me, therefore I will deliver him. I will set him on high, because he has known My Name. He will call upon Me, and I will answer him. I will be with him in trouble, I will deliver him and honor him. With long life I shall satisfy him, and show him My salvation."

Several amens rang out from the crowd. Weston made his way back to the stage pew. As he did, he realized that as soon as he had begun reading, he had no longer been nervous. This was the first time in his life that he had spoken in public and not been afraid. It had to be a miracle. Weston marveled that God had heard his simple prayer and answered it within seconds.

After church, Weston and his family spoke with Pastor Pete and Elder Andre in the foyer.

"So, Millers," Pete began, "it looks like our meetings are almost finished."

"Yep," Weston agreed.

"What do you folks think about all getting baptized together?" he asked.

"You mean at the same time?" Ally questioned.

"Well, no," Pete laughed, "I mean one after another. On the same day. We were going to do the baptisms at our church picnic in two weeks. We had access to a pool at the Mercers."

"What happened?" Ally questioned.

"Because of all the wildfires, the church board voted to cancel the picnic. We can't do any outside activities until all this smoke abates," he explained.

"I mean, that makes sense," Weston looked at Ally. The skies had been dark all week.

"So, in two weeks, we'll just do it here at the church. Next week, we'll cover the last few fundamental beliefs. And then on the day of the baptism, we will ask you to affirm publicly that you believe them," he explained.

"It sounds good," Weston stated. He turned to his wife and kids, "Millers, what do you think?"

"I can't wait to be baptized with Jesus," Charlotte exclaimed loudly.

Everyone smiled and laughed.

"I just want to warn you," Pastor Pete placed a hand lightly on Weston's arm, "in the past, I have seen that the devil really attacks people right before and after baptism to try and dissuade them. It could be a crisis with a distant relative, a medical emergency, trouble at work. The devil doesn't change tactics much. Remember, this is a sign that you're doing the right thing. We all just really need to be praying right now."

"I will," Weston promised.

Elder Andre suggested they pray right then. Everyone bowed their heads, and he uttered a short but fervent prayer for the Millers' protection and for them to stand firm on their new beliefs. After the prayer, Weston felt tremendous peace. It felt good to be on the right path.

That night, he and Ally sat on the couch, watching their favorite TV show, Law and Order. They had seen every episode from each season, including SVU seasons, which were a bit more graphic. Currently, one of the officers was interrogating a child molester, who seemed to be gleefully toying with the detective.

"West," Ally spoke up reluctantly.

"Yes?" he replied.

"Can you mute it for a minute?" she asked.

He looked over at her. Something was wrong.

"Ok," he stated, turning towards her, "are you ok?"

She paused for a few seconds. "Remember in the studies we went over Christian living?"

"Yes."

"And it seems like we're doing a lot of that already. But it said a Christian should be very careful what they say, what they listen to, and...what they watch," she added.

He turned towards the TV. One of the detectives was pursuing a suspect through the streets of New York on foot, gun in hand.

"You mean this show," he stated matter-of-factly.

"Well," she answered slowly, "yes. It is violent. And I've been thinking... if we're going to do this thing, I think we should go all the way. I've been feeling a conviction. Pastor said I should listen to that when I feel it."

He knew exactly what she was talking about.

"Ally, I've been feeling the same thing."

"You have?" she asked, surprised.

"Yes," he answered, "it's just hard to change habits. I'm realizing that what we watch on TV, movies, and phones is not very good for us. I grew up in front of a television. My earliest memories are not of family stuff but of TV. My parents were taking me to rated R movies when I was five."

"It's sad," she lamented.

"Yeah," he agreed, "I do think you're right, though. Let's go all the way with this thing. Let's call in the kids too, and tell them what we think?"

Ally looked reluctant.

"Why not?" he joked, "The worst they can do is totally and completely disagree with us."

She laughed at that.

"Ok," she agreed.

They turned off Law and Order and called in the kids. Weston relayed what they had just been talking about.

"Dad," Dylan exclaimed, "we already stopped watching The Walking Dead two weeks ago."

"And now we only watch Veggie Tales or The Chosen," Charlotte added.

Braden nodded in agreement.

Weston and Ally exchanged glances. Apparently, the kids had been way ahead of them on this one.

"Wow, out of the mouth of babes," stated Ally, "come here, all of you."

"That is it...wow," Weston agreed.

She hugged Braden first.

"My Brae-bear," she said, squeezing him.

"Mom, stop it," he protested.

"Fine," she answered, "Dyl and Char, give me a hug too!"

They both came in for squeezes.

"Alright, all of you back to bed," Weston ordered.

Later, when he and Ally were in bed, he turned on his phone to take in the nightly news. Ally looked over to see what he was doing.

"Well, I still need to keep up with the news," he stated defensively.

"Oh, honey, of course," she quickly replied, "I'm not giving you a hard time. I'm sure we will still watch some things...we are just going to be more discretionary."

"Yeah," he agreed.

He thought about when Ally had given the kids hugs. She had reached for Braden first, as she always did. Also, his nickname was more creative than Dylan's and Charlotte's. He was worried the kids would sense favoritism. Weston considered bringing this up, but he didn't want to start a fight.

He turned back to his phone. Local news was doing fire coverage, as usual. Currently, there were thirty-five active wildfires in California alone. It was hard to believe. The nearest one to them was over fifty miles away, but the problem was the air was totally polluted from that fire, as it was north of them and the prevailing winds were blowing south. When they went outside their home, they could only see about ten houses down. The smoke completely blocked everything beyond that.

Outside of California there were major fires in every western state save Utah. The newscaster on TV was currently interviewing a wildfire survivor from Susanville, CA.

"Thank you for joining us this evening," the anchor said to a man who appeared in his thirties. He had multiple burns on his face and neck, which were the only areas visible on the screen.

"Of course," he replied.

"So, tell us in your own words, when did you first realize something was wrong?" she asked.

The man hesitated. "I was out after work, I'm a mechanic...and we could see a wall of fire up on the ridge. But you could see the smoke long before the fire. It was shooting out towards us. We knew something was coming."

"What happened next," the anchor prompted.

"Huge flames...as tall as a telephone pole. How do they get so big?" he questioned, with a haunted look, "I saw the wall coming towards main street. It came too fast, you see, for those folks to get out of the way. It was violent, it was weird, ok?"

"Ok," the anchor stated, prodding, "so, what happened then?"

"It moved faster than a man. Maybe faster than a car. That fire was alive, eating up everything. It blew through us so fast. Millions of sparks were shooting out of it. A wave of heat was pouring out of it, before it even got to us. There was just no time for those people."

"How many would you say died?" the anchor asked with an inappropriate look of fascination.

"The whole town," he stated emptily, "I think. I'm the only one, I was told."

He started to tear up and was unable to speak.

"How did you survive?" the anchor prodded. She seemed determined to make this segment boost ratings, "How did you survive the inferno?"

"Simple enough," he said as he forced back tears, "I was next in the car wash line. I just drove in, and I guess the timing was right. I think too, it was because the fire ruined the machine...it didn't push me out. The water just kept pouring onto my car, it never stopped. Still got pretty burned though."

The anchor no longer seemed as interested and appeared ready to move on to her next segment.

"Miss?" the man inquired.

The anchor hesitated. "Yes?" she returned dryly.

"Do you think God is punishing us? I mean, this planet?" he questioned.

The anchor got a look of disgust on her face. She paused for a moment, then placed her finger on her earpiece.

"I'm just getting word of breaking news," she began, excitement rising again in her voice.

The split screen quickly went from two to one, jettisoning the man off the program as quickly as he had first appeared. Apparently, the interview was over.

Weston would have agreed with the man in the past about God punishing the Earth. But this very topic had just been covered in their baptismal studies. It was clear from Scripture that these bad things that were happening were not being done by God, but by the devil. It made Weston think of what they had talked about in the book of Job. As soon as God withdrew some protection from Job, the devil came in with bad men and even natural disasters, and killed almost all of Job's family. Apparently, he had that level of control over people, and even the elements of nature.

The thing that worried Weston currently was the natural disasters he was seeing around him. A thought kept nagging at him: was God now withdrawing His Spirit from the Earth, and was the devil moving in? Was time running out?

The two weeks had gone by quickly, and now Weston, Ally, Braden, Dylan and Charlotte were all huddled in the back room of the church, dressed in blue baptismal robes. Pastor Pete began to invite them one by one, to come into the baptismal tank. First came the children, youngest to oldest.

The Pastor called Charlotte, who looked at her mom, and then timidly walked into the large tank with the Pastor. Pastor Pete spoke of how Charlotte had inspired them with her fervor and simple faith. She had encouraged several other girls her age to start coming to church.

He then said he was now baptizing her in the name of the Father, of the Son and of the Holy Ghost, at which point she went down into the water. Weston had promised himself he would not cry, but as Charlotte came up out of the water, he lost control and started to tear up. As Dylan and Braden followed her, it only got worse. He looked over at Ally, and saw she was having the same trouble controlling her emotions.

"You ready?" he asked her.

She looked at him and smiled. The look in her eyes was one he had not seen in a long time. It was a look of absolute peace and unconditional love. It dawned on him that doing this act together was bringing them even closer. They had always been close physically and emotionally, but now a new element would be added to their marriage: the spiritual dimension.

"No turning back," she stated with determination.

"Ally Miller," Pastor Pete called out.

She moved forward and descended the steps to the baptismal.

Later, after the baptisms, they all posed together for photos and then went to eat at potluck in the fellowship hall. It was a wonderful, joyous time. Weston had never felt so close to his family as he did at this moment.

After church, the Millers went out with Elder Andre and several other church members to hand out books door-to-door. At first, Weston was pretty nervous about it. Even though he was excited about his new beliefs, he didn't want to pressure people by coming to their door or pushing anything on them. But, as they began, he realized it was not as bad as he had thought it would be.

They were simply going door-to-door and hanging books on the doorknobs; they were not knocking on the door and attempting to talk to each person. If any in their group happened to run into an individual, they were by all means encouraged to engage with them. This happened several times that afternoon, and while initially Weston was afraid, he gradually began to relax.

Several people seemed interested in the books and asked what church they attended and where it was located. One person commented that they 'respected folks who would come out and live their beliefs.' Another said they were 'clearly living in the last days,' and they would come to their church as soon as possible. Weston and Ally both tried to emphasize one basic theme in their conversations with people. It was a theme that Andre had advised them to stay focused on while they were doing this because it helped to stir people out of their lethargy: the message that Jesus was coming soon.

Chapter 10 - Falling apart

Time passed. It had been a cold winter. So cold that it had snowed three times already, and it was only December. Old-timers recalled that it hadn't snowed in the Sacramento Valley since around 2009, and it had only been for a few minutes.

The snows weren't just dustings either, but several inches had dropped and stuck for days. This of course had caused havoc with every area of life. Stores had been raided, traffic accidents had skyrocketed, and experts on TV were pounding the message that it was all because of climate change, which was destroying the planet.

The temperatures in Roseville had plummeted to single digits. No one could recall them ever getting down this low in the San Joaquin Valley. The ten day forecast showed no end in sight either.

The rest of the country wasn't faring much better. In Milwaukee, it was forty below. In Concord, New Hampshire, sixty below zero. Even Little Rock, Arkansas had clocked in at fifteen below. Records were searched to locate a similar temperature in the past there; it had last happened in 1899.

The nation was experiencing a deep freeze, and basic services were suffering. The supply chain had barely recovered from all the terrorist attacks, and now it was slowing down again because of the weather. On the east coast, Interstate 95 had experienced a pileup so large, authorities were still trying to reach survivors days later. With no incoming shipments from truckers, stores had emptied quickly, and rioting had begun in surrounding regions. Similar conditions existed on 80, and even Interstate 40.

The only positive to it all was that the fires, which had been threatening to wipe out a good portion of the Western United States, had finally been extinguished. But so many had died. Lutrell smirked as the thought occurred to him that the same forces of nature that had created the disaster had also terminated it.

As the President read his morning briefing, he felt sick to his stomach. The artillery phase had ended and ground war had begun in Iran. Marines had landed at Bandar Abbas and were fighting to take control of the airport and establish a foothold. It was not going well and casualties were high. The Iranian government was committed to fight, prepared to fight, and wanted to fight. It was bad enough having to deal with conventional fighting with the Revolutionary Guard, but there had also been wave after wave of suicide bombers. Apparently, Iran had an endless supply of fanatics, ready to kill themselves to hurt the Great Satan.

But, what made things even worse was how bad things had gotten at home. Reports were coming in of mass rioting in major cities. Antifa had moved into downtown areas and proceeded to destroy everything in sight. Street battles were taking place between rioters and police, and a nationwide curfew of 8 pm had been instituted. More terrorist attacks were happening too, which appeared to be coming from Hezbollah sleeper cells.

Blackwater had supplied armed security forces nationwide after the first terrorist attacks, but it had proven to not be enough. The National Guard had been deployed to St. Louis, Cincinnati, Charlotte, and half a dozen other major cities. However, neither the rioting nor the attacks had stopped.

The briefing was saying that nine police officers and three guardsmen had died in the line of duty in just the last week. Several movements within the country had claimed responsibility, including some he had never heard of: The Map Boys and the Pony Express. Hezbollah had remained silent. After reading what the Pony Express was, Lutrell concluded that America was going insane.

It seemed like everything was falling apart, and he had no idea what to do about it. Advisors were saying, and he kind of agreed, that the root cause of all the trouble was the calamities. Because of them, so many basic services were down. The earthquakes, the fires in the

West, and the intense cold throughout the country. That was causing general discontent in society. People were cold, hungry, and scared. Therefore, they were resorting to violence.

So, the disasters were the problem, but how could you fight Mother Nature? You couldn't. Besides, Lutrell wasn't convinced that was the real problem. Wouldn't a more noble society, a society of the past, have weathered these problems with grace and dignity? The reason his country was having these problems was, in Lutrell's opinion, because the soul of America was rotten. The bottom had rusted out, and the ship was sinking.

Lutrell had been a child of the seventies, and while that era had seemed bad at the time, it was tame compared to the psychosis of current society. Everything was now about self, sex, and violence. Everyone believed they were a star and were owed everything for doing nothing. The public schools were more concerned about pushing gender transitions than teaching. Lutrell dared not bring up any objections to that movement. They had been highly effective in silencing all dissent. Consequently, American kids had fallen grossly behind in academics. Children in almost every other part of the world were outperforming them.

TV and movies were reaching levels of violence no one could have imagined possible: and it had to be constantly increased in order to keep society's attention. Experts were now speculating that this had something to do with all the mass shootings and violence in the country.

Added to all that, church attendance and belief in God was at an all-time low. With all these factors, it was a wonder that America was still on top. While other countries were planning to attack the United States, America seemed unconcerned. No one was interested in righting the wrongs of the world anymore, or even preparing to defend their own nation. Instead, the overwhelming issue on American's minds was correctly identifying where each citizen landed on the gender spectrum. Lutrell believed social media, while maybe not causing the problem, had certainly sped up the decline.

The coalition of faith leaders that he dealt with on religious matters were all in agreement on the solution to the problems America faced: Seek advice from the Holy Father. They were adamant that he alone had the connection with God that could turn things around for the United States, and the world.

He had had a conference call with the Faith First coalition leader, Jeremiah Lauerer, yesterday. Faith First was the main lobbying group that represented the Protestant denominations of America, and Lauerer had been adamant that America's morality had decayed to the point where it was now an emergency. Lutrell agreed with him on almost everything, except the position the Pope should hold. Jeremiah had said he was God's sole representative on this planet, a claim which ruffled the President's feathers. It was quite arrogant. However, the Protestants didn't seem to have any answers, and the Pope did.

He had been toying with calling Pope Giordano for the last hour, but he was hesitant. He was still irritated from their last meeting: how he had been bulldozed by him and his agenda. There was something about the man that made him uneasy. Lutrell didn't believe he was seeing the full picture with Giordano. No, there had to be another way. Things were bad, but they were going to turn around; they always did.

Just then, Tim Blain hurried in, out of breath.

"John?"

"What is it, Tim?" he asked.

"Problems," he returned, "can we conference in ten?"

"Yes," he answered dully. He wished Doug Fauser was still alive.

The Millers were huddled around the fireplace, singing a song from the church hymnbook. 'All the way,' hymn number 516. Dylan and Charlotte sang the loudest. Weston had a roaring fire going from some seasoned oak, and they were soaking in its warmth while they sang. In addition, the heater was cranked, but it couldn't keep up. Weston had looked out the backyard at their patio thermometer earlier; it said one degree.

After they sang a few songs, Weston read a passage from Romans eight. It said, '*For I am persuaded, that neither death, nor life, nor angels, nor principalities, nor powers, nor things present, nor things to come, nor height, nor depth, nor any other creature, shall be able to separate us from the love of God, which is in Christ Jesus our Lord.*'

They said a family prayer, going around in a circle. Braden prayed for their neighbors to find Jesus, and Dylan prayed for the cold to end soon. Charlotte passed, as she was too shy to pray out loud. Ally petitioned for strength for them all to be true to His Word, and Weston closed it out, asking God to continue to lead and guide them. After they were finished, Charlotte spoke up:

"Dad?"

"Yes, honey?" he responded.

"Do you think Jesus will come soon?" she wondered.

Weston thought about it for a moment.

"I do," he said matter-of-factly.

"We're ready, right?" she inquired. She had a look of real concern.

"Honey, you've asked Jesus into your heart. You believe He died on the cross for your sins, and you've repented. All you can do now is live one day at a time, following Him. He will make sure you're ready," he answered with assurance.

Her look of concern eased. She appeared to have peace about it.

"Dad?" she asked again.

"Yes?"

"Can we sleep around the fire tonight?" she requested hopefully.

"Yeah!" Dylan and Braden chimed in, "Can we, Dad?"

The kids were clearly excited about the idea. Weston cast Ally a glance. He would have much preferred to sleep in their soft bed, cold as it was. Ally nodded approval towards him.

"Okay," he replied slowly, "go get your stuff out of your go bags."

"Yea!" The kids cheered.

After they all left for the garage, he looked again at Ally.

"A night on the floor," he said with mock enthusiasm.

"Yea!" she replied with equal enthusiasm.

They were all gathered in the briefing room for the emergency meeting Tim had asked for. Lutrell was not looking forward to whatever new problem had arisen.

"Well, what is it?" he asked impatiently, "Another disaster?"

"Not quite," Tim replied, "first, we've got a problem in Massachusetts. And it's likely going to spread."

"What?" Lutrell urged.

"They already had the lowest marital consent age at fourteen... but the MAP folks have been pushing hard in that state.."

"MAP?" the President asked. He had heard this acronym repeatedly but still didn't know what it meant.

"Minor Attracted Persons," Tim responded.

Lutrell was silent as he absorbed this.

"Well, they pushed it up the chain and they've had a huge victory. The state Supreme Court has ruled in their favor. Kids as young as nine can now legally marry an adult," Tim announced.

The President spilled his coffee on the conference table as Tim said the word nine. Everyone turned towards him.

"What?" he exclaimed.

"They made persuasive legal arguments, John. Love is love, that line of thought. Age being no barrier or boundary," Tim stated matter-of-factly.

"Are there any barriers left?" Lutrell exclaimed in disgust.

Tim ignored him and continued. "So, we are assessing all options, but we see this riding up to the Supreme Court, with a win for the MAP side, as there is already legal precedent for this line. And even if it loses, the adult in the relationship can just identify as a minor now anyway, regardless of actual age. There is case law on that, too. We may be looking at a nationwide phenomenon in the next year. We'll have to assess our stance."

"Our stance," Lutrell laughed, "our stance is that we won't tolerate this disgusting perversion. Our stance is that this is an assault on children - "

" - I understand that you feel that way, John, but in our current environment, as President, you just can't express views like that. You really can't. It's hate speech - "

" - It's called hate speech by the people who are committing the crimes! Don't you think that's strangely convenient?" Lutrell interrupted.

Tim paused. "Maybe we should move on...we've got bigger problems anyway."

Lutrell sighed. He was mentally exhausted. Half his staff, including Tim, was under fifty. This new generation was like an alien race to him. He could not relate to them on these social issues at all.

"We had a penetration a few days ago in Boston. They're taking every precaution, but the contagion wasn't located in time for real containment. They're trying to get their heads around it now, trying to locate patient zero," Tim said.

"What, Covid, JN.4? Spit it out, Tim," Lutrell asked.

Tim hesitated. "Ebola."

A chill went down Lutrell's spine.

No, he thought.

"Ebola," the President repeated, "how could Ebola be here? How many are sick?"

"Not many," Tim answered, "only fifty confirmed dead so far."

"Fifty!" Lutrell exclaimed, "Fifty Americans are already dead?"

"Yes, sir. But because the death rate is so high, Boston is optimistic this thing will burn itself out," Tim answered, trying to sound upbeat.

"We need to get our best people at the CDC out there tonight," he ordered, emphasizing each word.

"Agreed," Tim stated, "we're already on it."

"I just don't..." Lutrell hesitated. He placed his head in his hands and ran them through his hair. "I just..."

More hesitation.

His staff was all staring at him with concern.

How do I handle this?

He was at a total loss. It was just too much.

Terrorists had destroyed the White House. There were no plans in place to rebuild it. They had pulled off dozens of attacks nationwide and were continuing to strike in random places. Thousands of Americans were dead as a result. The war in Iran wasn't going well, earthquakes and fires had devastated the West, and extreme winter was causing death and famine all over. Americans were rioting and fighting in the streets en masse. A nationwide curfew was in place.

Additionally, the culture was literally coming apart at the seams. Pedophiles were gearing up to start legally victimizing children, and it seemed the Supreme Court was going to let them. Violence was filling the land, and the government appeared to be losing control. Now, Ebola, the most deadly contagion of modern times, threatened to burn through the population.

He decided it was time to call Jeremiah Laurerer and the Pope.

Weston was perusing the canned goods aisle at WinCo. Ally was looking for spaghetti, and he had been assigned sauce and parmesan cheese. Braden and Dylan were with her. Charlotte walked beside him pushing a shopping cart.

Nobody wanted to go out because of the cold. They also had been nervous because of all of the rioting. Fortunately, there was not as much of it in the suburbs as there was downtown, but it was still visible. They had seen several burnt-up cars on the way to the store, and multiple National Guard vehicles drove by them on the way. At least there were two armed guards here at Winco; it made Weston feel safer.

The store was crowded as usual, and devoid of any fresh food. In each aisle, dozens of shoppers grabbed whatever was available. Today's fare was mainly canned corn, asparagus, and string beans. Weston had hated canned beans ever since he was a kid. He grabbed two cans of each; this was the allowable limit for any particular item in the store.

Store rules were posted on several signs throughout the building; no more than two of the same item, one shopping cart per family, and absolutely no cash or stealing. Cash had been eliminated several months ago, and already Weston was getting used to not seeing it anymore. But they had had no problems with their FedNote cards, so Weston had no complaints about the new order of things. The last rule about stealing could only mean that store thefts must have dramatically increased.

Ally and the rest of the kids met up with Charlotte and him on aisle twelve, the cereal aisle.

"Any luck?" he asked, referring to the spaghetti.

"It was a bust," Ally replied, defeated.

"Same here," he echoed.

"Looks like another night of beans and rice," Braden announced with mock enthusiasm.

Everyone chuckled.

The cereal aisle, notorious for its many selections, was down to Grape Nuts and Cream of Wheat. Weston actually loved Grape Nuts, so he grabbed two. Reluctantly, he also grabbed the Cream of Wheat.

As they made their way to the checkout counters, he could see all of them were manned. Each one had a line of at least twenty to thirty people. It was going to be a long wait or as his old friends used to say, a slow roast.

Charlotte and Dylan were playing; Braden stared off into the distance, bored.

"I spy with my little eye, something brown," Charlotte announced.

"Bread," Dylan replied without hesitation. The bread aisle was right by the checkout counters.

"Hey, how'd you know?" Charlotte demanded, annoyed.

"I just do," Dylan replied, "alright, I spy, with my little eye, something red."

"Hhmmm," Charlotte looked around, unsure. She twirled her chestnut hair with her finger. It bunched up around the neck of her heavy winter jacket. "The candy?"

"No, goob," he answered, "the checkout number. See it?" he pointed.

"Oh," she replied, embarrassed.

Suddenly, the power went out.

Groans and grumbles went out amid the crowd. Backup lights immediately turned on, but the store was still pretty dark.

They must have a working generator, Weston thought. *Apparently not enough power to work the registers though.*

He could see that all the register lights were off.

"It should come back on soon," he said to Ally, hoping but not really believing.

He noticed that they were one of the last people in line. If the power didn't come back on soon, none of these people would be leaving with food today. The only way to buy anything was with a FedNote card.

The crowd settled in for a long wait, and people began having conversations, which all blended into a general low hum of noise. Occasionally, someone yelled out how the situation was unfair or something needed to be done.

After a while, a tall young man dressed in a Winco uniform hauled himself up onto one of the checkout counters. Weston could tell he was the store manager, as a large picture of him was displayed by the front exit, along with other upper management staff. The Blackwater guards now moved into the store and stood near the exit, watching the crowd.

"Excuse me," the manager raised his voice, "excuse me! Ahh, I'm sorry everyone, but we don't have any power to operate the cash registers."

The crowd moaned. Several voices yelled expletives.

"That's fine," he continued, "look, I'm sorry, but we're not able to complete your purchases today because we don't allow cash or check. If you will just leave your carts where they are, store employees will return items to shelves. You'll have to leave and return tomorrow. Our store closes in one hour anyway."

The crowd was getting loud now and drowning him out.

"I'm very sorry," he continued, trying to raise his voice above the noise.

Angry voices were everywhere. One man in the front could be heard above the rest.

"Ain't no way," he yelled, moving his full cart through the register coral and pushing toward the exit. Several others followed his example.

The guards moved swiftly. The one nearest him, dressed in all black but with a blue bandana on his head, shoved him so hard that the man and his shopping cart of food items went sprawling across the tile flooring. Glass jars broke, and milk jugs burst, sending a river of green and white across the dirty floor. The man lay on the ground, shocked by the sudden and swift response.

"Hey!" yelled several patrons near the front, "That ain't right!"

Three or four new men moved towards the guards in a threatening manner. Bandana man quickly pulled out his sidearm and shot into the ceiling several times.

The reaction of the crowd was instantaneous. Almost everyone began ducking and crouching, moving away from the front exit. Women and children were screaming all around them.

Weston could see the aggressive response had the opposite effect that the guards desired. Now nobody could be controlled. People began grabbing whatever they could and running towards the back of the store.

Even more surprising, the aggressiveness of the guard had ignited the anger of some in the crowd even more. Several men and women moved toward the guards and began actively fighting with them, trying to take their guns. Multiple shots rang out, echoing in the cavernous box store.

"Let's go!" Weston yelled, grabbing Ally and the kids. He had to pull Braden and Dylan away as they stared, mesmerized at the fighting. He grabbed each of them, corralling them towards the back of the store.

"Run, come on, run!" he yelled.

He continued pushing his family towards the rear of the store.

Multiple groups were jogging toward the rear exit, away from the shooting. Some were parents with arms around their kids. Others were younger, their arms full of stolen goods. As they neared the rear of the store, Weston was shocked to hear a new sound: the deafening report of AR-15s firing.

All the Millers now ducked down, continuing to run. They passed through the large double doors by the meat aisle and into the recesses of the store. Huge shelves filled with boxes lined the walls and went from floor almost to ceiling. The cavernous area was dark, and no store employees could be seen anywhere. All the patrons were running in a line towards a red exit sign.

A box of canned goods nearby exploded from stray gunfire. The sound of screams and glass shattering could be heard out in the main store. They were almost out now. As the Millers followed everyone out the door, they emerged into a large back alley. It was shocking to go from the warmth of the warehouse area to the cold outside. Everyone's breath came out in plumes.

Weston could immediately tell they were still in trouble. People were running in all directions, but many were fighting, swinging fists at each other. Others had bottles and even knives in their hands.

A young teen with a crazed look in his eyes moved towards Weston. He had a short black knife in his right hand.

"I'm gonna mess you up, man," he declared.

Ally and Charlotte screamed. Weston shoved them behind him in a protective move. The main thing was to keep his body in between them and the assailant. Weston desperately looked around for something to defend themselves with.

Braden and Ally tugged on his shirt sleeves, begging him to get away. Since they were near the rear dumpsters, multiple boxes, pallets, and pieces of wood lay spread across the pavement. Suddenly, he noticed a broken 2x4. It looked to be about two feet long. He quickly lunged toward it and grabbed it. He extended it towards the knife wielder without saying a word.

The expression on knife-wielder's face changed from excitement to uncertainty. He stopped advancing towards them and scowled. It appeared they were at a standoff.

Weston continued to push his family towards the side of the building. After they had moved twenty more feet, the attacker seemed to lose interest and turned away. Weston and his family ran full speed around the side of the store to the front parking lot. Shots could still be heard ringing out inside the store. Either the guards were just killing people now, or people had managed to get their guns and were going on a spree of their own. Either way, they needed to get out of here.

As they reached their van, multiple sirens could be heard in the distance. Weston clicked the remote, and everyone piled in. He started the vehicle and peeled out of the parking lot towards home. The shopping trip resulted in them leaving with less than they had started with. Somehow, in all the commotion, Weston had lost his wallet.

That night, he reported his FedNote card stolen. A representative assured him a new card would be sent within the week. Having returned from the shopping trip empty, they re-assessed their food situation. They still had a full pantry, which, among other things, contained several months of pasta, rice, and beans. They had about three weeks of canned fruits and vegetables stockpiled. Weston was concerned however, because he knew it wouldn't last long. He wasn't looking forward to returning to the store.

"Could we go somewhere else?" Ally wondered.

"Yes," he answered, "there's a Raley's. It's further away and more expensive. But I think we should go there instead."

"Yeah," she agreed, "I think the kids are going to be too traumatized to return to WinCo."

"Understandably," he echoed.

"I was thinking," she continued, "about moving - "

At the word moving, he started to get upset.

" - moving out of California."

"Really," he said with annoyance, "and where do you imagine we will go?"

She stared at him with irritation.

"You want your family to stay here?" she asked, "Weston, I don't know if you've been paying attention, but this place is turning into a dump. You almost got killed by a gang member - "

" - Nobody was going to get killed," he interrupted her.

In truth, he had thought he might, but he was angry at Ally now and didn't want to give on any point.

"You almost got killed, and your family would have watched. Charlotte said she doesn't feel safe. The boys and I don't feel safe," she stated.

"When was someone planning on telling me?" he questioned her, annoyed, "We can't afford to leave, and even if we did, we are not moving to Louisiana with your brother Ronnie! He is so annoying with that oath he makes you take on your birthday - "

" - My brother is...different. Look," she stated, "if you want to stay here...fine."

"Fine," he returned flatly.

She left the room, and he was glad. He was so irritated with her. How would they just pick up and move? He was not going to subject his family to crazy Ronnie.

He turned on the TV to cool down. It was a nature show. After a minute, he realized he had gotten too heated over nothing. She was just trying to talk to him. He felt ashamed. He just needed a few minutes to cool down.

All of a sudden, the television changed. The program was gone, and now the screen said, *'local broadcast interrupted: Presidential address.'* He changed the channel quickly, frustrated. Each channel was the same, with the Presidential logo on the screen. Finally, President John Lutrell appeared on the screen, with a hallway behind him containing all of the world's flags. It seemed to be a virtual background.

After a brief pause, the President looked at the screen and began:

"My fellow Americans,

As you know, our country is experiencing an unparalleled crisis. Terrorist attacks at home, war abroad, natural disasters due to our treatment of the Earth, pestilence, and in some ways, worst of all, total moral decay of our society.

As some of you already know, in the last few days, a new crisis has emerged. In Boston, cases of Ebola have been detected throughout the - "

" - Ally!" Weston yelled, "Ally!"

"What!" she yelled back.

"You have to see this, now!"

Ally emerged from the other room while Weston turned up the TV. She stared at the screen. There was a video of healthcare workers, clad in protective gear, moving around stacks of full body bags.

"Where is this?" she asked.

"Boston," he replied.

" - so I'm calling up our best physicians around the globe," the President continued, "to work together, to fight this new Ebola crisis. Together, we are stronger. Our global community can overcome this new challenge that has arisen.

We must realize that these crises have come upon us because of our treatment of the Earth. We have made enormous strides in reducing coal and oil usage, replacing gas vehicles, converting traditional power plants to biomass stations, and increasing wind and solar energy. However, these efforts have not been enough."

The President paused. Now, an odd expression came over his face.

"But we can learn something from the past. During the Covid 19 epidemic, when all the movement of man finally slowed down, it was a beautiful time. The Earth was finally able to heal. So today, I'm signing a new bill called the Green Sunday Initiative. It requires that all Americans do NO work on Sunday. It asks that, as Americans, we rest, spend time with our families, refrain from traveling, emitting as little of these deadly emissions as humanly possible.

In two weeks, on February twentieth, I'm calling on all Americans to step forward and make this commitment. To lead the way globally, as we always have. Keep in mind this is not a request; this is now law, and there will be repercussions for those who make the choice to endanger us all by breaking that law. But let us remain positive and focus on how we can work to solve this crisis. Together, we can turn the tide for our nation and the world. Goodnight."

With that, the TV returned to a reality show in progress.

The phone rang. It was Rick.

"You see it?" he asked.

"Yep," Weston responded, "all along....you were right. It's happening."

"This is just the beginning."

"How much time do you think we have?" Weston asked.

"Not sure. It could be a year or two. Maybe just months now. Now's the time to really start watching the news, but mainly, now's the time to get serious."

"Definitely," Weston agreed.

"The good news is, Jesus is coming soon," Rick stated.

"Jesus is coming soon," Weston repeated.

"I'll call you tomorrow."

"Goodnight, Rick," Weston said.

"Goodnight," Rick replied.

That weekend at church, the pews were full. Multiple people stood in the back, and some were seated on the floor before the pews. The praise team seemed more enthusiastic than ever, and several additional choruses of 'Jesus is coming again' were sung spontaneously.

Pastor Pete was bursting with energy as he took the pulpit. His sermon was on the ten virgins: five wise and five foolish. Now was the time for soul searching, he declared. Numerous amens rang out from the crowd as he raised his voice in consternation; would they be ready to meet their Lord? He gave a rare altar call, and a dozen newcomers came forward to surrender their lives to Christ.

After church, Ally and Weston walked out holding hands. The kids followed behind.

"What a beautiful service," Ally commented.

"It was moving," Weston agreed.

"Kids," Ally said, "go on ahead and meet us at the van."

She handed Braden the keys. All three of the kids ran ahead of them.

"West?" Ally said.

Something was on her mind.

"Yeah?" he replied.

"Is there going to be trouble soon?" she asked.

Weston hesitated. He was staring at a large black van parked a short distance away in the parking lot. It faced the church foyer entrance, even though all the other cars turned away. He noticed several men were inside, even though church had just gotten out.

They wore dark suits and sunglasses. They were taking pictures of church members as they emerged from the building.

"I think there will be," he answered matter-of-factly.

The news shows that night were all buzzing about the new law. It was set to take place tomorrow, and multiple questions were coming into the Channel 40 viewer questions box. There was a lot of confusion on what could and could not be done on Sunday.

The anchor said they would have an expert to explain the Sunday Green Initiative in greater detail shortly, and viewers were also directed to SunGreenLaw.org for more information.

Weston changed to another channel. It was three commentators with a host, arguing different points of the law.

" - and we can only conclude this will lead to nothing good. We've already given up our cash. They control that. Now the government is going to tell us what to do every Sunday? Look at China and their social credit system. This is leading to a similar tyranny," a middle-aged man in a gray suit stated.

"That's an exaggeration, Tom, and you know that," a purple-haired man in a strapless dress interrupted, "I've been to China, and they are some of the happiest people I have ever seen."

"You would try to appear happy too," Tom countered, "if to look unhappy meant possible arrest and internment in a death camp."

"No, no, no, Tom! You are displaying such white fragility and colonialism right now. Ha ha," the third commentator laughed heartily.

She was a young, gothic-looking white woman with rainbow glasses, "you talk about the Chinese as though you have any right to do that. You don't understand their culture."

"I understand that they are killing Christians because they are Christian," Tom countered.

"That's a cultural issue," goth-lady countered, "our former President Biden said it best when he said that their government's oppression of their people is ok, because culturally, each country has different norms they are expected to follow. How dare you get up on your white horse and judge. Your fake allyship deserves a trigger warning to all our viewers out there."

"Alright, alright, alright," broke in the host, "we all know China is one of the best countries to live in. But now, what about what's happening in our country? Tomorrow, we're set to implement this new law. Is it a good idea, or is it tyranny as Tom says?"

"What we need," stated purple girl dude, "is submission to authority in every possible spectrum right now. Look at what's happening around us! We need to surrender our identity, surrender our reality, our bodies, and our property to the global collective. It's hivemind; it's about the passage of time and the significance of the passage of time. It's fluid-think, and it works."

"I don't know what most of that means," Tom replied, "but the last time I checked, we still had a Constitution that gave individual Americans a set of basic rights - "

" - Ahhhgg," interrupted purple girl dude, "don't bring up the Constitution, please! The greatest example of toxic colonialism and white privilege. Please! It needs to just go away, the sooner the better."

"You do realize, ahh, John, is it? You do realize that without the First Amendment, legally we wouldn't even be allowed to have this conversation right now? Before 1776, we would have been thrown in jail," countered Tom.

"Wait, what? Are you deadnaming me right now? Are you actually deadnaming me?" yelled purple girl dude. "It's either Ze, Zie, or CandyCane to you. But that's fine, you just go on with it then. It's binary of you, baby, but look, what Snow White here doesn't realize is we need to destroy the Constitution. We need to destroy it. Individual rights is what has gotten us in the mess we are in now."

"Look," broke in goth lady, "this Sunday law is good in my opinion. Mother needs her rest - "

" - By Mother, you mean planet Earth?" Tom asked.

"Obviously I mean planet Earth," goth lady mockingly emphasized each word, "Mother needs to rest. Climate change is killing her, and she needs to take a little nap every Sunday. And if you had any sense of climate justice, you would start doing your own part and just sit on your bare floor all day, in your house that you don't own, and take small shallow breaths and hold in all your waste as long as possible. The white emissions out of this country are just so off the charts I can't even give you statistics - "

" - Because you don't have any," Tom interrupted.

"But if a way of life needs to die," goth-lady continued, ignoring him, "it's this life of privilege. His toxic masculinity is so triggering. Why is he even on this show mansplaining about tyranny?"

Purple girl dude started laughing.

"But millions and millions need to die," goth lady continued, "millions of people for her healing, that's beautiful. We need a cleanse. That's 'The Great Reset.' You will own nothing, have nothing, eat almost nothing, be nothing, do nothing, and you will be so happy the entire time, and when you do finally expire, you'll have fulfilled your global purpose and it's beautiful. It's all about that."

"It sounds great," Tom responded sarcastically.

Weston turned off the TV, shaking his head. He had heard enough.

What was America now?

It was not what he had referred to all his life as America. It had become something...else.

He checked all the doors and windows, and joined Ally in bed. She was already asleep. He placed his Smith and Wesson on the night table next to him and patted it, feeling very little reassurance. In the distance, he could hear gunshots: a full blown firefight. It was just another night in Roseville.

That Sunday, the Millers went out to go shopping for groceries. They did not attempt to go back to WinCo. Instead, they drove a little farther to Raley's.

Along the way, they could see that almost everything was in fact closed. Occasionally, they would see an open store, but there would be multiple police vehicles parked out front. Weston was not surprised when they pulled into the Raley's parking lot and found it empty. All the store lights were off.

"Well, that's a bust," Ally exclaimed.

"We had to try," said Weston.

On the way home, three more large National Guard vehicles drove by them, headed in the opposite direction, towards the foothills.

In his rear-view mirror, Weston noticed a police car following behind his van. He wasn't sure how long it had been there. Suddenly, the lightbar came to life, but no siren.

"Agghh, great!" Weston exclaimed.

Ally turned her head behind her.

"Oh no," she spoke as she saw the siren.

"We're getting pulled over," Weston complained, stating the obvious.

"Dad, just pull over," Dylan said. The kids all looked scared.

"What did you think I was going to do exactly," Weston chuckled, "make a run for it?"

"Dad!" the kids all yelled, clearly upset.

"Relax, I'm pulling over," he stated amusedly.

He found a spot with a large shoulder off to the side and pulled over, stopping the car. The police vehicle moved in behind him, lights blazing. The officer paused momentarily, then got out and started walking towards them.

"What should we say?" Ally asked urgently.

The officer was almost to his window.

"I don't know," answered Weston quickly.

The officer tapped on his window. Weston quickly hit the control button on his door, rolling it downward.

"License and registration, please," the officer asked.

"Of course," Weston replied, quickly fishing them out of his wallet and handing them to the officer.

He took them and walked back to his police cruiser. Upon returning, he handed them back.

"Do you know why I pulled you over today?" he asked.

"Was I speeding?" Weston asked.

The officer glared at him for several seconds.

"As I'm sure you know, travel is not permitted on Sundays now except in the case of emergencies. Are you experiencing a life-threatening emergency?" he asked.

"No, sir," Weston answered.

The officer stared at him for a moment. Then he glanced at Ally and the kids.

"I will let you off with a warning... this time."

"Oh, thank you, officer," Weston gushed.

"Your non-compliance has been recorded in our system, though. Don't get another one of these. Don't travel on the first day of the week," he instructed.

"Oh, I won't," Weston replied. "Thank you, officer!"

The policeman stared at him again momentarily, then turned and returned to his car.

The following Saturday, there was a line outside the church. The Millers were not even able to get inside the sanctuary. Speakers had to be hauled out of storage, hooked up, and placed in the foyer so those who didn't get there early enough could even hear the sermon.

Weston looked around. Families were sitting on the floor, with Bibles open, soaking up every word of Pastor Petes. It did not even seem to matter that they could not see the speaker. Every available space was taken up on the floor. Weston had never imagined it could be like this.

He had been told repeatedly that a Sunday Law would be a bad thing, but looking out over the sea of people, it seemed to him it was having the opposite effect. Families had materialized out of nowhere. Church attendance hovered around two hundred on a typical Sabbath, but there must be at least twice that now. All seemed eager to have the Bible explained to them.

A system was set up where current members, including the Millers, would be assigned one of the new families. They would invite them into their homes, fellowship with them, and study the Bible together.

The Millers' adopted family was the Kovalenkos: Ivan, Darynala, and their two children, Artem and Alina. Since Artem was thirteen and Alina was nine, the Miller kids paired up with them nicely.

The Kovalenkos had never been to a church, but they expressed a desire to be baptized into the Seventh-Day Adventist movement. Weston and Ally began studying the Bible with them with a set of study guides that covered the beliefs of the church.

All was going well until one day, while studying at the Kovalenkos house, Darynala's father showed up unannounced. As he came in, introductions began.

"Weston, Ally, this is my father, Anatoliy," said Darynala nervously.

Anatoliy smiled faintly and nodded his head. He was looking around the room and eyeing the open Bibles.

He was not a large man but seemed intimidating nonetheless.

"Darynala, what is this?" he asked, "You are studying Bible?"

"Yes, Father. Studying about the last days, which we are living in," she answered quietly.

"So I raise you your whole life, and now you are becoming Christian?" he complained, his voice rising.

"Papa, this book is - "

" - It is fairy tales!" he shouted, interrupting her, "Fairy tales. If your mother could see what I now see."

"Anatoliy," Ivan interjected, "we are - "

" - You shut up!" Anatoliy snapped, pointing a finger at his son-in-law.

Alina started crying. Charlotte just stared wide-eyed at Anatoliy. Weston and Ally glanced at each other; the situation seemed like it could become dangerous. Anatoliy appeared to be very controlling and possibly violent.

"It is because of you this is happening," he announced to Ivan, advancing toward him, "I never should have allowed..."

Suddenly, Weston arose from the couch. He was angry. Angry at what was clearly a spiritual attack taking place through this ignorant man to stop the spread of God's Word. Angry at the scared look he had produced in the children's eyes. Ally reached for Weston's arm to get him to sit back down, but he shook her off.

As Weston stood, Anatoliy's voice trailed off. He began sizing up Weston. He did not seem intimidated by him at all. However, he began glancing towards Ivan, who was also standing and seemed ready to fight. Apparently, the pair of them made him less confident.

"You will regret this," he announced to his daughter, pointing a finger in her direction.

As he turned to leave, he glared at Weston one last time before walking out the front door.

Chapter 11 - The Summoning

The Ebola virus continued to rage on in Boston. The WooSox stadium, where Boston's AAA baseball team played, was being used as a makeshift morgue, and it was half full after just a month.

Everyone in Boston knew someone who had died, and quickly. It wasn't unusual for extended family members to find out someone had the disease after they had already passed away. Seven days was about the longest most people could take before succumbing. From the statistics that were available, there appeared to be about a fifty percent chance of survival.

Progress was being made on slowing the spread however, and it appeared there was reason to begin having hope. Medical experts were saying this was because the virus killed its victims so quickly. Therefore, each victim had less time to spread the illness to others.

But then cases started springing up in nearby Providence.

It was at that point that the decision was made to cut off the entire region. From Portsmouth, New Hampshire, all the way to New Haven, Connecticut, a large semicircle of America was now cut off from normal life. It was called The Zone. An over two hundred square mile swath of land had now become a militarized zone, a no-man's-land. Its borders were swarming with National Guardsmen, Black Hornet Reconnaissance systems, and even Apache helicopters. But no one dared go inside. Twin seven-foot chain link fences with barbed wire stretched across the hills as far as the eye could see, separating the possibly infected from the healthy.

The stories coming out of The Zone were horrendous, if they were true. Reports circulated that hordes of Americans were starving and trying to get out, and were being turned away at the new two hundred mile border. Most had nowhere to go and would simply remain at the fenceline and die, or charge the fences and be gunned down. There was even a story that extermination squads of

Blackwater personnel were moving through The Zone and systematically killing, simply because they could. Law and order did not seem to exist there.

It was all becoming too much for Weston, and he slowed down on watching the news. He certainly didn't have it on when the kids were around. He and Ally still wanted to try to shelter them, as much as could be done in the world they now lived.

It was Sunday, and Weston was bored, but he dared not attempt to leave the house again. The Internet, radio, and TV were all saying there would be a $750 fine for the first offense. The only exception would be if one was traveling on Sunday due to an emergency.

He wanted to get some work done around the yard, so he got out the lawn mower from the detached garage in the backyard. He started mowing the grass in the back.

He walked back and forth with the mower, working the grass down in neat rows. Weston looked around. Their backyard led to a shared alley that ran to cross-section streets a block or two away. He could see seven or eight houses while standing in his yard. No one was out at any of the houses, and all the blinds were closed. It looked like no one was home. However, he knew that people were there because, other than church, no one was allowed to go anywhere on Sunday anymore.

Once finished, he moved to the front yard. He cranked the mower to life again and adjusted the throttle. He began going over the front now, slowly clipping down the grass, starting in the corner by the driveway.

He noticed his neighbor across the street, Ms. Anderton, was staring at him through her kitchen window. As he stared back, she quickly shut her blinds.

"Hello, neighbor!"

Weston turned quickly. It was Rick. He released the control bar to shut the motor off.

"Hey, man. How are you doing?" Weston asked.

"Good as can be," Rick replied, "say, none of my business, but I don't think we're allowed to mow anymore on Sunday."

It dawned on Weston that his actions were now against the law.

"Oh, no! I didn't even think," he replied. He felt so stupid. "Force of habit, I guess."

"We have been doing it our whole lives," Rick said in a conciliatory tone, "neighbors are watching, though. We have to be careful now."

"You mean Ms. Anderton?" he asked.

"And probably others," Rick stated matter-of-factly.

"I'm just unsure how to do all this, you know?" Weston stated, "I want to stand up to what's happening. I want my light to shine, but I don't want to blind anybody with it."

Rick chuckled.

"You know, that gives me an idea," he stated.

"What?" Weston asked reluctantly.

"They're curious. Let's satisfy their curiosity. I'm gonna go grab something. Wait here."

Weston watched Rick disappear into his garage. He moved the mower off to the side of the house and waited for Rick to return.

Rick came out with a medium-sized box. It was full of books. Weston grabbed one; it said 'The Great Controversy.' He was familiar with it because he had just finished reading it.

"Let's pass these out in the neighborhood," Rick said excitedly.

"Oh, I don't know," Weston said nervously. The thought of going door-to-door made him feel sick to his stomach.

"Weston, these people need to hear the message, same as you did. Time is short," Rick stated with conviction, "all we have to do is give them a book."

"You're right," Weston relented. He knew Rick was right no matter how uncomfortable this was going to be, it was God's will, and people needed to hear the truth. Who knew how much time was left?

"And don't worry," Rick added, "I'll do most of the talking!"

They began on their side of the street, moving left. At the first few houses no one answered the door, so they left a book on the front porch. Occasionally, Weston would glance back at Ms. Anderton's house. He noticed she continued to stare from the window.

At the next house, someone finally answered the door. It was a middle-aged man.

"Yes?" he asked, "May I help you?"

Rick explained they were his neighbors and were passing out this book, which explained that they were living in the last days and told what was about to take place.

The man seemed interested and promised he would read it.

More doors started to open, but at most of them, the people did not seem interested. Some would take the book hesitantly, and others would outright refuse it. Some would only speak through the door, citing concerns with the Ebola virus.

They were now at the end of his street, getting ready to cross and start on the other side. At the last house on this side there was a very loud, busy intersection.

They knocked. Weston was shocked at who opened the door.

It was Anatoliy.

He looked at Rick with no expression, but his eyes narrowed as he saw Weston.

"How dare you come to my door!" he said angrily.

"You know each other?" Rick asked in surprise.

"Anatoliy," Weston stated in shock, "I didn't know we lived on the same street."

"What are you doing here?" he asked icily.

"We're here giving people this book, which outlines what's going to happen in the last days," Rick interjected, handing him the book.

Anatoliy made no move to receive the offered item.

"You people," he began, "you think you can get whatever you want."

Rick realized there was bad blood between Anatoliy and Weston.

"Sir," he began, "we're sorry we disturbed you today. We only wanted - "

" - Get off my property," he spoke coolly, emphasizing each word. He turned to Weston, "and stay away from my daughter with that filth!"

He glanced at the book and spat in their direction.

Weston stared in shock at Anatoliy. He had never been spit at in his life, and he felt violated. His blood pressure began to rise. Fortunately, Rick took control of the situation.

"You have a good day, sir," he said, grabbing Weston's arm and leading him away. They began walking towards the crosswalk at the busy corner. Anatoliy continued to stare.

"Don't come back again," he yelled from his door, "or else!"

They continued to make their way down the other side of the street. Fortunately, Anatoliy had gone back inside. Weston's pulse was still racing from the encounter, but Rick seemed to have moved on and was his upbeat self again with the next neighbor, a young woman.

"Yes?" she asked.

"Ma'am, we're here today to give you this book outlining the history of the world, from Jesus first coming to His second coming. He is coming soon," Rick announced.

The woman immediately burst into tears.

"Ma'am, are you alright?" Weston asked, concerned.

She attempted to compose herself and speak, drying her eyes with the sleeve of her sweater.

"You came here to give me a book about Jesus?" she asked.

"Yes," Rick replied.

Her face squished up, and she began crying again. Through tears, she said:

"A few minutes ago...I grabbed my...Percocet," she paused, struggling to speak, "I was going to take them all. I was ready. I had them all in my hand like this. I felt I should say one last prayer. I have not prayed since I was a kid. I asked Jesus, if You're real, show me a sign and a way to learn who You are. Within a few seconds, the doorbell rang. Are you really coming to give me a book about Jesus?"

She burst into fresh tears.

Weston was shocked. He struggled to remain composed.

"Miss," Weston stated, "this book will not only show you who Jesus is, it will prepare you to live with Him forever in Heaven. He is coming soon. He wants you to be with Him."

"I think He sent you to my house today," she choked out between sobs.

"What's your name?" Rick asked.

"Rosita," she answered.

"Rosita," Rick continued, "I want you to start reading this book. And I want you to come to our church this Saturday."

"Saturday?" she asked, confused.

"Yes, this Saturday," Rick answered, "and here's my personal number. We're your neighbors, and that should mean something more than just people who live by each other, wouldn't you agree?"

"Yes," she replied, nodding her head.

"You are valuable, Rosita," Rick continued, "valuable and loved desperately by God. The devil wanted you to take your life, but Jesus intervened. Never forget that. It's not me or Weston here. We were just the instruments. Jesus intervened to save you. Now He wants you to commit your life to Him."

Their conversation continued, with Rosita surrendering her life to Jesus. They prayed that He would lead and protect her in her new life with Him. Rosita seemed to have a new peace as they left her door. She promised to read the book and call later for directions to the church.

Rick and Weston were amazed at how God had used them to intervene in someone's crisis. What if they had not gone door-to-door today? It was incredible to think about what God had just done. He had saved Rosita's life. They hit the next few doors with new enthusiasm and success.

Eventually, they reached the house directly across the street from Weston's. It was Ms. Anderton's home. Weston suddenly felt panicky as they made their way to her front door. After ringing the doorbell and knocking once, she opened the door.

"What is it?" she questioned with a scowl.

"Hello, Ms. Anderton," he hesitantly began, "it's me, Weston, your neighbor across the street - "

" - I know who you are," she interrupted, "whatever you're selling, I don't want any."

"Oh, we're not selling anything," he chuckled nervously.

"Figure of speech," she mumbled.

"We're just here giving away this book, The Great Contro - "

" - Don't want it," she stated gruffly, "I told you, I don't want anything from you. You people are the problem, you know."

"We are the problem? What do you mean?" Rick asked.

"All of it. Country's falling apart. The world's falling apart. Your little cult is the cause of it all. I know about you people."

"I assure you, Ms. Anderton, we are not a cult," Weston answered, "Our church's motto is Sola Scriptura. The Bible and the Bible only."

She stared at Weston as she pulled out a cigarette. Her glare was intense. She was old and haggard but tall and slender. Suddenly, a change seemed to come over her. She appeared younger and edgier, almost dangerous-looking.

"You don't get with the program; you're all gonna die," she stated in a strange voice.

Weston got chills down his spine. He was taken aback and didn't know what to say.

"Miss," Rick stepped in, taking a more direct approach, "it's imperative that you read this book. Something worse is coming, and we want you to be prepared."

The look in her eyes was one of intense hate. Without a word, she slammed the door in their faces.

A fierce wind howled in The Zone, running and whipping through trees, over hills, and into dark gulleys. It was dusk and growing cold. A beautiful sunset was spanning the western skies, but it was foreboding and baleful. It signaled another night of potential horrors in no-man's-land.

Down below, a mass of bodies lay on the frigid ground near the endless fence line, piled on top of each other. Twelve lifeless forms lay still in the dark grass. The soldiers who shot them were laughing and making their way back to their Humvees.

The dead group had been two families trying to make their way out: the Saldos and the Bentleys. They had traveled for two days from the nearest town. The families hadn't experienced any real trouble along the way other than occasionally hiding from an Apache helicopter flying by, and the twelve-hour days of walking. As they neared the fence line, they grew excited at the prospect of freedom.

Unfortunately, unbeknownst to them, a UGS or Unattended Ground Sensor had sealed their fate. It was only about the size of an alarm clock with a small antenna, but it was spiked into the ground and hidden among the grasses. These passive seismic sensors had been placed near the fenceline, all along The Zone's border. They were small enough that you would not be able to see them until it was too late.

The UGS nearest to this group sensed movement as they approached it. It alerted and awakened a nearby stealth infrared trail camera mounted in some pine trees, which transmitted to the network, classifying the threat movement as a pack of infected survivors. Immediately, the nearest mobile base station, a group of Humvees, was alerted and dispatched.

The confrontation had been over really before it even began. The two husbands had been hunched down on their knees, trying to cut through the first set of chain link fences, when a sniper from Humvee One had gunned them down without warning. Humvees Two and Three had closed in from the other side. Those soldiers had exited the vehicles at a trot and immediately opened fire on every other individual. The entire fight, if you could call it that, had lasted twenty-four seconds.

The wind continued to blow, and the corpses were already starting to grow cold. Suddenly, there was a stirring amid the victims. Little twelve-year-old Sarah came to, opened her eyes, and gasped in pain. She could not move because her mother, a larger woman, lay on top of her. Her mother had flung her body in front of Sarah when the shooting began and had taken almost every bullet meant for her daughter. Every bullet, except for the one that had gone through Sarah's right arm. She could barely move it, and the pain seared through her right upper extremity and into her brain. But she had to move; she was suffocating under the weight of her mother. The first two attempts to push mom off had failed, and she was beginning to panic. She could not breathe well.

Then, she remembered something she had learned in self-defense at school. She rotated her left hip upward as hard as she could. Her mother actually moved upward a bit. She continued the hip movement and agonizingly slid her body out, bit by bit, until she was free. She gasped at the pain from moving her arm. It was sharp and brought tears to her eyes. But, at least she was free.

Sarah looked at her right arm. Blood oozed down underneath her jacket to her hand. She could not see the wound but felt it gingerly. She could tell it was clotting. Sarah grabbed a shirt from her nearby backpack and wrapped the wound outside her jacket. It would have to do for now.

She turned towards her mother. She didn't want to look at her the way she was. Sarah put her good arm around her mom's still body and sobbed. After several minutes, she knew it was time to let her go. Her mother had sacrificed her own life to save hers. It was too overwhelming to think about.

Sarah crouched down, cautiously looking upward toward where the soldiers had been. She had heard their vehicles racing off but needed to be sure.

How could they have just mercilessly slaughtered us, she thought, *we're Americans!*

There hadn't even been a warning given.

How did they even know we were coming?

As she turned her head to the right, she saw it. A small black box on the ground with an antenna sticking upward. She wasn't sure exactly what it was, but it looked military and didn't belong. It must have been what alerted the soldiers to come here for them. She noticed that one of the bullets from the soldiers had gone clean through its metal casing, and its electronic guts were splayed out on the ground.

Good, she thought, *You little bastard.*

At least now she could move, and it wouldn't rat her out again.

She got up and slowly made her way to the top of the hill. As she reached the fences, she could see for miles. In the distance, there were lights. That meant civilization, and that was where she needed to head. She was sick and in desperate need of help.

The sickness had only come upon her yesterday, and everyone else in the group had been puzzled because none of them felt ill. They had questioned her repeatedly, but she had not told them the truth. The truth was, she had visited her close friend Natalie the day before they left, and Natalie had been coughing and sneezing the entire time. Natalie had even sneezed in her face, but Sarah had been hoping and praying that it wasn't what she feared it was.

Now, Sarah was coughing too, and feeling feverish. Chills and aches were racking through her body, and she was tired. She knew she had to press on though, to civilization. Maybe there was a medicine that could help her. She just knew she didn't want to die like those other Ebola victims she had seen die. Crashing and bleeding out from every orifice.

She grabbed the bolt cutters from her father's hand without looking at him. Sarah stifled a scream and tried not to cry as his lifeless hand released the tool. He would want her to be strong now, not weak. To be strong and survive. She couldn't think about what had happened here, not now anyway. She began cutting through the chain links one at a time. It was good to have something to do, something to keep her mind distracted.

She quickly made her way into the narrow space between the first fence and the second. She glanced cautiously in both directions. No one was around or seemed to realize she was there. She cut through the next fence and was free. Finally, free from The Zone. Her only objective now was to find a doctor and a cure. She began slowly walking towards the lights in the distance.

President Lutrell sat with Tim Blain in the backseat of their limousine, staring out the window at the streets of Rome. Opposite him were two secret service agents and several representatives from Faith First, including their leader, Jeremiah Lauerer.

He was tired. It had been a fourteen-hour flight on Air Force One with a refueling stop. Then, a landing in Rome Fiumicino Airport to Vatican City, which was only ten miles from the airport. Traffic was backed up, and they crawled forward at twenty miles an hour. They were traveling in a fleet of three, with Secret Service in limousines in front and behind.

As they neared the main gate at Via Sant'Anna, Lutrell was impressed. There were four or five Gendarmerie in their flat hats, black jackets, and pants, armed with machine guns. Alongside them were several Swiss guards in traditional uniforms. He had heard they were armed to the teeth, although you couldn't tell by looking at them. The metal gate was at least twenty feet tall and currently open to receive the guests. It looked formidable.

The entourage moved through the extensive Vatican Gardens, making their way along the streets of Vatican City to the Apostolic Palace, where Pope Giordano was waiting. Beautiful marble statues and rows of cubed-shaped trees lined the streets. Lutrell took in its splendor and old world charm. He needed a distraction from what was coming. He was sure this meeting would be worse than the last. Part of the reason was he was pressured to have Faith First present. He stared at Jeremiah, who was preening in his side mirror like a teenager on a prom date. On the flight, he went on and on about how the Pope was basically God. Lutrell had had to hold his tongue the entire trip, and he was exhausted by him.

They were greeted outside the large white building and ushered via elevator to an expansive library, where Giordano was waiting with an entourage of cardinals dressed in red. Lutrell was annoyed as he realized this was not a private meeting like before. Now, at least twenty other world leaders and himself had to wait in line to even greet the Pope. Additionally, he saw that each politician knelt before Giordano and kissed his ring.

No way, Lutrell thought.

As they made their way to the front of the line, Giordano saw Lutrell. He began to speak to his interpreter. Whatever was said, it wasn't conveyed to the President.

As Lutrell moved to face the Pope, he hoped they would just shake hands like before. Greet each other as equals. However, Giordano held out his ring, indicating homage must be paid.

Lutrell glanced around. His hesitation had created a stir, and now every head of state, cardinal, and staff member was staring at him. He realized this was more than just a greeting or a formality; this was a test. It was putting everyone in their place, letting them know who was in charge.

Lutrell hesitated and then bowed on one knee before the Pope, kissing his ring. Normal conversation resumed again in the library.

The Faith First leaders were next in line behind him. He noticed with irritation that Jeremiah swiftly prostrated himself on all fours and kissed the Pope's feet.

Apparently, the ring isn't enough for this lapdog.

A few minutes later, Pope Giordano began to address the group via his translator.

"May I have your attention, please? Your attention, please? My friends, you have been called here today because of momentous events taking place in our world. Wars, famines, fires, floods, and disease. Disasters of every kind are ravaging our planet.

As we know, these problems have arisen due to our lack of care for the Earth," he continued, "this global warming has been a wake-up call for this generation, and we have seen the damage it causes.

And it would be that simple, and the solution would be more simple, if it were only environmental. However, it is not. These calamities are more than just from the physical. This is spiritual. These are judgements from a displeased God. He is displeased, and he is warning us to change course.

In our lifetimes, we have seen the constant downward slide of our societies. Downward into vice, debauchery, and violence. Our cultures are on the brink of ruin. What can we do?"

He paused.

"We have brought the Lord's day to the forefront once again. We have asked all people to rest on it, and we have met with success. Hindus, Buddhists, Muslims, Taoists, and even atheists have begun refraining from work and activity. It has been a success, my friends. But this is not all that God wants. God is a spirit, and those that worship Him must worship Him in spirit and in truth. God wants to be WORSHIPPED.

And so, that is what we must do. We must tell the world, not just to rest, but to worship their Creator on the day He has so richly blessed. The day He rose in triumph. When we honor Him, He will honor us. Right now, in the world, He is not being honored fully. But, we will make it so He is again. We will right this great wrong that the adversary has done. The world will be united in worship to God.

So, at this time, we ask that you pledge your assistance to help us. To help mankind. Because we cannot continue to sustain this kind of damage and these catastrophic losses in our nations, I would ask at this time that you all move into Conference Room A for a short presentation on how this will be implemented in your various nations.

God bless you all."

They were ushered into Conference Room A and made to wait while a young man in a business suit made last-minute adjustments on his laptop for a slide presentation.

"Good afternoon, good afternoon," he said awkwardly in a thick Italian accent, "we are so glad that you could be with us today. We are going to go ahead and get started. So, what we are looking at is a global platform. A uniformity. We have the connectivity capability, we have the satellite networks, and the bandwidth. And so now we have the platform to work with to accomplish it."

He changed slides to a logo showing a chain of individuals holding hands, all connected and raised upward towards the sky.

"Mandate," he continued, "is the answer. A high-powered app that brings excellent user experience together with great design functionality. When used in combination with a HPC that has high volume data transfer with low network latency, and now via the new Starshield satellite network, it packs the punch that is needed for this job."

"Excuse me," said the German Chancellor, "that all sounds like a bunch of tech jargon. I'm confused. What is it and how does it work?"

Ambassador Bianchi, as if on queue, walked in from a side door and answered smoothly:

"It will download easily on every smartphone from existing platforms. All Androids and iPhones will take it," he stated confidently, walking into the center of the room. He paused, "Every device in the world will have Mandate soon, ladies and gentlemen, I can assure you of that."

He turned and stared momentarily at President Lutrell. There was no jovial smile on his face now. He seemed to barely recognize him.

"But what is it, you asked? It is a way to track, if you will, every individual's choice," he paused for effect, "their choice to attend their unique place of worship on the Lord's Day, or to make a different unfortunate choice. Many will continue to go in person and worship corporately, we know that. For them, the app is simply a check-in device at the door. But there will be many more who cannot go in person or will not go. But, they will log in and be counted, and be a part of that worship experience in their homes.

With new cutting-edge technology, Mandate will track their virtual attendance, provide real-time two-way monitoring. Even assessing their level of enthusiasm while singing the morning's hymn or watching the sermon. It will do all this because it is a virtual worship environment. All those who log on will have their own personal avatar who must participate in the digital environment of their preference. Christians will have a church environment, Muslims a mosque, Jews a synagogue, etc."

"Excuse me," the British Prime Minister asked, raising his hand, "what about bandwidth? This is on a much larger scale than anything I've ever heard of, and more users will be on at once. Will you have the bandwidth?"

"I assure you," he answered in a bored tone, "we have it."

"What assurances do we have from the Pope that this will turn the tide of all these disasters?" asked someone in the back that Lutrell couldn't see.

"The Holy Father has given full assurance that this is the will of God. It will turn the tide. Next question," he answered dismissively.

"What about enforcement?" questioned Saudi Prince Abadi, "You can't just force a population to go on to an app."

"Oh, but you can," Bianchi replied eagerly.

His original enthusiasm seemed to have returned.

"Most will comply, but we all know there will always be outliers. Conspiracy theorists, the homeless populations, flip-phoners, atheists. All you need are laws, ladies and gentlemen and non-binaries, and those laws are already in place, just waiting to be enforced."

He paused to look at President Lutrell again.

"Even the great United States," he resumed in a patronizing tone, "land of the free, correct? You jailed citizens in the past for breaking Sunday laws. Anything is allowed, if it is determined by the government for the common good. Your governments need only decide that this is for the common good and general welfare of your own individual populations, and they will comply!

Those that don't, punish them. But I would assert that you make an example of them, because the very existence of our world is at risk! Those are the stakes here. Our world must continue, and so we have to make hard choices. Let history not look back on this moment and decide that we all made the wrong choice here today, if there will even be people to look back on us at all."

His voice had risen, but now he seemed to calm down.

Lutrell felt that strange light-headedness again. The feeling he had experienced when he had his meeting with the Pope at the Pentagon. What was going on?

"This is what we ask of you. I believe you will find that in no time at all, things will be back as they were, and we will all be able to look back on this time and thank the Holy See for such guidance in our hour of need. Remember, he is the vicar of God, and ultimately he is in charge of this world. We only need follow his direction.

If there are any more questions," he paused briefly and scanned the room. "If not, then I will dismiss you all and bid you safe journey to your respective homes. Bless you."

Lutrell sat in shock. What was happening? Whatever it was, it was happening fast, and he hadn't been a part of it. He seemed more a spectator now than a world leader of a powerful nation.

He looked over at Giordano, his arms raised while several Japanese leaders were genuflecting before him. He seemed to receive energy and power from these worshipers, almost like he was taking from them their life essence.

Who was this man, and how had he suddenly come to be in charge of everything?

Chapter 12 - Paranoid

The Millers were seated together eating potluck after church. Several other families were gathered around, and they were all discussing the new law requiring Sunday observance.

"What about just turning on the app but not really even paying attention to it?" An older gentleman asked.

"You won't be able to do that," Rick answered, "it's a virtual worship environment. Your avatar is literally going to do whatever you're actually doing at home. You'll have to sit down in a virtual pew, listen, sing, kneel, etc. It's a VR environment, using this Mandate app, which is using your phone. If you don't comply - "

" - Why don't we just do it?" said a woman in her twenties, "what's the harm? It just seems like a dumb video game."

"It would be honoring the beast, Joan," an older man answered, "taking the mark."

"He's right," Rick agreed, "the purpose of this app is to be a substitute for people who can't worship in person. So even though it might all look like a video game, it's the same thing as being there in person."

"I still don't understand how going to church on a Sunday can be the mark of the beast," interjected a newcomer, a middle-aged man, "if I'm worshipping God at a church, how is that something God doesn't approve of? The mark of the beast must be something else."

"Revelation thirteen specifies that the mark of the beast will be about worship," Weston spoke up. "The verse right before the mark of the beast is brought up says that as many as would not worship the image of the beast would be killed. So, clearly whatever act they're trying to get us to do, it is worshipping. And it has to be worshipping God, because the first beast is hyper focused on counterfeiting God, not counterfeiting some pagan deity or something.

Interestingly, a lot of tests in the Bible have revolved around worshipping the right or the wrong way. Cain and Abel, the three Hebrew worthies, Elijah and the prophets of Baal on Mt. Carmel, Jesus verses the Pharisees regarding the Sabbath, etc. Since the Papacy is the first beast of Revelation thirteen, and they say changing the Saturday Sabbath to Sunday is their mark, it seems clear. But, if you have a better theory, I'm willing to listen. This is too important to not hear all ideas."

The man remained silent.

Weston groaned inside. What was he going to do? The first RWE, or Required Worship Experience, was scheduled for 11am Pacific Standard Time for his region in just one week, or next Sunday. He would be tracked either in person or by his phone.

He knew this because the Mandate app had already downloaded onto his phone and given him several reminders. It also reminded him that, should he be traveling and find himself in a different time zone or part of the world on Sunday, Mandate would assist him in logging in to the local RWE for that region.

Almost as much of a concern too, was the absence of Pastor Pete. He had been gone from church for two straight weeks, and no one seemed to know where he was. He certainly should have been here. If ever there was a time they needed his leadership and guidance, it was now.

As Weston lay down to sleep that night, he was restless. The gunshots and the sirens in the distance didn't help; they were a nightly occurrence now. There were also homeless on their street now, camping right on the sidewalks. He had no idea how they were surviving in the cold. Two men camped right in front of his house in separate tents. Other tents littered the sidewalk sporadically.

One of them seemed somewhat normal and kept to himself, but the other was clearly suffering from mental illness. He would frequently yell out in the night and harass the Millers as they came and went. Weston had called the police, but they had shown no interest in helping.

He tossed and turned, trying to think of a way out of this Sunday law situation. He hadn't really anticipated being put over a barrel like this with the technology. Somehow it had all seemed so much easier when he read about the mark of the beast in the past. You would just simply refuse to take it.

Easy.

He had never really thought about the forces behind all this and how much pressure would be placed upon people to take the mark. With this app on one's phone, it seemed there would be no way out. He realized he needed, more than ever, to pray. After talking to God about it for some time and receiving no immediate answers, he drifted off to sleep.

He did not know what time it was when he awoke. It seemed to be the middle of the night. He thought he had heard sounds, like tiny alarms or the noises one might hear when receiving a text message.

He remained still and listened intently.

Nothing.

Then he noticed a dim light flickering in the next room. It seemed to get brighter and then fade again. The pattern kept repeating. Bright flashes, and then a duller continuous light. He quietly got out of bed so as not to wake Ally and creeped toward the light in the next room.

As he turned the corner of his bedroom doorway, he saw it was coming from his cellphone. He had placed his phone on the living room ottoman so that it could charge at night and so that he would not look at it while in bed.

As he moved closer to the phone, he could see the screen better. A flurry of code was rushing across it from left to right. Occasionally, apps would open and close.

Weston stared at it in horror as it continued its frantic activity. Was someone controlling his phone? What were they doing to it?

He quickly grabbed it and pulled the charger cable out of the port, picking it up to look closer. Within a few seconds, the code stopped running across the screen, and every open app slid upward and disappeared. His phone appeared normal again.

There was no way to tell that anything out of the ordinary had ever happened. He swiped his thumb from bottom to top to display any open apps.

Nothing.

Next, he restarted the phone, but it continued to appear as it always had. He went into applications to see if something new had been installed. He could not tell that there was, but he also realized he was not very familiar with what apps had been on his phone before.

He stood there in the dark, holding the phone, unsure what to do. Frustrated, he crept back to bed and fell asleep.

The temperatures continued to hover in the single digits that week. Weston was thankful that he had inside work; they were installing split-jambs and doors inside a spec home. He had learned to be careful with his tool placement. They had had three tremors just in the last two weeks. The last one had been pretty bad. Everything had started shaking violently and an impact wrench had gone flying into Weston's face. Another coworker had fallen off a ladder. Thankfully, no one was hurt badly.

He couldn't imagine working outside. It had been over a month of arctic temperatures, and it was starting to wear on everyone. The supply chain hadn't recovered. Food was sparse at the stores, and more than once the Millers had watched physical altercations take place over an item. Weston and Ally tried not to take the kids out anymore.

They were now down to bare essential meals like beans and rice and mac and cheese. Their pantry stores were holding, but the future didn't look good unless something changed soon. Weston tried not to think about it.

That Sabbath, Weston noticed that Pastor Pete still wasn't present. He asked around but didn't get answers. After church, he cornered Elder Andre in the bathroom.

"Andre, is the pastor ok?"

Andre hesitated.

"I think so," he answered.

"He hasn't been here in three weeks. People are starting to get concerned," Weston complained.

"Actually, he called me last night," Andre continued, "but he sounded strange. He assured me that everything was fine, though."

"But you're not sure," Weston said.

"He's scheduled for the pulpit next week, so I'm sure everything's fine," Andre replied.

"With all that's going on, I just don't understand why he would choose now to disappear," Weston stated.

"I wish I knew," Andre agreed.

As the Millers were getting ready to leave, Rick and Kathleen approached them in the foyer. Rick had a set of keys in his hand. He handed them to Weston.

"What are these?" Weston asked.

"We were hoping you could watch the house," Rick stated.

"Oh, yeah. No problem. How long?" Weston asked.

"At least a couple of weeks. We'll be going up to Kathleen's father's cabin in Idaho. Maybe for a while."

"Is everything ok?" Weston questioned.

"Things are heating up a lot here. We want to get away from it all," Rick said.

"I get it. Well, we'll watch her for ya," Weston stated.

Rick leaned in and lowered his voice.

"You guys should get out of dodge, too. It's going to get bad here," he declared.

"You're probably right," Weston agreed.

"I mean it," Rick insisted, "you need an escape plan."

"I will, I will," Weston promised.

Rick gave Weston a firm handshake. Weston moved in and hugged him. At first, Rick stiffened, but then he leaned in, too.

"See ya, man," he said, pointing upward, "if not here, then up there."

With that, they turned and left. Weston had the feeling that he wouldn't see them again in this life.

After church, they received a knock at the door. Ally answered it and found two well-dressed men and a lady. They introduced themselves from the Tower of Zion Baptist Church down the street. They were canvassing the neighborhood, inviting everyone to attend their services this Sunday and reminding them attendance was mandatory. After a few friendly exchanges, Ally was able to put them off. She was non-committal and vague. The eldest gentleman's smiling veneer seemed to wear off towards the end as he said:

"You all get to church now. It ain't an option anymore. You understand?"

Ally tried to remain friendly and assured them they would talk about it.

"Ain't nothing to talk about," he said as they finally walked away, "we'll see you this Sunday."

Ally and Weston called the kids into the living room. It was time to talk. Weston had told Ally about the recent phone incident, so they decided to leave their cell phones in the backyard, just in case. Weston had heard a rumor that the phones could listen and record you. It sounded conspiratorial, but they couldn't take chances.

"Well," Weston began, "as you know, tomorrow is the first RWE."

He looked around the room. All eyes were on him.

"Your father and I have decided that we are not going to attend in person or log on to Mandate," Ally stated, "but we wanted to talk to you kids so you understand the ramifications."

Braden, Dylan, and Charlotte sat in silence. They looked worried.

"The letter we received threatened possible fines," Ally continued, "up to $1,000."

Braden gasped. "Can we afford that?"

"We can," Weston responded, "but there's more we're worried about."

"It also mentions," Ally stepped in, "possible imprisonment."

Charlotte appeared ready to burst into tears.

"Guys, we just have to trust in the Lord right now, more than ever," Weston encouraged, "we believe we have to stand firm and follow the commandments of God versus the traditions of men. We believe this is the final test described in Revelation thirteen. More than anything, we have to be faithful now. We believe Jesus is coming soon."

"Dad, you can't go to jail," Braden insisted.

"I know, I know, son," he agreed, "your mother and I are discussing our options. One of them might be leaving home."

Groans filled the air.

"I realize this is hard," Ally sympathized, "and it is so cold outside. But there is just nothing we can do about it. Now, we want each of you to get your go bag from the garage and bring it into your room. Gather the warmest clothes you can, only absolute essentials. We need to be ready for anything now."

"Now let's say a quick prayer for guidance and our safety," Weston added, "we need direction now more than ever."

With that, Weston and Ally took turns praying for protection, guidance, and for God's will to be done in their lives. The kids gathered their go bags, and everyone went down for the night.

At 11am on Sunday morning, Weston and Ally's phone began chiming. It sounded like electronic church bells. It was the worship reminder from Mandate.

Today's church attendance had been the elephant in the room all morning, and everyone was avoiding the subject. Now, the moment was here.

"Maybe they won't do anything?" Ally stated.

"I wish," Weston said.

"Maybe we should just log in?" she suggested.

"Ally!" Weston exclaimed. Her momentary weakness alarmed him. Probably because he was feeling it himself. It would be so easy. The phone was within reach. He could see the Mandate app had opened itself, and a login screen was flashing insistently.

This didn't seem like the ultimate test that Revelation thirteen had described. Maybe they had it all wrong? Weston paused. No, they had studied this out, studied the history, the Bible symbols. It all made sense. Suddenly, he felt a new resolve. This was the final test, and he was the spiritual priest of the house. The Bible said so. He must lead them to safety, to Heaven.

"I'm sorry," she said, "I'm just kinda freaking out. What are we going to do? You can't go to jail, honey!"

"More than ever," he answered confidently, "we need to follow what we know and pray for guidance and strength. Let's do that now."

They prayed together. When they got up from their knees, Weston felt better. A look of resolve spread across his face.

"I think I have a plan," he confided.

Betsy Rhan was excited. She hadn't been to church in years. She watched Elizabeth, her younger sister, attend Calvary United every week. They had both attended there their whole lives, first as children with their parents and then after their parents passed, on their own. Elizabeth had married once, but Betsy had just never met the right man. Now they were old, and Betsy's legs wouldn't allow her to leave the house anymore.

She always encouraged Elizabeth to go, but secretly she resented her sister's ongoing freedom. She would just sit at home and watch church on livestream. But it wasn't the same.

But now, this Mandate app promised her an immersive experience! She could participate again. She opened the app on her phone. The first step was creating a profile. She quickly created one with login and password. Then she had to do something strange with an 'avatar,' as it was called. The app pushed her through a series of screens where she fashioned a little digital character to look just like herself. When she tried to give it pink hair just for fun, Mandate gave her an error stating:

'YOUR HAIR COLOR IS GRAY.'

Well, that was no fun!

Apparently, it already knew what she looked like. She remembered that in the beginning it had made her hold the phone very still. It must have been scanning her or something.

Now the screen asked for her worship preferences. It said:
'CHRISTIAN CHURCH

SYNAGOGUE

MOSQUE

TEMPLE

GONG'

The list went on. Betsy selected Christian church. The screen flashed:

'YOUR REQUIRED WORSHIP EXPERIENCE WILL OPEN MOMENTARILY.'

There was a flashing symbol fading in and out, indicating the program was loading. It was a symbol that looked like those coexist bumper stickers Betsy saw everywhere. It had every major religion symbol in a little sphere.

Now organ music began to play, and a pair of doors appeared before her. The screen said:

'PLEASE MOVE TOWARDS THE DOORS AND OPEN THEM.'

Oh, boy. Betsy hadn't realized she was actually going to have to move. She slowly got up with the help of her walker and started moving forward. She was holding the phone awkwardly in one hand. Immediately, her avatar began moving towards the doors. Fortunately, she could see that it moved much faster than she did. It was already to the doors by the time she had taken two steps. Now the program said:

'OPEN THE DOORS AND FIND A SEAT.'

With her right hand, she reached for the virtual door on the screen. It opened, and she moved forward into the sanctuary. It was an expansive, modern-looking Christian church. Every seat seemed already taken. As she moved her head slightly to the right, her avatar's head moved, shifting the whole view to the right. The same thing happened when she turned left.

She hated technology. She had never really kept up with all the gizmos and gadgets. This felt like a video game. Her avatar was still standing in the aisle, waiting there. She was tired and just wanted to sit down in real life. Suddenly a robot-looking figure floated over to her. It was dressed in a black, three piece suit with a flashy red tie.

'MAY I HELP YOU FIND A SEAT?'

"Yes," she said awkwardly, out loud.

It immediately responded:

'FOLLOW ME, PLEASE.'

The bot directed her to a few open seats near the front. Once she maneuvered around a younger couple, the bot left. The problem now was she wanted to sit down, but she had walked halfway across the room. Her sofa was five feet away. Now Mandate said:

RECALCULATING PEW LOCATION. PLEASE FIND ACTUAL SEATING. YOU HAVE 10 SECONDS FOR RECALIBRATION.

Wow, bossy little thing, wasn't it?

Well, at least she could go sit down now.

As the service began, Betsy grew annoyed. The program was heavily monitoring her. If she didn't sing loud enough during a hymn, she would get a message:

'PLEASE SING LOUDER.'

When the prayer time came, and she didn't kneel, the program said:

'YOU MUST KNEEL.'

When she stayed seated, it repeated the phrase again. Then another message came up, saying:

'MEDICAL EXEMPTION?'

She then had to go into a separate login screen again and state that she could not kneel for medical reasons. Then it made her fill out her doctor's contact information to verify she wasn't lying!

When the sermon started, she hoped it would at least be interesting. However, it was given by another bot-looking figure, and it was lifeless and boring. It did not seem very spiritual, and she exited the program when it was all over, feeling empty and dissatisfied.

When Elizabeth came home, Betsy asked her how church had been.

"Oh, the same," replied Elizabeth, "there were just lots more people! The only thing different was, I had to open that Mandate app and scan my phone in a little machine at the door. How was your church?"

Betsy paused for a moment.

"I'm gonna go to Dr. Suiex this week," she declared, "and see if I can get cleared to go back to a REAL church again!"

"That good, huh?" Elizabeth asked.

They both laughed.

Weston was bored, as usual. Sunday used to be a day he could catch up on stuff around the house, but now he couldn't work outside openly. They couldn't stop him from walking around outside on his property, though. There was no crime in that.

He went out his front door and started walking around his yard. The grass was dead from winter, and their hydrangea bushes were bare. Beyond his yard, it was a disaster. Trash was heaped in piles next to the ragged tents. One of the homeless men, the crazy one, lay lifeless, sprawled out on his back on the cold sidewalk. Weston had learned this was normal. Both men remained in a comatose-like state for most of the day but became extremely animated and loud at night.

He glanced across the street. There was no Ms. Anderton at least. As he gazed further down he noticed a black Ford van parked a few doors down on his side. It stood out because he had never seen it before. It also stood out because all the windows were tinted. He could tell the degree of tint was not legal.

It was facing his house. Weston had the feeling that someone inside the van was watching him. He quickly looked away, pretending that he had no interest in it. He yawned, stretched, and slowly made his way back into the house.

Once inside, he ran to the window and peered through the curtains, watching the van. There was no movement or activity at all. After about fifteen minutes, he became bored and decided to go do something else. He realized he was being paranoid. It was probably just someone visiting one of his neighbors.

That Sabbath, as expected, Pastor Pete was back. He exchanged greetings with the Millers, but Andre had been right. He seemed off. He gave his usual enthusiastic sermon however, and Weston would have thought it was all nothing but for one short sentence near the end.

The Pastor had been talking about David's unfaithfulness with Bathsheba and Uriah. He was normally unequivocal that sin was sin, but as he was finishing, he said:

"God knows we don't always obey, but the important thing is that we just try."

It seemed a bit trite to Weston, considering the enormity of David's sin. It rubbed him the wrong way. No one else in the congregation seemed to notice it however, so he let it go.

Another week went by without much change. They continued to ignore the Mandate app that Sunday as well. Weston was almost starting to believe nothing would really happen.

It was Wednesday night, and he decided to give Ally a break from grocery shopping. He procured a list from her. He was not sure they would be able to find much of anything anyway, but maybe there would be something.

As he made his way through the grocery store, he noticed things were a little better. There were no people fighting over canned tuna or a bag of carrots like the last time he had been to the store. Perhaps, it was the greater armed presence. There were now armed security guards patrolling the aisles instead of just sitting up front.

Weston was also pleasantly surprised to see peanut butter. It was on his list, and Ally would be so pleased. He also found some dilapidated broccoli, but it was the best he'd seen in a month. After perusing several more aisles, he made his way out to the checkout lines. They were still longer than the old days but they moved fairly quickly since nobody had much in their carts.

As his turn was next, he placed the separator bar on the conveyor belt and loaded his items. The cashier was a younger woman with tattoo sleeves on each arm, up her neck, and on her face. Multiple piercings filled her nose and ears. Weston tried not to stare as she wrung up his items.

"That'll be $100.56," she stated flatly.

He pulled out his FedNote card and held it to the POS machine's receiver.

After a pause, the screen said: *card declined.*

"Your card's declined, mister," tat-girl announced.

Weston was shocked. He was sure they had plenty of money in the account.

"Can I run it again?" he asked.

"Sure," she replied, hitting some keys on her register.

Again it said: *card declined*.

"Two - One," tat girl spoke over the intercom microphone at her register.

"What's that?" he asked.

The girl pretended not to hear him, avoiding his stare. He could see a manager moving towards them.

"Sir?" the manager called out to him. Several Blackwater guards were also walking in his direction.

"Umm... I gotta go," he said to tat girl, stuffing his card back in his wallet. He quickly walked towards the nearest exit without looking back.

"Sir! Wait!" The manager yelled more insistently this time. The Blackwater guards started jogging towards Weston. Tat girl just stood there watching the whole affair with a grin on her face.

As soon as he passed through the automatic doors, he looked around. There was only one guard standing at the other entrance about a hundred fifty feet away. He paid no attention to Weston. Trying to look casual, Weston jogged towards his vehicle, fishing the keys out of his pocket as quickly as possible.

The store manager was now outside with a security guard.

"Excuse me, sir!" he yelled.

Weston reached the van and jumped in. He turned the ignition and revved the engine, pulling out as fast as he could towards the street. As he glanced back in his rear-view mirror, he saw one of the Blackwater guards standing outside with the store manager. He was speaking into his walkie-talkie and watching Weston leave.

Chapter 13 - The War

It was Saturday, and it was snowing again. As they drove to church, the wind pushed thousands of tiny flakes onto the windshield. It made an ordinary drive seem magical, almost like they were moving through a white miniature forest of microscopic trees. But after a month of arctic temperatures and near-constant snow, they were weary of it.

As they pulled up to their church, they could tell that something was wrong. There were cars in the parking lot as usual, but everyone was gathered near the front entrance.

The Millers walked up to the crowd. Weston saw Elder Andre.

"Andre, what's going on?" he asked.

"We're shut down," Andre responded.

"You're joking," Weston said.

"See for yourself," Andre said, pointing towards the front doors.

Weston made his way to the large double doors. There was a chain with a padlock around the door handles and a large sign taped to the door. It said:

'NOTICE - DO NOT ENTER

THIS CHURCH IS TO REMAIN CLOSED AT ALL TIMES.

GATHERINGS ON THE SEVENTH DAY OF THE WEEK, OR SATURDAY, ARE UNLAWFUL AND ARE PUNISHABLE BY A FINE OF UP TO $1000 AND/OR IMPRISONMENT. THIS IS TO INCLUDE GATHERINGS ON THESE PREMISES, AS WELL AS AT ANY OTHER LOCATION. PER AB9191.54.

CITY SHERIFF'S OFFICE 916-773-5050.

02/10/35.'

Just then, two sheriff's vehicles pulled slowly into the parking lot. They sat in their cars, engines running, staring at the crowd.

"Folks," Andre announced, "we must start meeting in small groups in our homes. We can't meet here anymore."

"But the sign says it's illegal to meet on Saturday," a young woman questioned.

"I know, I know," he replied, "you will have to decide what you're willing to do. What God wants you to do. But remember the words of Peter in Acts, where he said we ought to obey God rather than man. The Bible says obey your authorities, but only if that doesn't conflict with your duty to God. I think that applies in this circumstance."

Heads nodded in agreement.

"It may not be safe to use our phones anymore for this kind of thing," he went on, "so right now, I'll give you all a couple of addresses to meet at this week."

"Our phones could be listening right now," a younger gentleman stated. He glanced towards the police cars.

It was getting colder, and the wind was whipping snowflakes into their faces.

Andre paused to consider that.

"Just keep this piece of paper on you," he said. He began tearing up little pieces of paper, writing on them, and handing them out. "It has a location and time on it."

"Why isn't Pastor Pete here?" a lady asked in an irritated tone, raising her voice above the wind.

"I don't know, Jackie," Andre answered matter-of-factly.

The officers had now gotten out of their cars, and were making their way over to the crowd. Everyone stuffed their papers inside their jackets.

"Folks, folks," a gruff overweight officer with red thinning hair barked, "you all cannot be here. This gathering is illegal."

"Officer," Andre replied, "please give us a few minutes. We just found out. We need to regroup."

"I don't care when you found out," he replied nastily, "you find yourselves off this property right now... or I will throw every one of you in jail!"

"Yes, sir," Andre answered meekly.

"And don't even think about regrouping...and gathering somewhere else, sonny," he growled, pointing a finger in Andre's face, "that will also get you thrown in jail."

The two men stared at each other for a moment.

"Matter of fact," Red continued sarcastically, "I already have probable cause. Don't think I didn't see your little handoffs. Why don't we do ourselves a little search right now?"

Just then, a cacophony of gunshots echoed in the distance. Both officers looked at each other.

"Officer," the younger gentleman chimed in, "please be lenient. We weren't aware of this law. How were we supposed to know?"

"Listen, you," he shot back, "that's enough. Don't take me for a fool. This law was well publicized."

"Where?" Andre asked.

Red glared at Andre for several seconds before answering.

"On our official police website."

Red appeared to have more to say and continued to glare at Andre. Suddenly, his radio mic blared.

"29-11. John?"

He grabbed the mic and keyed it without looking away from Andre.

"Yeah, here," he replied.

"Code three, officer down, 2100 Atlantic Parkway," a female voice spoke in a garbled tone.

Both officers turned and immediately started back to their vehicles. The gunfire continued sporadically in the distance.

The wind picked up even harder, pushing the crowd slightly.

"Don't think this is over, sonny," Red warned, looking over his shoulder, "we'll catch up with ya all real soon."

That Monday night, Ally had a strange look on her face. After dinner, which consisted of canned beans and brown rice, Weston pulled her aside.

"What's wrong, honey?" he asked.

Ally hesitated. All the kids were listening.

"Let me show you something," she answered as she walked to their room.

Once in their room, she handed him a letter. It was from the Placer County Sheriff Department. It said that due to Ally and him missing three RWEs, enclosed was a fine of $3,000. There was a separate bill in that amount, with a due date of twenty days. The letter stated if a fourth RWE was missed, a warrant would be issued for both of their arrests, which meant up to six months of imprisonment.

Ally started crying.

"What are we going to do?" she exclaimed.

"We will have faith," he answered sternly. Weston was angry. Not at Ally, but at the situation they were in. "We may have to leave here soon."

"Well, I don't know if you've noticed, Weston," she replied between tears, "but that van you told me about is back. How are we going to get away if they're watching us all the time?"

"The black van?" he questioned, surprised.

"Yes, and it's been here all day," she sobbed.

"I'm going to go look," he announced, moving downstairs.

"Weston, don't go out there!" She raised her voice, reaching for him.

Just then, the doorbell rang. They both froze and looked at each other.

"Are we expecting someone?" he asked.

His adrenaline was pumping.

She shook her head. They both headed to the front door. Weston looked through the peephole.

It was Pastor Pete.

He opened the door.

"Pastor?"

"Hello, Weston, Ally," he said, "may I come in?"

"Certainly," Weston responded as he moved aside to let the Pastor in. As Pastor Pete moved past him into the living room, Weston stared down the street. The black van was still there, sitting in the same spot it had been in before.

They aren't even trying to hide the fact that they're watching us, he thought.

After greeting the kids, and exchanging preliminaries in the foyer, the Pastor asked if they could talk in private, just adults. Weston and Ally sent the kids to their rooms, while they and the Pastor sat in the living room on their couch. Nobody said anything for several seconds.

"So," Weston began, "can we get you anything to drink?"

"No, no," he answered, "I'm fine, thank you."

"What brings you out here, Pastor?" Ally asked.

Pastor Pete hesitated.

"I'm visiting with various church members, not all, but some," he started, "we are living in momentous times - "

" - You could say that again!" Ally exclaimed.

"And it's so important that we do the right thing during these times, because there are such severe consequences now if we don't," he continued.

"Agreed," Weston affirmed.

"That's why I'm recommending to church members at this time that they rethink their stance on the seventh day Sabbath," he stated.

"What?" Ally cried out in disbelief.

"Yes," he replied, "after much study, I have come to the conclusion that we don't really know what day the seventh day of the week is, anyway."

"Huh?" Weston asked, confused.

"Weston, the calendar has been changed, so we don't really know... and as your Pastor, I'm not ok with asking members to risk their lives over a non-salvation issue."

Ally was clearly upset now, raising her hands. "A non-salvation issue?"

"Look, I've come to believe that it doesn't matter what day of the week we worship God...I worship Him seven days a week. We're all going to Heaven anyway, as long as we love God and love man, that's what matters," he stated.

"Umm, you taught us that it does matter to keep all of the ten commandments," Weston argued, "are we now able to pick and choose which ones we think are important? And actually," a thought just came to him, "the commandment says six days shalt thou labor, but the seventh day is the Sabbath of the Lord thy God."

"So?" Pastor Pete asked in a confused tone.

"So, that means you don't worship God the same way every day, like you just said. You must work for six days and do something unique and different on the seventh day," Weston answered.

The Pastor got an irritated look on his face but made no answer.

"Wait, so what day are you going to church, then?" Ally asked, her voice fluctuating with emotion.

"Sunday...the Lord's Day," he stated matter-of-factly. He did not look either of them in the eyes as he spoke.

"So, you're saying we can't know for sure what day Saturday is anymore, but you seem to somehow understand when Sunday comes," Ally said sarcastically.

"Look," he replied, more annoyed than ever, "if you don't follow this new law, you will be put in prison. And something worse is coming. If you remain in this stubborn belief, they're going to kill you."

"I'm willing to follow other great men," Weston said, staring the pastor in the eyes, "men like John the Baptist, James, Peter, Huss, Jerome, Tyndale."

"And you will follow them," Pastor Pete answered quickly, "and lose your life over a belief."

"How are we even having this conversation?" Weston asked angrily, "You are a Pastor. Of a church whose motto is Sola scriptura. I feel like I am talking to someone else right now. Look, Jesus said be faithful unto death, and I will give you a crown of life. He said, blessed are those who keep His commandments, that they might have right to the Tree of Life, and enter in through the gates into the city. Revelation thirteen literally spells out that they're going to do the very thing they are now actually doing. We can see it happening all around us. The next thing after that is Jesus comes! Now is not the time to falter!"

"You've become quite the theologian," Pastor Pete answered sarcastically, "I was sent here to try to persuade you, but if persuasion won't - "

" - Wait!" Ally interrupted, "Someone sent you here?"

The Pastor sat in silence, staring at the coffee table in front of him. He seemed to realize he had said too much.

"Who sent you here?" Weston demanded, raising his voice.

"Well," the pastor said, as though nothing strange had just happened, "this visit has been nice. We'll have to catch up again sometime soon."

He stood to leave.

"What did they do to you?" Ally demanded, her voice full of emotion.

A bitter smile came over Pastor Pete's face. It left as quickly as it had appeared. He seemed as though he wanted to say something, but then an iron resolve took its place.

"Good day," he said sullenly as he walked himself to the door.

"Pastor, wait," Weston pleaded, following Pastor Pete to the door. He now regretted how poorly the conversation had gone. He regretted how angry he had gotten. Perhaps if they could just talk some more, come to some understanding. They loved this man. He had baptized them and helped them find the way to everlasting life.

"This isn't the way, Pastor. Please."

"Good day," he said hollowly, without looking at either of them. He quickly opened the door and walked out.

Weston turned to Ally in disbelief. She moved towards him. As they embraced, she started crying. Weston tried hard to hold back his own emotions.

Out on the street, Pastor Pete looked to his right and left. He noticed a black van sitting a short distance away. He shrugged off the cold and walked to his car, got in, and drove off.

The van was parked two doors down from the Millers, silently sitting in the dark. A barrier separated the cab from the cargo area. In the back, two agents hovered over a set of laptops, listening to Pastor Pete's Tag 5 Phantom wire for any further conversation with the Millers. It appeared the engagement was over and had gone poorly.

The senior officer looked over at his subordinate with a grin.

"Mark 'em," he stated flatly.

The desert wind howled on the empty streets in Sirjan. Sand blew in Sgt. Kyle's face and mouth. He pulled his scarf over his mouth and nose. He looked over at his men and could see they had already done the same. His squad had just pushed into town and were scoping out the nearby buildings and houses for signs of activity. They were in the lead and about forty-five minutes ahead of 2nd Battalion and the Coalition. The Coalition consisted of IDF, British, and Canadian outfits.

2nd squad had been weirded out the further they had advanced into this country. The tactics of these Iranians were cold-blooded and chilling. It required a constant state of alertness. Yesterday, there had been a wave of five suicide bombers, all at once. Fortunately, none of them had made it within range. Their lead sniper, Moose, had been watchful and waiting for such an attack. But their ears hadn't stopped ringing until this morning from the explosions which had almost engulfed them.

Then, a few minutes ago, they had moved through fields of lifeless gray trees, all

with stones hanging from them. Large stones. Kyle had no idea what the significance of it was, but it was alien. He didn't understand this culture. He missed his all-American hometown of Kingsport, where everything was normal, predictable, and safe.

Moose lay next to him in the sand. He pushed his digital night-vision goggles on his helmet down, scanning for signs of life.

"Anything?" Kyle questioned. He pushed his own goggles into position as well.

Moose hesitated, moving his head back and forth.

"Negative...zilch," he responded.

Well, no time like the present.

Time to draw fire, if they were out there. He knew they were, they always were. Kyle looked over his shoulder and waved his arm vigorously.

"Move out," he spoke hoarsely.

Kyle pushed himself up and started moving forward in a crouched run towards a cinder block shed. All eleven Marines followed behind him, pushing themselves toward houses, cars and whatever cover they could find.

Nothing.

No response.

Ahead of him lay a dark, deserted street. It seemed to hold several businesses, going down two long rows on each side. Trash and sand blew across the road from the wind. The road meandered ahead for about two hundred yards straight to their objective, a dark five-story building. Intel had it that that building housed the region's local Hezbollah headquarters. It looked like an abandoned warehouse or an old factory. Kyle was sure they would get it once they got within one hundred yards of the place.

2nd squad pushed forward in groups of twos and threes. Ready to provide covering fire, two men would aim their rifles forward while one soldier would sprint to a car or a door jam of a small business. That soldier would then kneel down, rifle ready, while the other two would follow. In this way, they made their way up the street towards the towering, dark behemoth in front of them.

They were at the end of the row of businesses now, and there lay between them and the warehouse only empty sand. This little no-man's-land made Kyle especially nervous. It was a perfect spot to get picked off by snipers. Moose was scanning the windows and roof. Kyle started doing the same.

Looking through the googles, everything had a green hue and appeared sterile and disconnected from reality. Some shades of green were lighter and some darker, but no signs of life appeared anywhere. As he gazed into windows he could see some large machinery, but not much else. The roof appeared empty. No menacing heads popped up to look down upon them.

Kyle sighed. He gave Billygoat a hand signal and quickly pushed his cheek against the butt of his M27. He was ready to push lead at anything that appeared in front of him.

Let's rock, he thought.

Billygoat ran full speed towards the corrugated metal wall of the building, little puffs of sand pushing out behind his feet. He almost ran into the wall before stopping himself and crouching down.

No response.

Again, in groups of twos and threes they pushed across the sand and gathered against the wall. Once everyone was there, they began moving toward a large door in the middle of the structure. As they passed by windows, they would crouch down, rifles ready.

Billygoat was already at the door when Kyle got there. He looked at the lockset which was a regular knob with two deadbolts. It was an exterior metal door.

"Breech it," he ordered.

Billygoat placed his EBAD Breecher strips on the hinge side. Attaching his detonator wire, he spooled it out about ten feet and ducked down. Every Marine watching took his queue and kneeled, lowering their head.

"Charge!" he yelled, pushing the detonator.

The strips exploded, pushing debris away from the building and into the air. The door instantly distorted and rocked outward, barely hanging on the jam. Smoke oozed from its hinges.

Moose moved forward and gave the door an enthusiastic kick with his boot. It flew into the room and crashed onto the floor. Everyone poured past him into the room, rifles raised and adrenaline pumping, ready to blow away any living thing.

They found themselves in a dark, cavernous area. It looked like an airplane hangar or factory of some sort. Large machinery was spread out across the floor. Kyle examined the light switch near the door while the squad pushed toward a set for rooms at the far end.

It didn't look tampered with in any way. He flipped the switch, but nothing happened. No lights.

"Clear!"

He could hear his men shouting as they pushed through the various rooms. The whole first floor of the building was actually just a large warehouse, but there were about six sheet-rocked rooms at the far end. A set of stairs sat at the end of the building, leading upward. Billygoat covered these with his M27.

Kyle could tell that everything had been cleared by his team. Unless there were terrorists upstairs, there was nobody home.

Where was everyone?

The whole town, the whole area, was deserted. They had not seen anybody since yesterday morning. It was weird.

"Sergeant!" Moose yelled at the top of his lungs.

It sounded urgent. Kyle double-timed it towards the room where Moose was. Billygoat stayed at the stairs while several other men patrolled the exterior.

He entered a room about 15x10 feet wide. The walls were unfinished sheetrock and there was no window or other doorway. Seven or eight of his men were gathered around an object in the center of the room.

"It's counting down. One hour left," Moose announced.

Kyle walked up to what looked like five or six fifty gallon drums covered in operational green camouflage. Weathered velcro straps ran along the tops and bottoms, as well as the sides. Attached to each was a camo green box about the size of a piece of luggage, and strapped to each top was a laptop with two or three USB cables feeding from the computer into the sides of each device.

"What is it? A SADM?" Kyle asked. He meant a Special Atomic Demolition Munition, or backpack nuke.

"It's a SADM," Edge responded immediately, tension in his voice, "five."

Edge was their EOD specialist, and had probably seen everything that went boom in the world.

"Yield?" he demanded.

"I think," Edge hesitated, combing over the devices, "one megaton."

"That's four or five clicks. We've got time to retreat if battalion gets here," he thought out loud, "can you disarm it?"

"Normally, yes," Edge replied, "I'm not sure why it has timers, though. That's way Hollywood."

"Look it over," he ordered, "I'm calling out now."

"Yes, sir," Edge replied, touching the device.

Kyle jogged to the main hangar area and called over his radio.

"Charlie Whiskey six, Charlie Whiskey six, copy?" he asked.

A distant, static-filled voice responded. It was the battalion comm officer.

"Charlie Whiskey six. Over."

"Roger, we need evac asap. Like five clicks out in thirty mikes. We have a SADM. Repeat, Sierra, Alpha, Delta, Mike. I repeat we have a SADM, estimate one megaton. Can you evac us?" Kyle asked.

"Ah, wow. Copy, that's Sierra, Alpha, Delta, Mike. We will be there in ten mikes. Charlie Company," the officer responded.

"I copy that. Out," Kyle replied, relieved.

They were going to get them out! If they could get at least five miles away, they would survive the blast. Then they could worry about getting further to try to avoid some of the radiation. They would still get hit, but at least they would not die.

Kyle hadn't wanted to admit it, but his knees had been shaking. He was sure they were dead when he had first seen it, but he had tried to hold it together for the men's sake. Nuclear detonation was not the way you wanted to go out. The thought of being vaporized completely freaked him out.

He jogged towards Edge to see how he was doing and tell them the good news. When he came back into the room, Edge was pouring over the bomb, removing one of the laptops with its cabling. His face looked like death, and he was covered in sweat.

"Charlie's ten mikes out. We'll be evac'd," Kyle announced.

"Something's wrong," Edge stated, his voice shaky.

"What?" Kyle demanded. Suddenly he felt sick.

"The laptops aren't even connected, Sergeant," he mumbled in fear, "they don't hook up to anything. They're just stuffed into the casing."

Edge and one of the other soldiers started ripping the camouflage material off a canister. As they removed part of the casing a new device was exposed. It was a camouflage box, strapped to the side, with six fat antennas on it and a digital screen which was lit. The box had multiple wires leading into the bomb itself. Edge's eyes grew wide, and he turned to face Kyle. Fear surged into every fiber of Kyle's being.

Remote detonator.

"Everybody go, now!" he screamed.

Kyle started grabbing men by the arm and yanking them towards the door, pushing them through it. Edge just sat there, crouched down, staring at the bomb.

"Move!" he screamed at Edge, grabbing onto his ballistic vest and hauling the two of them through the doorway.

Whatever spell had been cast over Edge seemed to dissipate, and he began sprinting after the rest of the men. All of his men were running as fast as they could towards the main door.

"Go!" he yelled to Edge, who seemed to have found new reserves of energy.

Edge had almost caught up to the rest of the squad. Now Kyle was the furthest one back. He willed his legs and arms to pump faster. Suddenly, in the background he heard what sounded like an old-school telephone ringing. It was coming from the bomb. There was silence. Then a second telephone ring.

In the next second, the backpack nuke detonated. Everything filled with ionizing radiation and blinding whiteness. This moved at the speed of light, which was 186,000 miles per second. A five mile radius around the bomb instantly heated to the tune of one hundred million degrees Celsius.

Fortunately, for Kyle and the rest of the 2nd squad, the chemo-electric thought process in their brains could only travel at 256 feet per second, so the blast velocity had them beat. There was no time for their minds to process the pain their bodies experienced in that brief second as they vaporized.

Charlie Company had been hauling it in fast to get to 2nd Squad. They were about half a mile away and were instantly vaporized as well. On the outskirts, an additional battalion of Marines was out on one of the deserted streets of the neighboring town about three miles away. They were sitting down in groups of twos and threes, eating MREs. With them sat a coalition of IDF, Canadian, and British troops.

All that now remained of these soldiers were blast shadows in the concrete showing where they had once existed. Each shadow looked like the shape of a man, and it extended away from the detonation. The blastwave had not even reached them yet, and they were already gone. When it did, it knocked down every building and military vehicle in the area with a thunderous crash. A powerful, howling wind and dynamic pressure increase followed that would have blown the soldier's eardrums, had they still been there.

At ground zero, a large orange mushroom cloud ballooned upward into the sky, dominating everything for fifty miles. The fireball brilliantly lit up the night, casting strange shadows behind what buildings and trees did remain. The sound of a thousand thunderbolts roared out continuously through the countryside, terrifying every living thing in the entire region.

Tim Blain was calling on line two. President Lutrell was having a rare conversation with his wife, Joan, and he was annoyed. It never seemed to stop around here; the issues, the problems, the interruptions. He let Joan know he had to go and picked up line two.

"Yes?" he said curtly.

"John, can I see you?" Tim asked.

"Come on in," Lutrell answered him.

"Be right over," he replied hurriedly.

I can't wait, Lutrell thought sarcastically.

A few minutes later Tim walked in. He came right to the point.

"John, Ebola's back."

Lutrell chuckled.

"Tim," he replied condescendingly, "it never went away! They're estimating at least fifty citizens dying each day."

"I'm not talking about The Zone, Mr. President," he answered briskly, "new cases have been reported in West Virginia."

"What?" Lutrell spoke, raising his voice, "What are you talking about?"

"Ebola has gotten outside of The Zone, John. Someone got out. They found a breech in the fence line," he reported.

"Well... how?" he yelled, "Who?"

"We don't know," he answered meekly, "a hole in the fence was found. We don't know who it was. We can assume they are dead by now, anyway."

"How can this happen?" Lutrell grumbled, mostly to himself. He felt like he was going to lose his mind, "What are we going to do? I'm asking, Tim! I'm at the point where I DON'T KNOW what to do."

"John..." Tim spoke softly. "John, I think..."

In the background, they could hear multiple footsteps running towards them. Voices were yelling.

"What the...?" Tim exclaimed, moving slowly towards the door.

"What is that?" Lutrell asked, standing up behind his desk.

Suddenly, multiple Secret Service agents burst into the room. A tall, African American agent named Kent spoke first.

"Mr. President, we must get you to Air Force One now."

"What? What's happened?" Lutrell asked with uncertainty.

"Now," Kent stated emphatically, motioning with his right hand to come, moving toward the President. Lutrell could see General McCarthy was amongst the group.

"Ok," Lutrell, stated. He moved from behind his desk, and the whole group began racing down the hall towards the heliport. All the agents formed a circle around him as they ran to the exit doors. Lutrell could see his Sikorsky Sea King was already starting up, rotors slowly whirling. The group was running as fast as they could. Kent was communicating with the pilot over his radio.

What was going on?

Once on board, he turned to General McCarthy.

"What is it?" he shouted over the roar of the rotor blades.

"We got nuked!" McCarthy shouted, emphasizing each word.

Lutrell's eyes went wide.

"Where? Here?"

"No," McCarthy answered quickly, "Iran."

Lutrell sat in silence, trying to absorb this new reality.

"We lost at least three thousand men, sir," McCarthy went on, "to a low-yield nuclear bomb. We lost over two whole Battalions. Our coalition all lost hundreds of men. It happened in Sirjan, Iran."

"They bombed their OWN country to kill us?" Lutrell asked incredulously, "Their own country?"

"They're extremists, sir," McCarthy stated.

"They're animals!" he shouted back.

They were lifting off now and headed in the direction of Andrews Air Force Base. Lutrell could see endless rows of neighborhoods flying by below them. Neighborhoods where families lived, families who had given up their boys and girls to go and fight terrorism.

"Should we go to DefCon One now, Mr. President?" McCarthy asked.

"Yes," Lutrell ordered, his voice shaking, "go to DefCon One."

They are going to pay for this, he thought.

They had put both of their phones in the backyard and turned on music. Weston and Ally were in their bedroom talking about what their next steps were. Weston had a plan.

"Ok, here's the situation, and I think I know what we need to do," he stated.

"What?" Ally asked.

"If we stay here, eventually you and I get arrested, and they take our kids...I think we both agree that's unacceptable, and not God's plan," he said.

"Definitely not," she agreed.

"We need a way to transport our family out of the city. We have two cars and two ways out. The Caravan and the Camry. The driveway and the back alley, but they're watching both."

"They have the van out front, and I'm sure that white sedan out in the alley is for us too. It's been there for several days now. There are two men in it," she advised.

"Right. So, we can't just drive out of here. Rick and Kathleen gave us the keys to their house. We have access to their vehicles, but he's right next door and Adventist. We have to assume that house is also being watched just as closely," Weston went on.

"So, what do we do?" Ally asked, feeling hopeless.

"I'll go shopping in the Camry," he announced.

"The Camry?" she asked.

"It handles better," he stated.

"Huh?"

"I'll go shopping, and the sedan will follow me, right?"

"Ok, right," she echoed.

"On the way, I'll lose them," he declared.

"You'll lose them?" she repeated, in a sarcastic tone.

"I'll have to," he said with determination, "or this won't work. Once I lose them, I'll double back as fast as I can. I'll park the Camry a few streets down, in front of a house. I doubt they'll ever notice it. It's a silver Camry; they're everywhere."

"Ok?" Ally was confused.

"Then when we're ready, we leave here...not in the Caravan, but on foot. Not from the front or the back, which they'll be watching, but over the fence," he pointed to Rick's house. "From Rick's, there's a greenbelt next door. That greenbelt has a culvert that goes under the road. We go through that tunnel, out the other side, and we're in the next neighborhood. I'll make sure the car's over in that area."

"Can we fit through that tunnel?" she asked, with new hope in her voice.

"We'll have to crawl, or crouch, but I think we can fit," he answered, "when I do this, I'll get a closer look at the culvert. So, what do you think?"

"Don't you think they'll notice the Camry never came back? Won't they start looking for it?"

"They might," he agreed, "but we'll have to hope, and pray, that they don't find it. I figure, don't let them see any of us again, and maybe they'll think I just went to stay somewhere else."

"We could stage a fight on the phone," she suggested, "if they're listening, they'll think you left to stay somewhere else."

"It's a good idea," he agreed, "I'm sure they're listening. But it kinda feels like lying. Let's play it by ear."

"Ok. How will you get back?" she asked.

"I'll come back to the house the same way that we're going to get to the Camry. I'll wait til night, sneak through the neighborhoods, go through the tunnel, hop Rick's fence."

He hesitated, "It's the best I've got."

She looked at him and gave him a weak smile.

"It's our best shot."

"It's all we can do," he agreed.

"West," she went on, "once we're free, really free, I mean, where do we go?"

"We head to the mountains, get to the high country," he answered matter-of-factly, "we have the gear. We haul as much food as we are physically able, and just use the water filters."

"And then?" she questioned.

"Then we wait this out. We know Jesus is coming soon. Winter is almost over. We wait it out in the Sierras. I spent a lot of my childhood backpacking up there. I know some spots. We are soon to be outlaws, and so we can't be in society," he got a pensive look on his face, "like the early Christians."

"Ok," she agreed.

"I'll take the trip in the Camry and lose them tomorrow. After that, we'll play it by ear," he said.

"It starts tomorrow then," she agreed.

Lutrell felt the hard pull into his seat as Air Force One barreled down the runway and lifted gently into the night sky. He could hear the roar of the engines coming from outside the cabin. The plane pushed upward at a steep angle and then turned slightly to the left to get on flight pattern. Soon they would be able to take off their seatbelts.

Next to him sat Tim Blain. On the other aisle were six Secret Service, General McCarthy, and Judy Nguyen, along with a few others in his cabinet.

A few minutes later, the aircraft leveled out, and the seatbelt sign dinged. They all began getting out of their seats.

"Let's go to the comm room," Tim announced loudly.

The group walked through the dining area and Senior Staff meeting room, and upstairs to the Communications room. Several Secret Service stood outside the door. Once inside, they sat at two conference tables. Multiple flat-screen TVs were on, showing an image of a distant mushroom cloud rising out of a vast desert. The video appeared to have been filmed by Hezbollah, and excited crowds of terrorists could be seen in the shot shouting and firing off AK-47s into the sky. Some were dancing and singing.

"Where's the vice president, Judy?" President Lutrell started off the conversation.

"He's in Florida, sir. We're trying to reach him now," Judy responded.

"So, who hit us? Hezbollah...Iran?" he asked impatiently.

"Our intel indicates it was Hezbollah or Al Qaeda, and Iran. But not Hamas, they seem to be quiet right now. That's another issue," McCarthy answered.

"Well the only issue right now is, are there going to be more attacks, and what is our response?" Lutrell stated sharply.

"Yes, sir," McCarthy said.

"There is no ground advance at this point," Tim cut in, "all forces are on standby. We are at DefCon One here, and just holding current positions overseas."

"It doesn't seem Iran has the capability to launch a nuke at our boys," McCarthy added, "we know from the last communications from the squad who dealt with the bomb, that it was a small backpack-style nuke. We think they can only leave nukes in our path, and remote detonate them once we arrive."

"Well these nutcases don't seem to care about ruining their own country, so I say we give them some more," Tim stated heatedly.

"Tim," Judy said, with concern in her voice, "are we really advocating for nuclear strikes in Iran? Which could create a retaliatory strike, and a larger response?"

"Who's going to retaliate, Judy?" Tim shot back, "None of these terrorist nations can launch a nuke. We hit them with a couple of ours; they just have to take it. And after we melt a couple of their cities, they'll surrender, and more of our boys don't have to die going house to house - "

" - Ok...ok, Tim," the President interrupted, "I think we get your point."

At that, a look of relief came over Judy's face.

"And, I am inclined to agree with your assessment," Lutrell continued.

"What?" Judy gasped incredulously.

"History has shown this worked before," Lutrell insisted to Judy, "and we are under nuclear attack. They leveled it up to this, not us. I don't want to have to tell more American families that their boys have died unnecessarily. I can prevent that. Iran has shown they would rather commit suicide, of their people and their land, rather than give it up to us."

"There has to be another way," Judy declared.

"I think this is it," Tim answered her, more gently now.

"So, what will be our strike?" McCarthy asked eagerly.

"Going back to history again," Tim answered, "I would think, two cities? That did it before."

"I agree," Lutrell answered, "let's hit Tabriz...and Tehran. Show them we mean business. Knock the country to its knees."

Judy sat silently in her chair with a sick look on her face. She looked like she was about to cry.

The next day was spent mainly in preparation. Everyone took everything out of their backpacks and went over them together in the living room. Only essentials were kept, and some essentials were shared amongst the family. This time the phones were kept inside, but everyone began getting in the habit of carrying around a small notepad with them and writing things down instead of saying them. Sometimes they would speak, but they would try to keep the conversation vague. If they had something important to say about leaving or preparing, they wrote it on the notepad.

They had two four-man tents, but Weston took the tents apart and spread the pieces into different backpacks, to distribute the weight better. Everyone had a knife and a water filter, which was also unnecessary. He paired four backpacking stoves down to two. As far as clothes, Weston and Ally helped the kids pack just two pairs of everything, and they made sure it was their warmest gear. Only wool and synthetics. The goal was to get Ally and himself under forty-five lbs, and the kids at about 20% of their body weight.

Water was not going to be an issue. They would head to the Tahoe National Forest; it was remote, and there were many lakes from which they could filter water.

The problem was food. Even though they were no longer able to go to the grocery store, they had plenty of non-perishables in the pantry at home, but they could only haul so much food on foot.

There was only one food source they could utilize in the Sierras; lake trout. Weston would bring fishing gear with them, but you couldn't rely on it to sustain a family or even one person. He had never been able to consistently catch fish. He had tried live bait, lures, and even sprays, but it had always been hit and miss.

Then there was also the issue of how long ago the different lakes had been stocked, and if they had been fished out. The way the world was now, he doubted the government had stocked any lakes with fish in a long time.

So they would bring a couple of poles and some fishing gear, but they would have to pack in most of their food, and they had no idea how long they would have to remain there. Weston had been studying the last days in the Bible extensively, but it was difficult to tell how long of a time period extended from the mark of the beast until Jesus actually came.

There were two indicators, however, that led Weston to believe it would not be long. The plagues of Egypt were in many ways very similar to the seven last plagues, except there were more of them, and they lasted approximately one year. Additionally, as one read the description of the seven last plagues, it became clear life on this planet could not be sustained for very long under the conditions described.

They would mainly pack dehydrated meals, which were actually delicious. They would supplement with beans, rice, and dried fruit.

They were ready to flee. But now it was all up to Weston. No, to God really. It would take a miracle. It was what felt like an impossible task. Weston would have to lose a government tail that was surely assigned to highly professional agents.

The hour was approaching when he would have to leave. It was already getting near dusk. He didn't want to leave at night because, while it would make it harder for them to spot him, it would also make it harder for him to tell if he had ditched them. He needed to be sure.

He knelt down and prayed with Ally and the kids in the backyard, away from the phones. If things went wrong, it could be the last time he ever saw his family. Weston prayed that they would all be sealed with the seal of God, if they weren't already, and not receive the mark of the beast. Everyone took turns pleading and petitioning God for his safety and success, and that the family would not be separated. Ultimately, each member asked that God's will be done, and that they would all be in Heaven together shortly.

Lutrell, McCarthy and Blain stood together in front of the Comms console, with a service member from Air Force One at the keyboard. Several Secret Service surrounded them. General McCarthy placed a large briefcase, known as the football, on the floor. It was made of black leather, with three separate compartments. On the Comms computer, McCarthy instructed the serviceman to issue a watch alert to the U.S. Strategic Command. He typed for several minutes.

"Ok, give me the biscuit," Lutrell ordered nervously.

"Yes, Mr. President," McCarthy responded, reaching into the football and handing him the launch codes envelope.

Lutrell ripped open the breakable seal on a large, red envelope. From inside, he removed several laminated cards. Each card had codes on them. He grabbed the top one and glanced at it.

"Send the following to NORAD, please," he motioned to Tim, who asked the serviceman to scoot down. Tim sat down at the console and placed his hands on the keyboard.

"Ordering nuclear strike, repeat, nuclear strike, on the following selected targets: Tibrez, Iran. Next target: Tehran, Iran. Order is for immediate nuclear launch, requesting Columbia class launch from Arabian Sea. This is the President of the United States, John Samuel Lutrell. Authentication code Alpha, Alpha, One, Alpha, Tango, Nine, Charlie, Nine, Zero, Alpha. Repeat: Alpha, Alpha, One, Alpha, Tango, Nine, Charlie, Nine, Zero, Alpha. Confirm... Get them on speaker, please," he motioned to the serviceman.

The man hit several buttons. About ten seconds later, a distorted voice came over the line.

"NORAD standing by, Colonel Shaw. Confirm Alpha, Alpha, One, Alpha, Tango, Nine, Charlie, Nine, Zero, Alpha. Repeat: Alpha, Alpha, One, Alpha, Tango, Nine, Charlie, Nine, Zero, Alpha. Targets Tabriz and Tehran. Confirm strike?"

Lutrell looked over at Tim.

"Do you concur?" he asked. His voice had a tremor in it.

"Yes, Mr. President, I do," Tim answered, taking a deep breath. He looked green.

"Confirmed, Colonel. Proceed," he ordered to the voice on the other end of the line.

My God, what have I done? Lutrell shuddered.

A few minutes later, a single Trident II D5LE ballistic nuclear missile was launched from its Columbia class submarine thirty feet below the surface of the Arabian Sea. As its head and body popped above the ocean, an enormous jet of water burst into the air. The missile seemed to hang suspended above the water for a few seconds before its thrusters ignited, sending it rocketing upward. Almost immediately it pitched fifteen degrees north towards its target. A deafening continuous roar bellowed out over the sea as the weapon scissored into the sky. A contrail three times the length of its body pushed out its back as it strained to reach its top speed of 18,030 mph.

Ten minutes later, Iranian Air Command detected an incoming threat to the capital city of Tehran. Air raid sirens began to sound, several fighter jets were scrambled, and anti-aircraft guns were manned, but there was no point.

The Trident II missile actually contained eight black, cone-shaped nuclear warheads inside it. Each cone could produce a 475-kiloton blast and independently target a different location. The Trident was coming in at almost Mach 24 when four of its eight nuclear warheads separated from the others and headed toward Tabriz. The remaining four came down over Tehran and detonated at twenty-five hundred feet, incinerating almost the entire city and over a million of its inhabitants instantly. At 1:58:39 pm they were there. By 1:58:40 they were all gone.

Weston was nervous as he walked through the side yard to the Camry in his detached garage. He would appear to go shopping at Raley's about four miles away. This is what the agents would think. The reality was he could no longer set foot in any store, and he was going to have to figure out a way to ditch the agents before he got there. All this would have to be done without breaking any laws, since to break the law meant he would be sinning. If he passed the store and appeared to just be driving aimlessly, they would become suspicious and probably call in more personnel to follow him.

He opened the gas tank cover and filled up the Camry from his five gallon can. Fortunately, he had filled it and bought one more and filled it, several months ago. He closed the cap on the can and placed it in the trunk. He placed the second can in the trunk as well. This model Camry came with a large storage capacity, so he was pretty sure they would be able to fit all their gear. Worst case scenario, the kids could hold their backpacks on their laps.

He turned the ignition key and drove out of the garage and into the back alley behind their house. He stopped before entering the alley and looked both ways. To the right, he could see a white Ford Taurus sedan, facing his direction and sitting a few houses down in the alley. As he turned slowly left and proceeded towards the main road, the Taurus came to life and pulled out after him.

He stopped at Jepson Avenue at a busy intersection where he needed to turn left. The sun was almost setting, casting shadows across the street and onto houses. The light was currently red, and after about ten seconds, the Taurus pulled in right behind him. He looked in his rearview mirror to try and catch a glimpse of who was actually following him. He could see two middle-aged men in suits staring ahead.

The light turned green and he proceeded left onto Jepson. It was a four-lane road with a suicide lane. Traffic was busy as it was the time of the evening commute, when everyone was trying to get home. There were also lots of protestors moving in groups of four or five on the sidewalks. They all appeared to be walking in the same direction towards some larger gathering. Some were shouting slogans and some were screaming at cars as they drove by. Weston could not tell what their issue was, but he saw several signs that said something about 'Trad.'

He made a few more turns and eventually ended up on Roseville Parkway, the street that Raley's was on. Now the crowds were getting thicker. Some protesters were starting to spill out onto the street. He could hear people chanting and screaming. Multiple National Guard vehicles were parked at different locations, with armed Guardsmen watching the protests, pacing with guns drawn.

The sun was setting now, and darkness was just creeping into the eastern sky. Why had he waited so late in the day to set out? Soon there would be no light, and the Taurus would be just another set of indistinguishable headlights. Then it would be even harder to see if he had actually ditched them. Weston was nervous and began to sweat profusely. He only had about two more miles until he reached the store, and he still had no actual plan.

A busy intersection loomed up ahead. He was about two hundred yards away when the light turned yellow. He hoped to make it but realized he couldn't, so he slowed down and stopped. The light turned red. He was in the pole position at the intersection, in the middle of three lanes, and there were cars all around him in both lanes. The Taurus was separated from him by one car.

Suddenly, from the left a crowd emerged and moved off of the sidewalk into the street among the cars. As they came closer, they began chanting:

"Down with the Trads. Down with the Trads!"

The mob was hooting and shouting. People started kicking the cars with their boots, keying them, and smashing them with baseball bats. Weston turned, horrified, to try to see better. He saw a tall, thin young man holding a sign which said: *Trads are the problem, Trans is the answer.* Another walked with a billboard that said: *Traditionals; when will you all just die off?*

The thunderous chanting continued. A large man with balding, stringy long hair, wearing a tattered prom dress and combat boots, jumped in front of Weston's Camry and started screaming his own version of the chant:

"KILL all the Trads! KILL all the Trads!"

He had a huge smile on his face, and a crazed look in his eyes. On the chest area of his gown was spray painted: *Trans is holy.* Hidden behind the large bottom of his lavender dress was a metal baseball bat. He grabbed it and quickly began smashing it enthusiastically into the hood of Weston's car. The Ram truck next to Weston had had enough, and engine racing, pulled forward and right on red onto Jackson Avenue. There was no problem getting through the intersection as all traffic had come to a halt.

Weston saw his chance. All bets were off with traffic rules today. He could follow the Ram if he did so now. He quickly stomped on the gas pedal, sending Prom Queen flying up onto the hood. He proceeded to grab the windshield wipers and scream at Weston. Weston tried to focus ahead on the road, struggling to make the turn onto Jackson without hitting the median. As he turned harder, Prom Queen flew off the hood and landed on the pavement, taking the wipers with him. Weston could see in his rear view mirror that he quickly recovered and began running after the car, shaking his fist in the air. With one final act of hate he hurled his baseball bat in Weston's direction.

Behind him, the Taurus immediately reacted by pushing forward, but it was boxed in and couldn't move. The agent decided he was getting free anyway, and began slamming into the car in front of them, trying to force enough space to get by. After several more attempts to make room, the car in front relented and moved, freeing up the Taurus.

Weston knew this was his only chance. He pressed the gas pedal to the floor, swerving around the Ram truck and other vehicles. He looked in his rearview mirror and could see the Taurus pushing out into the intersection now. He turned the wheel hard right, tires squealing, onto another major street.

He was going too fast. Several cars were converging up ahead, and he swerved left to get into the suicide lane to avoid them.

Horns blared as he sped by, but now he could see he was freed up. He was going to be able to maintain some speed. Unfortunately, in his rearview mirror he could now see the Taurus was somehow closing in on him. The agent was driving like a maniac trying to keep up with him. So, it had all been for nothing, they were going to catch up to him anyway and now surely arrest him. All he had done was make things worse than they had been before.

Up ahead he saw another major intersection and the light turning yellow. He wasn't sure if he could make it, but the road in front of him was clear and he kept his foot pressed on the accelerator. He sped through the intersection just as the light turned red. As he passed through, he could see there were no cars waiting in the intersecting lanes to move forward on their green. The intersection was empty. He was sure the Taurus was going to run the light as well.

He watched in his rearview mirror. As expected, the government car didn't slow down at all, but pushed through the red light and into the intersection at full speed.

With startling swiftness, a fully loaded eighteen-wheeler appeared out of nowhere. It was moving quickly as the trucker had a green light. He had no time to react to the car that was suddenly in his way. The trucker t-boned the Taurus with such force that the front of the Peterbilt cab crumbled and the car went flying into a light pole. Debris flew hundreds of feet in the air. The agent's car came down off the pole to rest on its top, crumpled, and oozing smoke.

As the shock of what happened faded, Weston realized he was free now. He slowed down and tried to get his bearings. He had already passed their neighborhood. Making a u-turn in the suicide lane, he took a left into their section of houses. It was dark now. He began slowly driving down the streets a couple of blocks from their house.

Suddenly, he saw it. A dilapidated, unkempt home that appeared abandoned. None of the neighbors were out and no lights were on. It was an older, worn down area. A place where no one asked questions or knew their neighbors. Without hesitation, he stopped in front of the home, put the Camry in reverse, and turned off his lights. He slowly backed into the driveway so that the front of his car faced the street. The driveway went around the side of the house instead of in front of it, so his car would be even more hidden from searching authorities.

He turned off the engine and sat for a moment in the dark. No one had come out or looked out their windows. He didn't believe anyone had noticed he had parked here. He was sure tomorrow some neighbors would see the car, but hopefully no one would think much of it.

He quickly got out and locked the car manually so there would be no loud, annoying beep from his clicker. He then moved to the sidewalk and began walking in the direction of his neighborhood. No one was out and the streets and sidewalks appeared empty. In the distance, he could hear multiple sirens approaching.

Weston continued in the dark, walking briskly down the sidewalk. He was nearing the culvert that passed under the road into the greenbelt by Rick's house. He looked in both directions to see if anyone was watching. Then he hopped over the metal rail on the road and onto his hands and knees, sliding down into the drainage ditch that led to the culvert. His hands were getting scratched up as he slid his way to the bottom.

There was a small amount of water running at the bottom of the ditch, as well as algae, which was slippery. He tried to walk slowly so as not to lose his footing. As he continued to move forward, a darker hole than the darkness around him emerged in front of him. It was the culvert. He could tell it was smaller than he had hoped. It was about four feet tall and four feet wide.

He hesitated as he neared the entrance. He was going to have to crouch down and possibly get on his hands and knees to make it through, and the bottom was covered with algae and slime. He crouched down and peered through to the other side. It was about thirty feet long.

Oh, well. Let's just get it done, he thought.

He entered the tunnel, leaning over, and crouching down as low as he could. The sound of running water was much louder in the enclosed space, echoing off the walls. His feet were already getting wet since he was wearing sneakers. About halfway through, he suddenly heard several police cars coming towards him, sirens wailing and engines revving. He paused as they passed above him. The concrete above him rumbled as the vehicles roared overhead.

He emerged out the other side, and scrambled back up and into the greenbelt. He could now see Rick's house.

Making his way through thick, unmown grass, he came to the fence bordering Rick's yard. Rick had installed a gate in the fence to access a gravel area behind his house. Weston strained to reach over the fence and pull the latch to release the gate.

Once in Rick's yard, he snuck through the grass, watching the front street. No one could see him from here and the black van was not visible. He reached his own fence and cautiously peered over it. He could now see the van. However, if he moved further down he could hop over without anyone observing him.

The fence had been built with the smooth side and the frame side alternating every eight feet. He moved to the frame side where 2x4s were exposed. He grabbed the highest 2x4 and hauled himself over the wood. At the top, he teetered back and forth, almost falling. He quickly hauled his other leg over the fence and lept down, landing hard with a grunt.

He started to move towards the back door of his house, when he had a thought and turned around. He moved back to the fence and squatted down. Aiming for the fence boards just above the lowest 2x4, he began kicking several of them as hard as he could. After several kicks, some of the fence posts cracked. He began working them back and forth with his hands until they came off. He discarded the broken boards onto the grass. Now they had an easy exit out of their backyard, unobserved from the street, when they finally did flee.

Weston ran to the back door where Ally and the kids were waiting.

"You made it!" Ally exclaimed, throwing her arms around him, "Were you followed?"

"Where are the phones?" he asked with concern. They could be listening in right now.

"Upstairs, listening to the Heritage Singers," she said with a grin.

"Trust me," he answered her question, "I lost them."

Chapter 14 - The Appearing

Lutrell and his staff were assessing the damage in Tehran via a MQ-1B Predator drone's live camera feed. He could see the landscape on one of the screens in the Comm room. There were flattened buildings and out of control fires as far as the eye could see. The region had been annihilated; everything was gone.

A call was coming through on one of the secure lines.

"Make sure our forces hold their positions," Lutrell stated.

"Yes, sir," McCarthy replied.

"Mr. President?" a service man at the computer console announced, "The Vatican's on line three."

"You want to take that call?" Tim voiced what they all were thinking.

"Give me that phone," the President answered angrily. There was only one reason Giordano would be calling right now. He was tired of this old man trying to meddle in American affairs.

Lutrell paused before picking up the receiver.

"Better yet, send it to the Senior Staff room, I'll take it privately," he instructed.

Several agents followed him as he made his way to the room. Tim walked behind them. Secret Service waited at the door as he sat down and picked up the line that was blinking. Tim walked in and closed the door.

"Pope Giordano?" he asked as he picked up the receiver.

"This is Ambassador Bianchi," Bianchi replied, "the Holy Father is unavailable. I am authorized to speak for him."

"Fine," answered Lutrell. He was in no mood for this meddling today. "How can I help you?"

"Are we alone?" he asked.

"We are," Lutrell lied.

"What is going on in Iran? We are hearing of nuclear bombs being dropped," Bianchi questioned.

"That is correct," the President answered tersely, "We have targeted and hit two cities; Tabriz and Tehran."

"Mr. President, you should not have done this - "

" - Now you listen to me, Bianchi," Lutrell interrupted, speaking slowly, "the Vatican does not need to be interfering in the affairs of my country, my country is at war. We were attacked - "

" - You can be replaced," Bianchi stated flatly.

"What did you say?" Lutrell asked, thrown off guard.

"Do you remember what happened that sad, unfortunate day in Dallas? America was in such mourning," Bianchi went on.

"What?" Lutrell asked confusedly, "What are you talking about?"

"We were so happy to have America's first Catholic president," Bianchi stated, "you have no idea the struggle involved to make that happen in your bigoted land. Barriers that took decades to overcome. Unfortunately, Mr. Kennedy was so strong-willed. He did not wish to follow the game plan."

"The game plan?" Lutrell repeated sarcastically.

"And so he had to be eliminated," Bianchi continued matter-of-factly.

Lutrell paused on the phone. Suddenly the message was clear.

"Are you threatening me?"

Bianchi paused as well.

"It is not just about you, mind you. It is your country, your position. Hungry wolves are everywhere, climbing up the hill, who want to kill the alpha, and rule the pack. Currently you are on top, but that can change. Russia, China, even the British Empire. It could re-emerge! This could all happen quite suddenly," Bianchi stated excitedly.

"How dare you," Lutrell growled, "if you think you can sit there - "

" - Listen," Bianchi stated with authority, "we ARE in charge. You are not. You are like the bulldog who goes and fetches the kill. You are strong, but the dog is always on a chain around its neck. From time to time we must pull that chain."

Lutrell sat there in shock. Tim was standing there, mouthing, *what are they saying?*

Lutrell motioned for him to leave. Reluctantly, Tim walked out and shut the door.

"You have two choices," Bianchi continued, "you can follow the game plan. Cease these hostilities. Then follow our lead. The next step."

"What is the next step?" Lutrell demanded. He had a feeling if he didn't ask now, he would never find out what these bastards were up to.

"The calamities are not ending, even though we have asked the world to revere the Lord's Day," Bianchi said.

Lutrell sat there, listening in silence. He was furious, and his mind was racing.

"So, now we must escalate our methods. Those who will not revere the day we have appointed... must be punished. Severely. President Lutrell...they must die...and you must enforce it. You are, as they say, the 'world's policeman,'" he stated dryly.

"Die?" Lutrell blurted out. "Now you listen to me.. I will NEVER cooperate with you, you sick, twisted - "

" - Then we are left with the second choice," Bianchi said with authority, "you will meet with an unfortunate accident."

Lutrell's heart was now racing.

"Whatever you think you're capable of - "

" - And sadly, your beautiful wife and children will also die," Bianchi spoke with mock sadness, "but not right away, of course.

They will have uses, temporarily. We sublet this kind of thing out now, you know? There are so many groups in Mexico and Albania, who love to do work with women and children. The beauty of globalization."

The anger was subsiding, and fear was taking its place. Lutrell was thinking more clearly now. What if Bianchi was telling the truth? Had they killed Kennedy? If they could get to Kennedy, they could get to him. Many presidents had been attacked. Could they get to his family? He knew kidnapping and slavery were at an all-time high in the world. Bianchi seemed so matter-of-fact about it all. And the thought of what he implied would happen to Joan and the kids...

"You'll, ahh, never get Congress to sign off on it," he said, trying to play the only card he had left.

"Leave that to us," Bianchi replied in a bored tone, "we are persuading key members now."

"How much time do I have to decide... to play ball?" he asked quietly.

"You have twelve hours. Oh, and don't even think of retaliation. If anything happens to myself, or the Holy See, things will automatically be set in motion. We will deep-fake you agreeing with us, and you and your family will still die, anyway," Bianchi stated flatly. With that, he hung up the phone.

Lutrell sat there alone in total shock.

In Mecca, Saudi Arabia, it was a cool day of seventy-two degrees. Men had their business casual long sleeves rolled down and their jackets on. Women moved about with coats on and full hijabs over their heads. The sun was at its zenith in the middle of the sky, but it seemed to bring no heat for those used to one hundred plus degree temperatures.

Haggling and arguing could be heard going on at the marketplace. Huge crowds of people were perusing the bazaar, which until recently had been filled with local foods. Now produce and meat were scarce, and what remained in the wooden display cases demanded the highest prices. Violence and lawlessness were rampant. This was evidenced by the fact that armed security forces patrolled the streets everywhere.

As the chaotic market scene continued, a strange light could suddenly be seen near the fountain at the center of the marketplace. It appeared about a foot off the ground and ebbed rhythmically. Looking up, people could see inky streams of orange and yellow, sinking down from somewhere high above. It almost looked like tongues of fire slowly feeding the odd-looking light. There were no streetlights or sources of power anywhere nearby, and as it grew brighter and larger, more and more people began to stop what they were doing and stare in disbelief.

The light began to pulsate quickly now and change from a bright white to a yellow, then crimson. Now the entire marketplace had gone silent. Everyone was mesmerized by the strange apparition. Traffic on the nearby streets began to stop as well, and people were getting out of their cars.

The light suddenly flared so brightly that everyone averted their eyes. Women screamed and men began shouting. As one, the crowd began to back away from it. It dimmed again, and all eyes turned back toward it. As they watched, incredibly, a man stepped out of the pure white orb and onto the pavement in front of them.

Gasps erupted from the crowd and several women fainted, collapsing to the ground. Men began pointing and shouting in fear.

The figure was tall, with dark, shoulder-length hair, which flowed thickly around a majestic Middle Eastern face. He had a neatly trimmed beard, dark brown in color. He was broad-shouldered, and wore a long, flowing tan robe. His head and body seemed almost luminescent.

People stared in awe and began to back away as he moved towards the main group of onlookers. Some ran in terror, while others timidly held their ground. Several people began to record with their cellphones.

The man raised both hands in the air and spoke.

"Do not be afraid," he said in perfect Arabic. His voice had a powerful, melodic tone to it. It was mesmerizing.

"I am Isa, your deliverer. Do not be afraid," he repeated.

The mood of the crowd seemed to change a bit, and several men and women stopped their flight. On the street, news vans approached and screeched to a halt. Reporters scrambled out of their vehicles, frantically gathering up their television gear.

"Isa, save us, please!" yelled a fervent young man from the crowd, "Our world is dying."

"I am here to save you," Isa reassured them, "it is the will of Allah that not one be lost. But it is not Allah's will that all faiths be so divided, as they now are. It is time for the planet to worship Allah together, as one. One heart, one mind."

He paused.

"Every Sunday."

"Isa," cried a woman in desperation, "I know you can heal my son. He is here, with me. Please, Isa. He is paralyzed. Please."

A man was pushed in a wheelchair towards Isa and parked at his feet. He had a portable ventilator strapped to the side and a brace for his head, which extended upwards behind him. The man moaned and turned his eyes slightly to glance at his potential healer.

"He is a quadriplegic, Isa," she cried, "for five years. Please, I beg you."

"Your faith shall be rewarded, daughter of Ishmael," Isa announced. He placed both hands on the man's head.

The man closed his eyes, breathing slowly at first, but then rapidly.

Suddenly, his hands began to twitch. His mother gasped in surprise. He began to make little moaning sounds. With a struggle, he slowly began to move. First his entire upper body raised forward slightly on his elbows. Then the man reached forward with both hands and struggled to pull out his breathing tube.

Once it was removed, he spoke.

"What did you do to me?" he croaked, his voice choked with tears. Slowly, he pushed off of his handrails and tentatively stood to his feet.

The mother immediately passed out, teetering forward and falling headlong into the crowd. Several women screamed and men began to cry out in disbelief. Gradually, some began to prostrate themselves before the figure. Then as one, the entire crowd fell on their faces in worship.

"I have forgiven your sins, as I did when I was here two thousand years ago," Isa answered the man, "but more importantly, I have a message for all of you."

"Yes, Isa. Anything!" someone cried out.

"All flesh must come together to worship Allah... each Sunday," he spoke forcefully. "The reason why you lack food, why calamities attack the land, why bombs fall from the sky, the reason why you suffer, is because not all are doing this. Allah cannot be pleased until there is absolute unity."

"Yes, Isa!" many shouted, "Yes!"

The crowd, continuing to prostrate themselves before the figure, began moving their hands up and down in worship.

Suddenly, a man emerged from the crowd with a gun pointed straight at the Messiah. He screamed out:

"There is no God but God and Mohammad is his prophet!"

He began squeezing the trigger repeatedly, aiming directly at Isa from several feet away. Screams came from the crowd as people began to duck down for cover.

The assassin continued to fire the gun. With each pull of the trigger, an explosion of gunpowder sounded and the handgun recoiled, firing round after round into the healer. However, the projectiles appeared to have no effect on their target. Isa just stared at his assassin, smiling.

"You are weak," he spoke in soft tones, "but my strength is made perfect in your weakness."

Suddenly, the man cried out in pain, dropping the gun. It clattered to the ground and appeared to glow red hot. He moaned, nursing his hand, which looked horribly burnt. He gazed in horror at the gun and then looked up to the figure before him with wide eyes.

Now the camera crews were rolling. They jostled the crowd to get closer to the Messiah.

Isa continued to gaze into the man's eyes. He raised his right hand towards his would-be assassin. The man cried out in fear and began moaning and praying repetitively, falling to his knees. He seemed to be witnessing a great horror which no one could see.

"No, Isa. Please, no!" he begged, his voice shaking with fear, "I am sorry, Allah... please. Oh, please."

"I AM," Isa pronounced loudly, "a God of mercy."

At that, some relief seemed to pass over the man's face, but his moans and supplications continued, quieter now.

People began falling to their knees in worship again.

"But mercy must be mingled with wrath."

Horror came over the man's face again, and the moaning repetitive prayers grew louder.

Behind Isa, the orb began pulsating brighter again, in orange and crimson. He turned around and began walking towards it. As he reached it, it appeared to glow white hot. He turned one last time and spoke.

"Remember, unity above doctrine. Unity before truth. Unity is Allah's will, and it will save you. Follow this command, and live. Goodbye for now, my friends."

With that, he stepped into the orb. Both he and the orb disappeared instantly. In its place, there was only the fountain, with water flowing out of it.

More gasps emerged from the crowd. Those nearest to the assassin looked down towards him. He lay on the ground, dead. A look of terror was frozen on his face.

The Mahabodhi temple in Bihar, India was swarming with worshippers. It was a beautiful, clear day; monks sat nearby under a Banyan tree with wooden boards, focusing inward. Tourists stood and admired the high temple walls with their elaborate engravings, while others walked through the beautiful park grounds.

At the nearby Bodhi Tree, a brilliant light suddenly began flaring near its highest branches. It ebbed and flowed, brighter and then duller, in changing colors of white, yellow, and crimson. A continuous stream of strange light sank down from somewhere high above, seeming to feed the apparition. No power lines or industrial lighting could be seen nearby to explain this strange sight. Onlookers gasped and began gathering towards the tree, trying to account for the phenomenon. Cellphones emerged and began recording.

The light grew brilliant white, causing the crowd to cry out and shield their eyes. Just as quickly, it dimmed again. Then, unbelievably, a translucent figure emerged from the glowing white orb of pure light and slowly began floating down to the ground, near the base of the Bodhi Tree. Although in mid-air, he sat in the half-lotus position, with legs crossed and arms slightly raised, and appeared to be in deep meditation, as he made his way to the ground.

The man was tall, with dark, shoulder-length hair, which flowed thickly around a majestic Middle Eastern face. He had a neatly trimmed beard, dark brown in color. He was broad-shouldered, and wore a long, flowing tan robe. His head and body seemed almost luminescent.

At first people backed away in terror, but as the being spoke, more and more crowds began to converge into the area.

Hindus shouted out, "It is Kalki!"

Buddhists cried, "It is Maitreya, finally come!"

But, despite the disagreement, a deafening, continuous chant began to emerge from the crowd, at first unsynchronized, but then as one. It could be heard for miles around. As more and more picked up the strain, the roar of the chant grew so loud that motorists in the outlying towns began stopping and getting out of their cars to listen to the strange, thunderous refrain:

"Maitreya! Maitreya! Maitreya!"

Weston hadn't been to work in almost a week. Their last project had wrapped up, and his brother-in-law had decided things were getting too crazy, so he had left town. Weston was watching the news, as he normally did each day.

On the TV, breaking news was showing a live feed of a cameraman following a female news anchor. She was running through a corridor of some sort, pushing people out of the way. The cameraman was struggling to keep up with her.

Suddenly, she turned and entered an enormous room. It was the sanctuary of a megachurch, filled with thousands of worshippers. They were all chanting and shouting. It was difficult to make out what they were yelling.

"I'm here at Grace Calvary," the reporter began in an excited voice, "where reports are coming in that we are witnessing the second coming of Jesus Christ, the Messiah!"

She continued to jostle for position, pushing her way towards the stage area.

"Local media," she yelled, trying to make her voice heard above the chanting crowd, "please move!"

Now on the TV, Weston was able to see a figure on the stage. It was a man; tall, with dark, shoulder-length hair, which flowed thickly around a majestic Middle Eastern face. He had a neatly trimmed beard, dark brown in color. He was broad-shouldered, and wore a long, flowing tan robe. His head and body seemed almost luminescent. There was an extremely bright light behind him. He was surrounded by men and women on the stage. They were all prostrating before him.

The crowd was going insane, some screaming, and others chanting in unison:

"Jesus! Jesus! Save us! Save us!"

Some worshippers raised their hands, tears flowing down their cheeks. Others danced vigorously in circles, while some fell to the ground and writhed and twisted like epileptics during a seizure.

The chanting grew deafening:

"Jesus! Jesus! Save us! Save us!"

The figure raised both hands. The roar of the crowd slowly began to dissipate.

"Hey, Ally," Weston yelled, "you gotta come see this! Hurry!"

Ally popped her head in from the kitchen.

"It must be the false Christ we were warned about!" he exclaimed, "They say he's been showing up everywhere."

"You've got to be kidding!" Ally exclaimed as she came in and sat down next to Weston. One by one the kids trickled in too and sat on the couch, entranced.

The crowd in the megachurch had gone silent. The Messiah figure continued to hold out both arms.

"Peace be to you," he stated.

Several hoops and hollers came from the crowd.

"I love you, Jesus!" screamed a middle-aged man from the crowd.

"I love you, too. This is definitely a friendly crowd here today," he joked, "if you've read much about me, you know I'm not quite used to that."

Peels of laughter emerged from the congregation.

"But in all seriousness, we have difficult things to discuss today," he continued, looking sober now, "hard things."

He paused. Every eye met his gaze.

"We are near the end, friends," he continued, "and my father and I want each of you to be there with us in Heaven. We are excited to have our Earth family finally join us, and I'm sure you are excited as well... But, there is a problem."

Groans came from the crowd.

"What is it?" shouted a woman, "Tell us!"

"Many of you will be raptured, and some of you must endure the seven years of tribulation, but in order for that to even begin, there must be unity... and there is not. There is not. I'll tell you what I'm going to do. Let me tell you a story, to illustrate the problem," he began, "there was once a young mother, a widow. Her name was Sarah."

Everyone sat in rapt attention.

"Before her husband died, Sarah gave birth to a son... named Malek. Malek was a happy child, full of life and promise, sometimes...you see, Malek was very, very sick. He went to many different doctors, but no one could figure out what was wrong with little Malek. All they knew was most days, he was too weak and nauseous to even get out of bed, let alone study in school, or play with other boys.

As time went on, a discovery was made. Little Malek had something strange in his system. It was called Alimemazine, and it should not have been there. An investigation began, and it was discovered that something very, very bad had happened. You see...Sarah had something called Munchausen by Proxy. She was poisoning her own child.

The one who gave him life, who said she loved him more than life itself, who should have been his ultimate protector, was poisoning him everyday and denying him a happy, fulfilling life."

The sanctuary was quiet as he continued.

"In the same way, you want true life with your heavenly father. You are tired of this Earth, and long for your eternal home, eternal life. You were not made just for...this," he said, gesturing with his hands towards everything around them.

"But someone is holding you back, keeping you spiritually sick and weak. They are poisoning you with ideas, like, I do not exist, or, the seventh day is special. My friends, Sunday is the day I have commanded you to keep. Most of the world has begun recognizing the Lord's Day, but some have not. Some have refused, and those people are intentionally hurting everyone, like that mother with her son. They are holding you back from true life.

And now it is my father's will that all religions unite, put aside their doctrinal differences, and unite and worship on the day I rose... in victory. Your heavenly father will never come in all his glory with the angels in Heaven if this problem is not resolved."

Now the figure began moving behind him towards the light, which began to glow brighter.

"Be faithful and unite," he said, "and I will give you a crown of life! All religions, sects and denominations MUST unite."

The crowd began cheering and shouting again, drowning him out.

The figure waved and stepped into the orb. Both he and the circle of light instantly disappeared.

At that, the anchor turned to her cameraman.

"Well, folks, you saw it here first," she said, "Jesus Christ has come back. Jesus Christ has returned. We're going to go to Bob in the studio for commentary on the incredible message we've just heard - "

Ally shut off the TV and turned towards Weston.

"How much time?" she asked.

"We'll leave by the end of the week," he announced slowly with resignation.

The next morning, Weston was watching the news again. Things were not going well. The war in Iran had halted, due to the bombings.

However, shortly after those nuclear strikes, Jerusalem had been overrun by units from Hamas and Hezbollah, and completely overtaken by Islam. They were saying blood had not flowed in the streets like this since the Romans had sacked the city in 70 A.D.

But since the appearance of Isa, there had been a truce of peace, and the killing had finally stopped. All were worshipping now, on the same day, from the Middle East to Africa, from Europe to South America; praying for deliverance and relief from the calamities. But relief would not come.

Eloba was racing through the Eastern Seaboard; further spread seemed inevitable. The government did not seem willing to create another 'zone.' And it was now moving to other countries such as England and France.

Record weather systems continued to cause devastation throughout the entire planet. In America, hurricanes blew down south, hundreds of F5 tornadoes tore up the Midwest, and earthquakes were everywhere. Thousands were dying every day in the U.S., and abroad it was said to be in the millions. Whatever this worldwide unity and worship was doing, it had not stopped the catastrophes.

Weston turned off the TV and looked out his window for the van. It was not there. He looked again in disbelief.

Nothing.

Every day it had been sitting in the same spot, in front of Ms. Averly's yard. Now it was gone. He looked up and down the street, but saw nothing suspicious.

Weston hadn't been outside in a while, and he wanted to check the mail. He decided if he was going to go outside, he better do it quickly. He walked out of his house, but immediately noticed something was off. He was looking where his mailbox was supposed to be, but there was only empty space. As he moved closer he saw that it had been knocked out of its footing, and was lying on the sidewalk, horribly dented. It sat next to one of the homeless men's tents.

He stood there looking at it, when suddenly a voice yelled at him from the side:

"Hey, Sabbath-keeper!"

Weston whirled towards the voice. As he did, he was hit with several raw eggs. They exploded in his face and began oozing down onto his shirt.

Weston rubbed the disgusting slime out of his eyes and struggled to look in the direction of the attack. Several youths stood before him, grinning. One had a crowbar in his hand and another a bat.

"You better get with the program this Sunday," a red-headed teenager with a flattop announced, pointing his crowbar at Weston, "or we're going to pay your family a little visit."

Weston could tell from the way he said 'little visit' that it would not be a friendly social call.

"Or we can just get things going right now," he spoke slowly, a widening grin on his face. "You got a problem? You wanna do something about it?"

Weston stood there speechless. Flattop and the others continued to stare. He could see the tension in their bodies, the hidden rage, waiting to be released. They all looked willing and eager to fight, or worse.

"No problem," he managed to speak up. His heart was racing and it was difficult to speak.

"I thought so, Sab-freak," Flattop answered triumphantly, "you just think about what's gonna happen. You just think about it."

The grin had gone away, and a look of hate took its place in Flattop's eyes.

"All this destruction in the world," he said, pointing at Weston again, "it's all your fault."

"But we're gonna fix the problem," Flattop continued softly, the smile returning now, "we're gonna fix it."

One by one, the antagonizers slowly turned and walked away.

As Weston turned around to walk back inside his house, he saw it.

The entire front of his house had been spray-painted. Several neighborly and welcoming messages had been haphazardly written across his front porch, windows, and siding:

'Seven Dayer.

You're gonna die, legalist.

You're killing us all.

Murderer.'

His favorite and the winner of the most creative message was:

'Sabbath Suck Face.'

As he walked back into the house, Ally and the kids saw the mess all over him and ran over.

"What happened?" Ally asked, her voice strained, "Why did you go outside?"

"Nothing happened," he replied flatly.

"What do you mean nothing, what did they do?" she demanded.

"Just a little neighborly visit," he said in a joking tone of voice, "it doesn't matter. We'll be gone by the end of the week."

Chapter 15 - Flight

The kids had all gone to bed and Weston and Ally were talking about better times; when they had first met. Ally liked to remind him occasionally, and she did so now, that he was lucky she went out with him on a second date, since on their first date, he had taken her to see Rambo Nine.

"Hey," he shot back, "it was practically billed as a rom-com! It was finally going to show Rambo's emotional side. How was I supposed to know it was going to change the rating system for violence in cinema?"

They held hands and laughed and talked, in the dim light of their bedroom lamps.

It was almost like old times, Weston thought. *Simpler times.*

Soon he slipped into a deep sleep, and Ally followed shortly after. His last thought as his eyelids grew heavy, was he hoped he would not dream.

In the dark, his phone began to vibrate. He drifted slightly out of sleep, but there was no desire at all to move.

It will stop, his tired mind told him. *Just go back to sleep.*

The phone vibrated again, sliding ever so slightly on the wood surface of the nightstand.

Ally shifted in bed and called out dreamily:

"What is it?"

He continued to lie in a comatose-like state, but he was now more aware. Someone was calling him.

Why? What time was it?

Another vibration.

More sliding.

"West," Ally complained, "what?"

The phone would not stop. He turned his body towards the alarm clock and opened his eyes.

1:03 am.

"Who is it?" Ally croaked.

"I dunno," he mumbled.

The dumb phone would not stop ringing.

He grabbed the phone and looked at the screen. It was a local number, but unknown. Something told him he should answer it. He swiped up to answer with his thumb and put the phone to his ear.

"Hello?" he grumbled.

"You've got five, maybe six minutes," a male voice spoke quietly on the other end of the line.

"Huh?" Weston responded.

"You remember all those stories we used to hear as kids about Communism, secret police coming in the middle of the night? Once they came for you, no one ever heard from you again."

"Ok," Weston stated.

Apparently, a crazy person was calling, or someone trying to harass them some more. Weston regretted answering the phone. He wanted to get back to sleep.

"I'm hanging up now," he announced.

"Weston, they're coming for you. Now you've got maybe five minutes," the man continued.

"Hey, how do you know my name?" he said, sitting up in bed. Ally sat up next to him, "If this is your idea of a sick joke, we've had enough harassment - "

" - You know that black van sitting in front of your house?" the voice asked.

The man now had his complete attention.

"I was in it. That's all I can say, except, I listened to you for weeks...and now I'm a believer. I gotta go, I've been on too long already. They'll see me. Now you've got four minutes. You don't want to know what they'll do to you if you get captured."

With that, the caller hung up.

Weston's mind was whirling. This was it.

We're not ready.

"Ally, we gotta go now," he whispered in her ear, pointing at the phone, implying it was listening. "Get the kids, I'll get the packs, meet me out back! We gotta go now! They're coming!"

Ally's eyes went wide, and she leaped out of bed. They both simultaneously threw on clothes and shoes. Ally ran down the hall to the kid's bedrooms while he practically vaulted the stairs and started grabbing food from the pantry and throwing it in a backpack.

He could hear the kids stirring upstairs and Ally shushing them to be quiet.

After filling two day packs with beans, rice, and dried fruit, he tossed the packs in the backyard. He met Ally and the kids in the hall.

"Everybody, let's go," he said hoarsely, in a near whisper, "backpacks, jackets, and hiking shoes on. Meet me in the backyard in one minute!"

The kids looked frightened as they hurriedly looked for their outdoor gear. Weston had forgotten his backpack upstairs and was angry that he had to waste time going back up to get it.

"West!" Ally said loudly.

"What?" he shot back, without slowing down at the stairs.

"West!" she repeated.

"What?" he exclaimed, turning around and raising both arms.

"Catch!" she said as she threw him her cellphone. He immediately raised his hands and caught it.

"If they're using them to track us," she explained, "we leave our phones in the closet. It buys us some time!"

He finally understood. A smile crossed his face.

"I love you!" he announced.

"Hurry!" she stated.

In the distance, they could hear the sound of engines revving. Several vehicles were approaching fast.

They were coming.

Weston ran upstairs, grabbed his and Ally's cellphones, and threw them in the closet. He picked up his backpack, hoisted one strap over his shoulder, and ran down the stairs.

When he had left, everyone was in the kitchen, but now the house was empty. He could hear several vehicles pulling up in front of the house.

He poked his head through the backdoor and looked both ways. To his left, he saw Ally motioning for him to follow. Braden and Dylan had already gone through the hole he made in the fence.

Suddenly, he heard an enormous crash at the front door. From where he was in the kitchen, anyone entering the house wouldn't see him. He quickly exited the back door and quietly shut it behind him.

As he moved through the backyard, bright flashes came through the windows followed by loud bangs. He quickly followed his family under the fence into Rick's yard.

He gave one last look towards his house. The moment felt unreal, as though it was happening to some other family. Through the upstairs windows, he could see beams from flashlights slashing this way and that. Soon the police would realize they had been fooled and would start searching the backyard and surrounding area.

Before he stooped down completely to get under the fence, he pulled their barbeque grill in front of the hole as best he could. At least if someone was looking from the back porch, they wouldn't see the hole very well.

As he came through the fence, he saw his family was making their way through Rick's yard. He caught up to Ally at the gate into the greenbelt.

"We made it!" she exclaimed. She seemed surprised they had gotten this far.

"We haven't made it yet," he replied, carefully unlatching the gate while looking back towards their house. No one was outside yet. "Follow me!"

When they reached the entrance to the culvert, it appeared dark and menacing. Weston suddenly had a flashback to his tunnel dream. It seemed a lifetime ago. He shrugged it off and crouched down, moving into the tunnel.

"Dad!" Charlotte called out.

"What?" he answered.

"I'm scared," she declared.

"Oh, honey," Ally answered, "Jesus is going to take care of us. In fact, let's pray before we take one step further. Weston," she turned towards him, "will you, please?"

He wanted so badly to get moving. But she was right. They could try to do this on their own, but without God leading and protecting them, it would never work.

"Of course," he relented.

After a short prayer for protection, guidance, and the strength to be faithful through the power of the Holy Spirit, Charlotte said she felt much better, and they traversed the tunnel with the aid of Braden's flashlight.

Once through the tunnel, they scrambled up the side of the drainage canal and moved into the street. The streets were dark and empty, being only 1:30 in the morning. A thick fog had settled over everything making it difficult to see more than twenty feet ahead. An occasional streetlight pierced the gloom, casting eerie shadows around houses and cars. They could hear multiple sirens in the distance.

As they continued on, suddenly a figure appeared in their path. It was too late to avoid them, so Weston pushed ahead as though nothing unusual was happening.

As they came closer, Weston could see it was an old lady walking her dog. The woman got a look of surprise on her face as she saw the family of five, hustling down the sidewalk with full backpacking gear on.

"Evening, ma'am," Weston nodded, trying to act as normal as possible.

The elderly woman did not return the greeting, but instead smirked. She seemed to read the whole thing at a glance.

After walking about ten more feet, Weston turned around and glanced at her. She had turned as well and was staring at them. She had her cellphone out and appeared to be dialing a number. She disappeared into the fog.

"Ally!" he muttered.

"I know!" she replied, looking back as well.

"Kids," Ally announced, "let's double-time it!"

Everyone started jogging, with Weston in the lead.

Now the sirens were much louder. It was difficult to tell how many there were, but Weston estimated three or four police cars, in addition to the original police that had first come. He had never seen them, so he had no idea how many there actually were.

Weston was beginning to stress out because the fog was making it difficult to retrace his steps. He had not bothered to memorize street names the first time because he hadn't anticipated having to return in the fog. Just as he was about to fully panic, he saw a familiar house. A wave of relief swept over him as he recognized they were in fact on the correct street. Then up ahead he saw it; the rundown abandoned house where he had parked the car. The Miller's silver Camry emerged from the fog, right where he had left it.

They hurried to the vehicle and unloaded their heavy packs in the trunk. All of them fit, but just barely. Unfortunately, the packs were probably going to reek of gasoline.

They pulled out of the driveway, without turning on the lights, and made their way onto the main road. Once they reached the intersection, Weston breathed a prayer of thanks and turned on the headlights.

The normally busy street only had the occasional car driving down it due to the hour. Weston had to pay extra attention to the road for two reasons; one, they were clearly now wanted by the police, and two, they were without their cell phones and the navigation they provided.

As they drove by the neighborhood where their house was, Weston saw a strange sight. Through the thick fog, police lights were reflecting upward into the mist, in blue and red flashes. The whole family turned to look at the strange sight, trying to catch a glimpse of their home, which they would likely never see again.

As they neared the entrance ramp to Highway 80, the tension in Weston's body started to ease a bit; they would make it out after all. He entered the freeway ramp and picked up speed, heading eastbound towards Reno, and the Sierra Nevadas.

They had been driving half an hour in the dark. Braden, Dylan, and Charlotte had fallen asleep in the backseat. Braden's head leaned against the side window, rocking slightly with the car's motion. Dylan and Charlotte slept on each other.

"Should we turn on the radio?" Ally asked in a whisper.

"I don't want to wake the kids," he responded quietly, "besides, I think we know what it would say."

"We're never going back, are we?" Ally asked. Her voice broke as she finished her sentence.

"We just have to think about what we're going to do now. And what Jesus has prepared for us in Heaven," Weston replied, trying to comfort her. He paused for a moment, speaking reflectively, "We're going to see it really soon."

"West?" Ally asked.

"Yes, honey?"

Ally hesitated.

"Are we sealed?" she asked.

"I've been thinking about that," he answered quickly, "actually a lot. According to the Bible and the spirit of prophecy, at this point in Earth's history, we should be...but I don't feel sealed."

"Neither do I," she agreed, "it makes sense that if people have already taken the mark of the beast, either in the forehead or the hand, oh, by the way, I finally understand that now."

"Yeah?" he asked.

"Taking it in the forehead means believing it with all your heart. Taking it in the hand means just going along to get along, so you won't be punished by the government," she explained, "but that's why the seal of God is only in the forehead, not the hand too, because when you follow God there is no faking it or serving Him to escape a punishment. You either believe it with all your heart and follow it or you don't."

"Well said," he agreed.

"But I think we have the seal of God now, since the mark of the beast is happening now," she went on, "I feel like I have changed. I feel like Christ has transformed my character. I don't get as mad or impatient as I used to, I feel like my faith in Him is stronger...but, I still feel like an unworthy sinner. Unworthy of His grace, and by no means do I feel sinless, even though I cannot recall committing an actual sin for some time."

"I think we will always feel sinful and unworthy, even to the very end. And I'm going through some agony inwardly right now, to be honest, that there might be unconfessed sins in my past. And that there might still be sin in my life. But I know what you mean, I can't recall a recent sin, and that's new for me. I feel a repulsion towards it, that I didn't feel before. It's hard to explain," he stated.

"I understand," she agreed.

To Weston it seemed that they were in total unison, total agreement. There was a oneness now. They did not even need to speak the words. Something had changed in their relationship and it was good. He wondered if it was something closer to what their union would be like in Heaven.

It was now two o'clock in the morning, and they were passing through Auburn. They had lifted out of the fog about ten minutes ago. They could see the lights of the quaint downtown to the right, and Highway 49 pushing northward off into the distance to the left. The initial adrenaline was wearing off, and Weston was getting tired. Ally noticed.

"You want me to drive?" she asked.

"No, no. I'm ok. Maybe in a little bit?" he answered.

The freeway twisted and turned through the town. They had gone through the first two exits when they saw it. A large digital billboard that occasionally changed images. It had been displaying an advertisement for HealthNet when suddenly the entire Miller family appeared on the screen.

Ally gasped.

Weston stared at the image in surprise. It was a family portrait they had taken about a year ago. He couldn't believe the government had obtained it and downloaded it for public display so quickly. Underneath there was a message which read:

WANTED FOR QUESTIONING. IF SEEN, PLEASE CALL 1-800-479-2934.

Weston and Ally sat in silence. They were now fugitives. As the Camry crested a large hill, another surprise awaited them. Weston's heart sank.

Below them sat a police barricade on the eastbound side of the freeway. Several police cars were blocking all three lanes, lightbars flashing. All cars were being funneled into one lane where an officer was questioning each vehicle. There was no way to turn off and go around.

Weston kicked himself. If only he had exited earlier they could have figured out a way around this, but now it was too late. To stop now would invite a chase. The only thing to do was get in line and pray.

As the car slowed down, all the kids woke up.

"Oh, no," Braden exclaimed, seeing the barricade.

"Let's just pray kids, right now," Weston asked.

"Dear Lord," Charlotte began immediately, "You know we want to escape to the mountains, but these men are going to stop that, unless You do something... God, I know You can do something. The Bible says the Earth is the Lord's, and the fullness thereof. You own everything. Please send an angel to help us right now. In Jesus' name, amen."

Ally and Weston raised their eyebrows and exchanged glances. They were both amazed at their youngest child's simple but powerful prayer. This was the first time she had ever wanted to pray out loud.

"Ok, let's do this," Weston steeled himself to meet what was up ahead.

There were two cars in front of them. An officer was talking to a third car that was stopped with the window rolled down. There were two other cruisers with police in them, parked sideways in the freeway lanes. Both of those officers remained in their cars.

Weston could see that the main officer had a routine. He would go to the window, retrieve the license and registration, and return to his vehicle and check the identification on his computer. Then he would return to the vehicle, give back the items, and let the car move on.

A few minutes had passed, and now it was their turn. Weston was sweating and his heart was beating fast as he pulled up to the officer and stopped, engine running.

"Go ahead and turn off your engine for me," the policeman said as he came to the window.

He was a young man with brown hair styled in a crewcut. His arms bulged out of his service uniform. His nametag said: Chandler.

Everything in Weston fought against turning off the car. He keyed the ignition off.

"License and registration," he asked.

"Certainly," Weston replied nervously. He fumbled for his wallet, while Ally pulled the vehicle registration out of the glove box.

"What has you out this time of night?" the officer inquired.

"We're taking a trip," Weston replied curtly.

"Sunday is in two days," he lectured, "you make sure you don't travel then, you understand?"

"Yes, sir," Weston answered.

He took the identification and walked back to his cruiser.

"I'll be back," he stated.

Weston and Ally held hands and prayed. In the back, Dylan and Charlotte began praying, too.

Officer Chandler returned to Weston's window. Weston noticed one of the other officers was coming over as well. Chandler had his right hand resting on the holster of his service pistol.

"Sir, I'm going to need you to step out of the vehicle," he stated with tension in his voice.

Behind them, Weston could see another police cruiser pulling up to the roadblock. The vehicle parked and two new officers got out. Their lightbar stayed on, red and blue alternatively flashing into the night.

"Sir," Chandler ordered, "out of the car."

"Yes, sir. Sorry," Weston answered.

It was over. What would happen to Ally and the kids? He couldn't think about it.

Without even looking at Ally, he opened the door and got out.

The two new officers were making their way towards Officer Chandler.

"Turn around and place your hands on the vehicle," Officer Chandler ordered.

Weston slowly turned around, faced the Camry, and put his hands on the trunk. He was already being treated like a criminal. All a criminal could do was take orders, and be punished, which would be what was going to happen for the rest of his life now.

The other two officers approached them, presumably to assist in the arrest. They must have figured out by now who he was and that he had evaded them. He was a fugitive from the law and these additional officers were coming to help subdue him if he resisted. Weston had seen enough TV to know the futility of fighting, all that did was bring more and more police. And it was not God's will.

As a Christian, he knew Jesus would want him to submit to the authorities until that submission conflicted with following Him. But he had wanted so badly to get away, not end up in a cell. Perhaps this whole thing had just been him being selfish, wanting to be free. Weston reflected that their plan hadn't been very smart after all. It had been unrealistic to think they could subvert the system and get away. God seemed to have had other plans.

"Do you have any drugs or weapons on you tonight?" Chandler asked, frisking him.

"No," Weston answered, fighting back tears.

"What's the situation?" one of the new officers asked, coming up beside Chandler.

He was a tall, Caucasian man in his late twenties, with a large build. The other officer stood next to him, listening. He looked eerily similar to the first officer, but was Latino.

"Suspect is wanted for RWE violation and flight," Chandler answered briskly, "we have to take him in."

"Actually, you have to go," the Latino officer stated matter-of-factly, "we'll handle the arrest from here."

Officer Chandler turned and stared at them with annoyance. His body exuded tension. Then slowly his face took on a peculiar, sluggish look. He seemed to be gazing somewhere else, staring at something none of them could see. His eyes looked glassy.

"Could you go ahead and head into town, pick up some chow for the unit?" the first officer requested, "We're sorry relief came so late."

"Sure, ok," Officer Chandler responded dully.

He turned and headed towards his police car. He began talking to one of the other officers who had gotten out of his car to assist. They both turned and went back to their vehicles. Officer Chandler pulled out and headed down the highway in his patrol car.

The Latino officer turned to Weston.

"You're free to go now, sir," he said briskly.

Weston stared at the two men, fighting his emotions. Could they be what he thought they were?

"What? Are you...?" he asked, voice quivering. He was unable to finish the sentence.

A hint of a smile crept over the officer's face.

"Go ahead and head out, there's not much time," he answered.

Weston turned stiffly in obedience and got in his car. He turned the key in the ignition and placed his hands on the wheel. The lightbar was still flashing from the new officer's cruiser.

Ally's face was streaked with tears.

"What happened?" she demanded.

"I don't know," he responded in confusion, "but we're leaving. Just praise God for it."

As he pulled forward to move through the barricade the red and blue lights continued to flash. Suddenly, he noticed an absence of light. He glanced in his rear view mirror.

He could not see the Caucasian and Latino officers anymore. Their police cruiser was also gone. It had been less than ten seconds since he had spoken to them, but they were no longer there.

They only made one stop to refuel. Weston was glad he had placed the gas cans in the trunk earlier. As they continued to ascend the mountains, the first hints of sunrise were coming up in the east. Patches of faint orange and red began to streak the sky. Night was turning into day, and the Millers sang songs of praise as the car sped along the highway. In between songs, Charlotte continued to recount what had now been termed the 'angel encounter.'

"Honey, should we get out some breakfast?" Ally asked. She was now behind the wheel.

"Sure," Weston responded, "I am getting pretty hungry, actually. Kids, how about you?"

"Yeah, Dad," Braden answered.

A bag full of Cliff Bars and bananas was passed around. Dylan said grace, and they all began to eat.

"So, what exit is it?" Ally asked.

"It has been a while," he hesitated, "I'll know it when I see it, I hope."

They continued to drive. Partial snowy peaks ascended upward on both sides of the freeway, covered with thick pines. Occasionally, a pair of headlights would pass them going the other way, but they saw no more police.

Soon, they reached Soda Springs and turned right off the freeway, then northbound on the overpass. The two-lane road was old and windy. There were still remnants of snow on the mountains and in shady spots in the forest. As they passed by several empty ski resorts, Weston couldn't help admiring the beauty of the wilderness. He thanked God He had allowed them to stay free and escape the craziness of the city. It would be peaceful here. Hard but peaceful.

"Let's park here," Weston suggested as they neared a large abandoned parking lot.

Ally turned in and parked the car. They both sat there for a moment, surveilling the area. It appeared to be an old ski resort of some kind.

"It would be best if we moved the car out of sight," Weston suggested.

Ally nodded in agreement.

"What about over there," she pointed, "on the far side of that building?"

Ahead of them was the lodge. No one was in sight.

"Yeah," he agreed.

She drove to the backside of the building, away from the street and parked. They all got out of the car and began organizing their packs on the ground.

"I don't think anyone will be able to see it from the street," Weston noted, "it's good."

He looked around. He could not see a hint of anyone around them for miles in any direction, and they hadn't seen anybody for at least the last hour. Weston began taking all the food in the car and distributing it to each child. They quickly stuffed Cliff bars in their pant and coat pockets.

Weston looked to the far end of the parking lot. He knew just around the bend lay a trailhead for a path that would intersect the Pacific Crest Trail. They would get to that trail and reassess from there. He worried about running into people. He knew the PCT could be teeming with people in about a month. However, the era of section hikers and thru-hikers was surely over; people were just trying to survive. But just the same, he worried many would have the same idea.

"Everybody ready?" he asked, hoisting his pack over his right shoulder, then swinging his left arm through the other strap. He began buckling his waist and chest straps.

"Yeah," the kids answered.

Weston began walking and everybody followed, moving out in the direction of the trailhead. Soon they were hiking on the hard soil path, hidden among the pine trees. They moved up and down, through twists and turns, until they were immersed in the forest.

Through a space in the trees, Weston caught a glimpse of the parking lot and the car. He glanced at it one last time. A pang of sadness came over him as he realized he would probably never see it again. It was silly, as it was just a piece of machinery. But it had been a faithful servant to them, nonetheless. The car had helped them escape, and was their last link to their old life.

The trail, surrounded on both sides by tall pines, began to slope up in elevation, and everyone slowed down, pushing harder to get up the hill. As they reached the top, they emerged into a clearing and a stunning view awaited them. The sunrise cast long shadows of purple, orange and pink through the jagged peaks in the distance. They could see the faint outline of the Pacific Crest Trail winding up the next mountain range until it disappeared. As they stopped to take in the view, they shivered from the morning chill.

"Let's keep moving," Ally suggested, "it's cold."

By lunchtime it had warmed up and they stopped by a boulder to eat. To their left, an enormous valley swept below them, covered in low sagebrush and pine. In the distance, the valley ascended again to another mountain peak similar in size. To their right, an endless series of mountain ranges spanned the horizon.

They continued their hike through the afternoon without seeing anyone. By dinnertime, Weston estimated they had hiked over ten miles. Their water was gone and the kids were exhausted. He and Ally began looking for a place to camp for the night.

As they rounded a bend, they saw a lake not far ahead. This would be the perfect spot to camp. They could stop, filter water from the lake, and cook dinner with their backpacking stoves. As they got closer, Weston could see the lake was about half a mile long, with mountain peaks rising up from its base on the far side of the water.

They found a small clearing near the water, but it still had the cover of trees, so they felt safe. Weston took Dylan to filter some water while Ally, Braden, and Charlotte made camp. When they got back, the smell of a backpacking meal filled the air. Weston's stomach growled.

"Mmhh, smells good," he said.

"Mountain House's finest," Ally quipped.

"Good stuff," he returned.

"I'm starving," Dylan announced.

"Walking all day will do that to you," Ally said, "let's eat!"

After dinner they talked for a while and got ready for bed. The kids wanted to have a fire, but Weston and Ally decided against it. It would make them easier to spot, and they worried the authorities would be looking for them.

They had brought a Bible, and Weston asked Dylan if he would read Psalm 91. Dylan turned his flashlight towards its pages and began:

"He who dwells in the secret place of the Most High will abide under the shadow of the Almighty. I will say of the Lord, He is my refuge and my fortress, my God, in Him I will trust. Surely He will deliver you from the snare of the fowler and from the perilous pestilence. He shall cover you with His feathers, and under His wings you shall take refuge; His truth shall be your shield and buckler.

You shall not be afraid for the terror by night, nor for the arrow that flies by day. Nor of the pestilence the walks in darkness, nor of the destruction that lays waste at noonday. A thousand may fall at your side, and ten thousand at your right hand, but it will not come near you. Only with your eyes will you look, and see the reward of the wicked. Because you have made the Lord, who is my refuge, even the Most High, your dwelling place, no evil shall befall you, nor shall any plague come near your dwelling.

For He shall give His angels charge over you, to keep you in all His ways, they shall bear you up, lest you dash your foot against a stone. You shall tread upon the lion and the cobra; the young lion and the serpent you shall trample underfoot.

Because he has set his love upon Me, therefore I will deliver him. I will set him on high, because he has known My name. He shall call upon Me, and I will answer him. I will be with him in trouble; I will deliver him and honor him. With long life I will satisfy him, and I will show him My salvation."

"Well read, son," Weston complimented.

"Thanks, Dad," Dylan replied.

"I think those promises are so important right now," Weston began, "we're at the very end of history, and soon the seven last plagues will fall. But God promises to protect those who dwell with Him. Those who've developed that personal relationship with Him, that I know you all have. For me, what stands out too, is at the end He says He will be with us in trouble. Not necessarily remove trouble from us, but be by our side as it's happening."

Weston paused.

"These next few weeks, or months...or possibly years, aren't going to be easy. And I think from my studies it will be three to six months, tops. So, as we go through this tough time, remember what Jesus said, He said when you see all these things begin to come to pass, look up, and lift up your heads, for your redemption draweth nigh. Jesus is coming soon, and it will all be worth it."

Chapter 16 - The Pursuit

Their sore bodies slept well that night. Early in the morning, Ally awoke and started making breakfast. The smell of food began to rouse the family, and one by one the Millers emerged from their tents.

After breakfast, they packed up and got ready to move out again. Everyone was sore, and the thought of walking again was not a welcome prospect. Weston was glad he had bought everyone Altra shoes; their wide toe box prevented blisters.

"Where to, chief?" Ally asked playfully.

"To fresh hunting grounds," he joked, playing along. They were all packed up, and moving onto the PCT again. "Actually, I was thinking - "

" - Dad, look!" Braden yelled, pointing ahead.

Everyone turned to where Braden was pointing. Behind them, on the trail, a lone figure walked towards them. He was coming from the direction they had traveled yesterday. He had just rounded a bend and was only fifty yards away.

"West..." Ally said nervously.

"It's ok," he reassured her, "I'll check it out."

Weston moved in front of his family and walked towards the man. His kids slowly followed. Ally, resigned to the fact that they were all apparently going, took up the rear.

As Weston walked towards the stranger, he waved. The man waved in return. He was tall, thin, and appeared in his mid fifties. He had a full head of salt and pepper hair with a short gray beard.

"Where are you coming from, friend?" Weston asked tensely. He stood protectively in front of his family, ready for anything.

"Highway 80," he replied in a friendly tone, "you don't want to go that way. Police and military everywhere."

"Why would we want to avoid the police?" Weston asked, testing him.

The man gave him a smirk.

"We're all Adventists, aren't we?" he stated matter-of-factly.

"How do I know you're Adventist?" Weston challenged.

"Fear God, and give Him glory, for the hour of His judgment has come...that began in 1844," he added, "and worship Him who made, the heavens and the Earth, and the sea... that's a reference to the fourth command - "

" - All right, all right, you're Adventist," Weston stopped him.

"Name's Geoffrey," he introduced himself.

Ally and the kids came close, gathering around.

"I'm Weston," Weston answered, "this is my wife, Ally. My sons Braden and Dylan and my daughter Charlotte."

"So nice to meet you all," Geoffrey stated.

"Did you live in the Sacramento area?" Weston asked.

"Yeah, I went to Central," Geoffrey answered.

"We went to Roseville," Weston said.

"Ahhh," Geoffrey stated, "good stuff...So, they're down there. Near the trailhead, by the freeway."

"How many?" Weston asked.

"Lots. A dozen police. Several military units," he answered.

"Did they have dogs?" Ally asked worriedly.

"I don't know," he replied, "but I do think they're going to come up. Try to clear out the trails. I had to hide and move through thick brush to get past them."

"I think we're going to need to go off trail," Weston stated worriedly.

"Do you know how to do that, honey? I mean, no offense," Ally asked.

"None taken," he replied, "I mean, it's far from ideal. Easy to get lost...but, in a way, that's what we're trying to do now. Stay lost."

"I agree," Geoffrey chimed in, "we can't stay on the PCT. It's like a human highway. They'll be checking it. I think I can get us to Independence Lake. Should be about a day's walk from here... but, we have to be careful now. We need to get more remote than this. Get into the high country."

"I agree," Weston concurred, "we can't have unfriendly locals seeing us and calling the police. We need lakes for water, but some of these lakes have people. Streams or rivers would be better."

"Well... shall we?" Geoffrey asked, extending his arm towards the north.

They began walking single-file in the morning sun. After a few minutes, their stiff joints loosened and their cold hands and feet began to warm.

The sun was going into its final stretch for the day, beginning its descent below the mountain peaks. It had been a long day of hiking. They had gotten into a rhythm, but now everyone was exhausted. They were stopping for a quick water break. The adults sat side by side on a nearby log while the kids leaned against a large boulder. Weston was just getting ready to ask Geoffrey if he had any family, when they heard it.

At first, Weston thought he had imagined it. A repetitive rat-a-tat-a-pat-a-tat-a thumping in the distance. He turned to look at Ally. Geoffrey tilted his head slightly to listen.

"Did you hear that?" Weston questioned.

Ally didn't speak, but seemed frozen in place, straining to hear. The noise came again, but this time louder. It seemed to be coming from an adjacent valley, echoing off of mountains and canyons.

"What do we do?" Ally asked frantically.

"Get under cover!" Geoffrey yelled, "Follow me!"

He began running off the trail towards a large clump of pines a couple hundred yards away. Everyone followed his example and began scrambling in the direction of the trees.

As they closed in on the edge of the forest, the helicopter grew louder and emerged from behind a nearby peak. Weston and the kids didn't look back, but sprinted the last ten yards, their backpacks shimmying left and right, until they made it into the trees. Geoffrey and Ally were waiting for them.

"Do you think they saw us?" Braden yelled, gasping.

The noise from the chopper was even louder now. It appeared to be headed right for them.

"I don't know," Weston answered, trying to catch his breath.

The helicopter kept moving towards them and began hovering about two hundred feet above them. Weston could see men in the cockpit, looking down at them.

"We're caught!" Braden cried in dismay.

"It's ok," Geoffrey shouted above the noise of the blades, "they can't land anywhere!"

"But they'll direct them right to us," Ally yelled, turning to Weston, "we're sitting ducks! What are we going to do?"

Weston tried to think. He was beginning to panic. A voice told him to calm down, all would be well.

Lord, please help us, he prayed.

"Let's move deeper into the forest," he yelled, "maybe they won't see us if we move further in. Reinforcements could be over a day away, for all we know."

Everyone stood there, staring at him.

"Let's move!" he yelled, pushing through low brush and rocks.

They began to move deeper into the forest, through thick grasses, bushes and trees. The chopper tried to follow them, but after a while it began to fall behind, and then it started moving off to the left. It seemed to have lost track of them.

Soon, they emerged into a large clearing. It was dark and flashlights were broken out. The helicopter seemed miles away now. Geoffrey stated what they were all thinking:

"I'm sorry, but I think we're going to have to keep moving, at least for a while. We know they have a firm position on where we were. We have to put some distance between us and that location."

"I agree," Weston stated reluctantly, looking off towards the direction of the chopper.

They trudged on for another hour. Geoffrey had his compass and flashlight out and stated he could guide them further north to another lake. A short time later, the noise of the helicopter faded. Weston looked back periodically as they walked. The kids were clearly exhausted. Charlotte was now in the rear, dragging her feet. She looked beyond tired.

"Guys," he announced, "I think we should stop for the night."

Everyone agreed and they made camp in a small dirt area surrounded by large trees. The kids wolfed down bars and dried fruit. Ally broke out additional Cliff Bars and handed them to the men.

"We'll need to keep watch from now on," Geoffrey said to Weston, pulling him aside, "they'll be tracking us now."

"You're right," Weston agreed, "I guess I'll go first? Three watches: nine to twelve, twelve to three, and three to six?"

"Sounds good," Geoffrey agreed, "I'll take midnight."

"I've got three to six then," Ally chimed in.

"Get some chow and go to bed," Weston instructed Geoffrey, "I'll wake you up soon."

Weston's watch passed without incident. The forest was eerily silent. He stared up at the night sky almost the entire time. Here in the mountains, the number of stars was overwhelming. He was awed by its beauty. Around midnight, he woke up Geoffrey and went to bed next to Ally. He passed out due to sheer exhaustion. The night passed without incident.

In the morning, Weston was awakened by a high-pitched whine. Everyone got up, and came out of their tents. It was Charlotte who first saw them.

"Look!" she shouted, pointing to the east.

Silhouetted against the sunrise, six men flew a hundred feet in the air in tight formation. They appeared to be soldiers, and were headed in their direction. The sight appeared impossible, but as they drew nearer, Weston could see they were wearing military jet suits.

"Down!" Ally yelled, as the soldiers flew closer.

Everyone dove to the ground. It was unlikely they would be seen, but Weston was worried about the tents. Fortunately, the team of flying soldiers veered off to the left, about a thousand yards away. As they came closer to the hideaways, the sound of the jet engines grew louder.

Weston raised up cautiously to stare at them. They were all holding their arms straight out at their sides, small jet turbines on each arm, and pushing themselves forward. He could see they were heavily armed, with machine guns hanging from harnesses at their front.

Weston glanced worriedly at Ally.

"Military?" She whispered.

Gradually they moved off into the distance, the sound fading.

"They're looking for us!" Geoffrey exclaimed.

No one needed to be told what to do. They all hurriedly packed up and moved out behind Geoffrey. After several hours of brisk walking they stopped to eat, gazing at the blue mountains in the distance. Weston wanted to disappear into those mountains. It was late afternoon when they arrived at the lake Geoffrey was guiding them to.

"Well, this is it," he announced, walking point.

In the distance, they saw a large concrete dam, extending downward into a bed of boulders. From where they were standing, it was not possible to see the lake on the other side, but they could see trees pushing out around what appeared to be a body of water. They could now see a trail again, winding all the way to the top of the dam where a road transversed it. On the other side a tunnel appeared to bore into the mountain.

Weston was relieved to be back on a man-made trail and out of the bush, where one had to rely completely on a compass. As they slowly ascended the hill leading to the dam, Weston marveled at its size. It appeared to be hundreds of yards across.

Suddenly, a new sound could be heard in the distance: the barking of dogs.

Everyone turned in alarm towards the sound. Weston could tell it was coming from behind them. He recognized the wail of hound dogs. They were being followed.

"Dogs!" Geoffrey called out, stating the obvious.

"We're being tracked!" Weston declared, "Run for the tunnel!"

"Wait!" Geoffrey shouted, "We have to split up!"

Weston didn't like this idea. He gave him a look of disapproval.

"It'll slow them down!" he explained.

It was hard to argue with that. Weston knew he was right.

"Ok," he relented, "we'll meet up at the far side of the lake. That tunnel must come out near there."

"Right!" Geoffrey yelled, "We'll meet again soon!"

The Millers began running up the last bit of hill to the dam entrance. Soon they reached the top and began running on the paved road. Weston turned to look behind them as they ran. In the distance he could see a group of men running behind a pack of dogs. Behind them ran another group with rifles.

"Go!" he yelled, as he turned back towards the tunnel. The Millers picked up the pace, backpacks swinging uncomfortably from side to side. As they neared the entrance to the tunnel, a small chunk of concrete exploded about ten feet in front of them. A loud rifle report echoed through the mountains.

"They're shooting!" Ally screamed, not breaking stride.

"Keep going," he yelled, "we're almost there!"

A second chunk of concrete exploded to their left. The boom of the gun reached them a second later. Now they were in. The tunnel was alarmingly dark, causing them to slow down. Everyone leaned over, gasping and trying to catch their breath. It was difficult to see, but at least they were safe from the shooters. Weston fished a flashlight from Ally's pack. It was difficult in the blackness.

"They're trying to kill us!" Braden exclaimed.

Weston didn't know what to say. He turned on the flashlight and pointed it deeper into the tunnel. He could only see about thirty yards ahead. The tunnel was about twenty feet wide with a two lane road. On the walls, there was occasional piping and machinery. In the distance, he saw periodic green lamps. Weston got a chill up his spine. It was eerily like his tunnel nightmare. He shook off a foreboding feeling.

"Let's move," he ordered, "we'll punch out the other side and try to lose them!"

Needing little encouragement, everyone started running forward into the blackness. Weston pointed the flashlight ahead, its beam bouncing back and forth as he ran. The green lamps provided minimal light.

The sound of the dogs had faded, but now they could be heard again. The police were gaining on them. As they continued to run forward, Weston glanced behind him. He could see the entrance of the tunnel in the distance now. Outlined against it, he saw several dark figures entering.

As they continued to run towards the far end, the tunnel began to curve, and more and more water gathered on the ground. Soon their feet were splashing in water several inches deep. Weston turned back and suddenly saw another smaller tunnel moving upward to the right. It could only be seen when going back towards the front entrance. As he looked forward into the main tunnel, he could not see the end. However, from this smaller side tunnel, a faint light penetrated through the darkness. Suddenly, he had an idea.

"Ally!" he called out.

"What?" she cried.

"Give me your sweater!" he demanded.

Too tired and stressed to argue, she reached behind her, grabbed it, and handed it to Weston. He quickly took it and threw it as hard as he could in the direction they were headed. It flew about thirty feet and landed on the wet ground with a splat.

"Now follow me, quickly! Stay in the water," he ordered.

"Oh," Ally stated as they all ran to the smaller tunnel. She understood her husband was hoping the water would mask their scent. Once the dogs lost the trail, the authorities would spot the sweater and assume the Millers had continued in that direction. If nothing else, it might buy them some time.

They ran up a long set of concrete stairs, which was only wide enough for one person. Weston could hear the echoing of the dogs in the main tunnel. The Millers made a sharp left turn which caused the barking to fade. Weston's hopes rose as the light ahead grew brighter. He pushed harder.

As they rounded a final bend, his heart sank. Up ahead was the exit, but it was blocked by a metal gate. As they reached it, Weston tried the lock, then shook the gate in frustration. He looked up and down, but there was no way around it. The space between each metal slat was narrow, but not impossible to get through. Charlotte and Dylan had already taken off their packs, left them on the ground, and begun squirming through. Ally went next, taking off her pack and squeezing her body, with much effort, between the bars. Next went Braden. Unfortunately, he had gotten stockier in the last three months, and he could not seem to fit his chest through the limited space. Weston pushed on him, but finally Braden cried out to stop, and he came back in. Weston knew there was no way he was going to fit through those slats. A feeling of total hopelessness came over him. He saw the same in Ally's eyes.

"West!" she said, beginning to cry. She started to try to come back through.

"No!" he said firmly, "You, Char and Dylan will go on. You have to go on. Braden and I will try to sneak back out and get behind them...we'll meet at the far side of the lake."

Ally seemed to understand he was only trying to fool her.

"No," she sobbed, holding his hand, "that won't work. It won't!"

Suddenly, the sound of dogs grew louder, coming up behind them. Ally's eyes went wide.

"Weston," she cried.

"You have to leave!" he demanded, "Get going, or they'll catch you."

He and Braden began handing them items they would need: the water filter, sleeping bags, food.

"I'm not leaving you," she managed to get out, her voice shaking.

Charlotte and Dylan sobbed uncontrollably, holding onto the gate.

"You must leave," he demanded, looking into her eyes, "they cannot catch Dylan and Char. You understand? You meet up with Geoffrey. Braden and I will be fine."

"No, you won't," she sobbed.

"I love you," he said, looking into her eyes, then at his kids.

With that, he grabbed Braden and started running towards their pursuers. If he couldn't escape from them, at least he could divert their attention away from Ally, Dylan and Charlotte. By the time they were arrested, hopefully the rest of his family would have gotten away.

Weston began yelling at the top of his lungs. His son seemed to understand and began yelling too. As they rounded a corner, they came upon three loud, barking hounds with their owners. Behind them was a police officer with pistol drawn, pointed in the air. The dogs, already excited, went insane when they saw them. Their owners' eyes went wide, and they struggled to keep the hounds under leash. The officer immediately lowered his gun and pointed it at them.

"Get on the ground! Get on the ground!" he screamed, clearly startled.

The dogs continued their insane barking. The sound was deafening in the small space. Weston got down on his knees and raised his hands up in the air. Braden followed suit. Within seconds, half a dozen police and military-types surrounded them, forcing handcuffs on their wrists.

Weston was shoved roughly from behind. He and Braden struggled to stay upright. Several of the officers were laughing. He thought with bitter irony that they had been so successful in getting out of the city, but he had only been able to stay free for three days.

Lord, please don't let them find my family. Keep them safe, he prayed.

He glanced over at Braden, who returned his stare.

"Stay strong, son," he instructed.

From out of the corner of his eye, Weston saw a black object moving towards him. As he turned toward it, a billy club smashed into his face and everything went black.

Chapter 17 - Interrogation

It was dark and cold. Weston lay on the concrete floor, miserable, his body aching and head throbbing. Only a tiny amount of light emitted into the room from a small metal window ten feet above him. To his right, there was a shiny metal toilet and sink combo. There was nothing else in the room, which he estimated to be about ten feet long and five feet wide. There was no one else with him, and he could not see outside into the hall, thanks to a solid steel door.

It seemed like a week since he had last seen Ally, Dylan and Charlotte. He had no idea what had happened to them. After getting himself and Braden back to the highway, the authorities had separated them into different vehicles. Weston had not seen Braden since.

He had eaten only once since his capture. Last night, a tray of stale bread had been shoved through a slat in the door without a word. A metal cup of water had been included. He had quickly swallowed the water and wolfed down the bread.

Nights were spent shivering uncontrollably in the darkness on the cold, unforgiving concrete floor. He longed for even a thin mattress and a blanket. Days were spent in mind-numbing boredom.

Try as he might to stop it, his thoughts kept returning to Ally and the kids. Had they escaped? He replayed the final scenes in his mind again and again. He had told her to leave, but she had refused to move away from the gate. He continued to picture her face, her tears. The look of dread on Dylan and Char's faces.

It had been a two day hike back to Highway 80, handcuffed and tethered to a soldier, and not a word had been spoken to him. He knew nothing, and it was driving him insane.

Not a word had been spoken to him since entering this place either. He hadn't seen another living soul, other than a pair of guards who had pushed him roughly into this cell. Weston was disoriented, starving, thirsty, but worst of all, racked with agony over the fate of his family. Especially Braden. Braden was surely somewhere within these walls. He prayed for strength for Braden and for his family. Prayed that they would find Geoffrey and he would help them remain free. There could only be a short time now: Earth's story was winding down.

As he passed the long hours, waves of panic would wash over him. He was trapped in this tiny cell and there was no escape. He was no longer in control of his life, and he could no longer protect his family. How he longed to be with them again, in the wide open spaces of the mountains. Time after time he would get on his knees and fervently pray, tears streaming down his cheeks. Pray for the Lord to take his mind somewhere else. He could be free in his mind, even if his body was trapped here.

Repeatedly, he turned to scriptures he could remember, verses here and there. Why had he not tried to memorize more of the Bible? It would have been such a comfort in this place. He rehearsed over and over what he could remember, and sometimes it seemed he could recite whole passages. Maybe not the exact words, but the scenes, and the order of them, and the concepts that Jesus conveyed.

He knew he should not worry about tomorrow. Jesus had been clear about that on the Sermon on the Mount. He knew he had to forgive his captors, and follow their orders, as long as it didn't conflict with his duty to God. One passage he had memorized brought him much comfort. It was from Matthew 5:

Blessed are the poor in spirit, for theirs is the kingdom of Heaven

Blessed are those who mourn, for they shall be comforted

Blessed are the meek, for they shall inherit the earth

Blessed are those who hunger and thirst for righteousness, for they shall be filled

Blessed are the merciful, for they shall obtain mercy

Blessed are the pure in heart, for they shall see God

Blessed are the peacemakers, for they shall be called sons of God

Blessed are those who are persecuted for righteousness' sake, for theirs is the kingdom of Heaven

Blessed are you when they revile and persecute you and say all kinds of evil against you falsely for My sake

Rejoice and be exceedingly glad, for great is your reward in Heaven, for so they persecuted the prophets who were before you.

After reciting the passage several times, Weston felt an unusual peace. God was with him and watching him. He need only to abide in Him. He fell into a peaceful sleep.

It was dark when the cell door abruptly flew open. Two guards stood at the door, staring at Weston as though he were a lab rat.

As they came into the room, he struggled to his feet.

"Turn around!" one of the guards commanded, "Hands behind your back!"

The quiet one had his baton out and seemed eager to use it. Weston had felt it once and wasn't ready for its touch again. He quickly complied and placed his hands together. The vocal guard roughly grabbed him, mumbling curses, and shoved the handcuffs on tightly. Weston was hauled forward, wincing at the pain in his wrists.

He was brought out into the hallway. He looked right and left. To his left, a guard sat at a desk, staring at him. Beyond the desk, the hallway turned out of sight. The guards hauled him to the right, towards another large hallway.

After passing a series of cells, he was pushed through a door into a new room. In front of him sat a desk with two chairs. He was shoved down into the nearest chair and a second set of handcuffs was attached to his handcuffs and the chair. The two guards left the room.

Weston sat there, his mind going numb with boredom for almost an hour. His wrists and arms ached. He was beginning to wonder if they had forgotten him, when a man walked in with two new guards behind him. He came around to the other side of the desk, while the guards took up positions behind Weston. The man sat down and stared.

He was tall, Caucasian, with dark, short hair, combed to the side. He was well built, and gave off an aura of ex-military. The thing that struck Weston most was his eyes. They were the lightest shade of blue, and seemed to pierce through you.

He wore ambiguous clothing, a pair of black jeans and a green sweater. He gave off no hint of rank or office held. He was eating a thick bagel, stuffed with cream cheese. Weston continued to stare at him and longingly at the bagel. The man continued to stare back, taking large bites and smacking his lips until the treat was completely gone. Finally, he spoke:

"Weston Miller. I've been looking forward to meeting you for some time," he stated matter-of-factly. He had a slight British accent.

"Really?" Weston asked, taken off guard.

"Your antics have been the stuff of legend lately," he continued, a twinkle in his eyes, "the cell phones in the closet...that threw off our SWAT team. They wasted thirty seconds trying to get you to come out, but you weren't there! Getting past the blockade...we're still not sure how you managed that one. And running towards your pursuers so your family could have time to get away...well, that was just brilliant."

Weston tried to hide his excitement. The man seemed to be indicating his family had escaped.

"But, the candle that burns twice as bright lasts half as long," he went on jovially, "you were fighting above your weight class."

He seemed about to break into laughter.

Weston stayed silent and stared. This man was strange, and not what he expected. The whole thing seemed like a big joke to him.

"I'm John, by the way. I will be your interrogator, your inquisitor, your investigating officer, if you will," he said nonchalantly, "I just think introductions are important. Mission statements, too."

A sick feeling began to form in the pit of Weston's stomach. This man seemed crazy, and possibly evil.

"Where's my son... Braden?" Weston asked.

John ignored him and continued his monologue.

"You see, mission statements give organizations a set of guiding principles, a sense of purpose. Right now things aren't going so good in the world, and we need to get them back on track. You belong to an organization that is preventing that. In a sense, you're like a disease, a cancer, that needs to be eliminated from the body...in order for it to thrive and be healthy again," he explained, "I and these fine gentlemen behind you, in a sense, we are the cure. The chemo. We see ourselves as heroes, just ordinary men, doing the kind of work that most folks don't have the stomach for.

So, here's the thing, Weston Miller. You're a Seventh-Day Adventist. For whatever dumb reason, you decided to join the only church that wouldn't go along with the program. You've had your fun, but now we need you to recant those beliefs and start worshiping with the rest of us. You'll be happy to know there's a sanctuary right here in this building. You can begin right away."

Weston's heart was racing. He struggled to control his voice as he spoke:

"I'm just following the Bible. I must worship on Saturday," he said.

Suddenly, John's face went from jovial to serious. He glared at Weston from across the desk.

"The Bible," John stated, "you mean the dead book. We have new information now. In case you're the last moron who wasn't aware, your Jesus already came back last month. He was very clear on what our stance should be. We worship on the Lord's Day."

"That wasn't Jesus," Weston managed to say, his voice shaking.

A burst of laughter escaped from John's lips. He began giggling and looked at the guards behind Weston. They also began chuckling.

"It sure looked like Jesus to me," he replied.

"It's not. Jesus warned - " Weston answered.

" - At any rate," John interrupted, "we need to move this conversation forward. Here's how this is going to work. Myself and these fine gentlemen behind you specialize in what's called enhanced interrogation techniques. These men are talented. They're artists really, in pain and torture. So, you're either going to sign an affidavit stating that you renounce your membership in the Seventh-Day Adventist church, and you no longer believe in the Sabbath, or we're going to put you in the box."

He gestured towards the door behind him.

Weston's heart raced. His throat was dry and he struggled to speak. A thought came to him that calmed his mind somewhat.

John the Baptist went through this. Many others. Jesus helped them all.

"I won't," he stated, voice shaking, but resolute.

Without a word, John nodded at the guards. They moved forward and unlocked first the handcuffs that tied him to the chair, and then the handcuffs on his wrists. Weston immediately grabbed his arms and began to massage them. The guards grabbed him and shoved him into the next room.

Weston saw a box laying horizontally on a set of stands. It was about half the size of an adult coffin. It sat with its lid open.

John followed them into the room.

"Go ahead and warm him up a bit. Let's get him accommodated," he said nonchalantly.

Without warning, Weston was struck with a baton. He felt an enormous surge of pain as it connected with his right elbow. His vision went to stars and he collapsed to the ground, reaching for his arm. Additional explosions of agony racked his back, calf and hand as more blows rained down on his writhing body. Wails escaped his lips, but no words came out. Tears streaked down his face as he was lifted upward, carried, and thrown into the box with a thud. He struggled to look up as the lid was slammed shut and darkness enveloped him. He heard the click of a lock. He was sealed in. Weston began to shake uncontrollably.

Time had passed. How much, he wasn't sure, but the insane throbbing had finally subsided. He wasn't sure how injured he was because it was difficult to move. He would flex his pelvis upward, so that his legs, butt, and back could be off the floor for a few seconds. He had learned over time that he could squeeze his body, while kinking his neck, and turn from his right side to his left. Unfortunately, he could not straighten out but remained in a constantly squished position.

The real confinement was to his mind. There was a complete absence of light or routine. He did not know how much time had passed since he had been put here, and he was afraid to think about it. Afraid that if he did think about what was happening to him for too long, he would go insane. That his mind would crack, his psyche permanently fracture. There had to be more to life than endlessly struggling to find relief in an impossibly tight space, and he was worried, because more and more he just wished he would die.

The only thing that brought him relief was prayer and the Word. He would recite the blessings Jesus gave at the Sermon on the Mount, identifying with them as he never could have before. And he would pray, sometimes for hours. He joked with God that he finally had that prayer life he always wanted, because he was forced to. But it was hard. His body needed food, water, and movement. He begged for those things from God, begged to be taken out of this box. He would be happy to receive any other kind of torture than this. At least with another form of torture, he could interact with a human being.

And still it went on. And on, and on.

When the lid finally opened, Weston was so thankful, he blessed his inquisitors. Not with words so much, because it was hard to speak. He mumbled praises as tears streaked down his face. They lifted him out of his tomb and dragged him back to the chair. It was no longer necessary to handcuff him, as he could hardly move. He was given a restraint around his chest however, to prevent him from sliding off the chair and onto the floor.

As he sat there waiting, he attempted to stretch his neck, arms, and legs. They had forsaken him and would not respond to his commands. However, with much effort he could make little movements, and it brought him joy to try.

"This is why I tried to flee to the mountains," he mumbled to himself, and began laughing uncontrollably.

As he continued laughing hysterically, John and the guards walked in. John gave him an amused look as he came around the desk and sat down.

"Well, I can see you had fun," he said, "I'm glad you enjoyed the box."

As John pulled out another bagel, loaded with cream cheese, Weston's laughter ceased. He began to stare intensely at the food, drooling uncontrollably.

"Oh, this," John said, looking at the bagel, then taking a huge bite, "sorry mate, I missed breakfast. Working with dimwits such as yourself, I need to keep up my strength."

He paused, finishing up the bagel, while smiling and staring at Weston the whole time.

"So, what did we learn in the last three days?" he asked in a condescending tone.

"Three days?" Weston asked in wonder.

"You certainly learned how to go to the bathroom all over yourself. Well, if you didn't learn a thing, I guess we'll just have to put you back in there," he stated nonchalantly.

Weston's eyes went wide.

"Relax," he said, laughing, "we've got other new and fun things to move on to. Variety is the spice of life, haven't you ever heard that before, Weston?"

This man loves this. He is evil.

"But we're not animals, Weston. Tom, give this man some water," he instructed to one of the guards.

A bottle of Aquafina water was brought in, and placed in Weston's hands. He struggled to hold it, desperately trying to get it to his lips. About a quarter of the bottle spilled down the front of his shirt as he opened the bottle and put it to his mouth. He began excitedly sucking down the liquid.

"So," John began, "have you had some time to think about our little talk? You remember our talk, don't you, Weston?"

"Yyyeess," he choked out, between gulps.

"Here's the affidavit. You'll read and sign it. Then we'll take you to the nearest courtroom, where you can publicly announce your conversion back to common sense, your desire to be on the winning team again," he came around the desk, handing the paper to Weston, "after that, you'll be free to go."

Weston grabbed the paper as best he could, and began reading:

I, Weston Miller, being of sound mind and body, and without any form of coercion whatsoever, do now at this time formally renounce my belief in the seventh day Sabbath and my faith in the Seventh-Day

Adventist church as a movement of God. I believe that I was diluted by doctrines of devils, and I acknowledge that I have caused much harm and loss of life because of my stubborn beliefs. I wish to make amends to all I have hurt, and to all I have infected with similar delusions in my proselytization attempts representing this church. I acknowledge that I am in part responsible for all the death and destruction in the world, and I solemnly swear to worship in accordance with the standards of the global community until I take my last breath.

Signed,

Weston Miller 03/01/35

"So," John began in a jovial tone, "how's it sound?"

Weston kept chugging the water.

"A little wordy, I know," he went on, "but lawyers have to cover everyone's butts these days."

"Could I have some more water?" Weston asked shakily.

John paused, staring at him.

"Certainly!" John replied. He had a smile on his face, but his eyes looked annoyed, "Get this man another of Detroit's finest!"

Tom left the room to retrieve more water. John continued to stare icily at Weston while Tom returned with another bottle. This time Weston had more control of his hands, and was able to drink freely.

"Now," he continued, "will you sign?"

Weston chugged the last quarter of the bottle before answering.

"I can't," he replied nervously, looking down.

"Why not?" John demanded in an angry tone.

"I don't want the mark of the beast," he spoke softly. He took the piece of paper and placed it on the desk. His right hand remained on the desk, holding it.

"Well," John replied casually, nodding to the other guard, "you won't be able to sign it now, anyway."

Suddenly, a baton came slamming down onto the center of Weston's right hand. A tsunami of pain surged throughout his arm as he collapsed onto the floor, gasping and struggling to breathe. Weston attempted to speak, but all that came out were little moans and strings of snot. As he grabbed for his right hand, a new wave of pain washed over him again. They had broken his hand.

"I'm confused, Weston," John began, coming around the desk now, "I'm certain we had a conversation the other day, and I explained to you that the Bible is the dead book. Jesus already came back last month and explained that he had new information. Information that you were not following. When I explained this you seemed to understand my words."

"I did," Weston moaned, struggling to rise from the floor without using his right arm to help him.

"Are you slow, Weston?" John asked, "Mentally disabled? Were you able to support a family, hold down a job? I think your wife must have done these things because you are quite an imbecile, actually. You seem to have no brains at all. I think your wife is the one who evaded the police, and you just followed behind, drooling."

He and the other guards laughed, as Weston struggled to get up off the ground, nursing his throbbing hand.

"You've got water all over you, mate," John continued, pushing him back down onto the floor with his boot, "but your wife's not here to clean you up anymore. You really are a dumb bloke. Don't you realize we can just deep-fake you signing the confession? But where would be the fun in that?"

He paused, staring at Weston, as a predator might stare at its prey.

"Deep-fake it?" Weston croaked.

John ignored him.

"You know, water…it's the building block of life. We need it to survive, as you just demonstrated so elegantly here. Our body is made mostly of water…but, sometimes too much water is a bad thing."

He looked over at the guards again, who grabbed Weston's arms and dragged him back into the other room.

"No!" Weston cried, staring at the box. He began struggling.

"Oh, it's not that," John stated, "since you like water so much, we're just going to make sure you get properly hydrated."

As they moved into the next room, Weston saw a spinal cord immobilizer board that a paramedic would use. It had straps at the hands and feet, as well as a head immobilizer. The entire board was slanted downward towards the head.

"Secure him," John ordered.

Immediately, the guards forced Weston down onto the board and strapped his head, hands and feet. A medium-sized cloth was placed over his face and pulled tight by one of the guards. Fortunately, he could still breathe. Weston was scared, as he had heard of what they were about to do; it was called waterboarding.

"Let's get him some of that H2O he likes so much," John stated, motioning with his hands to begin.

Through the cloth, Weston could see Tom raise a gallon jug of water above his face. Weston took a gulp of air and held his breath. Tom tilted the jug and began slowly pouring water on Weston's nose and mouth.

As the water poured over his face, he kept his mouth closed, but he could feel it moving into his nose. Fighting panic, he began blowing out of his nose. Everything was fine again, except he already felt like he needed to take a breath.

After holding out a few more seconds, he reflexively opened his mouth to get air. Instead, what came in was water. He gagged now and struggled, spitting the water out, but it was only replaced with more water. He began pushing and thrashing against the head, arm and leg restraints. He was drowning and he just wanted to die, if that would make this awful thing stop. Struggle as he might, he could not move his head or body a single inch.

His mind understood that he was not underwater, but his body was sure he was drowning in an ocean of fluid. He struggled and fought, to no avail.

"Get him up," John stated flatly.

They unstrapped him and threw him on the floor, where he proceeded to cough, spit, and gasp for air.

"Go get the affidavit!" he told Tom, "He's ready!"

The guard dragged him back to the chair in the other room. This time Weston was able to stay in it without sliding off. Tom handed the paper to John.

"All you have to do is sign this, with your left hand, of course."

"No," Weston answered in between coughing fits. He was surprised that he had any resolve left to resist.

"No?" John repeated with wonder, "No?"

This time John forcibly dragged him back to the room himself, swearing the entire time. The guards forced Weston down as he struggled desperately against being strapped to the board. Tom wàs having difficulty securing Weston's legs to the board, so the other guard punched Weston in the stomach. He seized up and no longer had any strength.

Successfully restrained, they began again. This time, Weston didn't have the energy to try and hold his breath, and he began spitting, gagging and thrashing immediately.

Lord, I need strength. Please.

After what seemed like hours, he heard John.

"Get him up," he ordered.

Weston collapsed on the floor, coughing, gasping and moaning. John stood over him, watching him.

"You're not going to sign, are you?" he yelled.

Weston didn't answer, but continued to cough.

"Are you?" he screamed, kicking Weston firmly in the ribs.

Weston seized into a ball, holding his stomach in agony and struggling for breath.

"You look like a fish out of water, mate. Get this worm filth out of my sight," he ordered.

They dragged him back to his cell and threw him onto the floor, slamming the door.

As he wept, he cried out to God. Not with sorrow, but with thanksgiving. It was over. At least for now, it was finally over.

Chapter 18 - The Break

Over the next month, the 'sessions,' as John liked to call them, continued. It was difficult to track what day it was, as they had thrown him in solitary confinement. He no longer had a window, and so the only light he had seen for a long time was the artificial lighting in the interrogation rooms.

John called him his little minnow, because minnows love water. Weston was waterboarded almost daily, and John had remarked more than once that he had never seen anyone endure it like this. Weston knew he had provoked his interrogator the day he asked for that second bottle of water. He had regretted that mistake, each time he was waterboarded, or as they liked to call it, each time they played the drowning game.

But then, as they say, the devil you do know is better than the devil you don't. Who knows what they would be doing to him right now if it wasn't this? Weston didn't want to think about that. Besides the beatings with batons and fists and the box, the only other thing they had tried was electric shocks.

All he knew was that God had sustained him. He knew no mortal could endure this, physically, mentally, or spiritually. God had answered his prayer; he had been given the strength of the martyrs. The strength of Jesus. And at least they had started giving him occasional food and water. He knew it was only so he wouldn't die, but he wolfed down the watery soup they brought him.

Weston had learned to be thankful for the little blessings; the days when he wasn't summoned, when a half a slice of hard bread ended up in his gruel or when memories would emerge into his conscience. Memories of his old life: Ally laughing hysterically when he tried to moonwalk, the whole family playing Scrabble for hours, or the day they got baptized and dedicated their lives to Christ.

But those times were gone. Long gone, and now Weston's life was only about lecture after lecture, torture upon torture, and constant humiliation. They were trying to break him, turn him into a spineless, gelatinous mass of gleeful compliance. And they had not been able to do it. A fact which infuriated John, maddened him to no end, because apparently it had never happened before. John could not explain it. Nor could Weston, except he knew that Phillipians 4:13 promised 'I can do all things through Christ who strengthens me.'

Once, when John had demanded an explanation as to why his minnow was so strong, Weston had quoted that verse to him. He did not repeat the verse anymore as it had resulted in a severe beating.

But now, Weston sensed something had changed. There was a difference in John the last few sessions. It was as though it had all gone on too long, and the honeymoon, if you could call it that, was over. They had expected him to crack by now and he hadn't. Weston sensed this was a place where it was frowned upon to exceed expectations.

Today was like any other day, and he was seated in front of John as usual. Except that something was very different. John's face had three gigantic sores on it that oozed fluid. Additional sores could be seen on his arms, as he was wearing a short sleeve t-shirt. The guards also had sores. John scratched occasionally, causing bleeding. Weston could not take his eyes off of the sores.

He was wondering if this was the first plague?

John was going on another lengthy monologue.

"Did you know I have quotas, Weston? I have quotas to meet, just like you. Goals, markers, performance targets. I've got a review coming up. The corporate world is, well let me just tell you; it's brutal. I've tried with you, Weston. I've been on your side this whole time, trying to get you on board, but you're so stupid... it's not my fault, really. I tried to explain it to them."

Weston just stared dully at John's sores. The one on his forehead was oozing more than the others, into his face. He wasn't clear where this conversation was going.

"Because of you, I haven't met expectations. It's a dog eat dog world out there, and if I can't perform, there's a line of other folks out there willing to do this kind of good, honest, hard work. So, what am I supposed to do?" he asked, looking at Weston.

He stared at Weston for an uncomfortably long time. Weston tried to return his unfriendly gaze.

"So, why don't you have any sores?" he asked menacingly, changing the subject.

He continued to glare at Weston, Suddenly, he broke into a grin.

"Sometimes in the corporate world it's good to break up the routine, shake things up, keep clients on their toes, you know? We've gotten stuck in a bit of a rut lately, wouldn't you agree?" he asked.

Weston started to stare at the floor now. One of the sores had dripped onto the linoleum, creating a small puddle.

"Say, you were in construction, right?" he asked.

Weston was not sure where he was going with this new topic.

"Yes," he stated flatly.

"Solve the age-old debate for me. Milwaukee or DeWalt?" he asked.

Weston could see Tom was bringing in a plastic molded DeWalt carrying case. Suddenly his heart started racing.

"Hey, wait!" he spoke, struggling to rise from his chair.

Tom handed John the case, who began walking into the next room, while the quiet guard manhandled Weston into the next room.

"You're not a dumb as I thought," John remarked.

In this new room was a large wooden table, surrounded by chairs, with various sets of straps built into it. Weston was forced down into one of the chairs. They attempted to place Weston's hands into the straps, but he began struggling violently. Tom came over and punched Weston in the face. Normally he would have crumpled, but somehow the thought of what they were about to do gave him renewed strength.

Despite the lack of nutrition and a broken hand, for the first time Weston seemed to be holding his own. Tom and the quiet guard were having trouble securing his arms into the straps.

"What the - " John remarked, turning around and moving to assist.

Between the three of them, they managed to get his arm in place, and strap it down at the wrist. Weston kept resisting and howling in frustration. Soon, the other wrist was secured as well. Weston struggled and grunted, but he could not move his hands one inch.

"So, as I was saying," John continued, out of breath, "I have found that DeWalt makes as fine a tool as any. Now mind you, I am not a professional tradesman such as yourself, but it just fits so well in the hand, and feel the weight of it?"

John was pulling out the saw and turning it from side to side, admiring it. Weston was no longer listening, but just stared at the blade of the saw. John revved the motor several times.

"I know Milwaukee has an incredible reputation among electricians, but just listen to that precision!" he yelled above the noise.

"You're evil!" Weston blurted out, "Demon-possessed!"

"Oh, now, we've been over this before," John shouted over the noise of the tool, "you're the one who's evil, not me. You're the one who's stubborn, stupid beliefs are killing people, killing millions of innocent lives! I'm the hero, trying to stop the carnage out there. This whole thing is all your fault, and you have no one to blame but yourself for what's about to happen!!"

Tom placed a 2x4 on top of the table. He pushed it tightly between Weston's fingers and thumb, splaying his thumb outward away from the rest of his hand. Then he hammered it down into the table, immobilizing Weston's hand. John lined up the saw with Weston's right hand, squeezed the trigger, and began sawing along the 2x4 as a guide. The saw emitted a continuous high pitch squeal. John shouted over it:

"You're the one who has been so high and mighty, thinking you're better than everyone else, that you're so special and that you've got this truth that nobody else has!"

He continued cutting along the 2x4, using it as a guide. The blade moved closer and closer to Weston's right hand. He thrashed against the restraints.

"The problem with these sessions, it's suddenly so clear to me now," John yelled above the noise, "is you've always come away intact. You never truly lost anything for your 'beliefs!'"

As the blade came into contact with the space between his fingers and thumb, Weston roared out in pain. It surged up his arm and into the center of his brain. He saw a lot of blood and then everything went black.

When he awoke it seemed that no time had passed. He was groggy and severely thirsty. For once, he did not feel starved, because he was sick to his stomach. He lay on the hard floor on his back, hands splayed out at his sides. His first thought was that it all must have been a dream, it was too awful to not have been. But his hand hurt badly. It was excruciating. Nothing would relieve it.

He turned on his left side and wretched, but nothing came out. Only dry heaves.

He was scared, but he knew what he had to do. He did not want to really know, was terrified to know, but he had to explore what he had. Slowly, gingerly, he sat up, and began moving his left hand over his right. He came upon a large bandage at his wrist. He began working his way over the bandage.

Working up the courage, he moved to his fingers. He felt a pinky finger, ring, index and pointer; but as he came to where his thumb should be, there was nothing. Just touching the area brought fresh waves of pain and he cried out. Tears flowed freely down his cheeks.

"Why?" he repeated over and over.

Later, he awoke again. He was sure he was dreaming, because John was standing in the doorway. A light was also on. He had lived in this room forever, and he had no idea the room had a light bulb.

Then the dream spoke:

"You've looked better, mate," John began.

"I need pain medicine," Weston said shakily, beginning to cry, "please."

"I think our powertool session was a success," John declared, ignoring him, "I received accolades from several of my colleagues for ingenuity, spontaneity and the ability to problem-solve in real time."

Now Weston knew he wasn't dreaming. His own imagination could never make up the psychopathic speeches that John endlessly spouted.

"So, here's the thing," he went on, "playtime is over. No more boxes, no more drowning games, no more Mr. Sparky. We've been too easy on you. Now what's going to happen is this: every session you don't sign the affidavit, I use my DeWalt."

"No," Weston moaned in a panic, pleading, "please, no!"

"You just let that sink in, mate," he stated icily, "cause I'm done with you."

With that, he turned and walked out.

Some time later, he awoke to the sound of the lock clicking in the door. It pushed open and two new guards moved in, picking him off of the floor.

"See, I told you," one of them spoke to the other, motioning towards Weston, "nothing."

Weston guessed they were talking about his lack of sores. Both guards were covered with them. He cried out in pain as one guard grabbed his right arm, placing handcuffs on his wrists in front of his body.

"Where are we going?" he asked.

"Shut up," said the guard briskly.

They moved him out of the room and down the hall to the right. At first, he bristled as they neared the familiar interrogation room, but he grew curious as they walked past it.

Soon, they made their way into a new hallway, through a set of double doors and into a small courtroom. He was shoved into a seat in the back, along with a few other prisoners. He looked around for Braden, but did not see him or anyone he recognized, not even John. None of the other prisoners returned his glance, but all of them looked down at the ground.

Everyone in the room, except for one or two people, had the same disgusting sores on their faces.

Weston looked up at the front. It was an informal version of a normal courtroom. There was a judge sitting behind a small desk, with two sets of folding tables opposite the judge; presumably for defense and prosecuting attorneys.

Currently, there was a man sitting in a small metal chair being questioned by a tall, slender, and stern looking woman.

"After all the evidence presented, will you sign?" she demanded in a stern voice.

The man held his head down low, in a defeated posture.

"Yes," he said hesitantly.

The judge hit a gavel, and spoke.

"Counsel, I recommend parties sign doc nine and bring it to the clerk, after I call this case resolved. Prisoner 112 is to be removed once all parties verify signatures. Next case," the judge called out.

The prosecutor smiled smugly as she spoke:

"We call prisoner 847."

A guard roughly hauled Weston up out of his chair. They moved him forward and sat him at one of the tables, opposite the prosecutor. Next to him was a young man in a tattered business suit. Weston assumed this was his assigned attorney.

"Counsel," the judge spoke up, looking down at his desk, "what is your case?"

"Prisoner 847," the prosecutor began icily, "Weston Miller. Guilty of four plus RWE violations, evasion of authorities, resisting arrest and assaulting a police officer."

"How do you plead?" the judge asked in a bored tone, looking at Weston and his attorney. He had a large, festering sore, oozing down his neck into his shirt.

"Your honor, a moment?" his attorney stated, turning towards Weston.

"You need to plead guilty," he said to Weston.

"No," Weston stated emphatically.

The attorney turned back to the judge in disgust. Apparently, the attorney-client huddle was over.

"Client pleads not guilty," he said.

"Prosecutor?" he turned to her.

She stood and began speaking:

"Your honor, the prisoner has four RWE violations before he was lost track of. He did not attend any sessions of Mandate worship by app or in person. When authorities came to speak with the accused about the initial sessions, he fled, causing the need for an extensive manhunt into the Tahoe National Forest. He assaulted a police officer at a designated roadblock in Auburn. When the authorities attempted to remand the prisoner into custody for questioning in the mountains, he resisted arrest and assaulted several more officers, causing much harm and costly medical care to the department. The prosecution recommends the death sentence, barring signature of the affidavit. If signed, we recommend life in prison."

"Mr. Miller," the judge said, looking at him directly, "you have one minute to respond. Will you sign the affidavit?"

Weston looked around, realizing his whole case rested on him now, not the disinterested attorney sitting next to him. Against him were leveled multiple false charges, but Weston didn't care about those. He knew no matter what he said, he was already condemned. He had nothing to lose. They had been torturing him for months, without a trial, like so many Communist regimes in the past.

He began:

"Your honor, I did not attend church on Sunday, because it was mandated by the government. I saw that as a fulfillment of Revelation thirteen, which talks about a world power enforcing the mark of the beast. I have reason to believe the papacy has spearheaded this movement, and they have publicly identified Sunday worship as their mark of authority. The Bible also clearly identifies them as the beast. The Bible says those who will not take this mark of the beast, would no longer be able to buy or sell, and would be put to death. It also says a world power would enforce these things, not the papacy. Those things were all done to me, they are happening to me now, by a world power; the United States of America - "

" - Your honor," the prosecutor interrupted, "this IS ridiculous. I object."

"Overruled, for now. Prisoner, you have thirty more seconds."

"Because you, representing America, have fulfilled the words of Revelation thirteen in every way, I can only conclude that you are the second beast power which causes the world to worship the first beast, which is clearly the papacy, who is in league with Satan - "

" - Your honor!" the prosecutor interrupted again.

" - And so I must have nothing to do with you," Weston spoke up even louder, "or your laws, or this sinful - "

" - That's enough," the judge interrupted.

Weston raised his right arm, pointing to it. He was angry now, at the injustice, as this mockery of a trial.

"And your Gestapo agents, in the dead of night, came to try and kill me and my family. Once they got me, it has been nothing but inhumane torture day after day - "

" - Somebody shut him up," the judge looked towards the bailiff, annoyed.

" - and now they have maimed me for life! They said they're going to keep cutting me to pieces," he exclaimed, close to tears, "all because I want to worship according to my conscience."

Several guards rushed towards Weston, batons out. His attorney leaped out of the way as Weston received blows to the back, leg and head. As a baton connected with his right hand, a tsunami of pain shot up his arm, and everything went black.

As time passed, Weston cried and rocked his arm. Nothing could alleviate the intractable pain in his right hand, as well as almost every other part of his body; no position, no mindset, no touch. At least the bleeding had finally slowed to a slight ooze.

I can't let this happen again. I'll just have to sign the affidavit.

Immediately he regretted the thought.

I must pray, he thought next. *Somehow through this, I must talk to God.*

He began to pray:

Dear Jesus,

You are so precious to me. You went through worse than this for me. I think I get it now. The fellowship of Your sufferings. But You went through worse than this to save me. To save me from sin, and so sin must be the most horrible thing in the entire universe. And I want no part of it. I want to show the world, the universe that I want no part of it.

I know I will die here, Lord. That they will cut me to pieces. It's not the way I would have preferred to go, but Lord...

He began crying uncontrollably, tears flowing down his face.

...Lord, I'll do it. I'll do it for You. I'm willing. Just please give me the strength. Just please remember me at the resurrection. Please raise me back to life and restore me whole. All I want is You. And Lord, just please make it quick. I pray this will be the last session and I can die, if it be Your will.

In Jesus name I pray...I want to see You soon.

Amen.

He remained there for some time, eyes closed, on his knees, rapturous. He even seemed to see a faint glow behind his closed eyelids, as though Jesus' presence were here with him. God was so gracious to him, to give him this token that He had heard and answered. He felt that now he could endure anything, knowing Jesus, although unseen, was with him.

As he opened his eyes, he saw that the glow was not coming from some heavenly presence, but from the cell door, which was cracked open.

His initial reaction was one of horror, as the door was always closed. For it to be otherwise meant something was wrong. He looked around for John, but he was alone. Weston continued to stare at the door for several moments, frozen in place.

Eventually, with effort, he rose to his feet and made his way towards the sliver of light emanating from beyond the door. His right hand hurt tremendously, and he held it up, nursing it with his left. Cautiously, he touched the door with his left hand, which he had never done before.

With hands shaking, he pulled ever so slightly on the door. It pivoted on its hinges without a sound. He could see the hallway now, dimly lit by fluorescent tubes. They cast a dull, lifeless glow over everything. His heart was racing as he slowly peered to the left, sticking his head out enough to see if the guard was seated at his desk.

He was.

There was another man in the hallway. A maintenance man, mopping the floor. He was tall and broad shouldered, with thick, blonde hair. He wore ratty overalls with steel-toed boots. He somehow seemed out of place with the mop in his hand, working it back and forth on the worn linoleum.

The man looked up from his work, staring directly at Weston.

"You were willing to go back," he stated loudly.

Weston's eyes went wide, and he looked down the hall. The desk guard was less than thirty feet away.

"Oh, don't worry. He can't hear you," he said matter-of-factly.

Weston just continued to stare at the janitor and the guard. The guard made no indication that he could see or hear their conversation. He seemed to be engrossed in writing a report of some kind.

"You were willing to go back," the janitor repeated, "for additional sessions."

Who was this man and why was this happening? It had to be one of John's latest 'tests.' He would not allow himself to be tricked by John.

"I never claimed to be smart," he answered.

He knew John would agree with that.

"He likes that about you, you know. Your sense of humor. He has one too," the janitor answered.

"I doubt that," Weston smirked, thinking he was speaking of John.

The janitor gave him a return smirk.

"Anyway," he continued, "you were willing to go back... so now you go... out."

As he said the word out, the janitor pointed towards the left somewhere. Weston was confused.

"Escape," the janitor said, exasperated that Weston didn't understand.

"Look, just follow me," he instructed, shrugging his shoulders.

With that, he turned and began walking towards the desk guard. The janitor looked back at Weston, who stood frozen in the doorway. He gestured with his hand to follow.

Well, if it is a trap, they can't do anything worse to me anyway, he thought to himself. *I'll just go tell the guard my door is open.*

Slowly, his heart racing, he stepped out of the cell and into the hall.

He began tentatively walking behind the janitor, who, if this was a prison break, seemed in no hurry at all. Weston stared nervously at the desk guard. As he approached the desk, his hands began shaking and he experienced tunnel vision.

Even though Weston was only a few feet away, the guard would not look at him. He continued writing furiously on what appeared to be some kind of form. Around the corner, the janitor beckoned with his hand. Weston looked at the guard again and hesitated to walk past him.

"Come on!" the janitor exclaimed, emphasizing each word, as though he were talking to a small child, "I told you. He can't see you."

This didn't feel like a trap. Weston took a deep breath, and walked past the guard. He looked back over his shoulder. The desk guard was still busy writing; somehow he had not seen or heard him walk by.

The janitor made several more turns down different hallways. Now he followed the janitor a little closer, making several turns down new hallways. Weston glanced around nervously, terrified someone would walk by and see his escape. As they came to a locked door, Weston groaned. They had almost made it, but there was nothing to do now. Weston started thinking about how to get back. He would retrace his steps, find his cell and lock it behind him. If he was lucky, they would never find out he had tried this.

The janitor touched the heavy locking mechanism on the door. It clicked, and the door pushed out slightly away from them.

Weston stared in amazement.

"How did you do that?" he asked slowly.

The janitor turned and looked at him.

"How did you do THAT?" he said, emphasizing the word that, and pointing back towards where they had come.

Weston realized he was talking about the incarceration, the torture.

"I don't know...Jesus," he said thoughtfully, with conviction.

"Exactly!" the janitor replied, speaking slowly, "Same way I did this."

"Are you an angel?" he blurted out.

The janitor gave him another smirk.

"We gotta hurry now," he replied, ignoring the question, "next shift is coming soon."

They went down two flights of stairs, past another locked door, and through a large dormitory style room. Each time they encountered a guard or staff member, Weston would cringe, but no one showed any sign that they were aware of their presence. Apparently, they were invisible to those around them.

After passing through another hallway, and two industrial double doors, they moved out into a large lobby filled with officers. Beyond that, he could see outside. Weston's heart raced with the thought of freedom being so close. It had all seemed unreal, but now there was the possibility of freedom, twenty feet away. He tried not to, but Weston began to cry. The officers around them showed no indication that they were even there.

"Once you get outside," the janitor instructed, "make your way to the 7-11 two blocks that way."

"Why the 7-11?" Weston asked, sniffling.

"Because you'll find some great deals there," he answered sarcastically. "Look, there's food and water there. Don't worry, it's not stealing, the owners are long gone. Look in the back office. Hole up there if you can until this thing is over," he answered.

"Ok," Weston responded. He suddenly realized he was absolutely exhausted. He really hoped he wasn't dreaming.

"Don't forget the water!" the janitor exclaimed, looking at his watch, "Something new is coming, probably any minute now."

Suddenly Weston knew.

"The second plague!" he guessed.

"No, Einstein. The third," he answered, "where have you been? In a... well, anyway."

The janitor stared at him strangely for a second. He had seemed much older in the bad lighting inside, but now in the lobby he seemed young. But his personality and mannerisms reminded Weston of a seasoned, sarcastic, old man. His blonde hair was just a tad long, and his bangs settled down just under his eyes, which were brilliant emerald green.

"I want you to know I asked personally for this assignment," he stated to Weston. For the first time the sarcasm had disappeared and he seemed incredibly solemn. "What you did in there, through Him... other worlds are going to want to hear your story. It's going to actually magnify Him, Weston."

A drunk suddenly pushed in through the front double doors, yelling loudly. Several officers turned and started walking towards the man. Weston turned momentarily to see what the commotion was all about. When he turned back to the janitor, he was gone. It had been one or two seconds since he last saw him. Weston took several steps and looked to the right and to the left. Besides the drunk, the officers, and a male receptionist behind a large desk, there was no one else in the lobby. Each door was locked leading into the building. The janitor had not gone through the locked doors, nor walked past Weston to go outside. He was just gone.

In wonder, Weston turned and walked unimpeded out the front door to freedom.

Chapter 19 - The Plagues

Ally could not remember the last time they had seen a trail. They had trudged through valleys, thick forests, and rugged mountains. They were near the top of another of the endless peaks, and from this vantage point they could see for miles in any direction.

Ally watched their pursuers through Geoffrey's Bushnell Prime compact binoculars. They were making their way up the rocky passage the Millers and Geoffrey had ascended earlier. There were twelve of them, all walking single-file with guns drawn.

The worst part had been the Black Hornets. Even now, Ally watched as a soldier pulled something out of his pack and released it into the air. All the soldiers watched it leave. Ally could not see it but she had learned what it was.

The Black Hornet was a small military drone about the size of a man's finger. It was slightly louder than a large bumblebee. It could take pictures, send live video, and had a flight time of twenty minutes. That last part was the only thing that had saved them.

It had found them two days ago. They had been lying in their tents, when suddenly a whining insect noise had brought them out. The drone hovered over them, looking like a large, prehistoric dragonfly. It had taken pictures of them, and scanned the area all around, presumably to try and determine where exactly they were. They had thrown rocks at it, but its remote operator had easily outmaneuvered their missiles.

Now they could hear the faint whine of Black Hornets nearby.

He who dwells in the secret place of the Most High shall abide under the shadow of the Almighty. Lord, hide us under Your shadow now, Ally prayed.

Geoffrey, Dylan and Charlotte remained still and hid behind some rocks as the Black Hornets flew overhead. They paused and hovered momentarily near the group. Everyone held their breath. Then suddenly, the Hornets pushed forward and continued on.

Ally breathed a sigh of relief. Geoffrey came out from behind a rock.

"We have to keep moving," he insisted.

"I know," Ally agreed, "but we're starving. And we need water."

At the mention of water, Geoffrey and the kids looked at each other awkwardly, and then at the ground. They had come upon water yesterday. They had heard the beautiful, life-giving sound that only a rushing mountain stream makes, and had run through thickets and over rocks to get to its source. What they had come upon, was something that could have only come from a nightmare.

A heavy, roaring mountain stream. Pushing around bends and over rocks. All blood. Nothing but endless blood, thundering down the mountain.

"Well, they're gaining on us," Geoffrey continued, "and we have no other choice."

"Why don't we pray?" Ally suggested, motioning for everyone to come in, "Kids, gather around."

In a sense, she had become the spiritual leader since they had lost Weston. Time and again she had helped them refocus on the One who could sustain them through the cold nights, the days without food, and the pursuing soldiers. Not that she was anything at all, but she seemed to be constantly focused on Jesus now. Her faith felt invincible.

The first few days after losing her husband and son, she had been an absolute wreck. Inconsolable. But something had changed by the third day. A realization that all they needed to do was be faithful and abide in Him, moment by moment. He would help them get through everything, and soon, He would be returning to take them to their real home. They would all be reunited.

As everyone bowed their heads, each person took turns praying for God's protection, the ability to evade their pursuers, and for food and water. When they finished, Geoffrey pushed ahead and everyone followed his lead.

Ally craved water. Her stomach moaned for food. They had finished the last of the food three days ago, and the water last night. The hunger pangs were relentless and all-consuming, but the thirst for water was even more urgent. It scared her. She continued to pray through it, and God had given her strength thus far.

Well, at least I'll lose that last five pounds Weston kept saying I didn't need to lose, she joked.

She worried about the kids more than anything. Dylan and Charlotte looked haggard and withdrawn. But their prayers a few minutes ago had been sincere and fervent. She knew they were closer to Jesus than ever, and He would sustain them, too. But they looked worn out. Life in the wild was a brutish life; it aged you. She also worried about Weston and Braden. Not knowing what had happened to them was the most difficult thing of all.

They were walking single-file through some trees, with Ally holding the rear. As Geoffrey and the kids rounded the crest of a ridge, Dylan exclaimed:

"Mom, come quick!"

Exhausted as she was, she jogged to catch up with the rest of the group. As she rounded the top of the hill, what she saw caught her breath.

A large airplane had crashed in the valley below. It looked like a 767 cargo jet. She could tell the crash had happened recently. Huge swaths of trees were blown over in its path. Sections had separated and lay in different parts of the valley, here and there. Ally could not see any survivors or indications of passengers. The nearest piece was a couple hundred yards away.

Dylan and Charlotte were running towards a large, white chunk of aircraft. Ally followed behind, worried about the possibility of them getting hurt. Geoffrey, who had been hiking at a fast pace, was already there.

"Ally! Ally!" he said excitedly.

She made her way down the small valley and walked into a large section of the aircraft. Geoffrey and the kids were already inside.

"What is it?" she asked tentatively, ducking down to avoid a mess of tangled wires.

"The answer to our prayers," Geoffrey replied, voice trembling with emotion.

As she moved further inside she saw it. Bottles of water and boxes of food.

Dylan and Charlotte were already drinking from small Aquafina bottles, and wolfing down Kind bars.

"Here, catch!" Geoffrey said, tossing Ally a water bottle.

"I can't believe it, Mom!" Dylan exclaimed, laughing.

"Believe it, son," Ally replied, opening the water, "God has a thousand ways to provide for His children, of which they know nothing. A wise woman once said that."

As they finished drinking and eating, they began to resupply. Normally they hadn't carried their water, but filtered it. With everything turned to blood, they would have to carry not just their food, but their water, too. With the soldiers on their trail, they could not stay long. They continued to eat while stuffing water into Geoffrey's pack and bars into their pockets.

The kids were eating less urgently now, actually chewing their food. Dylan and Char gave each other a playful shove and laughed together.

"Wait, listen!" Dylan urged suddenly.

Everyone went silent, freezing in place. A dull humming could be heard outside.

It continued to grow louder.

Suddenly, two Black Hornet drones emerged at the entrance of the hull, staring at the group. Charlotte screamed as they moved into the broken fuselage. Dylan lunged at one of the drones, trying to swat it with his hand. It dodged his attack, but in the process slammed into the roof of the aircraft, knocking itself to the ground. Dylan immediately stepped on it, smashing it with his shoe.

The other drone watched this attack, reversing slowly out of the hull and into the clearing. Geoffrey ran outside and started picking up rocks and throwing them. Despite multiple attempts, he was unable to hit such a small target. After making a full circle, scanning the area, the drone turned left and raced across the ridge.

"It got what it needed!" Geoffrey shouted, "Let's go!"

Everyone began running towards the treeline on the far side of the valley. Ally, weighed down with food and water, willed her legs to pump harder. Several bars dropped on the ground as she swung her arms. As they neared the cover of the trees, she could hear the sound of multiple jet engines approaching. She turned to look. Half a dozen soldiers, flying in jetsuits, crested the ridge and, spotting the fleeing group, prepared to land. At the same time, several soldiers emerged over the hill they had so recently crested. The soldiers shouted and pointed at them as more began to pour over the ridge. Ally calculated there must now be a small army on the far side of this tiny valley. There was no way they were going to make it now. They would be killed.

Suddenly, a nearby tree exploded and the roar of automatic weapons firing echoed through the air.

"Everybody down!" Geoffrey screamed.

The group backtracked to an outcropping of boulders, crouching down behind them as best they could. Chunks of rock exploded around them and bullets whined as they whizzed by.

What are we going to do? Ally thought, *We'll never make it to the treeline now.*

Dylan lay protectively over Charlotte, a look of fear on both their faces. Geoffrey rolled up into a ball nearby, trying to make himself smaller. On the other side of the valley she could hear whooping and hollering. The soldiers were excited to finally see their prey.

"Let's get 'em!" one of the soldiers yelled, as they made their way towards the rocks. They pressed forward, laying down a barrage of fire from their M27s. They would never outrun them now. It was over.

Suddenly, Ally felt an enormous heat. She looked towards her kids, who stared back at her with fright. The air around her looked strange and blurred.

The firing stopped and several of the soldiers screamed.

"Get to cover," yelled one.

She could hear them scrambling, and yelling out in pain.

"What is it?" Geoffrey screamed from behind his rock.

"I don't know!" Ally shouted.

All around her Ally saw a thick haze. It had grown dark around them, like an eclipse. However, in the distance it seemed bright, too bright to be safe. She saw the forms of the soldiers running into a section of broken aircraft, but they appeared fuzzy, distorted. The heat was overwhelming. Ally began sweating profusely.

"It's the fourth plague!" she announced loudly, realizing what was happening.

"And men were scorched with great heat..." Geoffrey recited from memory, his voice shaking.

"But we're not affected," Dylan exclaimed.

"Not like them," Ally answered, gesturing towards the soldiers. She could see several of them lying on the ground, motionless. "I think we're being shielded. Thank You, God. Thank You!"

"If He can protect us lying here on the ground, I think He can cover us while we move. Remember the Israelites?" Georffrey thought out loud.

"Oh, God," Ally prayed loudly, "we pray we are not being presumptuous. We humbly ask that You protect us from the fourth plague. Help us leave this place to get away from these awful men. Shield us with Your cloud like You did with the Israelites in the wilderness. We ask this in Jesus' name, amen."

Tentatively, they all rose from where they were. They could not see the soldiers clearly, but they all appeared to be hiding from the heat in the wreckage. No one fired at them as they stood. They could see several soldiers lying motionless on the ground. Geoffrey and the kids looked at each other, and at Ally.

"Ok," Geoffrey stated loudly, a look of fear on his face, "let's try it."

He began to move forward, stepping out in faith towards the treeline. Ally and the kids moved after him. The dark blurry mass began to move with them, continuing to surround them.

"It's working!" Geoffrey yelled in surprise, "It's working!"

Ally raised her arms in the air and began openly weeping. Tears streamed down her face.

"We praise You, Adonai. Oh, my God, we praise You! Oh, we praise You!"

President Lutrell sat in the library of the Apostolic Palace in Vatican City, waiting for Ambassador Bianchi. He had been their lapdog, performing every command they gave him, time and time again. Violating rights, attacking smaller, helpless communities and even nations that wouldn't comply with the worldwide mandate.

He had done everything they asked, and they had kept asking for more. He had violated Americans, violated other creeds, cultures and religions. And he could no longer live with himself. He had hidden Joan and the kids away in a safe place where these people would never find them. Today, he would tell the Pope and Bianchi that he would no longer do their bidding, they could find some other bulldog to terrorize the world, another wolf as Bianchi had called it. They would take his life, but they would never find his family as they had promised they would.

Tim Blain sat at his side with only one Secret Service agent. They had been waiting for over twenty minutes and he was starting to get impatient. He glanced over at a receptionist who had been on the phone for several minutes. Finally, he rose from his chair and walked towards her.

"Miss, when is Pope Giordano going to begin this meeting?" he asked impatiently.

"Mr. President," she replied in a heavy Italian accent, "we are so sorry, but there is a situation."

She gestured outside.

Although it was the middle of the day, he noticed it had grown dark outside. Lutrell turned to look at Blain in confusion.

They all got up and walked towards the window overlooking the city. Noonday had turned to dusk and it was getting darker every second.

A solar eclipse? Lutrell wondered.

Outside the walls he could see thousands upon thousands of protestors marching. Suddenly, a nearby building exploded, sending debris rocketing in every direction. Several fires could be seen inside the Vatican City walls.

As Lutrell watched from the window, the main gate at Via Sant'Anna suddenly exploded, sending smoke billowing up into the air. As Lutrell peered into the clearing smoke, thousands of armed people could be seen running through the gate, shooting into buildings and nearby cars. More fires began to erupt through the area.

"Mr. President," the agent stated urgently, "we need to go!"

Lutrell turned away from the agent.

"Go where?" he asked resignedly.

"To safety," Blain answered urgently.

Lutrell was tired. And he was lost. They had made him lost, without a soul, without a conscience, one small compromise at a time.

That's how it always happens, Lutrell mused, *no one ever plans on being the bad guy*.

He slowly walked back towards the waiting room chairs, and sat down. All he knew was, he could hear the sound of gunshots and screams closing in on them, and he was just tired.

Chapter 20: The Return

They were almost upon them. Maybe five hundred yards away and closing fast. The soldiers were bridging the gap and they knew it. Ally could hear their whoops and hollers. Their triumphant shouts, the hunt almost over. At least half of them had survived the heat, which had ended yesterday, and they were angry. Angry at this defiant little band who continued to evade them and had cost them several of their own.

Ally could hear their cries and taunts in the distance.

"You're gonna die!" one shouted.

"Wait 'til we get you!" another screamed.

She ran behind her kids, jostling and shoving them onward, over branches, rocks, and endless pines. There was only running, endless running and trusting in the Almighty's promise that someday it would end.

Geofffrey, as usual, stayed in front. He ran as fast as he could in his weakened condition. From time to time he would look behind him, and encourage them on.

Ally glanced behind her. They were maybe two hundred yards away now. This wasn't working. Two starved adults and a pair of scared, weakened children were no match for these elite soldiers. It was time to think about surrender. But they couldn't do that. They would be killed out here in the wilderness, like so many martyrs before them.

Shots began to ring out again; bullets whizzing around them.

"Get down!" she screamed, "Find cover!"

Her children scrambled behind a couple large pines, making their bodies small. Sadly, they had become accustomed to the violence.

Geoffrey stood silhouetted on top of a large rock. He turned around to face Ally and the kids, looking for a spot to hide. Suddenly, an enormous burst of blood exploded from his side, a shot rang out, and he collapsed behind the rock.

"Geoffrey!" Ally screamed.

She began crawling over to where he lay. Gunshots continued to ring out. She glanced towards the soldiers, and saw that they were getting closer. As she reached Geoffrey, she saw he was splayed out on top of a large, smooth rock. He looked weak and deathly pale. Blood oozed freely from his left side, pooling over the rock and onto the ground.

"End of the road, Ally," he managed to say.

He tried to raise his head, but couldn't do so. He looked exhausted by the attempt. Ally stared at him, unsure what to say. She pulled out his shirt a bit; the wound looked severe.

"You must go," he squeaked out with enormous effort.

"I won't leave you - "

" - You must," he interrupted, relaxing now, "I'll see you. I'll see you."

He began to fade.

"Real... soon. Oh, wow," he managed, his head slowly tilting to the side.

Bullets flew all around her. She looked into Geoffrey's eyes, he was gone. There was no time to think about it now, no time to mourn. She had to figure out how to save herself and the kids. She dared to poke her head up over the rocks and a new hail of gunfire greeted her. Rocks and trees exploded around her and bullets ricocheted everywhere. They now appeared to be only fifty yards away.

"Kids!" she screamed.

"Yeah?" Dylan and Charlotte answered.

"We've got to - "

From out of nowhere a lightning bolt smashed down in-between the Millers and the soldiers. The explosion was so loud that Ally crunched into a ball reflexively; terrified to move. She noticed the firing had stopped. Thunder echoed away from them, making an incredible noise as it traveled over the mountains.

Ally looked up into the sky. She noticed dark, angry clouds had formed and were moving swiftly to the west.

She could not hear or see the soldiers, but knew they were there. What was she going to do?

Suddenly, another jagged bolt kissed the ground, exploding near the soldiers. Ally could see that Charlotte was screaming, but all she heard was the roar of thunder.

Additional bolts raced across the sky and touched the forest all around them. Ally curled up into a ball and covered her ears. The noise was overwhelming, and the power being unleashed was beyond comprehension.

Now the mountain began to shake, at first gently, but then violently. Ally tried to hold onto a nearby rock, which she quickly realized was not a good idea. They all laid flat on the ground as it roared.

Oh, God, please help us.

It continued to grow darker. More lightning streaked the sky, thunderclaps exploding and booming off into the distance. Between lightning flashes, she could see her kids were huddled next to each other with terrified looks on their faces.

The ground continued to shake, making a terrifying roar that came from deep within the earth. She could not see the soldiers anymore, but they had obviously stopped advancing.

A light hail began falling from the sky as lightning continued to strike. Ally looked around as the bolts lit up the sky. The hail extended as far as her eyes could see.

"Let's get to cover!" she screamed at Dylan and Charlotte, "Let's move!"

They turned towards her, soaking wet and shaking.

"Come on!" She gestured with her hands to follow.

As they stood up and began moving in the direction of the trees, the hail began to increase in size. There was no response from the soldiers as they rose to their feet.

They held their arms out sideways to try and balance, as the ground continued to shake. The noise of the earthquake, thunder, and hail combined was hurting their ears. Ally swore she could also hear a voice speaking from the heavens.

Now I'm truly losing my mind, she thought. *It sounds like it's saying My Law, My Law.*

From the corner of her eye, she noticed one of the soldiers rise up, raise his M27, and aim directly at them. He was having difficulty due to all the elements of nature going haywire.

Suddenly, the hail increased to the size of coconuts. Ally screamed and covered her head. There was no cover anywhere. The trees they had attempted to reach had been stripped bare. She saw the soldier drop the weapon and fall lifeless to the ground as this barrage of hail pulverized him.

All around them hail continued to fall, but the larger hail seemed to push away from them, as if there were some kind of current in the sky moving the bigger pieces away. Ally looked up in amazement. The larger hail came down on top of them, but then pushed to the sides about fifty feet above their heads. All the smaller hail continued to rain down on them. There was some kind of invisible shield above them.

From the east, a single note sounded on millions of trumpets. Ally and the kids jumped in terror. She had never heard anything like it in her life. They all whipped their heads towards the sound.

Bright light emanated from a break in the clouds. It seemed their dimension was being ripped apart and invaded by another, more powerful one. Angelic figures began pouring through this dimensional rift, flooding the sky. First hundreds, then thousands, then millions. Millions of angels, luminescent and dressed in pure white, flying in their direction. The earthquake, lightning, and hail were all dissipating now.

"Mom!" Charlotte yelled, pointing towards the north.

Ally stood speechless, as she saw several dozen people rise up from the earth near them and push into the air with their angels.

"Ally," a voice called out gently behind her.

She whirled around. Geoffrey stood behind her. He no longer had a fatal gunshot wound. He looked vibrant and young.

"You ready?" he asked, grinning ear to ear, nodding upward.

She stared in disbelief.

Another trumpet, louder than before, sounded throughout the air, causing her to turn towards the sky again. Behind the clouds of angels, an even brighter light now blazed out. Although some distance away, she could see a Being sitting on a large throne, a crown on His head, surrounded by angels.

"It's Jesus!" Dylan spoke softly, pointing upward.

"Let's go to Him," Ally stated with sudden conviction.

And just how am I supposed to do that? she wondered.

Without thinking, she acted on this new impulse, this overwhelming urge to meet Jesus in the sky. She gasped as they all began rising into the air. She looked down and saw the ground falling away below them. It reminded her of one of those camera angles used on rockets as they lifted off their launch pads.

"Mom, we can fly!" Charlotte yelled with glee.

Out of the corner of her eye, she saw three angels ascend from where they had recently been, and meet a fourth one in the sky. The pack moved directly towards them.

"Greetings!" shouted the lead angel, as they approached. He held out his hand, and gripping it firmly in Ally's, said, "How's your first flight going?"

Ally laughed with childlike abandon.

"Ok, I think!"

The other angels quickly paired up with Dylan, Charlotte and Geoffrey.

"You're doing great," he encouraged, "I'm Gabriel."

Ally's eyes went wide.

"The Gabriel," she exclaimed in wonder, "I've read about you!"

"No, not that one," he replied with a grin, "I'm a different Gabriel. I'm your guardian angel."

"Sorry!" she stated, embarrassed. Thirty seconds into her new eternal life and she had already put her foot in her mouth. Suddenly, she blurted out the first thought that came to her, "I think you're amazing!"

He smiled.

They continued to ascend upward, reaching the area where Jesus was. She could see Him much clearer now. Chills went down her spine as she gazed at His crown, face, and pure white robe. Light and power seemed to emanate from the throne He was on. It was difficult to see everything.

"What now?" she shouted to Gabriel.

"Follow Him," he yelled, pointing to Jesus, "you should be used to that."

More and more humans congregated with their angels, behind Jesus, forming a long train in the sky. Ally realized that many were singing, and the refrain was being picked up by more and more humans. An angel dressed in white, with a large blue sash over his shoulder, appeared to be leading the song. It was one she actually knew, from their church hymnal. It was called 'He Lives.'

Millions of voices were taking up the refrain in perfect cadence.

" - I serve a risen Savior, He's in the world today, I know that He is living, whatever men may say, I see His hand of mercy, I hear His voice of cheer, and just the time I need Him, He's always near. He lives! He lives! Christ Jesus lives today, He walks with me and talks with me - "

Ally, Geoffrey and the kids sang with all their hearts, like never before. What must have been a million more voices now belted out the anthem, hearts identifying with each word, as more and more people continued to fly up and join them.

Ally looked at the ground far below. Every few seconds, a grave would burst open and a man, woman, or child would emerge and rise into the air with an angel at their side, to join the enormous glory train.

"We're going around the world, following the sunrise," Gabriel stated, "it should take about sixty minutes."

"Every eye will see Him," Ally responded, more to herself than to Gabriel.

"That's right," he answered her, matter-of-factly, "but not all at the same time... but, everyone will be addressed within the next hour. Every soul who ever lived. It was all decided in the judgment."

Gabriel looked intently into a crowd of newcomers rising up to meet them.

"Somebody's coming to say hello, I think," he announced.

Ally turned and looked intently into the rising crowd. At first she didn't see anyone she recognized, but suddenly Weston, her precious Weston, emerged and came directly to her. They embraced for several seconds.

"I was worried about you," she announced, getting emotional, "you have no idea how much."

"I think I know," he answered, staring into her eyes, "I was worried sick that they'd caught you and the kids."

"Not a chance, with Him in charge," she stated boldly, pointing towards Jesus.

Gabriel continued to smile widely, observing the reunion.

"Ally," Weston looked at her in wonder, "you look younger, vibrant."

"You do, too," she remarked, "and what are you wearing?"

They both had on white robes, and seemed to emanate a faint light.

She looked down at his hands. He kept holding his right hand and massaging it.

"Is your hand ok?" she asked.

"It is now," he exclaimed with joy, "my thumb was gone, that was difficult... it's back now."

"Your thumb was gone?" she questioned.

The kids flew to their Dad.

"Kids!" he said, giving them hugs.

"It's a long story," he replied to her question, "where's Braden?"

"I don't know," she replied, "he must be trying to get to us."

Ally noticed a large, blonde angel hovering next to Weston.

"So, is this your guardian angel?" she asked.

"Who, this?" Weston replied, turning to the angel with a grin, "No, this...this is the janitor."

The two of them laughed at some joke they apparently had between them.

"Yes, I'm just the janitor," the angel replied, giving her a wink, "but I prefer the term sanitation engineer. Just joking, sorry, my name is Renauld. I am his guardian angel. Your husband has kept me extra busy lately."

"I understand!" she agreed, "You have my condolences."

The group laughed heartily.

As they continued to make their way around the globe, the train of the saved grew until it extended out dozens of miles behind Jesus and His throne.

Gabriel turned from looking at Jesus towards Ally.

"You ready for this?" he asked.

"For what?" she asked.

"It's over, now we go home," he said.

Suddenly the entourage began moving higher into the atmosphere. They moved through wispy clouds and into the stratosphere until they reached the exosphere. Then, released from Earth's grasp, they passed into the cold, dark void of space.

Weston felt a moment of fear and instinctively held his breath as they passed over.

"You don't have to do that," Renauld stated.

Weston opened his mouth and took a breath. Oxygen flowed into his lungs as it normally did on Earth.

"How is this possible?" Ally questioned.

"We're in what you might call a membrane. We'll go over all of it later," Gabriel answered.

"I'm not even cold," Weston observed, looking around in wonder.

"You're a bit more like us now than a human, but you're still what you were," Gabriel tried to explain.

As they continued on, the entourage passed other worlds, first Mars, then the asteroid belt, then Jupiter, Saturn, and the other planets of their solar system. The crowd grew quiet as they flew by the brilliant blue orb of Neptune. Ally could see its beautiful clouds being whipped by supersonic winds from one end of the planet to the other.

"It's so beautiful. It almost looks like Earth," she remarked.

"You will see greater things than these," Gabriel stated assuredly.

Chapter 21 - The New Jerusalem

Time passed swiftly for the Millers. Every hour the void of space seemed to provide some fresh wonder. As they drew closer to the Orion Nebula, they flew by Bellatrix, and then Betelgeuse. Weston stared in awe at the size of the red giant. What looked like dark orange coals flamed and swam within a lighter sea of fire. As Weston watched, several coronal mass ejections, thousands of miles in length, exploded off of the surface. Pushing their way out into space, these bright rivers of plasma, subject to the enormous gravity below, turned back in wide arches through space and returned home.

Renauld noticed he was watching.

"Each arch is several billion tons," he stated, "of highly magnetized plasma."

"I've never seen anything...so beautiful, or large," he replied in quiet awe.

"You could fit seven hundred of your suns within Betelgeuse. This is one of the largest ones," Gabriel advised, "that you know about, anyway."

Suddenly, he gazed into the distance.

"We're nearly there."

They had traveled thirteen hundred light years, and now in the distance they could see the Orion Nebula. Thick clouds of orange, pink, green, and red expanded outward for a million miles in every direction. Brilliant arms of cold blue streaked away from the main body of the nebula, reaching into space. As they came closer, Ally could see a new, brighter light penetrating out of the side of one of the thick red clouds. It was pure white and looked out of place.

"What is that?" she asked, pointing forward.

"Your new home," Gabriel replied matter-of-factly.

As they came closer to the red cloud, they began moving around its side. The bright light increased, and a new wonder slowly revealed itself inch by inch.

It looked like an enormous block of pure gold with smaller white blocks inside. It was a city in space! The New Jerusalem! A clear, jasper-like light emanated from its surface, penetrating into the darkness. The light reminded Ally of the aurora borealis as it slowly faded into the void of space.

As they moved closer, Ally saw a smaller wall encircling the entire city near the bottom. It had the transparent violet hue of a pure jasper. Ally gasped at the scale of the metropolis. It appeared to be several hundred miles wide and high. Looking to the wall again, Ally noticed it was much larger than she had previously thought. Now, it appeared hundreds of feet tall. Three enormous sets of gates were mounted into it. There appeared to be similar gates around the city, but she could only see a partial one to the right. The gates had the silvery pale tint of pearls. She could not imagine why such large gates would be necessary, or how they could be constructed, but they rose to the entire height of the wall itself.

As they neared the New Jerusalem's entrance, Jesus and His entourage disappeared behind one of the gates. Ally and her group were not far behind, and they soon reached the same gate. As they came to it they could see, on an enormous foundation, the word 'Judah' written in gold. All along the wall were other names. She could see Levi, Simeon, and Dan. They were the names of the twelve tribes of Israel, each written in the color of a different mineral.

Ally's heart skipped a beat. She saw Jesus was waiting there, greeting each human as they passed through.

"Ally Miller," Jesus said warmly, as they reached the entrance. He moved towards her and gave her an enthusiastic hug.

"I've been waiting for this moment for a long time," Jesus stated.

The Millers stood there and gazed at their Redeemer. Strangely, it seemed that time stood still, and there were not millions of others waiting in line behind them.

"And My precious Weston," Jesus turned, gazing into Weston's eyes, "what you passed through, My friend...I want you to know, I have special plans for you."

He gave hugs to Dylan and Charlotte as well, speaking kind words to both.

Weston was speechless. He felt unworthy to be in his Creator's presence. As one, the Millers bowed before Him.

"I love each of you so much," Jesus said, helping them rise to their feet, "and I have new names for all of you, but not now. For now, your angels will show you to your accommodations. I will be there to visit with you shortly."

"Ok, thank you," Weston managed to speak.

Their angels were beckoning them to move along into the city. As they began to walk away, Jesus said:

"I hope the accommodations are to your liking."

Walking through the city, the Millers could not stop looking up. Tower after tower of pure gold rose to inconceivable heights. Ally stared straight up as they neared one building with a base that seemed a mile wide. It went higher than her eyes could discern, ascending straight as an arrow into nothingness.

"What is that?" she asked Gabriel in awe.

"Living quarters, schools, review centers," Gabriel answered.

"Review centers?" she asked.

"For judgment. You'll see," he replied.

Soon they began ascending deeper into the hills and the residential areas. Gabriel turned into a long, winding walkway lined with huge Eucalyptus trees. After walking a couple hundred feet, they reached a house.

It took Weston's breath away. Constructed of decorative rock colored Nepeda green, it was interwoven with some material that resembled timbers. The house had a roof which appeared transparent. The incredible thing was, it was fused with Willows, Elms and giant Sequoias. Part of the home moved upwards into the trees. It appeared a master craftsman had built it.

As they made their way inside, Weston saw a beautiful interior, all made of stone and other materials he did not recognize. A large granite table stood in a spacious kitchen.

"There's no wood," Ally noted.

"Nothing is used that would have to die," Renauld stated, "your new home is made only of materials that were never alive. If it is alive, it remains so in the home."

"There's one more thing before we go," Gabriel announced, "as I think you've probably sensed already, you have gone through some... changes."

"We've noticed," Weston said, looking at Ally, who returned his glance awkwardly.

"You are no longer married in an Earthly sense," Renauld continued, "your bodies are not exactly what they were."

"You are still flesh and blood," Gabriel interjected, "but reproduction and waste systems are not needed here. Your bodies have changed in that way."

"Oh," Ally stated, glancing awkwardly at Weston.

"You can remain together and live here. No one will ever take away the bond you two shared on Earth, the marriage," Renauld went on, "or, you can separate to different areas if you would prefer. There is no right or wrong way, it is just the next phase of your commitment you made on Earth. Sometimes these things, we hate to use the word, 'evolve.'"

Weston and Ally looked at each other. There was no doubt.

"I think we'll be happy here, together," Weston stated for the both of them.

Ally smiled, but bitterly.

"Renauld," Ally asked, "where is my son? Where is Braden?"

Renauld and Gabriel exchanged glances.

"Jesus will be here shortly," Gabriel replied hesitantly, "to go over any questions you might have."

It was two days later when Jesus came to their door. When He knocked, everyone ran to greet Him. Soon, they were all sitting in the living room chatting and sipping glasses of water.

"So, how are you adjusting to things?" Jesus asked.

"Oh, it's wonderful," Weston replied, "yesterday we climbed the tree this house is built into. We must have been five hundred feet in the air. We saw multiple sunsets at the same time."

"It is very beautiful here," Jesus remarked.

"We are just...so grateful," Weston continued, staring at Jesus' hands now, "I mean...thank You. For...everything."

Jesus followed Weston's gaze down to His hands.

"Of course," he replied, "and I know this sounds hard to believe, but if your family was the only family that believed, I still would have...gone through that."

"Jesus," Ally changed the subject now. She and Weston looked at each other for several seconds. Everyone could hear the nervousness in her voice, "I have something to ask you."

"I know," he stated soberly.

"Where is my son Braden? Why hasn't he reached us yet?"

A look of deep sadness and pain came into Jesus' dark eyes. He stared at Ally for several seconds before speaking.

"Unfortunately... Braden was not able to be part of the first resurrection."

Ally looked shocked. Immediately, she began crying.

"Why?" she asked in horror, "Why?"

Charlotte began crying, too. Weston and Dylan sat in shock, staring at Jesus.

"Ally," Jesus answered her, "We tried. The Father, the Holy Spirit and Myself, We tried. Many times, to get through to Braden."

"But, why? Braden was baptized with the rest of us. He was saved like everybody else," she continued, sobbing. Weston, clearly upset himself, came over and held his wife, trying to comfort her.

"I know this is going to be hard to hear right now, but Braden was presented with all the facts, and, ultimately, he didn't want to come here. We couldn't force people to come, We tried to reason with them," Jesus said, "but I want all your questions to be answered. Come down to the review center and see the records for yourself."

"I just can't believe this is it," Ally sobbed, "I mean, are You sure You did everything possible?"

"Ally," Jesus answered her, "I came to Earth and died for Braden. I took all of his sins upon Myself, and bore the punishment to the full measure. It killed Me...If I would go through all of that, do you not think I would do everything possible to save that which I worked so hard for, gave everything up to possess?"

Ally quieted down and pondered this.

"That makes sense," she responded, sniffling, "no, You're right. That makes sense. Obviously, You would have left no stone unturned to try and save him since You died for him. I"m...I'm sorry I expressed doubt."

"It's ok," Jesus answered without hesitation, "We are here to answer questions. Myself, the Holy Spirit, the Father. This place, I know this sounds hard to believe, but it is all here for you. I know you are in pain right now, all of you. I want you to know, I understand this pain. My Father and I feel it with you...and we are all going to have to work through it, together."

"Jesus," Charlotte stated, "thank You for dying for my sins so I could be here. I...I love You."

Jesus' smile returned.

"Little Charlotte," he replied, "you are so precious to Me. You are all so precious. I want you to know that, I did it...I did it because I need you. The Father needs you. Heaven would not be Heaven, without you all here. Those who are not here, it is very painful to process. We are going to need time to heal. But, I believe in time, we will. Come down to the review center, Ally, all of you should. It is important to Me that you see the records. Like I said before, We want every question to be satisfied."

"I will, Jesus," Ally answered, crying less now, "thank You."

"I'll see you this Sabbath," Jesus said, getting up to leave.

"We can't wait," Dylan piped in.

"Goodbye," Jesus said, as He walked out towards the front walkway.

As they shut the door, Weston turned to Ally.

"Are you ok?" he asked.

"No," she answered, reaching for him. As they hugged, she began to cry again, softer this time.

Dylan and Charlotte moved in as well, comforting their mother. After a while, she seemed ready to move on. She spoke:

"I'm going to be alright, West," Ally stated, "and I know you all are hurting too, I'm not the only one. It's just going to take time, like He said."

"Dad, can we go up to the tree loft again? Maybe see the sunsets?" Dylan asked.

"Let's all go," Ally answered.

That Sabbath, the saved gathered together for worship. Everyone had a harp-like instrument, which also had a fretboard-type apparatus like a guitar.

There was no church, but a gathering place which everyone was calling the 'Sea of Glass.' Ally looked around, and decided there could be no way to count everyone, and there was no reason to, anyway.

They had been to the river, the water of life, which was a short walk away. It surely could sustain billions. As she drank from it, she had felt invigorated; water had never tasted so good or been so refreshing. She looked down into its depths. It was crystal clear all the way to the bottom. It seemed to emanate life and health.

The Tree of Life was growing from both sides of the river. There was no doubt that its fruit could sustain untold masses for several eternities. When standing at its base, Ally had not been able to see the top of it. Its branches hung low, making it easy for thousands of people at a time to grab its luscious fruit, but its higher branches seemed to reach dozens of miles upward and outward. The fruit itself felt life-changing as she took her first bite. An energy and vitality seemed to awaken within her as she chewed and swallowed. Its taste was beyond description, nothing on Earth had ever come close.

Jesus had told them this was the tree that had something in its fruit that would sustain eternal life. All one had to do was eat.

As the Father, Son and Holy Spirit entered the Sea of Glass, They sat on a throne, to be seen above the assembly. Everyone bowed down in adoration.

As they were bowing, an angel came to Weston.

"Jesus wants you up there by Him, to sing in the choir," he announced, "please come with me."

Weston glanced at Ally.

"Go to Him," she stated without hesitation.

A leading angel, wearing a brilliant gold sash, appeared near the Trinity. He struck the first note for the key of the song.

"Let's begin," he announced through some sort of public address. It had no wires or obvious speakers, but everyone could hear him.

The angel began playing a simple, but beautiful melody. After a bar, millions of others began joining in. Ally picked up the strain immediately. She had never been musical, but somehow her fingers followed along, making a haunting, gorgeous melody. Eventually, the song changed and became brighter and richer. It reminded her a little of Johann Brahms' Hungarian Dance.

A thrill went through her whole body. She had never experienced anything like it in her life. She imagined it must have been something akin to being in an orchestra back on Earth.

I *want to do this forever*, she thought.

She turned to Dylan and Charlotte, who were skillfully playing their own harps. They both looked tremendously happy.

After several repetitions of the melody the choir began to sing. It was a song none of them had ever heard, and it was beautiful. Ally could see Weston up near Jesus, grinning from ear to ear.

This is more wonderful than I could ever have imagined, she thought.

She glanced at Jesus, the Holy Spirit, and the Father. Somehow, even though she stood among untold masses, They each glanced back at her and smiled.

How could I have ever thought the things of Earth were more important than this? she wondered.

Later, at home, Ally and Weston sat together.

"Did you enjoy the worship?" Weston asked.

"It was beyond what I ever imagined," she replied, "and you, up there singing next to Jesus... you looked... happy," she stated.

"I was," he agreed.

"West?"

"Yes, love?" he answered.

"This is truly perfect. A perfect existence. I'm...fulfilled," she hesitated, "but, I'm worried."

"Why?" he asked, turning to her in surprise.

"After the Millennium, we're going back. There'll be a second resurrection...what if we see him?" she began crying again.

Weston held her tightly.

"It won't be easy," he remarked gravely, "but we'll get through it together. Like Jesus said."

"West?"

"Yes?"

"I have to know," Ally stated with conviction, "I have to know why my son isn't here."

"I understand," Weston replied.

Ally sat in a large cushioned chair surrounded by a thin transparent screen. She was on the 270th floor of the Abraham Review Center, high above the city. The room had been brightly lit, but once she sat down, the lights automatically dimmed.

An angel had greeted her at the front entrance, led her through a maze of corridors and two different elevators, and had now left her alone and was waiting outside. She had been given the instruction to 'take your time and let the interface guide you.'

Now she was alone in the dark, and she hesitated. What had brought her here? The need to know? Why did it matter? Braden was not here, and would never be. He was gone. All she knew was she was in pain. The irony had not escaped her, as she walked through beautiful groves, spacious gardens, past ivory towers and verdant hills, as she walked by the Tree of Life, that she was in the most wonderful place in the universe, and she had only been growing more unhappy by the day.

No, she needed to know. Jesus had said so. This 'review center' would give her the answers she required in order to move on. And she knew, even through her pain, that eventually she was going to have to move on from this.

As the lights dimmed, the transparent screen suddenly glowed pink and clouded opaque. She could no longer see the wall behind it. Then words appeared on the screen, accompanied by a soft female voice.

"HELLO, ALLY."

"Hello," she answered awkwardly.

"HOW MAY I ASSIST YOU?"

She hesitated. Ally had never been much for computers, but apparently they had them even here. There was something different about this one, however. She could not see wires or any hardware. Just a thin glass screen.

"I came to learn about Braden...my son," she said.

"BRADEN AUSTIN MILLER. ABOUT HIS FALL?"

"Yes, about his fall," she said, tearing up suddenly.

Apparently, this interface, whatever it was, was much smarter than any Earthly computer.

"PLEASE HOLD."

Suddenly, the entire room turned into an image of Braden, laying in his bed. The screen seemed to fade into the background. Ally seemed immersed in the image, part of the scene. It was late at night. She leaned forward, fascinated by the sight of her son, alive again. Everything was clear and sharp, giving her the sense that she was in the room with him.

The only light was emanating from his cellphone. His face was awash in it, and he was typing. Ally couldn't see the screen however, and she had no idea what he was saying, or to whom. She wanted to know so badly.

She reached out her hands, beckoning him closer. As she did, the entire room shifted and moved clockwise.

'ROTATE PREFERRED VIEW?' pulled up in small letters near the bottom of the 'screen.'

Wait.

Was this actually possible? She quickly raised her hands again, and began trying to move Braden towards her. Everything began rotating, controlled by her movements.

Incredible.

She was able to manipulate what she was seeing and view it from any angle! She quickly began rotating Braden until she was now watching over his shoulder as he typed. She zoomed in closer to his cell phone screen by motioning her hands towards her body.

'*When?*' someone typed on his screen, named GeckoThug.

Braden hesitated, apparently deep in thought.

'*When!?!*' the person repeated.

'*4. At your house,*' Braden typed.

'*That's the right decision, Brae,*' GeckoThug affirmed.

With that, the conversation ceased and Braden tossed his phone towards the bottom of his bed. He turned over and began staring at the wall.

Ally quickly rotated him around until he was facing her again. She stared intensely into his face. What was he thinking? What did this have to do with his fall? He stared back in her direction, looking troubled. She made little micro-adjustments until his eyes stared directly into hers. For a moment it gave the appearance of a connection between them, but Braden might as well have been a million miles away and in a different time. It was all an illusion.

Ally began to cry softly, when suddenly everything sped up tremendously. Braden began racing through the next day, eating breakfast, working out, and watching TV, while the family raced around him doing their own tasks. It slowed down again to a normal speed as Braden began walking eastbound down their street. Dusk appeared to be settling over the neighborhood. Ally watched him walk past the black police van that had been surveilling them for so long, and continue into another neighborhood. Whatever was happening, it was clear it was after he had been baptized. She could tell by the presence of the van.

What was he doing now? Occasionally he would text someone on his phone and continue on, turning a corner or running across a street. Eventually, he turned into the driveway of a rundown single story house, with multiple cars parked in the driveway and on the lawn. Ally noticed something odd. Several dark figures hovered on the front lawn, watching Braden approach the door. She could not see them clearly; they were more like shadows, out of place. Whatever they were, she decided they were not human. They must be evil angels. Apparently, with this device, she was able to see beyond the third dimension and into the fourth.

Ally rotated her view, looking over his shoulder now. As he knocked on the door, a young man with tattoos on his face and arms answered. After a friendly exchange, the two walked past a large group of young people drinking and went into a bedroom. The tattooed man pulled a bag of pills out of his pocket and handed them to Braden, who quickly shoved them into his front pocket.

Next, the man pulled out a small pipe, placing a rock-like substance inside it. Several evil angels suddenly materialized through the wall and entered the room, pressing around Braden. A sick feeling grew in the pit of Ally's stomach.

The man pulled out a lighter and took a long hit from the pipe, extending it towards Braden. Her son appeared to hesitate. Smoke began to fill the area around the air. The angels surrounded them, blocking Braden from her view. Ally rotated the image until she could see his face again.

She watched in horror as Braden quickly grabbed the pipe and took a long hit from it.

Ally placed her head in her hands and cried softly. So Braden had become a drug addict. Why? They had given him everything he had ever wanted, been a loving, normal family. Why had he chosen this?

Suddenly, she regretted coming here. Now she felt even worse, knowing this new truth about her son. It would have been better to be ignorant. But she had wanted answers, hadn't she? She was no longer sure.

Everything sped up again, drawing Ally's attention once more. Now Braden was back in his room, sitting on his bed. The drugs were laid out beside him on his right side. He now had a lighter and a pipe of his own. There seemed to be an internal struggle going on, as he held the pipe in his hand. His eyes darted back and forth from the paraphernalia to a portrait of Jesus on the wall. Two dark shadows, apparently evil angels, hovered over him, seeming to encourage him to take the drugs.

Suddenly, a strange light began washing over everything in the room. At first dull, it quickly became overpoweringly bright. The two angels looked up in surprise and immediately fled. Moments later, a powerful looking Being materialized through Braden's wall, accompanied by two figures in white. Ally immediately recognized the Being as the Holy Spirit. The two figures that entered with Him were good angels. Braden, unable to see them, remained staring at the pipe.

As Braden held the pipe to his lips, the Holy Spirit pressed around him. Both angels stood watch around his room, looking this way and that. Braden put the pipe down, hesitating. This process went back and forth several times. Ally willed Braden to make the right decision, to listen to the Holy Spirit's voice.

Now Braden made an odd face. He seemed totally discouraged, hopeless. He quickly placed the pipe to his lips, lit the substance inside, and inhaled deeply. After a few more hits, he fell back onto his bed in a stupor.

Ally watched in total dismay as, one by one, the beings of light left the room. The Holy Spirit's face affected Ally the most. He had a look of intense sorrow.

Now they were gone, leaving Braden alone in the room. Almost immediately, the dark shadowy figures returned in their place.

"I've seen enough," she spoke softly.

"OK, I'M CLOSING THE FILE THEN."

She raised herself up and turned towards the door. She needed to leave this place, get the images out of her head.

"ALLY?"

She turned back towards the screen, which had reappeared by the wall.

"Yes," she answered dully.

"I'M TERRIBLY SORRY."

Not knowing how to respond to this artificial expression of sympathy, she opened the door and walked out of the room.

Chapter 22 - Eternity

When the city began moving, it was not discernible to any of its inhabitants. However, one thousand years had transpired, and everyone was aware that it was time to go back. They began to move forward through the Orion Nebula, back towards Earth. What had been about a week's journey to get here went faster this time. They retraced their path, past the mighty Betelguese, Bellatrix, and eventually through the Oort Cloud, where the Sun's gravitational influence and heat could first be detected.

As they moved through the asteroid belt, Earth became visible in the distance. A tiny blue orb, outlined by the blackness of space. Every few hours Weston, Dylan, and Charlotte would go up into their treehouse, look out above the cityscape and see their former home.

Ally declined to come up, stating she had things to do. Weston knew she was dreading going back to Earth, that she was trying to distract herself from what was coming: the second resurrection.

They continued to move closer to Earth. Now a reversal took place. The massive city of New Jerusalem entered the atmosphere, and for the first time, it appeared small and the Earth appeared large. A miniscule block of brilliant gold, a speck outlined against the massive blue and white orb of Earth's wide circle. As it descended into the atmosphere, land masses began to show. Then mountain ranges and lakes could be seen. Eventually, Weston recognized the Mediterranean Sea, and the land of Israel. A few minutes later, they touched down on the ground: the New Jerusalem on top of the old.

They were waiting for them when they arrived.

Masses of people stretched out as far as the eye could see. Ancient armies and modern ones. People of every nation, tribe, and time period, all dressed as they had perished. In Roman military gear, ancient tunics, modern business suits and Marine uniforms. There were housewives, construction workers, paupers and kings. All had one thing in common though; each was amazed that they were alive, and most of them could not explain how.

They began to congregate in small groups, then into larger ones, by language, time period and occupation. In the midst of them walked luminescent beings, glorious figures dressed in robes of pure white. They seemed to be organizing everyone into companies. Among these beings, another walked in their midst, barking orders and pointing this way and that. All whom he walked by gazed at him in wonder, for he was a magnetic figure.

He was tall, with dark, shoulder-length hair, which flowed thickly around a majestic Middle Eastern face. He had a neatly trimmed beard, dark brown in color. He was broad-shouldered, and wore a long, flowing tan robe. His head and body seemed almost luminescent. But one thing above all made him stand out from the rest, and it made everyone stay out of his path. He had a look of rage that terrified those around him.

Twenty-four hours after the New Jerusalem touched down, he made his first speech. Masses of people crowded near him, anxious to find out two things; what was happening, and what was the plan.

"People of Earth," Satan began, his voice projecting by some unknown system, "I beg of you an audience. Some of you may remember me, many of you probably do not, but you know who I am, and you have followed my voice, whether you realized it or not.

Many of you are wondering why you are here, and how you are here. I want you to know that you are here because I have raised you for a purpose, to help me. I am your leader, I am one of the leading angels in Heaven. My name is Belial, and I need your help taking back what is rightfully mine."

The city was silhouetted behind him, and he turned and pointed towards it.

"The New Jerusalem!" he yelled.

The crowd roared. Shouts of approval sounded in the distance.

"Belial!" someone screamed, "We will follow you!"

"I want what's best for all of you," he stated warmly, "look around you," he exclaimed, waving his arms outward, "the Earth is wasted. We cannot sustain ourselves here.

I've given you life," he continued, "and I wish that that life could last forever...but unfortunately, it won't. You are like this barren Earth around you. You will all eventually die, yet again, unless something is done!"

Shouts and cries continued from the crowd.

"Behind those walls," he pointed back to the New Jerusalem again, "is a city. A beautiful city. But do you know what else is there?"

More cries emerged from the crowd, asking.

"The answer to your problem, and mine," he continued, turning and pointing now with both hands towards the metropolis, "within those walls, lies something that sustains life, eternal life. It is called the Tree of Life. Its fruit, once consumed, will cause you to live forever. All you must do is consume it regularly, and you will never die.

I won't lie. The New Jerusalem, just like the old, is well fortified. It will not be easy to gain entrance. But I know that together, we can take this city."

He hesitated, gazing out over the masses.

"Are you with me?" he screamed, "Shall we take it?"

A new roar emerged from the crowd, louder than the first.

"In one week's time," he screamed, trying to make his voice heard.

He raised his hands, begging for quiet. The noise began to diminish.

"In one week's time," he repeated, "you will assemble in your companies. Already, my soldiers are working on revitalizing and rebuilding the most state of the art weapons we can find. You will take up these arms, those of you that can. Those who cannot, will provide support for our army. We will march upon the city, hit it with everything we have, and we will take it."

He continued to raise both arms as the crowd hailed their new leader, Belial.

A week had gone by. For a full day, they sat in their house, listening to the sounds of war outside. The screams of advancing soldiers. The racket of machine gun fire and even rockets. Nothing had gotten through, which could only be due to the fact that the angels guarding the city seemed to be able to absorb any type of human attack.

Weston was sick watching it all, and came down from their treehouse. He was sitting down on their couch now, beside Ally, trying to comfort her. Jesus was also there, holding her hand.

"Ally," Jesus spoke, looking into her eyes, "we all knew this time would come. I need you to be strong now."

Ally stared at the floor, her face soaked with tears.

"I can't," she croaked.

"Honey," Weston spoke, "I think it would be healing for you to see him...one last time. Don't you think you would want to see him?"

"No," she replied.

Weston and Jesus exchanged glances.

"Ally," Jesus said, "I understand how you feel, and unfortunately, I must go. But I want to leave you with this thought: you do not have to watch what happens next. You do not have to go see your son, but..."

Ally continued to stare at the floor, tears running down onto the tile.

" ...this will be the last time you ever get to see Braden. You may not want to see him, but he wants to see you."

Ally turned and looked up at Jesus.

"I believe you need this, Ally, and so does he," Jesus stated with finality, holding her hands in His.

"Maybe," she managed to say.

"I must leave now," Jesus continued, "it's almost time."

Weston stood up and saw Him to the door.

"When the time comes," Jesus continued, "My Father and I wish that everyone would be there."

"We understand," Weston spoke for both of them.

"We'll see you soon," Jesus stated.

With that, He turned and walked out the door.

Satan paced back and forth in their makeshift army tent, furious. Onxyial, his lead angel, was giving the battle report.

"We are no further, my lord, in creating a breach than we were with the previous two waves, as I said," Onxyial stated.

Satan continued to pace.

"And we've lost over 250,000 soldiers in the last wave. As soon as they hit the wall...they were gone."

"You know I don't care about that," Satan reminded Onxyial.

"What weapons we were able to assemble and get working again, have also been ineffective," Onxyial went on, "as you know, His army has some kind of shield. We cannot penetrate."

"Those little insects cannot penetrate," Satan complained.

He stared off into the distance. Suddenly, a smile began to spread across his face.

"But I know something that should," he continued, "bring me the General."

A few minutes later, General Thompson walked inside the tent.

"Yes, my lord Belail?" he asked.

"I sent you to North Dakota. What did you find?" Satan inquired.

"My lord, we were able to salvage six missiles," Thompson answered positively.

"That's not very many," Satan countered, annoyed.

"Belial, it has been so long since they were maintained."

Satan turned and glared at him.

"No," he replied, "while you were taking your little thousand year nap, I made sure they were maintained. Don't tell me what condition they're in!"

"Even so, my lord, my men are telling me it has been at least decades... metal rusts, seals decay."

"I want two dozen missiles," Satan announced.

"My lord, we can't," the general stated plainly.

Satan now moved towards General Thompson, who suddenly levitated several inches off the ground, and began crying, grabbing for this throat. Onxyial stood there watching awkwardly, unsure what to do.

"I have issued a command, and there is no further need for discussion about that command. Get me more ICBMs, ready to fire, General. If you do wish to discuss this matter further, I will have you and your family nailed to crosses within the hour. Clear?" Satan asked.

"Yes, my lord," Thompson replied, choking.

With a wave of his hand, Satan released General Thompson from whatever mysterious grasp had held him. He collapsed onto the ground and lay gasping.

Satan turned again towards the General, annoyed that he was still there.

"Move, insect!" he cried, causing Thompson to scramble to his feet and out of the tent.

"Lucifer," Onxyial spoke slowly, "if we use their nuclear arsenal, we risk - "

" - I don't care about the risks!" Satan interrupted angrily, turning now to the tent opening, where the New Jerusalem stood in view. "I want back in that city."

Outside the city walls, encamped in tents, sat millions upon millions of professional soldiers, from all ages of time. Most of them congregated, fascinated, around the elite SEAL and Green Beret teams and their modern gear. They would shoot their M27s and FN MK46s at the city walls, even though they had no visible effect. At night Persian warriors and Roman centurions would stare through night vision goggles in wonder, watching the inhabitants of the New Jerusalem move about. All tried to catch a glimpse of the Tree of Life. The tops of its branches were barely visible from their vantage point.

The first ICBM came in at Mach 24 and deployed all eight of its 475 kiloton warheads onto one area; Judah's Gate.

Ionizing radiation, unbelievable heat and brilliant whiteness suddenly ballooned outward ten miles in all directions. The camps of soldiers and support personnel, millions of them, disappeared within the flash.

From a safe distance, Satan watched through binoculars with Onxyial in their command tent. He had a satisfied smile on his face. Within seconds, they felt the blast wave pass. The mushroom cloud continued to rise higher and higher. Eventually, the intended target became visible again.

As Satan continued to watch, his smile turned into an enormous grin. He chuckled.

"What is it?" Onxyial asked.

"See for yourself," he replied smugly, handing him the binoculars.

While Onxyial's vision was far superior to a humans, and he was certain Lucifer's was just as good, the binoculars helped him focus clearer on the section of wall that had just been hit.

He could see the enormous pearly gate, still sitting intact on its hinges.

"It's still there," he observed.

"Look closer," Satan replied, annoyed.

As Onxyial refocused the device, he now saw that there were black streaks running along the entire length of the wall.

"It looks like something smeared it," he noted.

"Not smeared," Satan corrected, "damaged."

"Lucifer, I don't know - "

Suddenly, several soldiers walked into the command tent. General Thompson led them, walking straight towards Satan and raising his voice:

"Just what is going on here?" he demanded, "You targeted a nuke right on top of my army, on top of your army...If I had known this was the plan, I would have never...they're all dead now!"

"I'm aware," Satan answered in a bored tone.

"What is wrong with you, you psychopath - "

As the General moved towards him, he suddenly tripped and fell, grabbing his throat and making choking sounds. The other military personnel slowly backed away, their glances alternating between Satan and their commanding officer struggling on the floor.

"Does anyone have any additional issues they care to raise at this time?" Satan stated icily.

One of the soldiers pulled out his Glock and began firing directly at Satan from about ten feet away. The rest quickly unholstered their sidearms and started shooting too.

As the shots rang out and the bullets hit their target, Satan did not move or seem to be affected at all. Once the magazines were emptied, Satan began laughing.

"You finished, insects? Bring me a new general to replace this dead one," he stated with disgust.

They gazed in horror at this supernatural being whom they had just attempted to kill. Their weapons had been ineffective. As one, they slowly backed away towards the tent exit. Each one glanced at Thompson who had been struggling on the floor. He now lay lifeless, a look of horror on his face.

"What is the plan, Lucifer?" Onxyial asked after the men left.

"Fire every nuke we have available at Judah's Gate. All of them," he commanded.

As one, the Trinity stood on an ascension platform and slowly began rising above the city walls. A myriad of angels of different rank, and wearing various colored sashes, gathered on either side.

The saved were encouraged to gather on top of the gate, to witness the executive judgment event. Some were afraid after the recent nuclear bombing, but Jesus assured them no additional attacks would be allowed.

Weston stood with Dylan and Charlotte on top of the wall. Ally had decided not to come. From where they were, they could see an enormous valley with mountains off in the distance. Every inch of the valley was filled with the lost. Some had guns, but those that did not carried swords, knives, and clubs. All seemed conscripted into battle, from the sixteenth century maiden to the modern housewife. Whether they desired this or not was uncertain, but among their ranks could be seen glistening white angels, spurring them on.

Suddenly, a series of trumpets began to sound. All of the saved turned to look towards the Trinity while the lost glanced up as well. The Godhead continued to rise higher and higher above the wall, eventually stopping in mid-air.

Out of nowhere, an enormous panoramic image appeared below the Godhead. It was replaying Jesus' life on Earth. Multiple scenes enfolded simultaneously, from Jesus' birth, to His temptation in the wilderness, to His agony on the cross. There was an added element to each scene though: it showed the seen as well as the unseen. Evil angels prodding the Pharisees to argue with Jesus, working amongst the crowd before Pilate's attempt to save Him, and Satan with an army of evil swarming over Christ on the cross.

More and more lost in the crowd began staring at Satan in disgust as they realized who he was for the first time. Hordes of them began backing away from him.

Weston was surprised when suddenly, Ally came up beside him.

"Honey, I thought - "

" - Jesus was right," she stated, "it took me a while to realize that. But I need to see this."

She began to scan the crowd, looking for Braden.

At first a few of the lost, moved by the panoramic scenes, began to bow down before the Trinity. No one around them mocked them. The masses seemed sobered as they realized the gravity of the situation and what they had rejected. Life. Eternal life. Offered as a gift, but spurned by every person in the crowd.

As the panoramic showed the nails being hammered into Jesus' hands, many of the lost began to openly weep.

"Weston!" Ally said shakily.

He turned towards her.

"What?" he asked.

He could see she was crying again and pointing straight ahead. As he followed her finger, he saw him in the distance, standing amongst a group of warriors. He looked haggard, injured and sorrowful.

"Braden," Ally choked out, tears running down her face, "Brae-bear."

Braden was staring directly at them, a look of panic in his eyes. He could see his father, mother, brother, and sister all staring back at him. It was clear from the look on his face that he realized his situation. He had spurned the love of his Creator, and it was about to cost him everything.

He dropped the weapon he was holding and fell to his knees, tears running down his face. Weston's heart was breaking. He could see that his boy, his little boy, was scared. At that moment he wished they could trade places. He would willingly do it, if it were somehow possible.

Bring him into the city, and put me out there in the death scape.

But then he remembered Jesus' words, and he knew Jesus was right: Braden had chosen not to be here. He would not be happy if he was forced inside.

As one, all began to bow and prostrate themselves before the Godhead, as though to acknowledge Jesus was in the right, and they were in the wrong. Onxyial, moved by the panoramic display, bowed to his knees too, acknowledging his former Master. Other evil angels, looking longingly at their former home, did the same. Satan looked around in dismay, but hesitantly, followed suit and slowly dropped to his knees.

For one moment, a stirring of repentance entered his heart. For all that he had incited: the idolatry, hatred, and incredible loss of life. Both temporal and eternal, to a billion souls created in God's image. Century after century, he had continued to entice man to rebel. Generation after generation, he had pushed humanity to constantly hurt, betray and kill his fellow man.

Now a thought emerged inside him, a thought that he had pushed down for so long.

He was wrong.

But then, just as quickly, a hatred arose. The hatred that had been nurtured for so many centuries, of Jesus Christ, his bitter enemy. Nurtured for so long, that it had built itself into the very pathways of his brain, and could not be ignored.

"I will not submit to this!" he stated angrily.

Satan quickly rose, grabbing Onxyial by the shoulder and dragging him over to a pair of remote launch interfaces.

"On my mark," he instructed, "turn your set of keys at the same time as mine. Row one, and then we work our way down. Launch everything!"

"Lucifer," Onxyial interjected, "I think we should - "

" - Just do it!" Satan screamed.

From the corner of his eye, Weston saw the Father raise both hands. Suddenly, from the sky, a mass of dark clouds formed. Fire began to rain down with fury upon the lost. Huge flames and waves of heat slammed into the ground, creating large explosions. Chunks of brimstone fell as well, crashing to the Earth and creating a strange chemical-looking fog. The noise was deafening, even inside the city. Many of the New Jerusalem's inhabitants crouched in fear and covered their ears.

Screams erupted from the crowd outside the city walls, but Weston noticed they were already beginning to die down. As far as the eye could see, the Earth was on fire, and massive waves of heat were washing up over everything, including the New Jerusalem.

Weston cringed as the sea of fire ballooned towards them, but noticed with relief that it did not get through; the flames could not penetrate into the city. Masses of hot air rose from the ground. Heat shimmer made it difficult to see clearly in any direction as the waves emanated upward. The entire horizon appeared distorted as light from above tried to make its way through the superheated air.

Weston continued to watch. He now saw that the lost appeared lifeless within the flames. It had all been mercifully quick: death had come in less than a minute. Thankfully, he had not been able to see his son, and he could not see him now. He tried not to think about what his last moments must have been like. At least it was over.

The only movement he could still see was a figure in the distance. He recognized it was Satan. He was lying on the ground and making slow, repetitive movements on his side as flames encircled his body. Within another minute, he appeared lifeless and still.

It was over.

They were at the star gate. Weston and Ally were excited. Jesus was sending them on their first mission. Dylan, Charlotte, Geoffrey, Rick, and Kathleen, as well as a host of others were there to see them off. They were to go to the planet Youltoni, and share their Earth testimony with the inhabitants there. Share what Jesus had done for them. Share about the evil of sin, and the goodness of God.

Much time had passed since the Earth had burned, and it was difficult for Weston to even picture it now. The Trinity had re-created the surface of Their world into something that must have been more like pre-Flood times. It was more beautiful than anything Weston could have ever imagined.

He gazed out over its surface. There were no more jagged mountain peaks or layers of exposed strata jutting out among the hills. These had all been signs of God's first destruction of the world. There were no signs of the second, final destruction. Weston realized this was because after the Flood, sin had continued on, and God mercifully kept signs in the Earth to testify that a judgment had taken place in the past. But after the second destruction, sin was finally eradicated. The planet itself now emanated that fact.

Everyone was chatting excitedly. Dylan and Charlotte were soon to go on their own missions. They would be traveling to Alpha Centauri. Weston chuckled to himself. He used to worry if his children left his sight. Now they would be going to another galaxy and he felt not the slightest worry or concern. The universe was now sinless, perfect, and safe. Nothing bad could ever happen to them again.

He turned to look at Ally. Her face beamed with excitement. For many days and nights that beautiful face had been streaked with tears, after watching the end of her firstborn. Jesus had spent many days with her, and all the Millers, comforting, explaining, and really, just being there.

Over time, whatever that meant now, they had all started to heal. What had surprised Weston the most though, was how Jesus seemed to need the healing too, seemed to be going through the same grief they were. He wondered if, in some ways, maybe they had helped Him, too? The thought seemed ludicrous. He was a God. But a memory kept resurfacing, although it was growing dimmer all the time. A memory from that awful day. As the hellfire had rained down on the lost, Weston had turned to look at the Godhead high above them: the Father, the Son, and the Holy Ghost. What he saw was not what he had expected to see from an eternal, all-powerful, all-knowing Trinity. They did not look happy, or stern, or even indifferent. They had been holding each other and crying. Crying, as They watched Their creation die.

It made Weston think of a verse from the Bible, which read:

'For God so loved the world, that He gave His only begotten Son, that whosoever believeth in Him should not perish, but have everlasting life. For God sent not His into the world to condemn the world, but that through Him it might be saved.' John 3:16-17.

God must have SO loved the world, loved it beyond what any human could ever understand. To love something was risky, and to lose it was extremely painful, and incredible as it seemed, this appeared to be true even for the Godhead.

Weston looked over at Ally. She was beaming.

"You ready?" he asked.

She gazed into his eyes.

"Honey," she spoke softly, gazing outside the city walls, beyond the platform into the vast expanse of stars, "we were made for this."

Renauld and Gabriel exchanged smiles. They were coming along for this first adventure, too. They had to lead the way to Youltoni, but after this, who knew? It was a first for all of them.

"Let's go, everybody. It's time," Gabriel announced.

They lifted up from the platform, soared over the city walls, and moved into the void of space. At first they flew slowly, but then they all began to accelerate. As they passed the speed of light, Ally could see weird distortions in her vision as the light particles around her began to actually move slower than she was moving. Again, they were not cold and they had no trouble breathing at all.

"It's so beautiful!" she shouted to Weston.

"It is," he yelled back, "because it's of Them. Let's go tell Youltoni what we saw!"

Ally looked around her at the expanse of space speeding by. She felt alive. She was one of God's perfect creatures, going on a mission for her Creator, through an eternal galaxy. There were memories of sin, of pain. But they were starting to fade, as all memories eventually do. She looked ahead, where Renauld and Gabriel were, leading the way. She let out a loud, guttural whoop. A cry much like a wolf might make as it hollered at the moon. She was free, for the first time truly free, and she was alive. Forever alive. And it was good.

Bibliography

Ellen White, Desire of Ages pg. 35, (1898): 61

348

Priest Brady, in an address, reported in the Elizabeth, NJ "News" (March 18th, 1903): 94

C.F. Thomas, Chancellor of Cardinal Gibbons, in answer to a letter regarding the change of the Sabbath (November 11th, 1895): 95

The Catholic Record of London, Ontario (September 1, 1923): 95

Julius J. Nam, Spectrum Magazine, Adventists in American Courts - The Sunday Law Cases (January 11th, 2013):109

Ellen White, Ministry of Healing, pg. 281 (1905): 300

About the Author

Toby Mikelbank lives in Tennessee with his wife, three children, two dogs and multiple farm animals. He is an avid student of prophecy and end time events.